Thereby Hangs a Tale

by

George Manville Fenn

Double 9
BOOKS

Thereby Hangs a Tale
by George Manville Fenn

ISBN: 978-93-61156-08-3

Published by

DOUBLE 9 BOOKS

2/13-B, Ansari Road
Daryaganj, New Delhi – 110002
info@double9books.com
www.double9books.com
Tel. 011-40042856

This book is under public domain

ABOUT THE AUTHOR

George Manville Fenn was a very productive author of novels, a writer, an editor, and an educator from England. He was born on January 3, 1831, in Pimlico, London. He mostly learned on his own; he taught himself Italian, French, and German. During the years 1851–1854, he went to Battersea Training College for Teachers and then became the head of a state school in Alford, Lincolnshire. In the early 1850s, Fenn started to write short stories and pieces for newspapers and magazines. The Old Forest Ranger, his first book, came out in 1856. Afterward, he wrote more than 100 books, many of them for teenagers and young adults. He was one of the most famous writers of his time, and his books were well-liked and read by many people. He-- also worked as a reporter and writer for Fenn. Among the newspapers and magazines, he worked for was The Boy's Own Paper, which he ran from 1866 to 1874. He worked hard to make children's books better and was a strong supporter of education and reading. The Englishman Fenn passed away on August 26, 1909, in Isleworth.

CONTENTS

A Peep at Tolcarne

"Ed—Ward!"

"Yes, mum."

A stiff, high-shouldered footman turned round as he reached the breakfast-room door.

"Are you sure Sir Hampton has been called?"

"Yes, mum."

"And did Smith take up her ladyship's hot water?"

"Yes, mum."

"Are the young ladies coming down?"

"They went out for a walk nearly an hour ago, mum."

"Dear me! and such a damp morning, too! Did they take their waterproofs?"

"Please, 'm, I didn't see them go."

"Look if they're hanging in the hall, Edward."

"Yes, mum."

Edward walked stiffly out, closed the door, "made a face" at it, and returned at the end of a minute.

"Waterproofs hanging on the pegs, mum."

"Dear, dear, dear, dear! Then of course they put on their goloshes! Go and see if they're in the lobby, Edward."

"Did see, mum," said Edward, who was wise in his generation, and had learned the art of making his head save his heels—"goloshes is in the lobby."

"Goloshes is in the plural, Edward, and should be *are*—mind that: goloshes are."

"Yes, mum—galoshes are," said Edward; "and the letter-bag *are* just come into the kitchen. Shall I fetch it?"

"*Is*, Edward, *is*. Now do, pray, be careful. Nothing is more annoying to visitors than to hear servants make grammatical mistakes."

"Yes, mum," said Edward.

"Is the heater very hot?"

"Yes, mum—white 'ot."

"White *what*, Edward?"

"'Ot, mum! white 'ot!"

Miss Matilda Rea, a rather compressed, squeezy lady of forty-five, shuddered, and rearranged her black net mittens.

"Go and fetch the letter-bag, Ed-ward."

The footman made the best of his way out, and Miss Matilda inspected the well-spread breakfast table through a large, square, gold-rimmed eyeglass; walked to the sideboard, upon which were sundry cold meats; and finished with a glance round the handsomely furnished room, ready to be down upon a speck of dust. But the place was scrupulously well kept; even the great bay window, looking out upon sloping green lawn, flower beds, and clumps of evergreens, backed up by a wall of firs, was perfectly clean. So Miss Matilda preened her feathers, frowned, and waited the return of Edward with a locked wallet of leather, bearing the Rea crest—a peacock with expanded tail, the motto "*Floreat majestas*"—and, in large letters on the brass plate, the words, "Sir Hampton Rea, Tolcarne."

"Place it beside Sir Hampton's chair, Edward," said Miss Matilda.

The wallet was duly deposited in the indicated place.

"Now bring in the urn, Edward."

"Please, 'm, Sir Hampton said it was to come in at nine punctually, and it wants a quarter."

"Then go and be quite ready to fill it, Edward," said Miss Matilda, not daring to interfere with the Mede-like laws of the master of the house.

And Edward departed to finish his own breakfast, and confide to the cook his determination that if that old tabby was to be always worriting him to death, he would give warning.

Miss Matilda gave another look round, and then going to the end of the hearthrug, she very delicately lifted up the corner of a thick wool antimacassar, when a little, sharp, black nose peeped up, and a pair of full black eyes stared at her.

"A little darling!" said Miss Matilda, soothingly. "It was very ill, it was; and it should have some medicine to-day, it should."

The little toy terrier pointed its nose at the ceiling, and uttered a wretched, attenuated howl, cut short by Miss Matilda, who popped the antimacassar down; for at that moment there was heard upon the stairs a sonorous "Er-rum! Er-rum!"—a reverberating, awe-inspiring sound, as of a mighty orator clearing his voice before sending verbal thunder through an opposing crowd. Then came steps across the marble hall, the door handle rattled very loudly, the door was thrown open very widely, and entered Sir Hampton Rea.

The sounds indicated bigness—grandeur; but Sir Hampton Rea was not a big man—saving his head, which was so large that it had sunk a little down between his shoulders, where it looked massive and shiny, being very bald and surrounded by a frizzle of grizzly hair.

Sir Hampton came in stiffly, for his buff vest was as starchy as his shirt front and sprigged cravat, which acted like a garrote, though its wearer suffered it, on account of its imposing aspect, and now walked with long strides to the fire, to which he turned his back, threw up his chin, and made his bald crown double in the glass.

"Matilda, have the goodness to close the door."

"Yes, dear," and the door was closed.

"Matilda, have the goodness to ring for the urn. Oh, it is here!"

In effect, hissing and steaming, the urn was brought in by Edward, and the tea-caddy placed upon the table.

"Edward!"

"Yes, Sir Hampton."

"Tell Miss Smith to inform her ladyship that we are waiting breakfast."

"Yes, Sir Hampton."

The footman hurried out, and Sir Hampton took up yesterday's *Times*, which arrived so late on the day of issue that it was not perused by the good knight till breakfast-hour the next morning, his seat, Tolcarne, being three hundred and twenty miles from town, and some distance off the West Cornwall Railway.

Sir Hampton—tell it not in the far West—had made his money by tea; had been made alderman by his fellow-citizens, and made a knight by his sovereign, upon the occasion of a visit to the City, when the turtle provided was extra good, and pleased the royal palate.

While waiting the coming of her ladyship, Sir Hampton, a staunch Conservative, skimmed the cream of a tremendously Liberal leader, grew redder in the face, punched the paper in its Liberal wind to double it up, and then went on with it, shaking his head fiercely, as his sister smoothed her mittens and watched him furtively, till the door opened with a snatch, and a little round, plump body, very badly dressed, and, so to speak, walking beneath a ribbon and lace structure, which she bore upon her head as if it were something to sell, bobbed into the room.

Description of people is absolutely necessary on the first introduction, so a few words must be said about Lady Frances Rea. She was what vulgar people would have termed "crumby;" but, literally, she was a plump little body of forty, who, born a baby, seemed to have remained unaltered save as to size. She was pink, and fair, and creamy, and soft, and had dimples in every place where a dimple was possible; her eyes were bright, teeth good, her hair a nice brown, and in short she seemed as if she had always lived on milk, and was brimming with the milk of human kindness still.

"Ten minutes past nine, Fanny," said Sir Hampton, pompously, after a struggle with a watch that did not want to be consulted.

"Never mind, dear," said her ladyship, going at him like a soft ball, and giving him a loud kiss. "Matty, where's my keys?"

"In your basket, dear," said Miss Matilda, pecking her sister-in-law softly on the forehead.

"So they are, dear," said her ladyship, rattling open the tea-caddy, and shovelling the tea into the silver pot.

"Er-rum, er-rum!" coughed Sir Hampton, clearing his throat.

His sister fell into an attitude of attention, with one thin finger pressed into her yellow cheek.

"Er-rum," said Sir Hampton. "Punctuality, Lady Rea, is a necessity in an establishment like ours, and—"

"Now don't be so particular, Hampy," said her ladyship, watching the boiling water run into the teapot. "It's like having crumbs in bed with you. Ring the bell, Matty."

"But, my dear," began Sir Hampton, pompously, "with people in our position—"

The door opened and Edward appeared.

"Tell cook to poach the eggs and grill the cold turkey, Edward."

"Yes, my lady."

"And where are the young—oh, dear me! bring a cloth; there's that stupid teapot running over again."

"Turn off the water, dear," said Miss Matilda, with the suffering look of one who had been longing to make the tea herself.

"Oh yes, of course!" said her ladyship. "Quick, Edward, bring a cloth and sop up this mess."

"Yes, m' lady."

Sir Hampton rustled his paper very loudly, rolled his head in his cravat till it crackled again, and looked cross. Then he strode to the table, took his seat, and began methodically to open the letter-bag and sort the letters; and then, in the midst of the sopping process and the exclamations of her ladyship, a door was heard to open, steps pattered over the hall floor, there was a babble of pleasant voices, a scuffling as of hats and baskets being thrown on to a table, and then the breakfast-room door opened, and two young girls hurried into the room.

"Nearly twenty minutes past nine, my dears," said Sir Hampton, consulting his watch.

"Ah! so late, papa?" said one, hurrying up to kiss Lady Rea, and receive a hearty hug in return.

"Oh, never mind," said the other, following her sister's suit, and vigorously returning the maternal hug. "We've had such a jolly walk. Oh, ma, how well you look this morning!"

"Do I, my love! There, Edward—that will do. Now, the poached eggs and the turkey, quick!"

"Yes, m' lady," said Edward.

And he disappeared, as Sir Hampton was forgetting to be stiff for a few minutes, as he returned the salute of his eldest girl, Valentina.

"I'm sorry we're late, papa; but we went farther than we meant."

"But you know, Tiny," said Sir Hampton, "I like punctuality."

And he glanced with pride at the graceful undulating form, in its pretty morning dress; and then gazed in the soft grey eyes, looking lovingly out of a sweet oval face, framed in rich brown hair.

"Oh, bother punctuality, daddy!" said the younger girl, a merry, mischievous-looking blonde, with freckled face, bright eyes, and a charming petite form that was most attractive. "Don't be cross," she cried, getting behind his chair, throwing her arms round his neck, and laying a soft downy cheek upon his bald head. "Don't be cross; we've had such a jolly walk, and got a basketful of ferns. There! that'll make you good tempered."

And she leaned over, dragging his head back, and kissed him half a dozen times on the forehead.

"Fin! Finetta!" exclaimed Sir Hampton. "Now, suppose one of the servants saw you!"

"Oh, they wouldn't mind, daddy," laughed the girl. "Oh, I say, how your head shines this morning!"

And bubbling over, as it were, with fun, she breathed sharply twice on her astonished parent's crown, gave her hand a circular movement over it a few times, and, before he could recover from his surprise, she finished it off with a polish from her pocket-handkerchief, and then stepped back, looking mischievously at the irate knight, as he forced his chair back from the table and stared at her.

"Is the girl mad?" he exclaimed. "Finetta, you make me exceedingly angry."

"Not with me, daddy," said the girl placing herself on his knee. "Kiss me, and say good morning, sir."

The head of the family hesitated for a moment, and then could not resist the upturned face, which he kissed and then pushed the girl away.

"Now go to your place; and I insist Fin, upon your dropping—"

Miss Matilda started.

"I mean leaving off—using that absurdly childish appellation. I desire you always to address me as papa."

"All right, daddy," said the girl, laughing—"as soon as I can teach myself."

Sir Hampton snatched himself back into his place, and began to open letters; while Finetta went and kissed her aunt.

"Well, aunty, how's Pip this morning?"

"Pepine is very unwell, my dear," said Miss Matilda, coldly.

"You stuff him too much, aunty, and don't give him exercise enough."

"My dear you should not deliver opinions upon what you do not understand. Your papa's cup."

"Don't understand, aunty!" said the girl, passing the cup; "why, I know all about dogs and horses. You give Pip over to me for a week; I'll soon put the little wretch right."

Lady Rea saw the horror upon her sister-in-law's countenance, and catching her daughter's eye, shook her head at her, as she went on dispensing the tea.

"Have some poached eggs, daddy—pa?" said Fin, correcting herself with much gravity, and revelling in the look of suffering upon her aunt's face. "No? Tiny, give papa some of the turkey."

Sir Hampton fed himself mechanically, passed some letters to his wife and eldest daughter, and read his own.

"Is there no letter for me, Hampton?" said Miss Matilda, plaintively.

There was a grunt, indicative of "No," from the knight; and Miss Matilda sighed, and went on sipping her sugarless tea, and nibbling some very dry, butterless toast.

"I say, Aunt Matty," said Fin, merrily, "I mean to take you in hand."

"Take me in hand, child?" said the spinster.

"Yes, aunty. Now, look here; if, instead of stopping grumping here at home, you had had a jolly good run with us—"

Miss Matilda took a sip of her tea, which might have been vinegar from the aspect of her countenance.

"You could have gathered ferns, sipped the bright morning dew, come back with a colour, and eaten a breakfast like I do. Tiny, give me some more of that turkey."

"Your appetite is really ravenous, child," said Miss Matilda, with a shudder.

"Not it, aunty; I'm growing—ain't I, ma, dear?"

"Well, my love, I think you are filling out—not growing."

"Oh, but, ma," laughed Fin, with her mouth full, "I'm not going to be round and plump like you are, am I?"

"Fin!" exclaimed her sister, from the other side of the table.

"Oh, ma knows I don't mean any harm; don't you, dear? It's only my fun, isn't it? I shouldn't mind—I should like to be such a soft, loving old dear; shouldn't I?"

"Hush, hush, hush!" exclaimed Lady Rea. "I do think, though, aunty, a walk would do you good before breakfast."

"Perhaps it might do you good, too," said Miss Matilda, with some asperity.

"Er-rum, er-rum!" ejaculated Sir Hampton, laying down a big blue official envelope. "Lady Rea—my dears, I have something to communicate."

He sat back in his chair, and brushed a few crumbs from his buff waistcoat.

"Well, pa, dear, what is it?" said Lady Rea, out of her tea-cup.

"Er-rum, I have at last," said Sir Hampton, pompously, "received public recognition of my position. My dears, I have been placed upon the bench, and am now one of the county magistracy."

He looked round for the applause which should follow.

"Well, my dear, I'm sure I'm very glad if it pleases you," said Lady Rea. "Matty, give me another poached egg."

"It was quite time they did, Hampton," said Miss Matilda.

"I congratulate you, papa, dear," said Valentina, going up to him and kissing him; "and I'm sure the poor will be glad to have so kind a magistrate to deal with them."

"Thank you, Tiny—thank you," said Sir Hampton, smiling, and trying to look every inch a magistrate, before turning to his second daughter, who was intent upon a turkey drumstick.

"But I say, pa, what fun it will be!" she said at last; "you'll have to sit on the poachers."

"Yes, the scoundrels!" said Sir Hampton, and his cravat crackled.

"And send all the poor old women to quod for picking sticks."

"To where?" exclaimed Miss Matilda, in horrified tones.

"Quod," said Finetta, quite unmoved; "it's Latin, I think, for prison, or else it's stable slang—I'm not sure. But oh, my," she continued, seeing her father's frown, "we've got some news, too."

"Have you, dear?" said mamma, "what is it?"

"We saw Humphrey Lloyd this morning."

"Who is Humphrey Lloyd?" said Lady Rea.

"The keeper at Penreife."

"Penreife," said Sir Hampton, waking up out of a day-dream of judicial honours. "Yes, a beautiful estate. I would have bought it instead of this if it had been for sale."

"Well," said Finetta, "we met Humphrey, and talked to him."

"I think, if I may be allowed to say so, Finetta, that you are too fond of talking to grooms and keepers, and people of that class," said Miss Matilda, glancing at her brother, who, however, was once more immersed in judicial dreams—J.P., *custos rotulorum*, commission of the peace, etcetera.

"Tennyson used to hang with grooms and porters on bridges, and he's poet laureate; so why shouldn't I?" said Finetta, rebelliously.

"I don't think it's nice, though," said mamma. "Aunt Matty is quite right; you are not a child now, my dear."

"Oh, mamma, dear, it's only Fin's nonsense," said Tiny. "Humphrey is a very respectful, worthy young fellow, and he climbed up the big rocks down by Penreife for us, and got us some of those beautiful little aspleniums we couldn't reach."

"Yes, ma, dear," said Finetta; "and he says that the next time he writes to his old aunt in Wales, he'll tell her to send some of the beautiful little rare ferns that grow up on one of the mountains, in a place that nearly broke my teeth when I tried to say it."

Lady Rea shook her head at her daughter, who rattled on.

"Well, you know about Penreife belonging to Lieutenant Trevor?"

Lady Rea nodded.

"Well, Humphrey's got orders to go to town to meet his master, who has been on a cruise round the world, and his ship's paid off, and now he's going to settle at home."

"Who's going to settle at home?" inquired Sir Hampton.

"Lieutenant Trevor."

"Ah! a sailor person, and rough, I suppose—sailors always are," said Sir Hampton.

"Yes," cried Finetta, "they haul in slack, and cry 'Avast!' at you, and 'shiver my timbers!' But, I say—I like sailors; I shall set my cap at him."

"Finetta!" gasped Miss Matilda.

"Don't talk nonsense, child," said Lady Rea. "Don't you hear what papa says about sailors being so rough? I daresay he isn't a bit of a gentleman."

"But he's an officer, ma, dear," said Finetta; "and if Tiny hasn't made up her mind to have him, I shall. They are doing all sorts of things up at the house; and it's to be full of company, Mrs Lloyd says; and she looked as proud as a peacock, as she stood smoothing her white apron. We're sure to be invited; and won't it be a good job! for this place is so jolly dull."

"Ah, my child," said Aunt Matilda, "if you would only properly employ your time, you would not find it dull."

"What! knit mittens, bother the poor people, and read Saint Thomas à Kempis, aunty?" replied Finetta. "No, thank you. But Mr Trevor's coming—I say, ought we to call him lieutenant?—it's so absurd—ought to brighten up the place a bit; and of course, ma, you'll ask him here?"

"Er-rum!" ejaculated Sir Hampton, rousing himself from his day-dreams. "It is my wish that there should always be shown in my establishment the hospitality of—er—er—a country gentleman."

"And a knight," said Miss Matilda, softly.

"Thank you, Matilda—and a knight," said Sir Hampton. "But, my dears, I have great pleasure in announcing to you that I have made up my mind that we shall now pay a short visit to the great metropolis."

"How jolly!" said Finetta. "But what are we going for, pa, dear?"

"My dear, I have several things to see about," said Sir Hampton. "To engage a groom for one thing, to buy horses for another, and a gun or two for my friends. I intend to have, too, the west room fitted up for billiards."

"For what, Hampton?" said his sister.

"Er-rum!—billiards," said Sir Hampton.

"It is not often that I venture upon a word, Hampton, respecting your household management; but when I hear of propositions which must interfere with your fixture welfare, I feel bound to speak."

"And, pray, what do you mean?" said Sir Hampton, angrily.

"I mean that I gave way when you insisted on having cards in the house, because you said your visitors liked whist—"

"And you were always rattling the dice box and playing backgammon," retorted Sir Hampton.

"That is different," said Miss Matilda; "backgammon is a very old and a very innocent game."

"Oh!" said Sir Hampton.

"I have known great divines play at backgammon."

"And I've known a bishop play a good rubber at whist," said Sir Hampton.

"I am sorry for it," said Miss Matilda; "but I draw the line at billiards. It is a detestable game, played on a green cloth which is the flag of gambling, and—"

"If you will take my advice, Matty, you will hold your tongue," said Sir Hampton. "My guests will like a game at billiards, and I'll be bound to say, before we've had the table in the house a month, you'll be playing a game yourself."

"Hampton!"

"Same as you do at whist."

"I oblige your guests, and make up your horrid rubbers."

"But I say, aunty, you do like winning, you know," chimed in Fin.

"Oh, my dear, I—"

"You pocketed fifteen shillings—I won't say 'bob,' because it's slangy," said Fin, laughing mischievously.

"I protest, I—"

"Er-rum!—I will not hear another word. We start for town to-morrow; and, my dears, you asked me once for horses—you shall have them. Fin, my child, don't strangle me! There, now, see how you've rumpled my cravat!"

"Oh, thank you, daddy!"

"Now, if you say *daddy* again, I'll alter my mind," said the old gentleman, angrily.

"There, then, I won't," said Fin. "But I say, pa, we must have a groom."

"Of course, my dear."

"And riding-habits."

"To be sure."

"And we can get them in town. Oh, Tiny, do say 'Hooray' for once in your life."

"Er-rum! It's my intention," said Sir Hampton, "to patronise the sports of our country, and foster hunting, game-keeping, and the like. By the way, that man Lloyd might do some commissions for me. Matty, you will keep house till we return. My dears, we start to-morrow morning."

"Then all I've got to say," said Miss Matilda, sharply, "is this—"

"Yelp! yelp! yelp!"—a succession of wild shrieks from beneath the antimacassar, out of one side of which lay a thin black tail, in very close proximity to Fin's pretty little foot, and in an instant Aunt Matty was down upon her knees, talking to and caressing the dog.

"Er-rum!" went Sir Hampton, slowly crossing the hall to his library, followed by Lady Rea; and directly after Miss Matilda hurried away, with her pet in her arms.

"Now, Fin, that was cruel. I saw you tread on Pip's tail," said Tiny.

"Doing evil that good might come," said Fin, defiantly. "Look here, Tiny—pets were anciently offered up to save a row. If I hadn't made him squeal, there would have been pa storming, Aunt Matty going into hysterics, and ma worried to death; so that it was like the old nursery rhyme—"

> "I trod sharp on the little dog's tail;
> The dog began to shriek and wail,
> And poor Aunty Matty turned mighty pale:
> It stopped papa from blowing a gale;
> And that's the end of my little tale."

"Er-rum!" was heard from across the hall.

"There's daddy going to lecture me; and look here, Tiny, Edward will come in directly to clear the cloth. Now, then, here's a penny; let's toss. Heads or tails, who wins."

"Wins what?"

"Mr Richard Trevor, and Penreife. Now then, cry!"

"No," said Tiny, "I'll laugh instead."

And she kissed her sister on the cheek.

In Pall Mall

"Voilà!—the pilot-fish and the shark!"

The words were spoken by an individual idly smoking a cigar on the steps of that gloomy-looking pile in Pall Mall known as the Peripatetics. He was the being that, go where he would, uneducated people would set down as belonging to the division Swell; for there was *ton* and aristocrat in the fit of his clothes and every curve of his body. Women would have called his black moustache and beard handsome, and spoken of his piercing eyes, high white forehead, and wonderful complexion; but Podger Pratt—that is to say, Frank Pratt—said more than once he had never seen a barber's dummy that was his equal. He said it in a very solemn way; and when it came to the ears of the gentleman in question, he denounced Podger Pratt as a disgusting little cad, and the next time they met at the club Captain Vanleigh asked Pratt what he meant by it.

"What did I mean?" said Pratt, in a serious, puzzled tone of voice. "What did I mean?—oh, just what I said. It's a fact."

Captain Vanleigh stood glaring at him as if trying to pierce the imperturbable crust of solemnity on the speaker's face; but Pratt remained as solemn as a judge, and amidst an ill-suppressed tittering, the Captain stalked from the room, saying to his companion—

"The fellow's a fool—an ass—little better than an idiot!"

As for Podger Pratt, he looked innocently round the room as if asking the meaning of the laugh, and then went on with his paper.

But that was months before the present day, when Captain Vanleigh, gracefully removing his cigar from between his white teeth, said—

"Voilà! the pilot-fish and the shark!"

"The sucking-fish and the porpoise, I should say," remarked his companion, a fair young fellow, dressed evidently upon the other's model. "What big fellow Dick Trevor has grown!"

"You're right, Flick; sucking-fish it is. That fat, little, briefless barrister will fatten still more on Dick Trevor's chequebook. Ah, well, Flicky, it is a wise ordination of Providence that those men who have the largest properties are the biggest fools."

"Ya-as, exactly," said Flick, otherwise Sir Felix Landells. "I daresay you're right, Van; but don't quite see your argument. I s'pose may call 'self a wealthy man?"

"No rule without an exception, my dear boy; you are one of the exceptions. Odd, though, isn't it, how we have all been thrown together after four years?"

"Yes, 'tis odd; but think it's dooced nice of Dick to look us up as he has. You'll make one of the party, of course?"

"Well, I don't know. Certainly, town is empty. These sailor fellows are rather rough, though."

"Oh, come down. Besides, it's in the country."

"Such an infernal distance! — but there, perhaps I will."

As they stood talking, there came slowly sauntering along the pave a well-built young fellow, broad of shoulder and chest, and fining rapidly down to the loins. He seemed to convey the idea that he was rolling up to you on the deck of a ship with a sea on, and he carried his hands as if it might be necessary at any moment to throw them out to seize belaying pin or handrail. He was well dressed; but there was a certain easy freedom in the fit of his garments, and a loose swing pervading all, much in contrast with the natty, fashionable attire of the friends, whom he saluted with a pleasant smile lighting up his bronzed face and clear grey eyes. His hair was crisp, curly, and brown, seeming rather at war with the glossy new hat he wore, and settled more than once upon his head as he listened to the remarks of the little dapper-looking man at his side — Podger, otherwise Frank, Pratt, of the Temple.

Pratt was a solemn, neutral-looking fellow; but none the less he was keen and peculiar, even though, to use his own words, he had been born without any looks at all.

"There's the wolf, Dick," said Pratt, as they approached the club. "Who's that with him? Ah, might have known — the lamb."

"You seem to have kept up the old school tricks, Frank," said Trevor, "and I suppose it gets you into hot water sometimes. Bad habit giving nicknames. We shouldn't stand it at sea."

"It breaks no bones," said the other, quietly, "and seems to do me good — safety-valve for my spleen. How odd it is, though, that we four should be thrown together again in this way!"

"I was thinking the same; but I don't see why we should call things odd when we have shaped them ourselves. I was cruising about for days to find you all out."

"Well, it's very kind of you, Dick," said Pratt. "And let me see—I've won four pounds ten and six of you during the last week at pool and whist. Dick, you're quite a godsend to a poor fellow. Look here, new gloves—ain't had such a pair for a month."

"By the way," said Trevor, "is Vanleigh well off?"

"He was," said Pratt—"came in for a nice property. How he stands now I can't say."

"And Landells?"

"Landells has a clear nine thousand a year; but I've seen hardly anything of them lately. Poole dresses them; and how could you expect such exquisites to seek the society of a man who wears sixteen-shilling pantaloons, dines on chops, reads hard, and, when he does go to a theatre, sits in the pit? By Jove, Dick, you would have laughed one night! I did—inside, for there wasn't a crease in my phiz. They cut me dead. I was sitting in the front row in the pit, and as luck or some mischievous imp would have it, they were placed in two stalls in the back row, exactly in front of me, so that I could inhale the ambrosial odours from Flick Landells' fair curls the whole evening."

"Snobbish—wasn't it?" said Dick.

"Just half," said Pratt. "Landells is a good chap at heart; but society is spoiling him. He came to my chambers the very next day, with a face like a turkey-cock, to ask me if it was I that he saw at the theatre. I looked at him out of the corner of one eye, and he broke down, and asked my pardon like a man. Swore he wouldn't have minded a bit, if Van hadn't been with him. It's all right, Dick; I can read Felix the Unhappy like a book."

"Well, gentlemen," said Trevor, as they reached the steps, "it is settled for Wednesday, of course?"

"Well," said Landells, hesitating, "I—er—I—er—"

"Oh, you must come, Flick," said Trevor; "we've got all our old days to go over, and I've ordered the yacht round. Vanleigh, help me to persuade him."

"You might come," said Vanleigh, in a half-injured tone.

"Oh, I'll go if you are going," said Sir Felix, hastily; and then, correcting himself—"if you both really wish it."

"That's right," said Trevor; "take pity on my seafaring ignorance. I shall want some company down at the old place. Pratt has promised."

"Indeed!" said Vanleigh, fixing his glass in one eye. "I thought last night he couldn't leave his reading?"

"Obliged to yield, like you, to the force of circumstances," said Pratt, "and give way to our old friend's overwhelming hospitality. But you needn't mind, Van, old fellow, I won't disgrace you. Look here," he said, taking off his hat and speaking loudly, "new tile, fourteen bob—couldn't afford a Lincoln and Bennett; brand-new gloves, two-and-three; and I've ordered one of Samuel Brothers' tourist suits for the occasion."

"My dear fellow," said the Captain, after a look of disgust at Sir Felix, "I really do not want to know the extent of your wardrobe. In fact, mine is at your service—my valet—er—I beg your pardon, Trevor."

"I say, don't take any notice of that solemn little humbug," said Trevor, laughing; "you know what he always was. I—oh, my God!"

The exclamation was involuntary, for just at that moment a hansom cab was driven sharply out of the turning leading to Saint James's Square, the horse shied—Pratt afterwards swore it was at Vanleigh's eyes—and in another instant would have stricken down a faded-looking woman, who seemed to be crossing towards the club steps, but for the act of a passer-by.

The act was as quick as thought. With a bound he caught the woman, swung her round, and was struck by the horse full on the shoulder, to reel for a few yards with his burden, and then roll over and over in the muddy road.

The cabman pulled sharp up, and leapt off his perch with a face white as ashes, in an instant, while Trevor and Pratt ran to the fallen pair—the former to raise the woman, and carry her scared and trembling to the club steps, where Vanleigh stood looking as scared as the sufferer, while Pratt helped the gentleman to rise.

"Take me away, please; let me go—away," said the woman, shivering with fear.

"Are you hurt?" said Trevor, with his arm still round her.

"No, no; not hurt—only let me go."

"I couldn't help it, gen'lemen," began the cabman.

"No, confound you!—it was an accident, worse luck!" said the principal sufferer, "or you should have caught it sharply, Mr Nine-hundred-and-seventy-six. Here's a pretty mess I'm in!"

"Very sorry, sir," said the cabman, — "but —"

"There, that'll do. Is the lady hurt?"

"No, no," said the woman, hastily, and she glanced timidly at Vanleigh, and then at Pratt, who was watching her keenly.

Just then a four-wheeler, which Trevor had hailed, came up, and he handed her in.

"Where shall he drive you?" said Trevor, as he slipped half-a-crown in the driver's hand.

"Twenty-seven, Whaley's Place, Upper Holloway," said the woman, in an unnecessarily loud voice; and the cab was driven off.

"Thank you," said the muddy stranger, holding out a very dirty hand to Trevor, who grasped it heartily.

"Worse disasters at sea," he said, smiling.

"Yes," said the other, looking hard in his face, "so I suppose; but then you do get an action for damages, or insurance money. I don't insure my clothes," he said, looking ruefully at his muddy garments, and then at those of the man who had served him. "I say, that was very kind of you, though."

"Nonsense!" said Trevor, laughing in the bright, earnest, middle-aged face before him. "Come into the club, and send for some fresh things."

"Thanks, no," said the stranger, "I'll get back to my rooms. I must have something out of somebody, so I'll make cabby suffer."

The cabman rubbed his ear, and looked blue.

"You'll drive me home, cabby?" said the stranger.

"That I will, sir, for a week," said the man, eagerly.

"We may as well exchange cards," said the stranger, pulling out a case, and putting a muddy thumb upon the top card. "There you are—John Barnard, his mark," he said, laughing. "Thanks once more. I'll stick your card in here with mine; and now good-bye."

"Good-bye," said Trevor, frankly; and they shook hands.

"I shall know your face again."

Saying which, after a curious stare in Trevor's face, the stranger climbed into the cab, the driver touched up his horse, and the two street boys and the crossing-sweeper, who had been attracted to the scene, were about to separate, when the latter pounced upon something white and held it up to Pratt.

"Did yer drop this 'ere, sir?"

"No," said Pratt, looking at the muddy note; "but here is sixpence—it is for one of my friends."

Directly after, to the disgust of the two exquisites, Trevor, soiled from head to foot, was laughing heartily at the rueful aspect of Frank Pratt as he entered the hall.

"Look here," he said, dolefully, as he held out his muddy gloves. "Two-and-three; and brand-new to-day. Van," he added, with a peculiar cock of one eye, "have you a clean pair in your pocket?"

"No," said Vanleigh, coldly. "You can get good gloves in the Arcade; but not," he added, with a sneer, "at two-and-three."

"Thanks," said Pratt; "but I am not a simple Arcadian in my ideas. Oh, by the way, Van, here's a note for you which somebody seems to have dropped."

Vanleigh almost snatched the muddy note, which was directed in a fine, lady's hand; and there was a curious pinched expression about his lips as he took in the address.

"Ah, yes; thanks, much," he drawled. "Very kind of you, I'm shaw. By the way, Trevor, dear boy," he continued, turning to his friend, "hadn't you better send one of the fellows for some things, and then we might walk on to the Corner if you had nothing better to do? Try a suit of mine; those don't fit you well."

"No, I'll keep to my own style," said Trevor, laughing. "I don't think I could quite manage your cut."

Then nodding merrily in answer to the other's rather disgusted look, he sent a messenger to his hotel, and strolled off to one of the dormitories, while Frank Pratt went into the reading-room, where the others had walked to the window, took up a newspaper, furtively watching Captain Vanleigh and his friend, in the expectation that they would go; but, to his great annoyance, they stayed on till Trevor reappeared, when Vanleigh, with his slow dawdle, crossed to him.

"What are you going to do this afternoon, dear boy?"

"Well, I was thinking of what you said—running down to the Corner to look at a horse or two. Things I don't much understand."

"I'll go with you," said Vanleigh. "You'll come, won't you, Flick?"

"Delighted, quite!" was the reply, very much to Pratt's disgust—the feeling of disgust being equally shared by Vanleigh, when he saw "that gloveless little humbug" get up to accompany them.

No matter what the feelings were that existed, they sent for a couple of cabs, and a few minutes after were being trundled down Piccadilly towards what is still known as "The Corner" where that noble animal the "'oss" is brought up and knocked down day by day, in every form and shape—horses with characters, and horses whose morals are bad; right up through park hacks and well-matched high steppers, greys, chestnuts, roans and bays, well-broken ladies' steeds, good for a canter all day, to the very perfection of hunters up to any weight—equine princes of the blood royal, that have in their youth snuffed the keen air of the Yorkshire wolds; mares with retrousse noses and the saucy look given by a dash of Irish blood. Racers, too, are there, whose satin skins, netted with veins, throb with the blue blood that has come down from some desert sire, who has been wont in fleet career to tear up the sand of Araby like a whirlwind, spurn it behind his hoofs, and yet, at the lightest touch of the bit, check the lithe play of his elastic limbs at the opening of some camel or goat-hair tent, where half a dozen swarthy children are ready to play with it, and crawl uninjured about its feet—the mother busily the while preparing the baken cakes and mares-milk draught for her Bedouin lord.

First Encounters

"Clean yer boots? Brush down, sir?"

"Why can't yer leave the gent alone? I spoke fust, sir."

"Here y'are, sir—out of the crowd, sir."

Sixpence to be earned, and a scuffle for it, with the result that Richard Trevor stood a little out of the stream of passengers, stoically permitting a gentleman in an old red-sleeved waistcoat to "ciss-s-s" at him, as he brushed him most carefully down with an old brush, even though he was not in the slightest degree dusty.

"Now, look here, Dick, if I'm to go trotting about at your heels like a big dog, I shall bite at everybody who tries to rob you. I shan't stand by and see you fleeced. Is there something in salt water that makes you sailors ready to part with your money to the first comer?"

The speaker was Frank Pratt, as he drew his friend away towards one of the omnibuses running that day from Broxford Station to where a regular back and heart-breaking bit of country had been flagged over for a steeplechase course.

"You shall do precisely as you like, Frank," was the quiet reply.

"Very good, then—I will. Now, look here, Dick; you have now, I suppose, a clear income of twelve thousand a year?"

"Yes, somewhere about that."

"And you want to fool it all away?"

"Not I."

"Well, there was a specimen. You gave that fellow a shilling for brushing your coat that was not dirty."

"Poor devil, yes! He tried to earn it honestly, and we don't get such luxuries at sea."

"As honestly as Van earned forty sovs. of you after we left Tatt's yesterday."

"Don't understand you, Franky," said Trevor, with a twinkle of the eye, as he allowed himself to be caught by a shoeblack, and placed a slightly soiled boot upon his stand.

"Tut!" ejaculated Pratt. "There you go again. What a fellow you are, Dick! What I meant was that horse of his. You gave him a cheque for a hundred for it."

"Yes, I did, Franky."

"He gave sixty for it last week."

Trevor winced slightly, and said quietly—

"Dealer's profit; and he understands horses. Try another cigar, Frank."

Pratt took another cigar, lit it, and said, quietly—

"Now look here, Dick, old fellow, I'm afraid I'm going to be a great nuisance to you. You're so easy-going, that with this money of yours—to use your sea-going terms—you'll be all amongst the sharks; every one will be making a set at you. 'Pon my soul, I've been miserable ever since I won that four pound ten. The best thing we can do is to see one another seldom, for if I stay with you I shall always be boring you about some foolish bit of extravagance, and getting into hot water with the friends who take a fancy to you."

"My dear Frank," said Trevor, smoking away in the most unruffled fashion, "you will oblige me very much by letting that be the clearing-up shower as far as talk of leaving me is concerned. It is quite right. Here have I been to sea, middy and man, for twelve years; and now I come back to England a great helpless baby of a fellow, game for everybody. You think I'm a fool. Well, I am not over-wise; but my first act ashore here was the looking-up of a tried old schoolfellow, whose purse I've often shared, and who never once left me in the lurch—and," he added, slowly and meaningly, "who never will leave me in the lurch. Am I right?"

Frank Pratt turned one sharp, quick flash upon the speaker, and that was enough.

"Thanky, sir," cried the shoeblack, spinning up the sixpence he had received.

The friends turned towards one of the omnibuses about to make a start for the course.

"Beg parding, sir," said a voice, "just a speck left on your coat, sir!" And the man who had received the shilling for the brushing began to "ciss" once more.

"That'll do, sir! That's the next 'bus, sir! Good luck to you for a real gent, sir," he added; and then in a whisper, "Back White Lassie!"

Trevor turned sharply round, just time enough to encounter a most knowing wink, and the man was gone.

"Dick, I'm afraid that's a trap," said Pratt, gazing after the man. "Better not bet at all; but if you do, I don't think I should go by what that fellow says. Well, come along. Eh? what?"

"Consequential-looking old chap in that barouche, I said;" and Trevor pointed to where a carriage had drawn up by the railway hotel, the owner having posted down from town—"regular type of the old English gentleman."

"Now, if we are to get on together, Dick," said Pratt, plaintively, "don't try to humbug me in that way. Don't hoist false colours."

"Humbug you?—false colours?"

"Yes, humbug me. Now, on your oath, didn't you think more of the two ladies in the barouche than of the old gentleman?"

"Without being on my oath—yes, I did; for I haven't seen a pretty girl for three years. Get up first."

"After you," was the response.

And directly after the friends were mounted on the knifeboard of a great three-horse omnibus, brought down expressly for the occasion.

The vehicle was soon loaded in a way that put its springs to the test, for the exact licenced number was not studied upon that day. There was a fair sprinkling of gentlemen, quiet, businesslike professionals, and decent tradesmen with a taste for sport; but the railway company having run cheap special trains, London had sent forth a few representative batches of the fancy, in the shape of canine-featured gentlemen "got up" expressly for the occasion, with light trousers, spotted neckerchiefs, velvet coats, and a sign in the breast of their shirt or tie in the shape of a horseshoe pin. It is impossible to sit in such company without wondering whether the closely cropped hair was cut at the expense of the country; and when a quiet, neutral-looking man, sitting amongst them, accidentally clicks something in his pocket, you may know all the time that it is the lid of a tobacco-box, or a few halfpence, but you are certain to think of handcuffs.

You cannot pick your companions on an omnibus bound from a little country station to the scene of a steeplechase, and Richard Trevor and his friend soon found that they were in luck; for in addition to the regular racing attendants, London had sent down a pleasant assortment of those sporting gentlemen who used to hang about London Bridge Station on the morning when an event was to "come off," police permitting, some forty miles down the line.

In the hurry of climbing up, Pratt had not noticed the occupants of the vehicle but as soon as they had taken their seats he was for descending again, and he turned to whisper his wishes to his friend.

"All comes of being in such a plaguy hurry, Frank. Always take soundings before you come to an anchor. Never mind now, though the onions are far from agreeable."

The words had hardly left his lips, when a man on his left turned sharply, and asked why he hadn't ordered his "kerridge," subsiding afterwards into a growl, in which the word "sweeps" was plainly to be made out.

This acted as the signal for a little light chaff, and remarks began to fly about the dress of the friends. Moses Brothers and Whitechapel hags were mentioned, counter-jumping playfully alluded to, and permissions to be out for the day; and then a battery of exceedingly foul pipes came into play, emitting odours resembling anything but those of Araby the Blest, and driving Frank Pratt to ask his friend, in self-defence, for a cigar.

"Giv's that there light," said an individual on his right—a gentleman in velveteen coat, tight trousers, and eyes of so friendly a nature that they seemed ever seeking each other's society, and trying to burrow beneath the bridge of their owner's flat nose. He had no whiskers nor beard, but a great deal of mouth and chin, spotted all over with tiny black dots. His massive neck was swathed in a great belcher kerchief, with ample but useful ends; for besides supplying warmth, one was used occasionally to supply the lack of nutriment, and be nibbled by the owner's great horse-teeth.

Trevor took the vesuvian from his friend, and politely passed it to the man, who leered, grinned, stuffed it into his pipe-bowl, holding it there as he puffed for a few moments, and then, winking at a companion, he pitched the little incandescent globe upon Pratt's light overcoat.

Pratt started, flushed angrily, and brushed the vesuvian from his coat, but not until it had burned there a round black spot. But he said nothing; his face only twitched a little, as he began to make remarks about the country they were passing.

"Hillo!—eo—eo!" came from behind, as the omnibus slowly lumbered along; the driver drew a little on one side, and the open carriage, with its post-horses, that they had seen by the railway hotel, began slowly to pass, with the two young men eagerly scanning the occupants.

"Look at that old cock in the buff weskit," said some one on the omnibus—a sally which was followed by roars of laughter, as an elderly gentleman, of portly, magisterial aspect, half started from the back seat, filming and frowning in utter astonishment at so ribald an attack on his dignity.

"Going to ask us to lunch, guv'nor?" laughed a third.

"That's Brighamy Young and his three wives," cried some one else.

"Tell the postboy to go a little faster, Edward," the old gentleman called out to a footman on the box.

"Do you hear, Edward? Why don't you go on faster, Edward?—eh, Edward?" cried the first speaker, while the old gentleman leaned forward to speak to one of the young ladies opposite, who was evidently somewhat agitated; while, to make matters worse, the omnibus driver had whipped up his horses, and the great vehicle kept on thundering along abreast of the barouche.

This fresh movement was the signal for a volley from the fellow on Trevor's right; and he now made himself especially conspicuous, kissing his hand, and evidently goading the old gentleman into a state of apoplexy. A scene was evidently brewing, and something unpleasant must have inevitably occurred, had not, almost at one and the same moment, Pratt whispered a word or two in French to his friend, and the postboy given his horses a few cuts, which made them start forward with such energy that the barouche was soon out of sight.

"You're about right, Frank," Trevor said, leaning back; "it is not worth notice."

"P'raps you'll just use about as much of this here 'bus as you pays for," said the man seated dos-à-dos to him, and whom he had slightly pressed.

Trevor started forward; for the remark was unpleasantly made, and qualified with offensive adjectives. Pratt looked anxious, and would gladly have finished the distance on foot; but to stop the omnibus, and get down, would probably have made bad worse—especially as Trevor only smiled, and sat up quite erect.

"He've been taking more than his share of the 'bus ever since he got up," said the black-looking gentleman on the right, pressing closer to Trevor. "Keep yer own side, will yer?"

Very pale and quiet, Richard Trevor edged a little more towards his companion; but this was only the signal for renewed insult, the knifeboard being in possession of the fellow's friends.

"Where are you a-scrowging to?" said the fellow on Pratt's left.

And then, acting in concert, he and his companions forced the little barrister closer to his friend.

"Here, let's speak to the driver," said Trevor, quietly; but there was a dull red spot in each cheek.

"No, no!" said Pratt. "It's not much further; don't let us have a row."

"Mind your pockets, then," muttered Trevor.

"Ah, just as I thought," said the fellow who had been ringleader throughout. "They're a talking about pockets—button up, gents."

Here followed a roar of laughter, and a few more witticisms of a similar character were fired off. Then, seeing how patiently the two friends bore it all, a fresh crowding was tried, and one of the most offensive of the fellows called out to the man in velveteens—

"Why don't you leave off, Barney?"

"Tain't me," said Barney, grinning hugely; "it's these here two swell mob blokes."

There was another roar of laughter, which culminated in a shriek of delight when Barney of the black muzzle removed his pipe from his mouth, and designedly spat upon Trevor's glossy boot.

The young man started as if he had been stung; but there was a quiet, firm pressure of his arm, and he said, in French—

"Is it much further to the course?"

As he spoke, he quietly drew a white cambric handkerchief from his pocket, carefully removed all trace of the disgusting offence from his boot, and threw the handkerchief into the road, following it up by lighting a fresh cigar.

"My! what a pity!" said the fellow, sneeringly, as he watched with curiosity the young man's action. "I am sorry. Wouldn't you like the handkerchief—again?"

And he pointed to a boy who had just picked it up from the road.

The pressure was again upon Trevor's arm, but he did not speak, and the only movement was a slight twitching about the muscles of the face.

What more insult might have followed it is impossible to say, for the omnibus now stopped at a gate, and the occupants began to scramble off. Trevor rose, and waited for the gentleman called Barney to get down. But he remained; so Trevor stepped over him, and Pratt was about to follow, when the fellow thrust out his legs, and the young man tripped, staggered, and would have fallen from the omnibus but for the strong arm of his friend.

"Get down first," said Trevor.

"No, no—never mind," said Pratt, catching his arm.

"Get down first," said Trevor, as if he were on the quarter-deck.

"There's nothing to be gained by it," whispered Pratt.

"I'll come directly," was the reply; and facing round upon the fellow, who had risen, he looked him full in his closely-set eyes, face close to face, as he said, quietly—

"I think I shall know you again, my friend."

Before the fellow had recovered from his surprise, Trevor stepped lightly down, took Pratt's arm in an easy-going, familiar way, and the friends joined the string of people crossing the fields.

"Thank goodness!" said Pratt; "I do hate a row. You must be on the losing side. Lost anything?"

"No," said Trevor, thoughtfully. "But if that fellow had been at sea with me, and behaved like that—"

"You'd have had him flogged?"

"No," said Trevor, "I'd have pitched him overboard."

"Overboard?"

"Yes," said Trevor, with his face once more all smiles—"and fished him out!"

Rather Unpleasant

"Ah," said Pratt, after a brisk walk, "it might have been worse; it all comes of getting on knife-boards. I never do go on a 'bus but I'm sure to meet some one I don't want to see from that elevated position. Let's see: in somebody's fables one poor bird got his neck wrung through being in bad company, and getting caught by the fowler."

"And what has that to do with knife-boards?"

"Only this," said Frank, grimly; "I should uncommonly like to see that barouche; and the cocky old gentleman inside will be safe to give us credit for being the ringleaders of those rowdies."

"Well, never mind," said Trevor; "I wanted to see a steeplechase, though I don't suppose I shall like it any more than a ball."

No more was said then, for they had reached the ground flagged out for the course—a pleasant tract running round in front of a mound-like hill, affording the spectators from the various stands a capital view of the whole race; save where here and there a tiny copse intervened, so that it must inevitably hide the horses for a few moments.

They were in ample time, for twelve, one, and two o'clock upon racing cards are very different hours to those represented upon the time-tables at our various termini; so they had a stroll round, pausing here or there; but, no matter where they strayed, so sure as Frank Pratt turned his head, it was to see the evil-looking countenance of their companion on the omnibus close at hand, though whether Trevor had seen him or not he could not tell.

For, probably from a love of the beautiful, the young men's steps generally led them to where they could stand in pretty close proximity to the barouche—whose occupants seemed to have, for one at least, something of an attraction. And no wonder; for on the front seat were two fresh, bright-eyed English girls, whose eyes sparkled with animation, and in whose cheeks came and went the bright colour that told you of excited interest in the day's proceedings.

"I thought as much," said Pratt, as they passed once close by the carriage on their way to the stand, and a quick glance showed that they were recognised by the ladies, who coloured slightly, and turned away; whilst the old gentleman's countenance, as he stood up, gradually assumed the purply-red well known to all who have seen a turkey-cock at such time as he ruffleth his plumes, and scowled fiercely at the friends.

"The impudent scoundrels!" he said aloud, as he turned to the elderly lady at his side.

"That comes of being in bad company," said Pratt. "Dick, old fellow, I shall walk back. Here, my friend, I have feeling in my toe."

"Beg pardon, sir, I'm sure," said a fine, handsome, bluff West-countryman—a regular keeper, in brown velveteens; "I really didn't see you." And he passed on towards the barouche, the friends following him with their eyes, to see him touch his hat to first one and then another of the inmates, who smiled, and seemed to talk to him in a very animated way, the old gentleman ending by pointing to the box-seat, a good post for seeing, to which the young man climbed.

"Lucky dog!" said Frank Pratt, softly; and they took their places on the stand, from which, close at hand, they could readily command the movements of all in the barouche.

But there was the ground mapped out by the little flags; green field, ploughed piece, brook, road, double fence, bullfinch; a cluster of spectators by this dangerous leap; a pollard laden with human fruit there; oak branches bending, groups of mounted men, with here and there the flutter of veil and riding-habit; vehicles in pastures, lanes, and wherever a glimpse could be obtained of the course; and over all the bright unclouded sun looked down, gilding, with its mellow beams, brown stubble and changing leaf; while overhead, little troubled by the buzzing crowds, a lark carolled its sweet song.

The friends were in ample time; but at last the excitement here and there announced the coming of the horses, and one by one the sleek, fleet creatures made their appearance to give the customary canter down the field, and then be gathered together for the start.

At last a low, dull, murmurous buzz runs through the crowd. They are off—nearly all together. The first hedge—only a preparation for troubles to come—and the horses going easily over a ploughed piece, the young and ardent jockeys pushing to the front, the old stagers waiting their opportunity.

Another hedge. A refusal. One—two—four—six—nine over somehow or another, and one down.

Then a loud cheer, by no means pleasant for the fallen man; and "for the fun of the thing," as he said, Trevor began to back the grey mare known as White Lassie.

"How can you be so foolish?" said Pratt.

"So," said Trevor, laughing; and he doubled his stakes with another.

"I believe we should be better off there on the knoll," said Pratt, pointing to the spot where the barouche was standing hemmed in by the crowd.

And acting upon the suggestion, the two friends quitted the low, temporary stand, and managed to get a pretty good position on the little eminence, where they could see right down the valley with the horses running along its slope.

But Pratt saw more than this; he noted that they were within half a dozen yards of the barouche where the ladies were standing on the seats, with eyes sparkling and parted lips, whilst close at hand were Barney, of the omnibus, and a couple of his intimates, demonstrative in their comments upon the race.

Of the eleven horses that started, four had, in hunting parlance, come to grief; and now of the others only five seemed to be in the race.

"Twenty pounds fooled away, Dick," said Pratt, in a whisper, as they now made out, the last of the five, the white cap and pale blue shirt of the rider of White Lassie.

"Be quiet, raven," was the calm reply; "the race is not won yet. Look at that."

That was the downfall of the leading horse at the next fence, the poor beast literally turning a somersault, and then getting up to stand shaking itself, as the other competitors got safely over; White Lassie, still last clearing the obstacle with ease.

"Now comes the tug of war," said Trevor; and all eyes were strained in the direction now taken by the horses towards a tolerably wide brook running between stunted pollards; for this once passed, there was only a low fence, and a straight run in to the winning post.

The betting on all sides was now fast and furious, Pratt biting his lips with vexation as, in spite of the distance his favourite was behind, Trevor kept making fresh engagements.

"He'll lose as much in ten minutes as would have kept me for a year," Pratt grumbled to himself; and then he was all eyes for the race, as, on reaching the brook, the leading horse stopped short and shot his rider right into the middle.

The next horse leaped short, and came into the brook with his hoofs pawing the crumbling bank, the rider having to crawl over his head, and help him ignominiously from his position. But long ere this, a great bay had cleared the brook easily, closely followed by White Lassie, whose rider now seemed to press her forward till she was not more than a length in the rear, the two horses racing hard for the last leap.

At a distance it looked but a low hedge, but there was a deep dyke on the riders' side which would require no little skill to clear; and now, of course, the slightest slip would be fatal to either.

"Don't look so bad now, does it, Franky?" said Trevor.

"No," said the other between his teeth. "Look, how close they are. I couldn't have—bravo!"

For the mare had run up alongside of her great competitor, and together they literally skimmed over the obstacle in front, and landing on the stretch of smooth green sward, raced for home.

"King Dick!"

"White Lassie!"

"King Dick!"

"White Lassie!"

"White Lassie!"

"White Lassie!" rose in a perfect roar, as first one and then the other head appeared in front, till, within a hundred yards of the stand, the white mare's head—neck—shoulders—half-length—whole length appeared in front of her competitor, and, amidst the frantic cheers of the crowd, she leaped in, a clear winner.

"There," said Trevor, turning with a smile to Pratt, "what do—"

He stopped short, and seemed to have tried to emulate the last hound of the mare; for at that moment, all excitement as she watched the race, Trevor saw one of the occupants of the barouche give a sudden start, and nearly fall over the side.

The cause was simple, and was seen by Pratt at the same moment.

Barney, of the omnibus, for the delectation of his friends, had, the moment the race was ended, raised his stick, reached over the heads of the crowd, and given the old gentleman a sharp thrust in the ribs.

The result was a violent start, and, as we have said, the young girl was nearly precipitated from the seat upon which she stood.

A hoarse roar of laughter followed the clown-like feat; and then there was a dead silence, for a fresh character appeared upon the scene, and Barney was stooping down shaking his head to get rid of the dizziness caused by a tremendous blow upon his bull-dog front.

The silence lasted but for a few moments, dining which Richard Trevor caught one frightened glance from the lady in the barouche, and then there was an ugly rush, and he and his friend were borne down the slope of the hill.

The crowd seemed bubbling and seething with excitement for a few minutes, during which the voices of Barney's friends could be heard loudly exclaiming amongst them; and the gentleman named, in whose eyes the tears had previously been gathering from the excess of his mirth, was borne along with the others, still shaking his head, and feeling as if the drops that collected had suddenly been turned to molten metal.

"Come away, Dick; for goodness' sake come away."

"My dear Frank, if you fill a vessel quite full, it begins to run over. This ungodly vessel has been filled full of the gall of bitterness to-day, and now it is running over."

"But, consider—what are you going to do?"

"I'm going to thrash this fellow within an inch of his life."

"But, Dick—the disgrace—you can't fight; you've punished him enough. Think of what you're going to do."

"I am thinking," said Trevor, in a quiet, slow way—"thinking that he's an ugly customer, and that his head looks precious hard."

"Keep back!"—"Make a ring!"—"Let him have it!"

"Now, Barney!" shouted the bystanders.

"Here, let me get at him!" shouted Barney.

"Call up the police!" said a mounted gentleman. "You can't fight that fellow, sir."

"I'm going to try," said Trevor, grimly.

There was a buzz of voices, the crowd swayed here and there, and an opening was made—Barney having struggled out of his upper garments, and begun to square—when, to the surprise of all, he was suddenly confronted by the stout-built West-country-man, who had leaped off the box of the barouche, now on the other side of the hill; and before the fellow had recovered from his surprise, he was sent staggering back into the arms of his friends with a sensation as if a hive of bees, suddenly let loose, were buzzing and stinging in his head.

That was the end of the engagement, for there was a rush of police through the crowd, people were separated, and by the time Frank Pratt had fought his way out of a state of semi-suffocation, he was standing with his friend fifty yards away, and the constables were hurrying two men off to the station.

"Let's get back," said Trevor. "I can't let that fellow bear all the brunt of the affair."

Pratt felt disposed to dissuade, but he gave way, and they got to the outskirts with no little difficulty, just in time to see that the barouche horses had been put to, and that the carriage was being driven off the ground with the West-countryman upon the box.

"He's out of the pickle, then," said Pratt.

"There, come away, man; the police have, for once in a way, caught the right offender; don't let's get mixed up with it any more."

"Very well," said Dick, calmly. "I feel better now; but I should have liked to soundly thrash that scoundrel."

"It's done for you," said Pratt. "Now let's go and get in your bets."

"I'm afraid, Franky," said Trevor, "that you are not only a mercenary man, but a great—I mean little coward."

"Quite right—you're quite right," said Pratt. "I am mercenary because the money's useful, and enables a man to pay his laundress; and as to being a coward, I am—a dreadful coward. I wouldn't mind if it were only skin, that will grow again; but fancy being ragged about and muddied in tussle with that fellow! Why, my dear Dick, I should have been six or seven pounds out of pocket in no time."

"I wonder who those girls were in the barouche," said Trevor, after a pause.

"Daresay you do," was the reply; "so do I. Sweet girls—very; but you may make yourself quite easy; you will never see either of them again."

"Don't know," said Trevor, slowly. "This is a very little place, this world, and I have often run against people I knew in the most out-of-the-way places."

"Yes, you may do so abroad," said Pratt; "but here, in England, you never do anything of the kind, except in novels. I saw a girl once at the chrysanthemum show in the Temple, and hoped I should ran against her again some day, but I never did. She wasn't so nice, though, as these."

Trevor smiled, and then, encountering one or two gentlemen with whom he had made bets, a little pecuniary business followed, after which the friends strolled along the course.

"By the way," said Trevor, "I was just thinking it rather hard upon our friend of the omnibus; those policemen pounced upon him and walked him off, without much consideration of the case. Well, I don't want to see the fellow again; he made my blood boil to-day."

"Then you will see him, you may depend upon it," said Pratt. "That's just the awkwardness of fate, or whoever the lady is that manages these matters. Owe a man ten pounds, and you will meet him every day like clock-work."

"Why, Franky," said Trevor, laying his hand upon the other's arm, and speaking with the old schoolboy familiarity, "I can't help noticing these money allusions. Have you been very short at times?"

There was a pause of a few moments' duration, and then Pratt said, shortly—"Awfully!"

They walked on then in silence, which was broken at last by Pratt, who said in a hurried way—

"That accounts for my shabby, screwy ways, Dick, so forgive me for having developed into such a mean little beggar. You see, the governor died and left madam with barely enough to live on, and then she pinched for my education, and she had to fight through it all to get ready for my call to the bar, where, in our innocence—bless us!—we expected that briefs would come showering in, and that, once started in chambers in the Temple, my fortune would be made."

"And the briefs do not shower down yet, Franky?" said Trevor.

"Don't come even in drops. Haven't had occasion for an umbrella once yet. So I went out to Egypt with Landells, you know, and wrote letters and articles for the Geographical; and, somehow, I got elected to the 'Wanderers,' and—here's the gorgeous Van and little Flick."

"Ah, Trevor, my dear boy!" said the first-named gentleman, sauntering up, "thought we should see you somewhere. Flick, have the goodness to slip that into the case for me."

As he spoke, he handed the race-glass he held in his delicately-gloved hands to the young baronet, who looked annoyed, but closed the glass, and slipped it into the sling-case hanging at his companion's side.

"We should have seen you before, but we came upon a pair of rural houris in a barouche."

"Where?" said Pratt, sharply.

"Ah, Pratt—you there? How do?" said the Captain, coolly. "Over the other side of the course, in a lane. I couldn't get Landells away."

"Oh—come!" drawled the young baronet.

"Had his glass turned upon them, and there he was, perfectly transfixed."

"Boot was on the other foot, 'sure you," said Sir Felix. "It was Van first made the discovery. It was so, indeed."

"What, going?" said Vanleigh, as Trevor moved on.

"Yes; we were going to walk all round the course."

"No use to go houri hunting," said Vanleigh, maliciously. "The barouche has gone."

Trevor coloured slightly, and then more deeply, as he saw a smile on the Captain's lip.

"We shall see you again, I daresay, by the stand," he said, taking no notice of the allusion; and, laying a hand upon Pratt's shoulder, he strolled away.

"Well," he said, after a few minutes, "the barouche had not quite disappeared, Franky."

"No," said the other, shortly. "Better for its occupants if it had. I say, Dick, if I had sisters, it would make me feel mad every time that fellow looked at them."

"What—Landells?"

"Oh no, Felix is a good sort of fellow enough; getting spoiled, but I don't think there's a great deal of harm in him. I've taken a dislike to Van, and I'm afraid I'm rather bitter, and—look, there goes, the barouche! Quick, lend me your glass!"

"Thanks, no, Franky," said Trevor, quietly, raising it to his eyes, and watching the carriage, which was going down a lane to their left, the owner having apparently given orders for the postboy to drive them from place to place, where they could get a view of the races, which had succeeded each other pretty quickly. "Thanks, no, I will keep it; but, for your delectation,

I may mention that the ladies look very charming, the old gentleman very important; and—now they are gone."

He replaced the glass in its case, smiled good-humouredly at his companion, and they walked on.

"Dick," said Pratt, after a few moments' silence, "if I were a good-looking fellow like you, I should get married."

"And how about yourself?" said the other, smiling.

"Self? I marry? My dear old fellow, marriage is a luxury for the rich. I should be very sorry to starve a wife, and—I say, though, I'm as hungry as a hunter. Take me back to London, old fellow, and feed me, without you want to stay."

"Stay—not I!" said Trevor; "a very little of this sort of thing goes a long way with me. But about those two fellows?"

"Let them try to exist without our company, for once in a way," said Pratt, looking earnestly at his friend, who was busy once more with the glass; but, catching his companion's eye, Trevor closed the binocular, and they left the course.

The Writer of the Letter

"Woa! d'ye hear? woa! I'm blest if I ever did see sich a 'oss as you are, Ratty, 'ang me if I did. If a chap could drive you without swearing, he must be a downright artch-angel. Holt still, will yer? Look at that now!"

A jig here at the reins, and Ratty went forward; a lash from the whip, and the horse, a wall-eyed, attenuated beast, with a rat-tail, went backwards, ending by backing the hansom cab, in whose shafts he played at clay mill, going round and round in a perfect slough of a new unmade road, cut into ruts by builders' carts.

"Now, look'ee here," said the driver, our friend of the Pall Mall accident; "on'y one on us can be master, yer know. If you'll on'y say as yer can drive, and will drive, why, I'll run in the sharps, and there's an end on't. Hold still, will yer? Yer might be decent to-day."

The horse suddenly stood still—bogged, with the slushy mud over his fetlocks, and the cab wheels half-way down to the nave.

"Thenky," said the driver, standing up on his perch; "much obliged. I'm blessed!" he muttered. "Buddy may well say as mine's allus the dirtiest keb as comes inter the yard, as well as the shabbiest. 'Struth, what a place! Now, then, get on, will yer?"

The horse gave his Roman-profiled head a shake, and remained motionless.

"Just like yer," said the cabman. "When I want yer to go, yer stop; and when I don't want yer to go, off yer do go, all of a shy, and knocks 'alf a dozen people into the mud, and gets yer driver nearly took up for reckless driving, as the bobbies calls it. Come, get on."

Another shake of the head, but the four legs seemed planted as if they were to grow.

"Well, there's one thing, Ratty," said the driver, "we're about square, mate; for if ever I've give yer too much of the whip, yer've had it outer me with obstinacy. Look at this now, just when yer oughter be on yer best manners, seeing as I've come about the mischief as yer did; and then, to make it wus, yer takes advantage of yer poor master's weakness, and goes a-leading of him inter temptation sore as can't be bore, and pulls up close aside of a public."

For the spot at which the horse had stopped was at the opening of one of those new suburban streets run up by speculative builders—a street of six and seven-roomed houses, with a flaring tavern at the corner; and the houses, starting from the commencement of the street, in every stage from finished and inhabited, through finished and uninhabited, down to unfinished skeletons with the bricks falling out—foundations just above the ground, foundations merely dug, to end only with a few scaffold poles, and a brick-field in frill work.

"Stops right in front of a public, yer do," said the driver; "and me as thirsty as a sack o' sawdust."

The cabman looked at the public-house, to read golden announcements of "Tipkin's Entire," of "The Celebrated Fourpenny Ale," and the "Brown London Stout, threepence per pot in your own jugs," and his whip-hand was drawn across his lips. Then the whip-hand was set free, and forced its way into his pockets, where it rattled some halfpence.

"Must have 'alf pint now, anyhow," he muttered, and he made as if to fasten the reins to the roof of the cab, but only to plump himself down into his seat again, jig the reins, and give his whip, a sharp crack.

"I'll tell the missus on you, Hatty, see if I don't?" he said, "a-trying to get your master back into his old ways. Get on with yer, or yer'll get it directly."

He gave his whip such a vigorous crack in the air that Ratty consented to go, and dragging the muddy cab partially down the new street, its driver pulled up by where a knot of shoeless boys were ornamenting, and amusing themselves with, the new ill-laid pavement. One was standing like a small Colossus of Rhodes, with his grimy feet at either corner of a loose slab, making the liquid mud beneath squirt out into a puddle, while a companion carefully turned a naked foot into a stamp, dipped it in the mud, and printed a pattern all along the pave, till a third smudged it out, and a fight ensued.

"Hallo, yer young dogs," roared the cabman, and his long whip gave a crack which stopped the fray; "a-fightin' like that! Where's Whaley's Place?"

"First turn to the left, and first to the right," shouted two boys.

"And is it all like this here?" said the cabman.

"No; you should have gone round Brick Street. I'll show yer."

"Hook on, then," said the cabman, turning his horse; and, to the extreme envy of his companions, the little speaker "hooked on" behind, his muddy feet slipping about on the step; but he clung fast, shouting his directions till the driver reached the main road, made a détour, and arrived at last in Whaley's Place, where the present of a copper sent the boy off in high glee to spend it in some coveted luxury.

"Nice sorter cheerful spot this," said the cabman, taking an observation of the street, which was of a similar class to the new one he had left, only that the houses had fallen into a state of premature decay; quite half, too, had declined from the genteel private and taken to trade, with or without the bow window of shop life. For instance, one displayed a few penny illustrated sheets and an assortment of fly-specked clay pipes, the glass panes bearing the legends, "Tobacco" and "Cigars." Another house had the door wide open, and sundry squeaks issued therefrom—squeaks of a manufacturing tendency, indicative of grinding, the process being explained by a red and yellow board, having an artistic drawing of the machinery used, and the words, "Mangling Done Here." Then, after an interval of private houses, there was a fishmonger's, with a stock-in-trade of four plaice and ten bloaters, opposite to a purveyors, in whose open window—the parlour by rights, with the sashes out—were displayed two very unpleasant-looking decapitations of the gentle sheep, and three trays of pieces, labelled ninepence, sevenpence, and sixpence individually, apparently not from any variation of quality, but the amount of bone.

"A werry nice sorter place," said the cabman, gazing down at the numerous children, and the preternaturally big-headed, tadpoleish babies, whose porters were staring at him. "Said it was a little groshers shop. Ah, here we are."

It was only four doors farther on, and at this establishment there was a shop front, with the name "B. Sturt" on the facia. The stock here did not seem to be extensive, though the place was scrupulously clean. There was a decorative and pictorial aspect about the trade carried on, which was evidently that of a chandler's shop; for, in attenuated letters over the door, you read that Barnabas Sturt was licenced by the Board of Inland Revenue to deal in tea, coffee, pepper, vinegar, and tobacco. The panes of the windows were gay with show cards, one of which displayed the effects of Tomkins's Baking Powder, while in another a lady was holding up fine linen got up with Winks's Prussian Blue, and smiling sweetly at a neighbouring damsel stiff with regal starch. There were pictorial cards, too, telling of the celebrated Unadulterated Mustard, the Ho-fi Tea Company, and Fort's Popular Coffee.

Descending from his perch, the cabman stroked and patted his horse, and then entered the shop, setting a bell jingling, and standing face to face with a counter, a pair of scales, and a box of red herrings.

Nobody came, so he tapped the floor with his whip, and a voice growled savagely from beyond a half-glass door which guarded an inner room—

Waiting patiently for a few moments, the cabman became aware of the fact that Barnabas Sturt consumed his tobacco as well as dealt in it; and at last, growing impatient, he peered through the window, to perceive that a very thin, sour-looking woman, with high cheek bones, was dipping pieces of rag into a tea-cup of vinegar and water, and applying them to the contused countenance of a bull-headed gentleman, who lay back in a chair smoking, and making the woman wince and sneeze by puffing volumes of the coarse, foul vapour into her face.

"Better mind what you are doing!" he growled.

"Can't help it, dear," said the woman, plaintively, "if you smoke me so. Well, what now?" she said, waspishly, and changing her tone to the metallic aggressive common amongst some women.

"Been having a—?" the cabman finished his sentence by grinning, and giving his arms a pugilistic flourish.

"What's that got to do with you?" growled Mr Sturt. "What d' yer come into people's places like that for?"

"Because people says as they sells the werry best tobacco at threepence a hounce," said the cabman. "Give's half-hounce."

"Go an' weigh it," said Mr Sturt.

The woman dropped the piece of rag she held, and passed shrinkingly into the shop, took the already weighed-out tobacco from a jar, and held out her hand for the money.

"Now then," growled Mr Sturt from the back room, "hand that over here, will yer?"

The cabman walked into the room and laid down the money, slowly emptying the paper afterwards into a pouch, which he took from a side pocket.

"This here's twenty-seven, ain't it?" said the cabman then.

"Yes, it is twenty-seven," cried Mr Sturt—our friend Barney of the steeplechase—and he seemed so much disturbed that he leaped up and backed into a corner of the room. "You ain't got nothin' again' me, come, now."

"No, I ain't got nothin' again' yer," said the cabman, quietly, but with his eye twinkling. "Did yer think I was—?"

He finished his sentence with a wink.

"Never you mind what I thought," said Barney. "What d' yer want here?"

"Only to know if Mrs Lane lives here."

"Yes, she do," cried the woman, spitefully; "and why couldn't you ring the side bell, and not come bothering us?"

"Because I wanted some tobacco, mum," said the cabman, quietly.

"Oh!" said the woman, in a loud voice; "with their cabs, indeed, a-comin' every day: there'll be kerridges next!"

"Just you come and go on with your job," said Barney, with a snarl.

"I'm coming!" said the woman, sharply. Then to the cabman—"You can go this way;" and she flung open a side door and called up the stairs—"Here, Mrs Lane, another cab's come for you. There, I s'pose you can go up," she added; and then, in a voice loud enough to be heard upstairs, "if people would only pay their way instead of riding in cabs, it would be better for some of us."

A door had been heard to open on the first floor, and then, as the vinegary remark of Mrs Sturt rose, voices were heard whispering. The cabman went straight up the uncarpeted stairs, to pause before the half-open door, as he heard, in a low conversation, the words—

"Mamma—dear mamma, pray don't notice it."

The next moment the door opened fully, and the pale, worn-looking woman of the accident stood before the cabman, who shuffled off his hat, and stood bowing.

"Jenkles, mum," he said—"Samuel Jenkles, nine 'underd seven six, as knocked you down in Pall Mall."

The woman stepped back and laid her hand upon her side, seeming about to fall, when the cabman started forward and caught her, helping her to a chair in the shabbily-furnished room, as the door swung to.

"Oh, mamma," cried a girl of about seventeen, springing forward, the work she had been engaged upon falling on the floor.

"It is nothing, my dear," gasped the other; though her cheek was ashy pale, and the dew gathered on her forehead.

"She's fainting, my dear," said the cabman. "Got anything in the house?"

"Yes, some water," said the girl, supporting the swooning woman, and fanning her face.

"Water!" ejaculated the cabman, in a tone of disgust. "Here, I'll be back directly."

He caught up a little china mug from a side table, and ran out, nearly upsetting Mrs Sturt on the landing and Barney at the foot of the stairs, to return at the end of a few minutes, and find the passage vacant; so he hastily ran up, to see that Mrs Lane had come to in his absence, though she looked deadly pale.

"Here, mum," he said, earnestly, "drink this; don't be afeard, it's port wine. A drop wouldn't do you no harm neither, Miss," he added, as he glanced at the pale, thin face and delicate aspect of the girl.

Mrs Lane put the mug to her lips, and then made an effort, and sat up.

"You was hurt, then, mum?" said the cabman, anxiously.

"Only shaken—frightened," she said, in a feeble voice.

"And my coming brought it all up again, and upset you. It's jest like me, mum, I'm allus a-doing something; ask my missus if I ain't."

"It did startle me," said Mrs Lane, recovering herself. "But you wished to see me. I am better now, Netta," she said to the girl, who clung to her. "Place a chair."

"No, no, arter you, Miss," said the cabman; "I'm nobody;" and he persisted in standing. "'Scuse me, but I knows a real lady when I sees one; I'll stand, thanky. You see, it was like this: I saw Tommy Runce on the stand—him, you know, as brought you home from the front of the club there—and I ast him, and he told me where he brought you. And when I was talking to the missus last night, she says, says she, 'Well, Sam,' she says, 'the least you can do is to drive up and see how the poor woman is, even if you lose half a day.' 'Well,' I says, 'that's just what I was a thinking,' I says, 'only I wanted to hear you say it too.' So you see, mum, thinking it was only decent like, I made bold to come and tell you how sorry I am, and how it was all Ratty's fault; for he's that beast of a horse—begging your pardon, mum, and yours too, Miss—as it's impossible to drive. He oughter ha' been called Gunpowder, for you never know when he's going off."

"It was *very* kind and very thoughtful of you, and—and your wife," said Mrs Lane; "and indeed I thank you; but I was not hurt, only shaken."

"Then it shook all the colour outer your face, mum, and outer yours too, Miss," he said, awkwardly. "You'll excuse me, but you look as if you wanted a ride every day out in the country."

As he spoke, the girl glanced at a bundle of violets in a broken glass of water in the window; then the tears gathered in her eyes. She seemed to struggle for a moment against her emotion, and then started up and burst into a passion of weeping.

"My darling!" whispered Mrs Lane, catching her in her arms, and trying to soothe her, "pray—pray don't give way."

"I've done it again," muttered Jenkles—"I'm allus a-doing it—it is my natur' to."

The girl made a brave effort, dashed away the tears, shook back her long dark hair, and tried to smile in the speaker's face, but so piteous and sad a smile that Jenkles gave a gulp; for he had been glancing round the room, and in that glance had seen a lady and her daughter living in a state of semi-starvation, keeping life together evidently by sewing the hard, toilsome slop-work which he saw scattered upon the table and chairs.

"She has been ill," said Mrs Lane, apologetically, "and has not quite recovered. We are very much obliged to you for calling."

"Well, you see, mum," said Jenkles, "it was to set both of us right, like—you as I didn't mean to do it, and me and my missus that you warn't hurt. And now I'm here, mum, if you and the young lady there would like a drive once or twice out into the country, why, mum, you've only got to say the word, and—"

"You'll excuse me, ma'am," said the sharp voice of Mrs Sturt, laying great stress on the "ma'am," "but my 'usban' is below, and going out on business, and he'd be much obliged if you'd pay us the rent."

The girl looked in a frightened way at her mother, who rose, and said, quietly—

"Mrs Sturt, you might have spared me this—and before a stranger, too."

"I don't know nothing about no strangers, ma'am," said Mrs Sturt, defiantly. "I only know that my master sent me up for the rent; for he says if people can afford to come home in cabs, and order cabs, and drink port wine, they can afford to pay their rent; so, if you please, ma'am, if you'll be kind—"

"Why, them two cabs warn't nothing to do with the lady at all," said Jenkles, indignantly; "and as for the wine, why, that was mine—and—and I paid for it."

"And drunk it too, I dessay," said Mrs Sturt. "Which it's four weeks at seven-and-six, if you please, ma'am—thirty shillings, if you please." The girl stood up, her eyes flashing, and a deep flush in her cheeks; but at a sign from her mother she was silent.

"Mrs Sturt," she said, "I cannot pay you now; give me till Saturday."

"That won't do for my master, ma'am; he won't be put off."

"But the work I have in hand, Mrs Sturt, will half pay you—you shall receive that."

"I'm tired on it," said Mrs Sturt, turning to the door; "p'r'aps I'd better send him up."

"Oh, mamma," said the girl, in a low, frightened voice, and she turned of a waxen pallor, "don't let him come here."

And she clung trembling to her arm as the retreating footsteps of Mrs Sturt were heard, and, directly after, her vinegary voice in colloquy with her husband.

"Here, I'll soon let 'em know," he was heard to say, roughly.

The trembling girl hid her face on her mother's shoulder; but only to start up directly, very pale and firm, as Barney's heavy step was heard.

"Blame me if I can stand this," muttered Jenkles.

Then without a word he stuck his hat on his head and walked out of the room, in time to meet the master of the house on the stairs.

"Now, then?" said Barney, as Jenkles stopped short.

"Now, then," said Jenkles, "where are you going?"

"In there," said Barney, savagely; and he nodded towards the room.

"No, you ain't," said Jenkles; "you're a-going downstairs."

"Oh, am I? I'll just show you about that."

He rushed up two more of the stairs; but Jenkles did not budge an inch—only met the brute with such a firm, unflinching look in his ugly eyes that the bully was cowed, puzzled at the opposition.

"You're a-going downstairs to send yer missus up; and jest you tell her to go and take a spoonful o' treacle out o' the shop afore she does come up, so as she'll be a little bit sweeter when the ladies pays her."

Then Jenkles walked back into the room, rammed his hand into his pocket, and pulled out a dirty canvas bag, out of which he fished a piece of rag tied tightly, in one corner of which was a sovereign, which had to be set free with his teeth. From another corner he tried to extricate a half-sovereign, but it would not come, the knot was too tight.

"Here, lends a pair o' scissors," he exclaimed, angrily.

"What are you going to do?" said Mrs Lane.

"To cut this here out," said Jenkles; "there, that's it. Here's a sov and a arf, mum, as was saved up for our rent. I never did such a thing afore, but that's nothing to you. I'll lend it you, and you'll pay me again when you can. There's my name on that dirty envelope, and you'll send it, I know."

"No," exclaimed Mrs Lane, in a choking voice, "I—"

At this moment Mrs Sturt entered the room, looking very grim; but no sooner did she see the money lying upon the table than she walked up, took it, said "Thanky," shortly, and jerked a letter upon the table.

Jenkles was following her, when Mrs Lane cried "Stop!" seized the letter, tore it open, and read it.

It was in reply to the second she had written, both of which had reached Captain Vanleigh, though she believed the first had been lost.

Her letter had been brief—

"Help us—we are destitute.
"A.V."

The reply was—

"Do what I wish, and I will help you."

No signature.

Mrs Lane clenched her teeth as she crushed the letter in her hand, then raised her eyes to see the cabman at the door, with her daughter kissing his hand.

"Oh, God!" she moaned, "has it come to this!"

The next minute Netta was clinging to her, and they wept in unison as the sound of wheels was heard; and Sam Jenkles apostrophised his ugly steed.

"Ratty," he said, "I wonder what it feels like to be a fool—whether it's what I feels just now?"

There was a crack of the whip here, and the hansom trundled along.

"How many half-pints are there in thirty bob, I wonder?" said Sam again.

And then, as he turned into the main road at Upper Holloway, he pulled up short—to the left London, to the right over the hills to the country.

"Not above four or five mile, Ratty, and then there'll be no missus to meet. Ratty, old man, I think I'd better drive myself to Colney Hatch."

All among the Ferns

An autumn morning in a lane. A very prosaic beginning. But there are lanes and lanes; so let not the reader imagine a dreary, clayey way between two low-cropped hedges running right across the flat landscape with mathematical severity, and no more exciting object in view than a heap of broken stones ready for repairs. Our lane is a very different affair, for it is a Cornish lane.

Do you know what a Cornish lane is like—a lane in a valley? Perhaps not; so we will describe the winding road, where, basket in hand, Tiny and Fin Rea, walking home, were seeking ferns.

In this land of granite, a clear field is an exception—the great bare bones of earth peer out in all directions; and however severe the taste of the first maker of a beaten track, unless he were ready with engineering tools and blasting appliances, instead of making his way straight forward, he would have to go round and dodge about, to avoid the masses of stone. Hence, then, many of the lanes wind and double between piled-up heaps of granite, through steep gorges, and rise and fall in the most eccentric way; while— Nature having apparently scoured the hill-tops, and swept the fertile soil into the vales along these dell like lanes—the verdure is thick and dense; trees interlace overhead till you walk in a pale green twilight flecked with golden rays; damp dripping stones are covered with velvet moss; a tiny spring trickles here, and forms crystal pools, mirroring delicate fronds of fern; gnarled oaks twist tortuous trunks in the great banks, and throw distorted arms across the road; half hidden from sight—here five, there fifty feet below the *toad*—a rapid stream goes musically onward towards the sea, singing silvery songs to the little speckly trout which hide beneath the granite shelves in their crystal homes. Verdure rich and bright on every side, and above all ferns—ferns of the tiniest, and ferns tall and towering, spreading luxuriant fronds, and sending up spikes of flowers, while lesser neighbours form patches of wondrous beauty—tropic palm forests in miniature.

"Now, then, who's going to take my picture?" cried Fin Rea, plumping herself down on a mossy stone, and snatching off her hat. "Should I do now, Tiny?"

Undoubtedly: for her lithe, slight form, in its grey muslin, stood out from the ashy brown of the oak trunk that formed the background, while a wondrous beauty of light and shade fell through the leafy network above.

"Oh, isn't it heavenly to be back? I couldn't live in London. I liked the theatres, and going to the race, and seeing pictures, but I should soon be tired of it all. It makes you so cross. I believe the blacks get into your temper. I say, Tiny, I wonder what Aunt Matty would be like if she lived in London?"

"Don't make fun of poor Aunt Matty," said her sister. "She has had a good deal of trouble in her life."

"And made it," said Fin, jumping up. "Oh, I say, look down there," she cried, pointing through the ferns at her feet to a cool, dark pool, twenty feet below; "there's a place. Oh, Tiny, if I thought I should ever grow into such a screwy, cross old maid as Aunt Matty, I think I should jump down there and let the fishes eat."

"Fin, that little tongue of yours goes too fast," said her sister.

"Let it," was the laconic reply. "Tongues were made to talk with. Let's go on; I'm tired of digging up ferns. Wasn't it funny, seeing Humphrey Lloyd at that race? And I wonder who those gentlemen were."

"Do you mean the people who stared at us so through the race-glass?"

"No, I don't, Miss Forgetful. I mean the big, dark man, and the funny, little fierce fellow with his hair brushed into points. You don't remember, I suppose?"

"Oh yes," said Tiny, quietly. "I remember, for I was very much frightened."

"Ah, I hope the knight-errant wasn't hurt; and, oh, do look, Tiny," Fin cried, putting down her basket. "What's that growing in that tree?"

As she spoke, she climbed from stone to stone up the steep bank, till she was stopped short by her dress being caught by a bramble.

"Oh, Tiny, come and unloose me, do. I'm caught."

There was nothing for it but that her sister should clamber up the bank, and unhook the dress, which she did, when Fin gave her a hand, and drew her up to her side.

"What a tomboy you do keep, Fin," said Tiny, panting; "see how my dress is torn."

"Never mind, I'll sew it up for you. What's the good of living in the country if you can't be free as the birds? Sweet, sweet, sweet! Oh, you beauty!" she cried, as a goldfinch sounded his merry lay. "Tiny, shouldn't you like to be a bird?"

"No," was the quiet reply. "I would rather be what I am."

"I should like to be a bird," said Fin, placing one foot on an excrescence of a stumpy pollard oak, and, making a jump, she caught hold of a low bough.

"But not now," cried Tiny. "What are you going to do?"

"Going to do?" laughed Fin. "Why, climb this tree;" and she got a step higher.

"Oh, Fin, how foolish! Whatever for? Suppose some one came by?"

"Nobody comes along here at this time of the day, my dear; so here goes, and if I fall pick up my pieces, and carry them safely home to dear Aunt Matty. 'And the dicky-bird sang in the tree,'" she trilled out, as step by step she drew herself up into the crown of the stumpy, gnarled pollard.

"Oh, Fin!" exclaimed her sister.

"Its all right, Miss Timidity. I'm safe, and I came on purpose," cried Fin, from up in her perch, her face glowing, and eyes sparkling with merriment.

"But what are you trying to do?"

"To get some of this, sweet innocent. You can't see, I suppose, what it is?"

"No, indeed, I cannot," said Tiny—"yes, I can. Why, it's mistletoe."

"Mistletoe, is it, Miss? Ahem!" cried Fin, resting one little fist upon her hip,—and stretching out the other—"Tableau—young Druid priestess about to cut the sacred plant with a fern trowel."

"Fin, dear, do come down. Don't touch it."

"Not touch it? But I will. There!" she cried, tearing off a piece of the pretty parasite. "I'll wear that in my hat all the way home as a challenge to nobody, and on purpose to make Aunt Matty cross. She'll—"

"Hist, Fin; oh, be quiet," whispered Tiny.

"Eh? What's the matter?" cried Fin, from her perch.

"Oh, pray be quiet; here's somebody coming."

"Never mind," said Fin. "You stand behind the tree—they can't see us—till I shout 'Hallo!'"

But Fin kept very quiet, peering down squirrel-wise, as a step was heard coming along the lane, and she caught glimpses through the trees of a man in a rough tweed suit and soft felt hat. The face was that of a keen, earnest man of eight-and-forty, with a full beard, just touched by life's frost, sharp dark eyes, and altogether a countenance not handsome, but likely to win confidence.

The newcomer was walking with an easy stride, humming scraps of some ditty, and he swung by his side an ordinary tin can, holding about a quart of some steaming compound.

"It's Saint Timothy," whispered Fin, from her perch. "Keep close."

Tiny drew her dress closer together, and pressed to the tree trunk, looking terribly guilty, while her sister went on watching.

The steps came nearer, and the stepper's eyes were busy with a keen look for everything, as he seemed to feast on the beauties of Nature around him.

"'I love the merry, merry sunshine,'" he sang, in a bold, bluff voice; "and—Hallo, what the dickens have we here?" he cried, stopping short, and setting two hearts beating quickly. "Lady's basket and ferns dug up—yes, within the last hour. Why, that must be—Hallo, I spy, hi!"

For as he spoke his eyes had been wandering about, amongst the brakes and bushes, and he had caught sight of a bit of muslin dress peeping out from behind a gnarled oak.

The result of his summons was that the scrap of dress was softly drawn out of sight, and a voice from up in the ties whispered—

"Oh, go down, Tiny, and then he won't see me."

"Hallo! whispers in the wind," cried the newcomer, glancing higher, and seeing a bit of Fin. "Is it a bird? By Jove, I wish I'd a gun. No: poachers—trespassers. Here, you fellows, come out!"

Jenkles's Confession

Sam Jenkles always boasted that he never kept anything from his wife; but he was silent for two days; and then, after a hard day's work, he was seated in his snug kitchen, watching the browning of a half-dozen fine potatoes in a Dutch oven before the fire, when Mrs Jenkles, a plump, bustling little woman, who was stitching away at a marvellous rate, her needle clicking at every stroke, suddenly exclaimed—

"Sam, you'd better give me that two pound you've got, and I'll put it with the rest."

Sam didn't answer, only tapped his pipe on the hob.

Mrs Jenkles glanced at him, and then said—

"Did you hear what I said, Sam?"

"Yes."

"Then why don't you give it me? Draw that oven back an inch."

"Aint got it—only half a sov," said Sam, leaving the potatoes to burn.

Mrs Jenkles dropped her work upon her lap, and her face grew very red.

"Didn't you say, Sam, that if I'd trust you, you wouldn't do so any more?"

"Yes."

"And you've broke your word, Sam."

"I aint, 'pon my soul, I aint, Sally," cried Sam, earnestly. "I've had my pint for dinner, and never touched a drop more till I had my pint at home."

"Then where's that money?"

"Spent it," said Sam, laconically.

"Yes, at the nasty public-houses, Sam. An' it's too bad, and when I'd trusted you!"

"Wrong!" said Sam.

"Then where is it?"

"Fooled it away."

"Yes, of course. But I didn't expect it, Sam; I didn't, indeed."

"All your fault," said Sam.

"Yes, for trusting you," said Mrs Jenkles, bitterly. "Nice life we lead: you with the worst horse and the worst cab on the rank, and me with the worst husband."

"Is he, Sally?" said Sam, with a twinkle of the eye.

"Yes," said Mrs Jenkles, angrily; "and that makes it all the worse, when he might be one of the best. Oh, Sam," she said, pitifully, "do I ever neglect you or your home?"

"Not you," he said, throwing down his pipe, and looking round at the shining tins, bright fireplace, and general aspect of simple comfort and cleanliness. "You're the best old wife in the world."

And he got up and stood behind her chair with his arms round her neck.

"Don't touch me, Sam. I'm very, very much hurt."

"Well, it was all your fault, little woman," he said, holding the comely face, so that his wife could not look round at him.

"And how, pray?" said she.

"Didn't you send me up to see that poor woman as Ratty knocked down?"

"Yes; but did you go?"

"To be sure I did—you told me to go."

"Then why didn't you tell me you had been?"

"Didn't like to," said Sam.

"Such stuff!" cried Mrs Jenkles. "But what's that got to do with it?"

Sam remained silent.

"What's that got to do with it, Sam?"

Silence still.

"Now, Sam, you've got something on your mind, so you'd better tell me. Have you been drinking?"

"No, I haven't," said Sam, "and I don't mean to again."

"Then I'm very sorry for what I said."

"I know that," said Sam.

"But what does it all mean?"

"Well, you see," said Sam, "I've been a fool."

And after a little more hesitation, he told all about his visit.

Mrs Jenkles sat looking at the fire, rubbing her nose with her thimble, both she and Sam heedless that the potatoes were burning.

"You've been took in, Sam, I'm afraid," she said at last.

"Think so?" he said.

"Well, I hope not; but you've either been took in, or done a very, very kind thing."

"Well, we shall see," he said.

"Yes, we shall see."

"You aint huffy with me?"

"I don't know yet," said Mrs Jenkles; "but I shall go up and see them."

"Ah, do," said Sam.

"Yes, I mean to see to the bottom of it," said Mrs Jenkles. "I haven't patience with such ways."

"They can't help being poor."

"I don't mean them; I mean those people they're with. I couldn't do it."

"Not you," said Sam. "But I say, don't Mr Lacy go next week?"

"Yes."

"And the rooms will be empty?"

"Yes," said Mrs Jenkles. "I have put the bill up in the window; he said he didn't mind."

Sam Jenkles went and sat down in his chair with an air of relief and looked at his wife.

Mrs Jenkles looked at Sam, as if the same idea was in both hearts. Then she jumped up suddenly.

"Oh, Sam, the potatoes are spoiling!"

They were, but they were not spoilt; and Sam Jenkles made a very hearty meal, washing it down with the pint of beer which he termed his allowance.

"Ah!" he said, speaking like a man with a load off his mind, "this here's a luxury as the swells never gets—a regular good, hot, mealy tater, fresh from the fire. It's a wonderful arrangement of nature that about taters."

"Why?" said Mrs Jenkles, as she emptied the brown coat of another potato on her husband's plate. "What do you mean?"

"Why, the way in which roast potatoes and beer goes together. Six mouthfuls of tater, and then a drink of beer to get rid of the dryness."

"I wish you wouldn't be so fond of talking about beer, Sam," said Mrs Jenkles.

"All right, my dear," said Sam; and he finished his supper, retook his place by the fireside, filled his pipe, glanced at the Dutch clock swinging its pendulum to and fro; and then, as he lit the tobacco—"Ah! this is cheery. Glad I aint on the night shift."

Mrs Jenkles was very quiet as she bustled about and cleared the table, before once more taking her place on the other side of the fire.

"Ratty went first-rate to-day," said Sam, after a few puffs.

But Mrs Jenkles did not take any notice; she only made her needle click, and Sam kept glancing at her as he went on smoking. At last she spoke.

"I shall go up and see those people, Sam, for I'm afraid you've been taken in. Was she a married woman."

"Yes," said Sam; "I saw her ring. But I say, you know, 'taint my fault, Sally," he said, plaintively. "I was born a soft un."

"Then it's time you grew hard, Sam," said Mrs Jenkles, bending over her work. "Thirty shillings takes a deal of saving with people like us."

"Yes," said Sam, "it do, 'specially when you has so many bad days to make up."

"You ought not to have to pay more than twelve shillings a day for that cab, Sam."

"I told the gov'nor so, and he said as it oughter be eighteen, and plenty would be glad to get it at that."

Mrs Jenkles tightened her mouth, and shook her head.

"Oh! I say, Sally," said Sam, plaintively, "I've been worried about that money; and now it was off my mind, I did think as it was all right. You've reglarly put my pipe out."

Mrs Jenkles rose, took a splint from the chimney-piece, lit it, and handed it to her husband.

"No," he said, rubbing his ear with the stem of his pipe, "it aint that, my dear; I meant figgeratively, as old Jones says."

Mrs Jenkles threw the match into the fire, and resumed her work for a few minutes; then glanced at the clock, and put away her work.

"Yes, Sam, I shall go to Upper Holloway to-morrow, and see what I think."

"Do, my lass, do," said Sam, drearily. Then, in an undertone, as he tapped his pipe-bowl on the hob, "Well, it's out now, and no mistake. Shall we go to bed?"

"Our next meeting"

Fin Rea stood gazing down for a few moments, and then said—"No, indeed, I can't, Mr Mervyn. Pray go."

"Oh, Mr Mervyn," said Tiny, softly, "don't tease her any more."

"It is hard to refuse such a request," said the newcomer; "but, as trespassers, you must leave me to administer punishment. And, besides, I owe Miss Fin here a grudge. She has been laughing at me, I hear."

"I'll never do so any more, Mr Mervyn—I won't indeed," cried Fin; "only let me off this time."

"Jump, you little gipsy, jump," cried Mr Mervyn.

"It's too high—I daren't," cried Fin.

"I have seen you leap down from a place twice as high, my little fawn. Now, then, jump at once."

Fin looked despairingly round for a few moments, then made a piteous grimace, and lastly sprang boldly down into the strong arms, which held her as if she had been a child.

"Now," said Mr Mervyn, "about the mistletoe?"

"Mr Mervyn, pray. Oh, it's too bad. I..."

"Don't be frightened, little one," he said, tenderly, as he retained her with one hand, to smooth her breeze-blown hair with the other. "There, come along; let me help you down."

But Fin started from him, like the fawn he had called her, and sprang down the great bank.

"Mind my soup," shouted Mr Mervyn; and only just in time, for it was nearly overset. Then he helped Tiny down, blushing and vexed; but no sooner were they in the lane, than Fin clapped her hands together, and exclaimed—

"Oh, Mr Mervyn, don't go and tell everybody what a rude tomboy of a sister Tiny is blessed with. I am so ashamed."

"Come along, little ones," he said, laughing, as he stooped to pick up the tin, and at the same time handed Fin her basket.

"How nice the soup smells," said Fin, mischievously.

"Yes; you promised to come and taste it some day," said Mr Mervyn; "but you have never been. I'm very proud of my soup, young ladies, and have many a hard fight with Mrs Dykes about it."

"Do you?" said Tiny, for he looked seriously at her as he spoke.

"What about?" said Fin, coming to her sister's help.

"About the quantity of water," said Mr Mervyn. "You know we've a big copper for the soup; and Mrs Dykes has an idea in her head that eight quarts of water go to the gallon, mine being that there are only four."

"Why, of course," laughed Fin.

"So," said Mr Mervyn, "she says I have the soup too strong, while I say she wants to make it too weak."

"And what does old Mrs Trelyan say?"

"Say?" laughed Mr Mervyn. "Oh, the poor old soul lets me take it to her as a favour, and says she eats it to oblige me."

"It's so funny with the poor people about," said Fin; "they want things, but they won't take them as if you were being charitable to them; they all try to make it seem like a favour they are doing you."

"Well, I don't know that I object to that much," said Mr Mervyn.

"They're all pleased enough to see us," continued Fin; "but when Aunt Matty and papa go they preach at them, and the poor people don't like it."

"Fin!" said Tiny, in a warning voice.

"I don't care," said Fin; "it's only Mr Mervyn, and we may speak to him. I say, Mr Mervyn, did you hear about old Mrs Poltrene and Aunt Matty?"

"Fin!" whispered Tiny, colouring.

"I *will* tell Mr Mervyn; it isn't any harm," cried downright Fin.

And her sister, seeing that she only made matters worse, remained silent.

"Mr Mervyn, you know old Mrs Poltrene, of course?"

"Oh yes, the old fisherman's wife down by the cliff."

"Yes; and Aunt Matty went to see her, and talked to her in her way, and it made the old lady so cross that—that—oh, I mustn't tell you."

"Nonsense, child, go on."

"She—she told Aunt Matty to go along and get married," tittered Fin, "and she could stay at home and mend her husband's stockings, and leave people alone; and Aunt Matty thought it so horrible that she came home and went to bed."

"Ha! ha! ha!" laughed Mr Mervyn. "Mrs Poltrene has a temper; but here we are—you'll come in?"

Tiny was for drawing back, but her sister prevailed. They had been walking along the lane, and had now reached a long, low cottage, built after the fashion of the district, with massive blocks of granite, and roofed with slabs of the same. There was a strip of garden, though gardens were almost needless, banked up as the place was on all sides with the luxuriant wild growth of the valley. On one side, though, of the doorway was the simple old fuchsia of bygone days, with a stem here as thick as a man's wrist—a perfect fuchsia tree, in fact; and on the other side, leafing and flowering right over the roof, a gigantic hydrangea, the flower we see in eastern England in pots, but here of a delicious blue.

"Any one at home," said Mr Mervyn, walking straight in. "Here, Mrs Trelyan, I've brought you two visitors," and a very old, white-haired woman, who was making a pilchard net, held her hand over her forehead.

"Sit down, girls—sit down," she said, in the melodious sing-song voice of the Cornish people. "I know them—they come and see me sometimes. Eh? How am I? But middling—but middling. It's been a bad season for me. Oh, soup? Ah, you've brought me some more soup; you may empty it into that basin. I didn't want it; but you may leave it. They've brought me up some hake and a few herrings, so I could have got on without. That last soup was too salt, master."

"Was it?" said Mr Mervyn, giving a merry glance at Fin. "Well, never mind, I'll speak to Mrs Dykes about it."

"Ay, she's an east-country woman. Those folks don't know much about cooking. Well, young ladies, I hear you have been to London."

"Yes, Mrs Trelyan."

"And you're glad to come back?"

"Yes, that we are," said Fin.

"Ay, I've heard it's a poor, lost sort of place, London," said the old lady. "I never went, and I never would. My son William wanted to take me once in his boot; but I wouldn't go. Your father was a wise man to buy Tolcarne; but it'll never be such a place as Penreife."

"You know young Trevor's coming back?" said Mr Mervyn.

"Ay, I know," said the old lady. "Martha Lloyd came up to tell me, as proud as a peacock, about her young master, talking about his fine this and fine that, till she nearly made me sick. I should get rid of her and her man if I was him."

"What, Lloyd, the butler?" said Mr Mervyn, smiling.

"Yes," said the old lady, grimly, "they're Welsh people; so's that young farm-bailiff of his."

"You know the whole family?" said Mr Mervyn.

"Why, I was born here!" said the old lady, "and I ought to. We've been here for generations. Ah! and so the young squire's coming back. Time he did; going gadding off into foreign countries all this time. Why, he's six or seven and twenty now. Ay, how time goes," continued the old lady, who was off now on her hobby. "Why, it was like yesterday that the Lloyds got Mrs Trevor to send for their sister from some place with a dreadful name; and she did, and I believe it was her death, when she might have had a good Cornish nurse; and the next thing we heard was that there was a son, and the very next week there was a grand funeral, and the poor squire was never the same man again. Ah! it was an artful trick that—sending for the nurse because Mrs Lloyd wanted her too; and young Humphrey Lloyd was born the same week. Ay, they were strange times. It seemed directly after that we had the news about the squire, who got reckless-like, always out in his yacht, a poor matchwood sort of a thing, not like our boots, and it was blown on the Longships one night, and there wasn't even a body came ashore."

"Rather a sad family history," said Mr Mervyn.

"Ay, sad enough," said the woman; "and now the young squire's coming home at last from sea, but he'll never be such a man as his father."

"Think not?" said Mr Mervyn, musing.

"Sure not," said the old woman. "Why, he was petted and spoiled by those Lloyds while he was a boy, and a pretty limb he was. Him and that young Lloyd was always in some mischief. Pretty pranks they played me. I've been out with the stick to 'em scores of times; but he was generous—I will say that—and many's the conger and bass he's brought me here, proud of 'em as could be, because he caught them himself."

"Well, Mrs Trelyan, we must say good morning," said Tiny, rising and taking the old lady's hand. "Is there anything you would like—anything we can bring you?"

"No, child, no," said the old lady; "I don't want anything. If you'd any good tea, I'd use a pinch; but I'm not asking for it, mind that."

"Where's your snuff-box, granny?" said Mr Mervyn, bringing out a small canister from his pocket.

"Oh, it's here," said the old lady, fishing out and opening her box to show it was quite empty. "I don't know that I want any, though."

"Try that," said Mr Mervyn, filling it full; and the old lady took a pinch. "That's not bad, is it?"

"N-n-no, it's not bad," said the old lady, "but I've had better."

"No doubt," said Mr Mervyn, smiling.

"By the way, Mrs Trelyan, how old are you?"

"Ninety next month," said the old lady; "and—dear, dear, what a bother visitors are. Here's somebody else coming."

For at that moment there was a firm step heard without, and some one stooped and entered the doorway, hardly seeing the group on his left in the gloomy room.

"Is Mrs Trelyan at home?" he said; and Tiny Rea laid her hand upon her sisters arm.

"Yes, young man," said the old lady, shading her eyes, and gazing at the strongly-built figure before her. "I'm Mrs Trelyan, and what may you want?"

"To see how you are, granny. I'm Richard Trevor."

"And—and—" cried the old woman, letting fall her net as she rose slowly and laid her hand upon his arm; "and only a minute ago I was talking about you, and declaring you'd never be such a man as your father. My dear boy, how you have grown."

"One does grow in twelve years, granny," said the young man. "Well, I'm glad to see you alive and hearty."

"Thank you, my boy," said the old lady; and then turning and pointing to the wall, "Look!" she said, "that's the very stick that I took away from you one day for teasing my hens. You were a bad boy. You know you were."

"I suppose I was," said the young man, smiling. "But I beg pardon; you have company, granny."

"Oh, that's only Mr Mervyn, my dear, and he's going; and those are only the two girls from Tolcarne. I let them come and see me sometimes, but they're going now."

"Mr Mervyn," said the young man, holding out his hand, which was taken in a strong grip, "I am glad to meet so near a neighbour; perhaps you will introduce me to the ladies?"

"That I will," said Mr Mervyn, heartily. "Mr Trevor!"

"It's Squire Trevor now, Mr Mervyn," said the old lady, with some show of impatience.

"I beg pardon," said Mr Mervyn, smiling. "Squire Trevor, your very near neighbours, Miss Rea, Miss Finetta Rea, of Tolcarne."

"Ladies whom I have had the pleasure of meeting before," said Trevor, with a smile.

And then, in a confusion of bows, the two girls made their retreat, followed by Mr Mervyn.

"Oh, Fin, how strange!" exclaimed Tiny; "it's the gentleman who struck that man at the race."

"Yes," exclaimed Fin; "and that horrid little creature's sure to be close behind."

Sam Jenkles Prepares for an Expedition

"There you are, Ratty," said Sam Jenkles, sticking a small yellow sunflower in each of his horse's blinkers, before mounting to his perch and driving out of the yard. "Now you look 'andsome. Only recklect 'andsome is as 'andsome does; so just putt your right leg fust for once in a way."

He walked round the horse, giving it a smooth here and a smooth there with his worn-out glove, and patting its neck, before walking back, and beginning to button-up for the day.

"Blest if ever I see such a tail in my life as he's got," he muttered. "Wonder what a hartificial one 'ud cost. It aint no kind o' use to comb it, 'thout you want to comb it all out and leave no tail at all I wouldn't care if it warn't so ragged."

It certainly was a melancholy-looking tail, but only in keeping with the rest of the horse's personal appearance, which was of the most dejected—dispirited. If it had only been black, the steed would have been the beau ideal beast for a workhouse hearse; as he was of a dingy brown, he was relegated to a cab.

"What's the matter, Sam?" said a cleaner, coming up—a man with a stable pail of water in one hand, a spoke-brush in the other, and a general exemplification of how, by degrees, Nature will make square people fit into round holes, and the reverse; for, by the constant carriage of stable pails, the man's knees had gone in, and out of the perpendicular, so as to allow for the vessels' swing.

"What's the matter, Buddy? Why, everythink. Look at that there 'oss—look at his tail."

"Well, he aint 'andsome, suttunly," said the helper.

"'Andsome!" exclaimed Sam; "no, nor he aint anythink else. He won't go, nor he won't stop. If you wants him to 'old 'is 'ead up, he 'angs it down; and if you wants him to 'old it down, he shoves it up in the air, and goes shambling along like a sick camel. He's all rules of contrairy."

"'Oppin' about like a little canary," chimed in the helper.

"'Oppin' about!" said Sam, in a tone of disgust. "I should just like to see him, if on'y for once in a way. I tell yer what it is, Buddy, I believe sometimes all he does is to lift his legs up, one at a time, an' lean up agin his collar. Natur' does the rest."

"Werry likely," said Buddy; "but you can't expect everything in a cab 'oss."

"Heverythink?" said Sam. "I don't expect everythink; I only want somethink; and all you've got there," he continued, pointing with one thumb over his shoulder at the unfortunate Ratty, "is so much walking cats'-meat."

"Yes, he aint 'andsome, suttunly," said Buddy again, screwing up one side of his face. "But why don't you smooth him over? Try kindness, and give the whip a 'ollerday."

"Kindness—whip—'ollerday! Why, I'm like a father to 'im. Look here."

Sam went to the little boot at the back of his cab, and tugged out the horse's nose-bag, which was lined at the bottom with tin, so that it would have held water.

"See that?" said Sam.

"Yes: what's it for?" said Buddy.

"Beer," said Sam, fiercely, "beer! Many's the 'arfpint I've poured in there along of his chopped meat, jest to cheer him up a bit, and he aint got no missus to smell his breath. I thought that 'ud make 'im go if anythink would."

"Well, didn't it?" said Buddy, rubbing his ear with the spoke-brush.

"Didn't it?" said Sam. "Lets out at me with his orf 'ind leg, and then comes clay mill, and goes round and round till he oughter 'ave been dizzy, but he worn't. There never was sech a ungrateful beast."

Buddy grinned as Sam stuffed back the nose-bag, the horse shaking his head the while.

"Try it on me, Sam," said Buddy, as the driver prepared to mount. "I won't let out with no orf 'ind legs."

Sam winked, and climbed to his perch.

"What's the flowers for, Sam?" said the helper.

"The missus. Goin' to call for her, and drive her to Upper 'ollerway," said Sam, "afore I goes on the rank."

"Oh, will you tell her," said Buddy, earnestly, "as Ginger's ever so much better, and can a'most putt his little leg to the ground? He eats that stuff she brought him like fun."

"What stuff was that?" said Sam, gathering up the reins.

"Sorter yaller jally," said Buddy.

"What, as smells o' lemons?" said Sam.

"Yes, that's it," said Buddy; "he just do like it."

"How long's he been bad now?"

"Twelve weeks," said Buddy; "and he's been 'most worn to skin and bone; but he's pulling up now. Takes his corn."

"Mornin'," said Sam.

He tried to start; but Batty moved sidewise, laid a blinker against the whitewashed wall of the yard, and rubbed it up and down, so that it had to be wiped over with a wet leather by Buddy; and when that was done, he tried to back the cab into a narrow stable door. After that, though, he seemed better, and began to go in a straight line.

"Tried that there game at a plate-glass winder t'other day," said Sam, shouting over his shoulder as he left the yard. "He'd ha' done it, too, if it hadn't been for a lamp-post."

Sam and his steed went gently out of Grey's Inn Lane towards Pentonville, where, in a little quiet street, Mrs Jenkles resided, and Sam began musing as he went along—

"I smelt that there stuff in the cupboard, and meant to ask her what it was, but I forgot. On'y to think of her making that up, and taking it to poor Buddy's little bairn! Well, she's a good sort, is the missus, on'y she will be so hard on me about a drop o' beer. 'Old that there 'ead still, will yer? What are yer lookin' arter, there? Oh! that cats-meat barrer. Ah! yer may well shy at that, Ratty; I don't wonder at it. Now, then, get on, old boy, the missus 'll be waiting."

On reaching Spring Place, where Sam dwelt, the horse objected. He was sawing along in a straightforward way, when Sam drew one rein, with the consequence that the horse's head came round, his long neck bending till the animal's face was gazing at him in a dejected, lachrymose fashion: Ratty seeming to say, as plainly as looks would express it, "What are you doing?" while all the time the legs went straight forward up Pentonville Hill.

They had got twenty yards past Spring Place before Sam could pull the horse up; and then he had to get down to take it by the head and turn it in a very ignominious fashion.

"Jest opposite a public, too," said Sam. "I never did see such a haggravating beast as you are, Ratty. Here, come along. It aint no wonder as fellows drinks, with a place offering 'em the stuff every five minutes of their lives, and when they've got a Ratty to lead 'em right up to it. Come on, will yer?"

Mrs Jenkles was standing at the door ready, in a blue bonnet and red Paisley shawl—for she was a woman of her word. She had said that she would go up and see those people, and Sam had promised to drive her.

Going the Rounds

Fin was quite right. They had not gone above a couple of hundred yards down the lane, with Mr Mervyn between them, swinging his empty soup tin, when they became aware of a loud whistling, as of some one practising a polka. Then it would cease for a few moments, and directly after begin again.

"There's somebody," said Fin; and then, turning a sharp corner, they came suddenly on Mr Frank Pratt, perched in a sitting posture on the top of a huge, round lith of granite, with his back to them, and his little legs stretching out almost at right angles. He was in his threatened tweeds, a natty little deerstalker's hat was cocked on one side of his head; in one hand he held a stick, and in the other a large pipe, from which he drew refreshment between the strains of the polka he tried to whistle.

Mr Frank Pratt was evidently enjoying the beauty of the place after his own particular fashion; for, being a short man, he had a natural love for elevated places. As a boy, he had delighted in climbing trees, and sitting in the highest fork that would bear him, eating cakes or munching apples; as a man, cakes and apples had given way to extremely black pipes, in company with which he alternately visited the top of the Monument, the Duke of York's column, and the golden gallery of Saint Paul's, where he regretted that the cost was eighteen-pence to go any higher. In these places, where it was strictly forbidden, he indulged in surreptitious smokes, from which his friends deduced the proposition that if not the cakes, probably the apples had been stolen.

The tail stone then being handy, Mr Pratt was enjoying himself, when he suddenly became aware of steps behind, and hopped down in a most ungraceful fashion to stare with astonishment so blank, that by the time he had raised his hat Fin had gone by with her chin raised in the air, and a very disdainful look upon her countenance, and her sister, with a slightly heightened colour, had plunged into conversation with Mr Mervyn.

Pratt stood half paralysed for a few moments, watching the party, until a turn in the lane hid them from sight, and then he refilled and lit his pipe, from which the burning weed had fallen.

"It's a mistake," he said at last, between tremendous puffs at his pipe. "It's impossible. I don't believe it. One might call it a hallucination, only that the beardless female face is so similar in one woman to another that a man easily makes a mistake. Those cannot be the same girls that we saw at the steeplechase—it isn't possible; but there is a resemblance, certainly; and, treating the thing philosophically, I should say here we have the real explanation of what is looked upon as infidelity in the male being."

A few puffs from the pipe, and then Mr Pratt reclimbed to his perch upon the stone.

"I'll carry that out, and then write it down as a position worthy of argument. Yes, to be sure. Here it is. A man falls in love—say, for the sake of argument, at first sight, with a pretty girl, quite unknown to him before, upon a racecourse. Symptoms: a feeling of sympathetic attraction; a throbbing of the pulses; and the heart beating bob and go one. Say he gets to know the girl; is engaged to her; and is then separated by three or four hundred miles."

A few more puffs, and sundry nods of the head, and then Mr Pratt went on.

"He there encounters another girl, whose face and general appearance are so much like the face and general appearance of girl number one, that his secondary influences—to wit, heart, pulses, and sympathies generally—immediately give signals; love ensues, and he declares and is accepted by girl number two, while girl number one says he is unfaithful. The man is not unfaithful; it is simply an arrangement of Nature, and he can't help himself. Infidelity, then, is the same thing in a state of change. Moral: Nature has no business to make women so much alike."

Mr Pratt got down once more from his perch, and began to stroll up the lane, to encounter Trevor at the end of a few minutes.

"Did you meet any one?" was the inquiry.

"Yes," said Pratt, "a gentleman and two ladies."

"Well?"

"Well?"

"Did you not know them?"

"Ah!" said Pratt, "then you, too, noticed the similarity of feature, did you?"

"Similarity?"

"Yes; wonderfully like the ladies we met at the steeplechase, were they not?"

Richard Trevor looked hard in his friend's face for a moment, and then they walked on side by side; for at a turn of the lane they met the young keeper, who had so suddenly changed the aspect of the encounter on the course.

"Ah, Humphrey!" said Trevor, "I'm glad I've met you. I'll have a walk round the preserves."

The young keeper touched his hat, changed the double gun from one shoulder of his well-worn velveteen coat to the other, whistled to a setter, and led the way to a stone stile.

"Another curious case of similarity of feature," said Trevor, laughing.

"Well, no—I'll give in now," said Pratt; "but I say, Dick, old fellow, ought coincidences like this to occur out of novels?"

"Never mind that," said Trevor, "the keeper here, who used to be my playmate as a boy, was as much astonished as I was—weren't you, Humphrey?"

"Well, sir," said the young man, "when I see you th' other morning, I couldn't believe my eyes like, that the gentleman who'd pummelled that fellow was the one I'd come up to London to meet. I saw you, too, sir," he said, touching his hat to Pratt.

"Yes, my man," said Pratt, "and felt my toe. I'm sorry to find you did, for you've blown up one of the most beautiful propositions I ever made in my life."

"Well, now then," said Trevor, "I'll see about matters with you, Lloyd; but, by the way, you had better be Humphrey, on account of your father."

"Yes, sir; Humphrey, please, sir," said the young man.

"Well, now then, as we go on," said Trevor, "if it don't bore you, Pratt, we'll have a talk about farm matters."

"Won't bore me," said Pratt; "I'm going in for the country gentleman while I stay."

"Well, then, Humphrey, how are the crops!"

"Well, sir," said Humphrey. "Ah, Juno! what are you sniffing after there?" This to the young dog, which seemed to have been born with a mission to push its head up rabbit burrows too small for the passage. "Well, sir, begging your pardon, but that dog's took more looking after than e'er one I ever had."

"All right, go on," said Trevor, following the man across a broad, rock-sided ditch, with a little brook at the bottom.

"Well, sir," said the keeper, "the corn is—"

"Here, I say, hold hard a minute! This isn't Pall Mall, Trevor," shouted Pratt. "How the deuce am I to get over that place?"

"Jump, man," cried Trevor, laughing and looking back. "That's nothing to some of our ditches."

Pratt looked at the ditch, then down at his little legs, and then blew out his cheeks.

"Risk it," he said, laconically; and, stepping back a few yards, he took a run, jumped, came short, and had to scramble up the bank, a little disarranged, but smiling and triumphant. "All right," he said, "go on."

"Corn is, on the whole, a fair crop, sir," said Humphrey.

"And barley?"

"Plenty of that too, sir. But I've a deal of trouble with trespassers, sir."

"How's that?" said Trevor, looking round at the bright, rugged hill and dale, with trees all aglow with the touch of autumn's hand.

"You see, sir, it's the new people," said the keeper.

"What new people?"

"The old gentleman as bought Tolcarne, sir."

"Well, what of him?" said Trevor, rather anxiously.

"Well, sir, he's a magistrate and a Sir, and a great City of London man, and he wants to be quite the squire. The very first thing he does is to get two men to work on the estate, and who does he get but that Dick Darley and Sam Kelynack; and a nice pair they are, as you may know, sir."

"Seeing that I've been away for years, Humphrey, I don't know," said Trevor.

"Well, sir, they was both turned out of their last places—one for a bit o' poaching, and the other for being always on the drink. They know I don't like 'em—both of 'em," said Humphrey, with the veins swelling in his white forehead; "and no sooner do they get took on, than they begin to worry me."

"How?" said Trevor, smiling.

"Trespassing on my land, sir—I mean yours, sir, begging your pardon, sir. They will do it, too, sir. You see, there's a bit of land at the corner where Penreife runs right into the Tolcarne estate—sort of tongue o' land, sir—and to save going round, they make a path right across there, sir, over our bit of pasture."

"Put up a fence, Humphrey," said Trevor.

"I do, sir, and bush it, and set up rails; but they knocks 'em down, and tramples all over the place. Sir Hampton's got an idea that he's a right to that bit, as his land comes nigh surrounding it, and that makes 'em so sarcy."

"Well, we must see to it," said Trevor. "I want to be good friends with all my neighbours."

"Then you've cut out your work," said Pratt, drily.

"You won't be with Sir Hampton, sir, you may reckon on that," said Humphrey. "Lady Rea is a kind, pleasant lady enough, and the young ladies is very nice, sir, and he's been civil enough to me; but he upsets everybody nearly—him and his sister."

"Never mind about that," said Trevor, checking him. "I wish to be on good terms with my neighbours, and if there be any trespass—any annoyance from Sir Hampton's people—tell me quietly, and I will lay the matter before their master."

"Or we might get up a good action for trespass," said Pratt. "But, by the way," he said, stopping short, and sticking one finger on his forehead, "is this Sir Hampton the chuffy old gentleman we saw at the steeplechase?"

"Yes, sir; and as told me I might get up on the box-seat. That was him, you know, as that blackguard prodded with his stick."

"Phew!" whistled Pratt. "I say, Dick," he whispered, "the old chap did not see us under the best of auspices."

"No; it's rather vexing," was the reply.

They walked on from dense copse to meadow, through goodly fields of grain, and down in deep little vales, with steep sides covered with fern, bramble, and stunted pollard oaks.

"Poor youth!" said Pratt, and stopped to mop his forehead. "How low-spirited you must feel to be the owner of such a place. It's lovely. Nature's made it very beautiful; but no wonder—see what practice she has had."

Trevor laughed, and Humphrey smiled, saying—

"If you come a bit farther this way, sir, there's a capital view of the house."

Pratt followed the man; and there, at about half a mile distance, on the slope of a steep hill, was the rugged, granite-built seat—Penreife—half ancient, half modern; full of buttresses, gables, awkward chimney-stacks, and windows of all shapes, with the ivy clustering over it greenly, and a general look of picturesque comfort that no trimly-built piece of architecture could display. The house stood at the end of one of the steep valleys running up from the sea, which shone in the autumn sun about another half-mile farther, with grey cottages clustering on the cliff, and a little granite-built harbour, sheltering some half a dozen duck-shaped luggers and a couple of yachts.

"Ah," said Pratt, "that's pretty! Beats Ludgate Hill and Fleet Street all to fits. Is that your master's yacht?"

"The big 'un is, sir—the *Sea Launce*," said Humphrey; "the little 'un's Mr Mervyn's—the *Swallow*."

"By the way, who is this Mr Mervyn?" said Trevor, who had sauntered up.

"Well, sir," said Humphrey, taking off his hat and rubbing his brown curls, "I don't kinder know what he is. He's been in the navy, I think, for he's a capital sailor; but he's quite the gentleman, and wonderful kind to the poor people, and he lives in that little white house the other side of the cliff."

"I can't see any white house," said Pratt.

"No, sir, you can't see it, 'cause it's the other side of the cliff; but that's his flagstaff rigged up, as you can see, with the weathercock on it, and— Here, hi! you, sir, come out of that! Here, Juno, lass, come along."

"Has he gone mad?" cried Pratt.

For Humphrey had suddenly set off down a steep slope towards a meadow, and went on shouting with all his might.

"No," said Trevor, shading his eyes, "there's a man—two men with billhooks there—labourers, I should think. Come along, or perhaps there'll be a quarrel; and I can't have that."

The Lion at Home

Sir Hampton Rea was out that morning, and very busy.

He had been round to the stables and seen the four horses that had arrived the night before, and bullied the coachman because he had said that one of them had a splinter in its leg, and that the mare meant for Miss Rea had rather a nasty look about the eye.

"You're an ass, Thomas," he said.

The man touched his hat, and Sir Hampton walked half across the stable-yard.

"Er-rum!" he ejaculated, half turning; and the coachman came up, obsequiously touching his hat again.

"Those horses, Thomas, were examined by a veterinary surgeon."

"Yes, sir," said the man.

"Er-rum! And I chose them and examined them myself."

"Yes, sir."

"You've made a mistake, Thomas."

"Very like, sir," said the man. "Very sorry, sir."

Sir Hampton did not respond, but gave a sharp glance round the very new-looking stable-yard and buildings, saw nothing to find fault about; and then, clearing his throat, went into the garden as the coachman winked at the groom, and the groom raised a wen upon his cheek by the internal application of his tongue.

"Er-rum!—Sanders!" cried the knight.

And something that had worn the aspect of a huge boa constrictor in cord trousers, crawling into a melon-frame, slowly drew itself back, stood upright, and revealed a yellow-faced man with a scarlet head and whiskers.

Perhaps it is giving too decided a colour to the freckles which covered Mr Sanders's face to say they were yellow, and to his hair to say it was scarlet; but they certainly approached those hues, "Er-rum! Sanders, come here," said Sir Hampton.

Sanders leisurely closed the melon-frame and raised the light a few inches with a piece of wood, and then slowly approached his master, to stop in front of him and scrape his feet upon a spade.

"Er-rum! I'm going to inspect the grounds this morning, Sanders," said Sir Hampton.

Sanders, head gardener, nodded; for he was a man so accustomed to deal with silent objects that he seldom spoke, if he could possibly help it; but here he was obliged.

"Shall I want a spade?"

"No; certainly not."

"Nor a barrow?"

"No!" sharply.

"Maybe ye'll like me to bring a billhook?"

"Er-rum! No. Yes; bring a billhook."

The gardener went slowly off to his tool-house, and returned as leisurely; Sir Hampton the while fiercely poking vegetables about with his stick—stirring up cabbages, as if angry because they did not grow—beet, for having too much top-onions, for not swelling more satisfactorily—and ending with a vicious cut at a wasp bent on a feast of nectarine beneath the great, new, red-brick wall.

Wasp did not like it. Ignorant of any doctrine concerning *meum* and *tuum*, he looked upon all fruit as *pro bono publico*, as far as the insect world was concerned. The nectarines might be choicely named varieties, planted by Sir Hampton's order, after having been obtained at considerable expense—the wall having been built for their use; but fruit was fruit to the wasp, so long as it was ripe, and he resented interference. Pugnacity was crammed to excess in his small, yellow body, and prevented from bursting it by a series of strong black rings; so it was not surprising that the insect showed fight, and span round the new magistrate's head with a fierce buzz.

"Css! Get out! Sh!" ejaculated Sir Hampton; and he struck at the wasp again and again. But the little insect was no respecter of persons. He had been insulted, and, watching his opportunity, he dashed in, and stung the knight in the tender red mark where his stiffly starched cravat frayed his neck, gave a triumphant buzz, and went over the wall like a yellow streak.

"Confound! Ugh!" ejaculated the knight; and then, seeing Sanders coming slowly back, he played Spartan, and preserved outward composure, though there was a volcano of wrath smouldering within.

He strutted off, with the gardener behind, fired a couple of shots at gardeners two and three, who were sweeping the lawn, and then entered into a general inspection of the garden.

"How—Er-rum!—how is it that bed is not in flower, Sanders?" "Done blooming," said Sanders, gruffly.

"Done blooming, Sir Hampton!" exclaimed the knight, facing round.

"Done blooming, Sir Hampton," said the gardener, slowly; and he looked as expressionless as a big sunflower.

"Take off that branch," said the knight, pointing to an overhanging bough; and it was solemnly lopped off.

"Er-rum!" ejaculated the knight, when they had gone a little farther. "How is it that patch of lawn is brown?"

"Grubs," said the gardener.

"Grubs, Sir Hampton," said the knight, fiercely.

"Grubs, Sir Hampton," said the corrected gardener.

"Ha!" said Sir Hampton, and they went a little farther.

"Those Wellingtonias are not growing, Sanders."

"Two foot this year," said the gardener.

"That's very slow."

"Fast," said the gardener.

"Fast, Sir Hampton," said the knight.

"Fast, Sir Hampton," said the gardener, corrected again.

"Er-rum! Ah! This won't do. This clump must be moved farther to the right," said Sir Hampton, pointing to a cluster of shrubs.

"Kill 'em," said Sanders.

"Then we'll set more," said the knight; and he went on to the farthest entrance of the garden, and the paths cut through the plantation, with a general desire exhibited in his every act, that as he had, so to speak, made the place and planted the grounds, it was absolutely necessary that he should have all the trees pulled up at stated intervals, to see how the roots were getting along.

There was a small iron gate at the end of the plantation walk, and this the gardener opened for his master to pass through, closing it after him, and sticking the billhook in his breast.

"Er-rum! Where are you going, Sanders?" said the knight, sharply.

"Back," said Sanders—"'taint garden here."

His domain extended no farther.

"Come along this moment, sir; and stop till I dismiss you."

The knight looked purple as the gardener slowly unlatched the gate, and followed him about a quarter of a mile, to where the estate joined that of the Trevors; and here, as they neared the pastures, angry voices were heard.

"Quick, Sanders," cried Sir Hampton—"trespassers!"

The next minute they were upon an angry group, consisting of Trevor, Pratt, Humphrey, a man with a sinister look and a mouth like a rat-trap, and a stumpy fellow, who was armed with a long plashing hook.

"Er-rum! what's this?" exclaimed Sir Hampton, with the voice of authority.

"These men of yours, Sir Hampton," said Humphrey, flushed and angry, "always trespassing across our ground."

"My servants would do nothing of the sort, fellow," said Sir Hampton.

"But they have done it, Sir Hampton," said Humphrey. "There they are; there's their footmarks right across the field; and they're always at it, and breaking down the bushes."

"Hold your tongue, Humphrey," said Trevor. "I beg your pardon—Sir Hampton Rea, I believe?"

The wasp sting, kept back so long, now came out.

"And pray, sir, why are you trespassing on my grounds?" exclaimed the knight, furiously.

"Excuse me, I am on my own," said Trevor.

"Your own! I never heard such insolence in my life. Who are you, sir? What the devil are you? Where do you come from?"

"Well," said Trevor, with a red spot coming into each cheek, but speaking quite coolly, "my name is Trevor. I am the owner of Penreife, and I have lately returned from sea."

"Then—then—go back to sea, sir, or get off my grounds; or, by gad, sir, my labourers shall kick you off."

The men advanced menacingly; but, with a face like fire, Humphrey rolled up his cuffs.

"Humphrey! Stop; how dare you!" exclaimed Trevor, angrily.

The young keeper drew back, grinding his teeth; for the others continued to advance, and the rat-trap-mouthed man, finding Juno, the dog, smelling about him, gave the poor brute a kick, which produced a loud yelp.

"Excuse me, Sir Hampton, but—"

"Get off my grounds, sir, this instant!" roared the knight.

Wasp sting again.

"Look here," said Pratt, "if it's a question of boundary, any solicitor will look through the deeds, and a surveyor measure, and put it all right in—"

"Who the devil is this little cad?" exclaimed Sir Hampton.

"Cad?" cried Pratt.

"Yes, sir, cad. Oh! I thought I knew you again. Yes; you are one of that gang on the omnibus who insulted me the other day. And—and—" he stammered in his rage, turning to Trevor, "you were another of the party. Get off my grounds, sir—this instant, sir. Darley, Sanders, Kelynack—drive these fellows off!"

The three men advanced, and Sir Hampton took the general's place in the rear, quivering still with rage and the poison of the wasp. Trevor was now flushed and angry, and Humphrey evidently ripe for any amount of assault or resistance, when Pratt stepped forward and laid his hand upon the arm of the angry knight.

Hebe

"Stand back, sir—get off my ground, sir!" cried Sir Hampton, furiously. "Look here, men, this is—er-rum—an assault."

"No, it is not, Sir Hampton," said Pratt, coolly. "Look here, my good man."

"Your good man, sir?"

"Yes," said Pratt, quietly; and there was something in the little fellow that enforced attention. "You are, I believe, a magistrate here—for the county?"

"Yes, sir; I am, sir; and—er-rum—"

"Be cool—be cool," said Pratt, "You called me a cad just now."

"I did, sir; and—"

"Well, I am a barrister—of the Temple. There is my card."

He stuck the little piece of pasteboard into the magistrate's hand.

"Confound your card, sir! I—"

"Now now, look here," said Pratt, button holing him, "don't be cross. Let me ask you this—Is it wise of you—a justice of the peace—to set your men on, right or wrong, to break that peace?"

Sir Hampton Rea stopped short for a moment or two, and then gasped, seemed as if he would choke, and ended by snatching his coat away from Pratt's grasp.

"Darley, Sanders, come back—go back," he said at last. "These people shall hear from me."

The rat-trap man stood looking evilly at the young keeper, and the Scotch gardener took a pinch of snuff. Then they slowly followed their master, and the coast was clear.

"You're sure, I suppose, about this tongue of land?" said Pratt. "By Jove! what a rage, though, the old boy was in."

"Sure? yes—oh yes," said Trevor. "Wasn't it here that they sunk the shaft for the copper mine, Humphrey?"

"Yes, sir, twenty yards farther on, under that clump. It's 'most filled up, though, now."

"To be sure, I recollect the spot well enough now. But this is a bad job, Franky," he continued, in an undertone. "I wanted to be on the best of terms with my neighbours."

"'Specially that neighbour," said Pratt, meaningly.

"With all my neighbours," said Trevor.

"You've made a nice beginning, then," said Pratt.

"If there is any fresh upset, Humphrey, let me know; but don't pick a quarrel," said Trevor. "I shall not go any farther to-day."

"Very well, sir," said the keeper; and then in an undertone, as he stooped and patted the dog, "Kick you, would he, Juno, lass? Never mind, then, he shall have it back some day."

The dog whined and leaped up at him, as he rose again, and looked after his master.

"Well, he's grown into a fine, bold-speaking gentleman," he said to himself; "but I should have liked it better if he'd tackled to and helped me to thrash them two ill-looking blackguards."

Meanwhile Trevor and his old schoolfellow had been walking sharply back towards the house, where they were evidently being watched for by the old butler, Lloyd—the remains of a fine-looking man, for he was bent now, though his eyes were clear and bright.

"I saw you coming across the park, Master Dick," he said, his face shining with pleasure. "You'll have a bit of lunch now, won't you?"

"Early yet, isn't it?" said Pratt.

"I don't think so, sir," said the old butler, austerely. "I am sure Master Dick requires something after his long walk."

"Yes, yes—that he does," said a rather shrill voice; and an active, grey-haired woman of about fifty came bustling out. She was very primly dressed in black silk, with white muslin kerchief, white holland apron, in whose pockets her hands rested; and her grey hair was carefully smoothed back beneath her plain white muslin cap.

"No, no; it's only twelve o'clock, Mrs Lloyd," said Trevor, good-humouredly. "I lunch at one."

"You take my advice, Master Dick, and have it now," said the butler.

"Yes, Lloyd, have it brought in, and ask Master Dick if he'll have some of the old claret," said the woman.

"My dear Mrs Lloyd," said Trevor, smiling, "this is very kind of you—of you both—but I'm not ready for lunch yet. You can both go now. I'll ring when I'm ready."

He led the way into his handsomely furnished study, the beau ideal of a comfortable room for a man with a mingling of literary and sporting tastes.

"Here, let's sit down and have a cigar," he said, pushing a great leather-covered chair to his friend; "it will smooth us down after our encounter."

"No; I'll fill my pipe," said Pratt, suiting the action to the word, and lighting up, to send big clouds of smoke through the large room.

"You mustn't take any notice of the old butler and housekeeper, Frank," said Trevor, after a pause.

"Don't mean to."

"You see, they've had their own way here since I was a child."

"And now they don't like to give it up?"

"I suppose not. But they mean well. They were always, I can remember, most affectionate to me."

"Yes; they seem to like Master Dick."

"Pish! yes, of course—their way. Sounds stupid, though, Franky; but you can't wonder at it."

"I don't," said Pratt. "But I should put my foot down, I think."

"That I most decidedly shall, and before Van and the little Baronet come down."

"Oh, by Jove!" said Pratt, starting, "why those two fellows are coming to-morrow."

"Yes; they'll be here about five."

"And what in the world are you going to do with them?"

"Oh, there's plenty to do—billiards, and cards, and smoking indoors; fishing and yachting out of doors."

"Yes," said Pratt, with a sigh; "but they'll both be murmuring after the flesh-pots of Pall Mall. You'll have your hands pretty full."

"Never fear," said Trevor; "I shall be able to entertain them. How strange it all seems, though—such a little while since we were boys at Eton, and now Van a perfect exquisite."

"Landells an imperfect ditto."

"You a barrister."

"Yes," said Pratt, "very barrister, indeed; and you altered into a tawny tar, regularly disguised by Nature."

Here there was a tap at the door. "Come in," said Trevor, who was sitting in a low, big-backed chair. And then, as the door opened, "Who is it?"

"Hebe!" said Pratt, softly.

"Eh?" said Trevor.

"If you please, sir, Mrs Lloyd said I was to bring this in," said a pleasant little voice; and Trevor swung himself round in his chair, to gaze upon a pretty little very round-faced girl of about seventeen or eighteen, with smooth brown hair, clear white complexion, rather large eyes, ruddy lips, and a face like fire with confusion. There were the faint traces, too, of tears lately wiped from her eyes, and her pleasant little voice had a plaintive ring in it as, in answer to Trevor's "Eh?" and wondering stare, she repeated her words—

"If you please, sir, Mrs Lloyd said I was to bring this in."

"And pray what is this?" said Trevor, glancing at the salver the girl carried, bearing a good-sized silver flagon, with chased lid, and a snowy napkin placed through the handle.

"If you please, sir, it's a pint of new milk beat up with three eggs, three glasses of sherry, and some lump sugar," said the girl.

"And who's it for?" said Trevor.

"For you and the gentleman, sir; Mrs Lloyd said the sea air must have made you faint."

"Well," said Trevor, "hand it to Mr Pratt, there."

The girl bore the flagon to Pratt, who took it, but emitted such a volume of strong tobacco smoke that the girl sneezed, and choked, and then looked more scarlet and confused than ever.

"I beg your pardon," said Pratt; and then he raised the flagon to his lips, and took a long draught, wiping the brim afterwards with the napkin. "Splendid, old fellow!" he said. "Take it to—your master."

"And pray who may you be, my dear?" said Trevor, looking critically at the girl, but relieving her from his gaze the next moment, in compassion for her confusion.

"If you please, sir, I'm Aunt Lloyd's niece," said the girl.

"And are you anything here—housemaid, or—?"

"Oh no, sir, if you please. I am here on a long visit to my aunt; and she said I was to help her."

"Well," said Trevor, setting down the flagon, "tell her the milk was excellent; but she is not to send anything in again without I ring for it. Well, what's the matter?"

The girl was looking in a pitiful way at him, and she remained silent for a few moments, when he spoke again.

"Is anything the matter?"

"Must—must I tell her that, sir?"

"Yes. Why not?" said Trevor.

"Because—because, if you please, sir, I..."

The girl did not finish, but uttered a sob, and ran out of the room.

"Cornwall promises to be a queer place," said Pratt; "but that stuff was heavenly—did you finish it, Dick?"

"Not quite, I think," said Trevor.

"And you sent it away. Oh, Dick!"

The little maid had hardly got outside the door, when Mrs Lloyd came across the hall, followed at a short distance by the butler, rubbing his hands, smiling feebly, and looking anxious.

"Crying?" said Mrs Lloyd, sharply. "You little goose!"

"I—I—couldn't help it, aunt, indeed," sobbed the girl.

"'Sh! not a sound," said Mrs Lloyd, sharply; and she caught the girl by the arm. "Did he drink the milk?"

"Yes, aunt."

"Did that other gentleman take any?"

"Yes, aunt—a lot."

"As if he couldn't come home without bringing such a pack with him. Now come into my room, and I'll talk to you, madam. Lloyd, take that waiter."

She led the way into the housekeeper's room, as her husband obediently bore off the flagon to his pantry; and then, shutting the door, she took her seat in a stiff, horse-hair-covered chair, looking as hard and prim as the presses and cupboards around.

"Now listen to me," she said, harshly.

"Yes, aunt."

"I'm not going to boast; but what have I done for you?"

"Paid for my schooling, aunt, and kept me three years."

"Where would you have been if it hadn't been for me?"

"Living with Aunt Price at Caerwmlych."

"Starving with her, you mean, when she can hardly keep herself," said Mrs Lloyd, sharply. "Now, look here, Polly, I've taken you from a life of misery to make you well off and happy; and I will be minded. Do you hear me?"

"Yes, aunt."

"Then do as I tell you exactly. Do you hear?"

"I'll try, aunt."

"Try? You must. Now, then: Did he speak to you?"

"Yes, aunt."

"What did he say? Come, speak, child!"

"He asked me who I was, aunt; and what I had come for."

"Of course, you silly little thing. There, no more tears. It's dreadful treatment, isn't it, to make you go in and attend to him a little?"

"Please, aunt, I don't mind that," said the girl.

"No, I should think not, indeed," said Mrs Lloyd. "He's an ogre to look at, isn't he?"

"No, aunt, I think he's a fine, handsome man."

"Not a finer, nor a handsomer, nor a nicer in all Cornwall: and you ought to be fine and pleased to be in the house. And now look here, madam—no more tears, if you please."

"No, aunt."

"And you're always to be nicely dressed, and do your hair well."

"Yes, aunt."

"And keep yourself to yourself, madam. Recollect, please, that you're my niece, staying in the house, and not one of the servants."

"Yes, aunt."

The door opened, and the butler put in his head.

"It's lunch-time now, and I am having the things taken in again."

"That's quite right."

"Do you want to come?"

"Not now; only Mary shall bring in the vegetables."

"Hadn't William better help?" said the butler.

"No, not to-day. There will be a pack more people here to-morrow, and she can't come then. Here, child, take these clean napkins and be ready to carry them into the dining-room."

"But my face, aunt—won't they see?"

"What—that you have been crying?" said the housekeeper, critically. "No; they won't. Stop here a minute while I go out into the hall."

The girl, from being scarlet, was now pale, but quite a little "rustic beauty" all the same; and she stood by the linen press looking very troubled, while Mrs Lloyd went back into the hall, where Trevor had stepped out to speak to the butler.

"Oh, there you are, Mrs Lloyd," he said, in a quiet, decided tone of voice. "I was just speaking to Lloyd about one or two little matters. Of course, I feel the highest respect for both you and your worthy husband."

"Thank you, Master Dick," said the housekeeper, stiffly.

"Yes, that's it," said Trevor. "And of course you can't help looking upon me as the boy you were almost father and mother to at one time."

"Of course not," said Mrs Lloyd, stiffly; "but you don't mean to turn us away now you have grown a man?"

"God forbid!" said Trevor, earnestly. "While I live, this is your home, and I shall interfere but little with you in the conduct of the house. But I take this opportunity of saying that I must ask of you both to remember—old friends as well as old servants of the family—that I have now come back to take my position here as the master of Penreife, and that, in speaking to me before visitors, 'Master Dick' sounds rather childish. That will do, Mrs Lloyd. Yes, Lloyd, you can bring in some of the claret."

He walked into the dining-room, the quiet, calm man of the world, with enough dignity and self-assertion to show the housekeeper that the days of her rule had departed for ever.

"That's going to sea, that is," she muttered. "That's being used to order people about, and being an officer. But we shall see, Master Dick—we shall see!"

And with a quick, spasmodic twitching of her hands as she smoothed down her apron, she went back muttering to her own room.

Mishaps

Lunch at Tolcarne that day was not one of the most pleasant of meals. Sir Hampton had come in, looking purple instead of red with his walk, to pause at the hall door and dismiss Sanders, the gardener, who stood mopping his face.

"Er-rum! Look here, Sanders!" he exclaimed.

"Yes, sir," said Sanders.

"Yes, Sir Hampton, man!"

"Yes, Sir Hampton," said Sanders, slowly and impressively, as if he were trying to fix the formula in his mind.

"I'll see you in the morning about a new bed on the lawn, and—er-rum—don't let this affair be talked about."

"No, sir—Hampton," said Sanders.

He went heavily down the new path, while his master stood apparently loading himself—that is to say, he thrust what seemed to be a white gun-wad into his mouth, before turning into the hall, and letting off a tremendous "Er-rum," which echoed through the house. The wad, however, was only a digestive tablet, an antidote to the heartburn, from which Sir Hampton suffered; and he strode into the dining-room, where the family was already assembled for luncheon.

"Oh, dad—papa," cried Fin, "such news for you."

"Don't worry your papa, my dear," said Miss Matilda, smoothing her handkerchief, which, from being sat upon, resembled a cambric cake; "wait till he has had some refreshment. He is tired. Hampton, will you take a cutlet?"

"Don't, pa. Have some chicken pie."

"Shall I send you a poached egg, dear?" said Lady Rea, who was in difficulties with the mustard-pot, the protruding spoon of which had entangled itself with her open lace sleeve, and the yellow condiment was flowing over the table.

"No," said Sir Hampton, gruffly.

"Tut, tut, tut," said Lady Rea, making matters worse by trying to scrape up the mustard with a spoon.

"Hadn't you better let Edward do that, dear?" said Miss Matilda, with a pained expression of countenance, as she played pat-a-cake once more with her handkerchief.

"They do make the mustard so horribly thin," said Lady Rea. "Finetta, give papa some of the pie."

Fin looked mischievously across at her sister, and then cut a large portion of the patty, enough to have called forth an angry remonstrance at another time; but though Miss Matilda looked perfectly horrified, Sir Hampton was too angry and absorbed to notice it; he only went on eating.

"Well, Finetta, dear," said Lady Rea, "what's the grand news?"

"Seen the sailor, ma, dear; been introduced to him. Such a nice fellow."

"Seen whom?" said Lady Rea, making a last scrape at the mustardy cloth.

"Mr Trevor, ma; met him at old Mrs Trelyan's. Such fun."

"My dear Finetta," began Miss Matilda; but a shot fired by Sir Hampton stopped her in dismay.

"Er-rum—what's that?" he asked. "Have you met that person?"

"What person, papa?" said Finetta. "That—that Penreife man—that Trevor, or whatever his name is?"

"Yes, pa, we met him this morning; and he's the same—"

"Er-rum, I know!" exclaimed Sir Hampton, upsetting a carafe in his excitement, and making Miss Matilda start back to save her silk. "I ought to have bought Penreife—it's one of those persons we saw—I know; I met him this morning—trespass—an insulting—ugh! ugh! ugh!"

"Oh, pa!" cried Finetta, "you shouldn't get in a passion with your mouth full; and so much pepper as there is in that pie."

For Sir Hampton had begun to cough furiously, his face growing deeper in tint, and his eyes protruding, so alarming Lady Rea that she bustled round the table and began to hammer his back, while Miss Matilda offered a glass of water.

"Ugh! ugh! ugh! Sit down—sit down!" gasped Sir Hampton. "I—er-rum—I forbid all fixture communication with that—that fellow. If he calls here, I'll have the door shut in his face. Insulted me grossly this morning, on my own grounds, and a dirty little jackanapes with him talked to me in such a way as I was never spoken to before."

"Oh, Tiny, it's the horrid little man," whispered Fin.

"Why, my dear Hampy, whatever is it all about?" said Lady Rea. "There, do drink some water, and get cool."

Sir Hampton glanced at his wife and sister, and poured himself out half a tumbler of sherry, which he drained, and then began to cough once more.

"Eat a bit of bread, dear," said Lady Rea. "Quick, you won't mind mine—I haven't touched it."

Saying which she held a piece out to him on a fork.

"Frances!" ejaculated Miss Matilda.

"Ugh! Any one would think I was a bear upon a pole," coughed Sir Hampton; and he wiped his eyes as he grew better.

"But, Hampy, dear," said Lady Rea, "it will be so strange. Suppose Mr Trevor calls?"

"Tell the servants to shut the door in his face," growled Sir Hampton. "An insulting puppy!"

"Oh, pa, dear, don't be so cross," said Fin. "Take us out for a drive this afternoon, and let's see if the box has come from Mudie's."

"Disgraceful—and on one's own land, too," growled Sir Hampton, not heeding his daughter, but still muttering thunder.

"But you will take us, papa?" said Fin, leaning on his shoulder.

"Such insolence!" muttered Sir Hampton.

"Was he trespassing, Hampton?" said Miss Matilda.

"Yes, and a pack of fellows along with him," cried Sir Hampton, firing up once more.

"You'll take us out, pa, dear?" said Fin, getting her cheek against his.

"No, no! well, there, yes," said Sir Hampton; and then, looking like a half-mollified bull, he submitted to having his cheeks patted, and his stiff cravat untied and retied by the busy fingers of his pet child.

"In half an hour, dad?"

"Yes, yes; only don't bother. Er-rum!" he ejaculated, as Fin flew to the bell, "tell them to bring round the waggonette."

Sir Hampton rose and left the room, firing a shot as he crossed the hall. Then the footman came in to receive his orders, and directly after Lady Rea looked admiringly across at her daughter.

"Ah, Fin, my dear, I wish I could manage your papa as you do."

"Really, Frances," said Miss Matilda, bridling up, "I don't think that is a proper way for you to speak respecting a parent to a child."

Poor downright Lady Rea looked troubled and distressed.

"Really, Matty," she began.

"Oh, it's all right," said Fin, coming to the rescue. "It's because you don't understand, Aunt Matty; only married people do. Why don't you marry Mr Mervyn?"

Miss Matilda rose from her chair, smoothed her skirts, gazed in utter astonishment at her niece, and marched out of the room.

"Oh, Fin!" exclaimed her sister.

"You shouldn't do it, my dear," said Lady Rea, in whose gentle eyes the tears were gathering.

"I should!" said Fin, stamping her foot and colouring with passion. "I won't stand here and hear my dear mother snubbed in that way by any one but papa; and if Aunt Matty only dares to do such a thing again, I'll—I'll—I'll say something horrid."

The next moment she had flung her impetuous little self into Lady Rea's arms, and was sobbing passionately; but only to jerk herself free, and wipe her eyes directly in a snatchy fashion.

"It's so vexatious, too, for papa to turn like that, when Mr Trevor's one of the nicest, dearest, handsomest fellows you ever saw. Isn't he, Tiny?"

"I thought him very pleasing and gentlemanly," said Tiny, flushing slightly.

"She thought ever so much more of him than that, I know, ma," said Fin, nodding her head. "But isn't it vexatious, mamma, dear?"

"It'll all come right, my dear," said Lady Rea, kissing her child fondly. "There, now, go and get ready, or papa will be cross."

Fin felt ready to say "I don't care," so rebellious was the spirit that invested her that day; but she set her teeth, and ran to the door.

"You're coming, mamma?"

"No, my dear, Tiny will go with you. I shall stay in this afternoon."

"And leave Aunt Matty to say disagreeable things to you. Then I shall stay, too."

"No, no, dear, go—to please me," said Lady Rea; and the girl ran off.

The waggonette was round, and Sir Hampton was drawing on his gloves, the image of punctuality, when Fin came rushing down, closely followed by her sister, and the party started for the little station town, Saint Kitt's, passing on the road another handsome new waggonette, with a fine, well-paced pair of horses.

"I wonder whose turn-out that is?" said Sir Hampton. "Strange thing that everybody gets better horses than I do."

"I know whose it is," said Fin, demurely.

"Whose?" said Sir Hampton.

"Daren't say," replied Fin. "Ask Edward. Edward!" she cried, "whose carriage is that?"

"Think it's Mr Trevor's, ma'am," said the footman, touching his hat.

"Er-rum," ejaculated Sir Hampton, and Fin nudged her sister and made her colour.

The box was at the station, and it was put in the waggonette by a tall porter, whom Fin spoke of to her sister as the signal post, and then she proposed that they should wait and see if anything would come by the train due in a few minutes.

Now, Sir Hampton expected something by that train, but he had been so crossed that day, and was in such a contrary mood, that he exclaimed—

"Er-rum, absurd; certainly not. Drive back at once."

Fin made a grimace at her sister, who replied with a look of remonstrance; Sir Hampton sat back and frowned at the landscape, as if he thought it too green; and away they bowled just as the whistle of the engine was heard in the distance.

Something has been said before about the Cornish lanes, and the way in which the granite bones of Mother Nature peer out and form buttresses to the banks, huge pillars, and mighty corners. The lane they were traversing on their way back was not one of the least rugged, though the road was good; and they had gone at a pretty sharp trot for about a mile, when a cart came rattling along just at a turn of the road where it was narrow; and in making way—*click*! the box of one wheel caught against a granite buttress pushed forth from the bank, the wheel wriggled about, and fifty Yards farther came off and went trundling down the hill—the coachman fortunately pulling his horses up short, so that the waggonette sidled over against the ferny bank, and no one was hurt.

"Such abominable driving," exclaimed Sir Hampton.

"Very sorry, sir," said the coachman.

"Oh, pa, it was those other people's fault. I saw it all," said Fin.

The coachman gave her a grateful look, and the footman helped all to alight.

Five minutes' inspection showed that the wheel was so much injured that it would take time to repair, and there was nothing for it but to send to the little town to get assistance.

"Shall I send Edward with one horse, Sir Hampton, and ride the other home and fetch the barouche."

"Yes—no—yes," said Sir Hampton, waking to the fact that they were yet eight miles from home, and he had done quite as much walking as he cared for in one day.

At this moment the sound of wheels was heard, and the waggonette they had before passed came up, evidently from the station, with two gentlemen inside, the coachman pulling up on seeing that there was an accident, while the gentlemen leaped out.

"I trust," said the elder, raising his hat, "that no one is hurt."

"Er-rum! none; no one," said Sir Hampton, stiffly.

"What misfortune!" said the younger, fixing his glass in his eye, and looking in a puzzled way at the ladies. "Under circumstances, Vanleigh?"

"Yes, of course," said the other, and then raising his hat to the ladies, "as my friend here observes. You will allow me to place the carriage at your disposal?"

Sir Hampton looked at the speaker, then at the carriage, then at his own. That was Trevor's carriage, but these were strangers, and he was not obliged to know. His legs ached; it was a long while to wait; and he was still pondering when the first speaker said—

"Allow me," and offered his arm to Tiny, who glanced at her father, and seeing no commands against the act, suffered herself to be led to the whole waggonette, the other stranger offering his arm to Fin, who just touched it, and then leapt in beside her sister.

"Will you follow, Mr—Mr—?"

"Er-rum! Sir Hampton Rea, at your service, gentlemen," said the knight, stiffly.

"I beg pardon, Sir Hampton—strangers, you see. My friend here is Sir Felix Landells; my name is Vanleigh—Captain Vanleigh."

"Guards," said Sir Felix, in the midst of a good deal of formal bowing; and then, all being seated, the waggonette drove off, Sir Hampton, in the conversation which ensued, being most careful to avoid any reference to the destination of his new friends, merely requesting to be set down at the end of the lane leading to Tolcarne, the party separating amidst a profusion of bows.

"What a pair of dandies!" said Fin.

"A most refined gentleman that Captain Vanleigh," said Sir Hampton.

"What did you think of the other one, dad?" said Fin.

"Aristocrat. Er-rum! aristocrat," said Sir Hampton. "Blue blood there, for a certainty. I hope they'll call. By the way, Tiny, I thought you unnecessarily cold and formal."

"Did you, papa?" said Tiny. "Indeed, I did not mean to be so."

Here they reached the hall, and the girls went to their room.

"Dad's hooked," said Fin, throwing herself into a chair. "Tiny, that dandy would come to grief if I knew him long. I should feel obliged to singe his horrid little sticky mustachios; and as for the other—oh, how I could snub him if he looked and talked at me as he did at you."

"I sincerely hope," said Tiny, "that we shall never see them again."

Polly's troubles

"By the way, Pratt," said Trevor, as they were strolling through the grounds, "what aged man should you take Vanleigh to be?"

"Close upon forty," said Pratt; "but he takes such care of himself, and dresses so young, that he keeps off the assaults of old Father Time."

"He can't be so old as that," said Trevor, thoughtfully; "and yet he must begetting on. He was much older than we were, you know, in the old days."

"Yes," said Pratt; "bless him, I love Van dearly. I suppose they'll be here soon. H'm!"

"Eh?" said Trevor.

"I said H'm!" replied Pratt.

"Yes, I know," said Trevor, laughing; "but what does H'm mean?"

"Shall I make mischief, or shan't I? Well, I don't know that it would be making mischief, for it seems quite natural."

"My dear Frank, don't play the Sphinx, please, for I'm one of the most dense men under the sun. Now, then, speak out."

"Only thinking, and putting that and that together," said Pratt, relighting his cigar. "Well?"

"Well—handsome young bailiff seen in the copse yonder; pretty girl is seen going rather hurriedly along path leading to copse; and elderly lady who holds post of housekeeper, and who, by the way, seems to know it, is seen to peer through window, and then to come to door, as if in search of pretty girl. I say only, what does it mean?"

"Means a bit of sweethearting, apparently," said Trevor, laughing. "Well, I suppose it's all right!"

"Not if the old lady catches them, perhaps; so let's go and talk to the old lady."

Trevor shrugged his shoulders, and the couple walked back towards the house, where Mrs Lloyd was standing, evidently fidgeted about something or another.

"I tell you she must have gone out," she was saying as they came up.

But just at that moment the sound of carriage wheels was heard, and the waggonette drew up at the door with Vanleigh and Landells.

"Jove!" said the latter, "what out-of-the-way place, Trevor. Thought never get here."

A sharp sniff drew his attention to Mrs Lloyd, who stood with her husband just inside the door.

"Not bad," said Vanleigh, superciliously.

"Ah, you'll like it when you've been down a day or two," said Trevor. "I'm heartily glad to see you both."

"Thanks," said Vanleigh, as his host led the way into the hall. "Ah, quite mediaeval."

"Mrs Lloyd, you've got the oak room ready for Captain Vanleigh?" said Trevor.

"No, Master Dick, I've ordered the blue room for him."

Trevor's brow clouded, but he only bit his lip.

"Then you've arranged that Sir Felix shall have the oak room?"

"No, Master—sir," she said, correcting herself in a very stately way, "Sir Felix will sleep in the chintz chamber."

Trevor flushed, but he turned it off lightly.

"These are our old butler and housekeeper, Vanleigh," he said. "Mrs Lloyd there was almost like a mother to me as a child."

"Indeed," said Vanleigh, superciliously; and Sir Felix fixed his glass and had a good stare at the old lady, who looked every whit the mistress of the house.

"Grey mare?" he said, in a whisper.

"Old favoured servants," said Trevor, in return; and the young men walked into the drawing-room.

"Don't stand staring there," said Mrs Lloyd, fiercely, to the footman; "take up these portmantees."

The man gave her a surly look.

"He'll go to ruin, that he will," said Mrs Lloyd, in a voice of suppressed anger, to her husband, as soon as they were alone; "and there you stand without a word to say for yourself."

"Well, what can I do, my dear?" said Lloyd, feebly.

"Nothing—nothing; what you have always done—nothing. But I'll stop it soon. I won't be made quite a nonentity of. Where's that girl? Go and look for her. Or, no, you must see to the dinner; and mind this, Lloyd—she's to be kept out of sight while these fine sparks are here. I don't like the looks of that dark fellow at all."

Mrs Lloyd hurried away to meet Polly, just about to enter the housekeeper's room.

"And pray, where have you been, madam?"

"Only out in the grounds, aunt—it was so fine," was the reply.

Mrs Lloyd looked at her till a red glow overspread the girl's face.

"Look here," said Mrs Lloyd, catching her by one hand; "you are not a fool, Polly. You understand what I mean, don't you?"

The girl looked up at her with a shiver, and then her eyes fell.

"Don't you try to thwart me, mind, or you'll be sorry for it to the last day of your life. Now, look here, do you mind me?"

"Yes, aunt."

"You are to keep in the housekeeper's room here till those friends of Master Dick's are gone. And don't you try to deceive me, because I can read that pink and white face of yours like a book."

Mrs Lloyd flung the little maiden's hand away from her, walked to a drawer, and brought out some new linen, which she set the girl to sew, while she went about the house seeing to the arrangements for her master's guests.

As a matter of course, little Polly had "a good cry," making several damp places on the new linen; and then, with a sob, she wished herself safe back at her old aunt's in the Welsh mountains, where she was poor, but happy and free as the goats.

"I'd go to-morrow if I could," she sobbed, and then the needle hand fell upon the stiff, hard work, and she closed her wet eyes till a faint smile came across her face like a little ray of sunshine; and she whispered softly to herself, as if it were a great secret, "No, I don't think I would."

Mrs Jenkles's Morning Call

"Been waiting, old lady?" said Sam Jenkles, throwing open the apron of the cab as he reached his wife's side.

"Not a minute, Sam; but why weren't you driving? Is he restive?"

"Restive!" said Sam; "I only wish he was. I'd give 'arf a sovrin' to see 'im bolt."

"And suppose I was in the cab!" said Mrs Jenkles.

"There, don't you be alarmed. Jump in. Ratty wouldn't run away with you inside, my dear—nor any one else."

Sam rattled the apron down, hopped on to his perch, chirruped to Ratty, and, for a wonder, he went decently out on to Pentonville Hill, past the Angel, along Upper Street, and round by the Cock at Highbury.

"What do you think of that, old lady?" said Sam, opening his little lid to peer down at his wife. "Comfortable?"

"Comfortable—yes," said Mrs Jenkles, looking up and beaming. "And you said he wouldn't go."

"He knows as you're here," said Sam; "and that's his aggrawating nature. He's a-selling me."

"Selling you, Sam?"

"Yes; a-making out as I grumbles without cause. Sit fast; I'll bowl yer up there in no time."

"No, Sam, don't—pray, don't go fast!" said his wife, in alarm.

"You sit still; it's all right, I tell yer. Good wives is scarce, Sally, so you won't be spilled."

Only half convinced, Mrs Jenkles held on very tightly by the sides of the cab, till, well up now in the geography of the place, Sam ran round by the better road, and drew up at B. Sturt's grocery warehouse.

"No," said Sam, as Mrs Jenkles made for the shop; "side door, and ring once."

As he spoke, Barney's ill-looking face appeared at the door; and as Mrs Jenkles went and rang—

"Mornin'," said Sam.

Barney scowled, and blew a cloud of tobacco at him.

"Keb, sir?" said Sam, mounting to his perch.

Barney growled, and then spat.

"Run yer up to town in no time. Cheap trains to S'burban 'andicap," said Sam, grinning.

But Barney turned his back as the cab drove off, and asked his wife— "What, them people wanted with kebs now?"

Mrs Lane admitted her visitor, and, in a hesitating way, asked her upstairs, where her daughter, looking very pale, was seated by the window, working for very life at the hard, blue cloth garments upon which they were engaged.

The girl rose as Mrs Jenkles entered, and bent towards her, flushing slightly beneath the scrutinising gaze to which she was subjected.

At the same time, Mrs Jenkles made a short bob, and then another to Mrs Lane, who placed a chair for her, which she declined to take.

"It was my husband, ma'am," said Mrs Jenkles, "who came up to you the other day."

"Yes," said Mrs Lane. "You have come from him. He brought you to-day?"

"I said I should come and see you," said Mrs Jenkles, looking sharply from one to the other.

"And he told you?" said Mrs Lane, hesitatingly.

"Yes; my husband tells me everything," said Mrs Jenkles, stiffly.

"Then you know how good he was to mamma?" said the girl, coming forward.

"My husband's one of the best men under the sun, Miss; only he has his weaknesses."

"Yes, it was weak," said Mrs Lane, with a touch of bitterness in her voice—"and to such strangers."

"If you mean about the money, ma'am," said Mrs Jenkles, in the same uncompromising manner, "I don't; I meant something else."

Mrs Lane directed an imploring look at her daughter, and the girl hastily took up her work, as did her mother, and stitched away.

"That may have been weak, and it may not," said Mrs Jenkles, who took in everything. "It all depends."

"It was a most generous act," said Mrs Lane, in a low, pained voice, "and will bear its fruit. But you will sit down?"

Mrs Jenkles seated herself on the very edge of her chair, bolt upright, while Mrs Lane drew out a well-worn purse, took from it half a sovereign, and laid it upon the table.

"I am ashamed to offer you so little of it back," said Mrs Lane, "but it was all we could get together in so short a time. You shall have the rest—as we can make it up."

"Thanky," said Mrs Jenkles, shortly; but without attempting to touch the coin.

There was a pause then, only broken by that weary sound of hard stitching, which tells of sore fingers and aching eyes.

"How much more have you got in that purse?" said Mrs Jenkles, shortly.

A faint flush of resentment appeared in the mothers face, and the daughter darted an angry look at the speaker. But it died out in an instant, as with a sad, weary action, Mrs Lane reopened the purse, and shook out two more coins beside the half-sovereign upon the table.

"Two shillings," she said, faintly; "it is all."

Mrs Jenkles sat very still, and the stitching went on like the ticking of two clocks, measuring out the short span of the workers' lives.

Mrs Jenkles's eyes were busy, and she saw, as they went over the room, how shabbily it was furnished, how thinly mother and daughter were clothed, how pale and weary was their aspect, while the girl's eyes were unnaturally bright.

At last Mrs Jenkles's eyes caught sight of a little white corner in one of the compartments of the open purse, and she gave a hysterical gulp.

There was a heap of thick cloth work lying on the table between the two women—the one coarse, unrefined, but comfortably clothed and fed, the other refined and worn to skin and bone—and this heap covered Mrs Jenkles's actions as she rose, walked to the table, and then, without a word, went out of the room.

"Has she gone?" whispered Netta, as Mrs Jenkles's retreating footsteps were heard.

"Yes," said Mrs Lane, with a weary sigh, and she worked on.

"It was very, very cruel," said the girl, with her voice shaking, and, in spite of her efforts, a heavy sob would make its way from her breast, and the tears stole down her cheeks. "Mother, darling, what shall we do?"

"Hope and wait," was the response, in a low, pained voice. "It was only their due. The husband was very kind."

"But the two shillings—for bread," sobbed the girl. "Mamma, does papa know—can he know of this?"

Mrs Lane leaned back in her chair, and held one hand over her eyes for a few moments; then, with a gesture to her child to be silent, she once more bent over her work.

Netta brushed the tears from her eyes, drew in her breath as if in pain, and worked on in silence for a quarter of an hour, when steps were once more heard upon the stairs.

The eyes of mother and daughter met, those of the latter in dread; but it was not the heavy step of Barney, nor the snatchy shuffle of his wife, but a quick, decided, solid footstep, and the moment afterwards Mrs Jenkles re-entered the room, and closed the door.

Mrs Lane rose in surprise, and took a step to meet her. Directly after, completely broken down, she was sobbing on the coarse, uneducated woman's neck; for she had seen at a glance that the money still lay upon the table by the empty purse—empty now, for the duplicate it had contained was gone—as, with a loving, sisterly movement, the cabman's wife slipped back upon her finger the ring she had been to redeem, and then, kissing her upon the forehead, whispered—

"My poor dear, what you must have suffered! Hush, hush! There, there!" said Mrs Jenkles, after a pause, with tears streaming down her own simple, honest face; and she patted and tried to soothe her forsaken sister as she would a child.

"There, there, there; don't you cry too, my pretty," she said, as Netta flew to her, and kissed her on the cheek. "Come, come, come, we must hold up. There, that's better; now sit down."

"And I said God had forsaken us in our distress," sobbed Mrs Lane. "I little thought what forms his angels took."

"There, there, there," said Mrs Jenkles, wiping her eyes with a rapid motion; "if you talk like that you'll drive me away. I told Sam I'd come up to see, for I didn't know; and he is so easily led away, and I thought all sorts of things. But, bless and save us, he never told me half enough. There, there, wipe your eyes."

As she spoke, with a delicacy for which one might not have given her credit, she turned her back, leaving mother and daughter sobbing in each other's arms, while she slipped the money back in the purse, and placed it on the chimney-piece. Her next act was to take off her bonnet and shawl, hang them behind the door, and take up Netta's work and chair, beginning to stitch away with a vigour that astonished the girl, as she tore herself away from her mother, and came to resume her toil.

"No, no, my dear; I'll give you a rest while you see about a bit of dinner; for," she said, with a cheery smile, "you'll let me have a bit with you to-day, now, won't you? I'll try and earn it."

The girl's tears were ready to flow again, but Mrs Jenkles's finger was shaken menacingly at her, and she turned to her mother, who rose, dried her eyes, and came and kissed the broad, smooth forehead.

"God will bless you for this," she said, softly; and then the work went on once more, with such sunshine in the room as had not seemed to enter it for weeks.

"Ah!" said Mrs Jenkles, as she bit off a fresh length of thread with her firm, white teeth. "Rents are dear up this part, I suppose."

"I pay seven and sixpence a week for this and the back room," said Mrs Lane.

"They'd be dear at half with such furniture," said Mrs Jenkles.

There was another spell of sewing, when Mrs Lane said that she would see about the dinner; and then, as if reading Mrs Jenkles's thoughts—

"I don't like letting Netta go out alone."

"And quite right, too, with her face," said Mrs Jenkles. "But she looks tired. You ought to walk out every day for an hour or two."

The girl gave her a pitiful look.

So the day wore on, Mrs Jenkles taking dinner and tea with them, and seeing that each of them partook of a hearty meal, leaving about half-past nine with a bundle.

It was sharp work to get home before Sam should arrive from the yard; but Mrs Jenkles managed it, had the table laid, the supper out, and the beer fetched, before he came in, took off his shiny hat and old coat, and seating himself began to fill his pipe.

"Well, old lady," he said, "what time did yer get back?"

"About a quarter of an hour ago," said Mrs Jenkles, as she took out some of the work upon which she had been engaged.

Sam whistled and stared.

"What's them?" he said, pointing with his pipe at the work.

"Only some slop-work I want to finish."

Mrs Jenkles seemed so busy, that she could not look up and meet her husband's eye. In fact, to use her own expression, she was all of a twitter, and did not know what Sam would say; for though she nominally ruled him, Sam had a will of his own.

"Well, and did you find out about 'em?"

"Yes, Sam," said Mrs Jenkles, without raising her eyes.

"Bad lot, aint they?" he said, puffing away at his pipe.

Mrs Jenkles shook her head.

"What, aint I been took in, then?" said Sam. "Aint they deep, designing people, as got hold of yer poor innocent husband, and swindled him out of thirty bob?"

"Oh, Sam, Sam!" exclaimed Mrs Jenkles, with her lip quivering, "I never see anything so pitiful in my life."

"Poof!" exclaimed Sam, bursting out into a guffaw, as he turned in his seat, hugged the back of the chair, and shook with laughter. "That's my poor, silly, soft old wife, as can't be trusted out. Did they offer to pay you any of the money back?"

Mrs Jenkles nodded.

"How much?"

"Half a sovereign, Sam."

"Well, that's something; and jolly honest, too!"

"But I didn't take it, Sam," said Mrs Jenkles, dropping her work, to go and rest her hands upon his shoulder.

"You didn't take it?"

"No, Sam, dear."

"Then you've been and let 'em have more."

"Yes, Sam, dear."

"There's a wife for you," he said — "there's a helpmate; and I aint made my guv'nor's money to-day by four bob."

"I couldn't help it, Sam—I couldn't, indeed," she said; bursting into tears; "it was so pitiful—she's a real lady, I'm sure, and her daughter, straining over that heart-breaking work; oh! it was more than I could bear."

"I wasn't such a werry great fool, Sally," he said.

"Oh no, Sam. Oh no. But I haven't told you all yet."

"You haven't?"

"No, dear."

"Well, put me out of my misery at once," said Sam, "that's all."

"Don't be angry with me, Sam, it'll come back to us some way, I hope; and if it don't, we shall only have done what thousands more would have done if they had only known."

"Let's have it," said Sam, gruffly.

"They're paying seven and six, Sam, for those wretched rooms, and the woman's a horrid creature."

"Yes, she is that," said Sam, nodding.

"And the poor young lady's frightened to death of the man, who insulted her once. He is a dreadful-looking fellow."

"Wuss, ever so much," said Sam, nodding at his pipe-bowl.

"And I—I—"

"Told 'em about our being about to be empty; that's about what you did," said Sam.

"Yes, Sam."

"Well, you're a nice one. Of course you've put the rent up?"

"No, I haven't, Sam," said Mrs Jenkles. "I've—"

"Asked only the same. Why, our rooms is a palace to theirs—not as I ever see a palace to know."

"They're smaller, Sam," said Mrs Jenkles.

"Precious little," said Sam. "Well, you've offered 'em at six bob, eh? Well, you are a nice one; and doing their work, too!"

"No, Sam, dear, I told them they could have them for five shillings a week."

"Five!" shouted Sam.

"Yes, dear," said Mrs Jenkles, pitifully; "don't be cross, dear. They said they wouldn't take them."

"That's a comfort," said Sam.

"But," exclaimed Mrs Jenkles, hurriedly, "I persuaded them to come. I told them that they would be saving half a crown a week, and that in twelve weeks they would have paid off the thirty shillings you lent them, and they're coming."

"And how many more weeks will it take to pay off the money you lent them?" said Sam, facing round sharply.

"Only three, dear; it was only seven and sixpence, Sam."

"You'll ruin me," said Sam. "You know as we're as poor as can be," he went on, with his eyes averted from her.

"No, Sam, we're not; for we've a comfortable home, and we always save a little."

"And you go and make jellies and give away."

"How did you know that?" said Mrs Jenkles, sharply.

"Ah! you women can't go on long in your wicked ways without being found out," said Sam. "I heerd on it."

"The poor child was dying, same as our poor little Dick was, Sam, and—and—"

Sam turned his head farther away.

"And now you invite poor people to come, as 'll never be able to pay their bit o' rent; an' the end on it all 'll be the workus."

"Oh, Sam; pray, pray, don't! Do I deserve all this?" and the poor woman burst out sobbing.

"God bless you! no, old lady," cried Sam, pulling her on to his knee, and giving her a sounding kiss, as she laid her head upon his shoulder. "It 'll all come right in the long run; see if it don't. Life aint worth having if you can't do, a bit o' good in it."

"Then you really aint cross with me, Sam?"

"Not a bit," said Sam. "Look at me. Sally, my old gal, it's my belief as them angels as takes the toll at the gate up above in the shiny way 'll let you go through free."

"Sam!" cried Mrs Jenkles, trying to lay her hand on his mouth.

"And look here, old lady," he continued, stroking her face; "when that does come off, which I hope it won't be for scores o' years to come, you keep werry, werry tight hold o' my hand, and then, perhaps, I shall stand a chance of getting into heaven too."

Love Minor

Little Polly wiped her eyes after her happy thoughts; for the shower had passed, and the gleam of sunshine augmented till her face grew dimpled, and she went on stitching busily. It was very evident that she had some consolation—some pleasant unguent for the irritation caused by Aunt Lloyd; for at the end of half an hour she was singing away at some old Welsh ditty, in a sweet, bird-like voice, filling up, when she forgot the words, with a melodious little hum, which was only checked on the appearance of her tyrant, that lady mating occasional incursions. Sometimes Aunt Lloyd required table linen; then she came to unlock the press where the dessert was laid out, and hand it to the footman, counting the fruit on the dishes as she did so.

"Now, Robert, what are you looking at there?" she said, sharply, as she caught the man's eyes straying in the direction of Polly. "Mind your work, if you please."

Polly did not get snubbed, for she had been bending diligently over her stitching, which, as soon as the tray of dessert had gone, came in for a close inspection; but, as it was very neatly done, there was no complaint.

"Hold out your hands, child," said Mrs Lloyd, suddenly; and she examined the finger roughened by the hard material and contact with the needle. "Ah, that stuffs too stiff; it shall be washed first. Mend those."

The linen was doubled up, put away, and some soft material placed in the girl's hands, over which she had been diligently at work one hour, when Mrs Lloyd returned for coffee from her stores, with which she again departed, muttering about "Such a set to bring down!" and Polly's musical little voice began once more.

Let's see: the dictionary says that an enchanter is one who calls down by chanting or singing—one who practises sorcery by song. Polly, then, must have been an enchantress, for her little ditty about the love of some deserted maid had the effect of bringing cousin Humphrey Lloyd through the shrubbery to the open window of the housekeeper's room; and just in the midst of one of the sweetest of the little trills there was a rustle amongst the laurels, and a deep voice whispered "Polly!"

"Oh, my!" ejaculated Polly, dropping her work, and starting farther from the window. "What will aunt say?"

Now, her instructions had been stringent; and knowing that it would be like high treason to speak to Humphrey, she determined that she would not, just as an industrious young needle, which had been warned not to get rusty by associating with common bits of steel, might have gone on busily through its work like the one Polly held in her hand.

But supposing that, instead of a common piece of steel, a magnet that had been rubbed with the loadstone of love should come in its way, what could the poor needle do?

Even as did little Polly—vow that aunt would be so cross; and then feel herself drawn, drawn closer and closer to the iron-barred window, till her little hands were caught in two strong, muscular fists, which pressed them so hard that they almost hurt.

"Oh! you mustn't, mustn't come!" sobbed Polly. "If aunt found it out she would almost kill me!"

"No, no, little one," said Humphrey; "why should she?"

"You—you don't know aunt," whispered Polly. "She's ordered me not to speak to you."

"Not to speak to me!"

"Yes; nor to any one else. She would be so angry if she knew. You don't want to get me scolded."

"No, no," he whispered—"not for worlds."

"Pray, pray, go then; and you must not speak to me any more."

"But Polly, dear Polly," whispered Humphrey, "tell me one thing, and then I'll go and wait years and years, if you like, only tell me that."

Humphrey stopped short, for a singular phenomenon occurred. Polly's fingers seemed to suddenly change from within his hands to his wrists, and to become bony and firm, a sharp voice at the same moment exclaiming—

"Who's this?"

Humphrey Lloyd was a man, every inch of him, and he spoke out boldly—

"Well, if you must know, it's me—Humphrey."

"Go round to the side door, and come to my room," said Mrs Lloyd, in a low, angry voice.

Humphrey was heard to go rustling through the laurels, as Mrs Lloyd exclaimed —

"Go up to your room, Miss, this instant; and don't you stir till I call you down."

Shivering with fear and shame, Polly made her escape to run up to her room, throw herself on the bed, and cry as if her heart would break, just missing Humphrey, who came round without loss of time.

"Now," said Mrs Lloyd, as soon as the door was closed, "what have you to say to this?"

"Only that it was my fault," said Humphrey—"all my fault; so don't blame the poor little girl. It was all my doing."

"Now, look here, Humphrey Lloyd," exclaimed the housekeeper, speaking in a low, angry voice, "you like your place here?"

"Yes, if you and he could treat me a little better."

"Never mind about that," said Mrs Lloyd.

"It's no use to mind," said Humphrey, bitterly. "If I had been a dog instead of your own flesh and blood, you couldn't have treated me worse."

"Treated you badly!" exclaimed Mrs Lloyd; "haven't you been well fed, educated, and placed in a good situation?"

"Yes—all that," said Humphrey. "And for reward you fly in my face. Now, look here, Humphrey. If you so much as look at that girl again, let alone speak to her, off you go. You shall not stay on the premises another day.

"Well," said Humphrey, "that's pleasant; but all the same I don't see what power you have in the matter, so long as I satisfy the young master."

"Then just content yourself with satisfying your young master, sir, and mind, that girl's not for you, so let's have no more of it. Now go."

"But look here," said Humphrey. "I told you to go," said Mrs Lloyd, pointing. "Your place is at the keeper's lodge. Go and stay there, and don't go thinking you can influence Master Dick—Mr Trevor—to keep you, because even if you could, the girl should go away, and you should see her no more. Now go."

"Poor little lassie," muttered Humphrey, as, in obedience to Mrs Lloyd's pointing finger, he slowly left the room, walked heavily along the passage, and out into the dark evening, to pass round the house, and cross the lawn, where he could see through the open windows into the dining-room.

"Nice for me," he muttered. "Forbidden to go near her—girl in my own station. What does the old woman mean?"

He stood gazing in at the merry, laughing party of young, well-dressed men.

"Nice to be you," he thought; "plenty of money to spend; people to do all you tell them to; nobody to thwart you. But I wonder what the old lady means."

He laughed to himself directly after, in a low, bitter fashion.

"No, not so bad as that," he said, half aloud. "She's ambitious, and scheming, but that would be going too far."

Kinks in the Line

Matters were not so pleasant, though, with the four occupants of the dining-room as Humphrey Lloyd believed. Vanleigh had his skeleton in the cupboard and was very impecunious; Sir Felix had wealth, but he was constantly feeling that his friend Vanleigh was an incubus whom he would give the world to shake off, but wanted the moral courage; Pratt suffered from poverty, and now told himself that he must be bored by his friend's affairs; lastly, Trevor had come down to his old home thinking it would be a bower of roses, and it was as full of thorns, as it could possibly be.

The dinner had been a failure. At every turn the influence of Mrs Lloyd was perceptible, and proof given that so far she had been sole mistress of the house.

"By the way, Vanleigh, try that claret," said Trevor, in the course of the dinner. "Lloyd, the claret to Captain Vanleigh."

The Captain tasted it, and set down his glass.

Pratt took a glass, and made a point of drinking it.

Trevor saw there was something wrong.

"Bring me that claret," he said.

The butler poured him out a glass of very thin, poor wine.

Lloyd was then proceeding to fill Sir Felix's glass, but he declined.

"I thought we had some good old claret," said Trevor, fuming.

"Yes, sir," said the butler.

"Fetch a bottle directly," exclaimed Trevor. "Really, gentlemen, I am very sorry," he continued, as the butler went out of the room. "It's a mistake. Here, Robert, what champagne's that?"

The footman brought a bottle from the ice-pail.

"Why, confound it all!" cried Trevor, "I said the dry Clicquot was to be brought—such fools!"

"Mr Lloyd did get out the Clicker, sir; but Mrs Lloyd said the second best would do, sir," replied the footman, glad of an opportunity to change the responsibility.

"Then all the wine is of the ordinary kind?" said Trevor.

"Yes, sir," said the footman.

"Look here, Lloyd," said Trevor, as the butler came into the room, "you made a mistake about that claret. See that the other wine is right; and if not, change it."

The butler looked aghast and hurried out, to return in a few minutes with a basket of bottles, which he changed for those already in the room.

Trevor said no more, but he was evidently making up his mind to suppress the mutiny with a high hand on the morrow; for, as the dinner went on, he became aware that in many little things his orders had been departed from. There was a paucity of plate, when an abundance lay in the chests; the dinner was good, by stretching a point, but not such as would please men accustomed to the *chefs* of Pall Mall; and when at last the coffee was brought in it was of the most economical quality.

"There," said Trevor, "I'll set all right to-morrow, I'm very sorry, Vanleigh; but things are all sixes and sevens here. Pratt, pass the claret. Landells, try that port."

"Never drink port, dear boy," said the Baronet.

"Then let's go into the billiard-room; or what do you say, Van—would you prefer my room and a rubber?"

"Don't much care for billiards to-night," said Vanleigh. "By the way, though," he said, "will your estimable housekeeper permit smoking in the dining-room."

"Oh, come, Van," said Sir Felix, "don't be hard on your host."

"Shall I ring for cigars, Dick?" said Pratt, reaching out his hand.

"Do, please," was the reply. "Smoke where you like, gentlemen, and make yourselves at home. I don't want to be hard on the old people. You see, it's a particular case. I've been away for years. I left a boy, and they have had it all their own way. Oh, Lloyd, bring in the cigar boxes, and brandy and soda."

"Here, sir?" said the butler, hesitating.

"Here? Yes, here directly," said Trevor; and he looked annoyed as he caught a glance passing from Vanleigh to Sir Felix.

"It's all right, Dick," said Pratt. "It's a nice estate, but weedy. Pull 'em up, one at a time."

"By the way, Van," said Sir Felix, "didn't tell Trevor of our 'venture."

"No," said Vanleigh, kicking at his friend beneath the table; "been so taken up with other things. Brought home some neighbours of yours—without leave—in the waggonette."

"Neighbours—without leave?" said Trevor, passing the claret. "We are all ears."

"Some of us," muttered Pratt, glancing at Sir Felix, and then looking perfectly innocent.

"Neighbours of yours—a Sir Hampton Court."

"No, no—Weir or Here, or name of that sort," said Sir Felix.

"Carriage broke down—two daughters—deuced fine girls, too."

"Vewy," said Sir Felix, arranging his gummy moustache.

"Good heavens!" exclaimed Trevor. "No one hurt?"

"Calm yourself, my friend," said Vanleigh, proceeding in a most unruffled way. "The ladies were uninjured, and we—"

"Brought back—home," said Sir Felix, feebly,

"I'm heartily glad of it—I am, indeed," said Trevor, earnestly. "Frank, old fellow, that will be an excuse for a call; and we can patch up the encounter. We were both horribly hot."

"Fever heat?" said Pratt.

"Yes, and I daresay the old fellow's as sorry now as I am. I'll—Well, Lloyd," he continued, as the butler came in, looking rather alarmed, and rubbing his hands softly, "where are the cigars?"

"Mustn't smoke!" said Vanleigh, in a whisper to Sir Felix, but heard by Pratt.

"If you please, sir, Mrs Lloyd thought you would like a fire in the smoking-room, sir, and I've taken the cigars in there."

"Bring—"

Trevor caught Pratt's eye, and he checked himself.

"Lloyd," he said, very quietly. "I don't think you understand me yet. Go and fetch those cigar boxes."

The butler directed a pitiful, appealing look at the speaker, and then went out, leaving Trevor tapping the mahogany table excitedly, till Pratt tried to throw himself into the breach, with a remark about Sir Hampton; but no one answered, for Trevor was hard at work keeping down his annoyance, Vanleigh was picking his white teeth with a gold point, and Sir Felix was intent upon the tints in the glass he held up before his eye.

In another minute the butler returned with the cigars, and then departed to fulfil the other part of his orders.

"Now, Vanleigh, since we are favoured," said Trevor, laughing, "try one of these. I know they are genuine, for I got them myself at the Havanna."

"Really," said Vanleigh, with a show of consideration, "I'll give up my smoke, and I'm sure Flick will."

"Oh, yes, dear boy; don't mind me."

"For goodness' sake, gentlemen, don't make bad worse," said Trevor; "take your cigars and light up. Hallo, Frank! Don't go out, man."

"Not going," said Pratt, who had already lit a tremendous cigar, and was puffing away as he took a chair to the window.

"Then, why have you gone there?"

"To smoke the curtains for the benefit of Mrs Lloyd," was the reply; and he proceeded to put his intention in force.

After an hour they adjourned to Trevor's room, where they had refreshments brought in, and were soon deep in a rubber of whist, Pratt being partner with Vanleigh, and playing his very worst; but all the same, luck and his partner's skill carried them through, so that they won rather heavily. Time glided away, and the cigars were so good that for the first time that evening Trevor felt comfortable.

"Well," he thought, "we shall have no more of Mrs Lloyd to-night, and to-morrow I'll set things right. Me to lead? Good that—there's a trump."

At that moment the door opened, and Mrs Lloyd appeared, bearing a waiter with four flat candlesticks, and looking the very image of austerity.

"The house is all locked up now, sir," she said, in a cold, hard voice. "It is half-past ten."

"Thank you, Mrs Lloyd," said Trevor, and his face twitched with annoyance.

"Is half-past ten—bedtime—Mrs Lloyd?" said Pratt, laying down his cards.

"Yes, sir, it is," said Mrs Lloyd, severely.

"And you've brought us our candles," said Frank, taking the waiter. "Thank you, Mrs Lloyd; don't you sit up. Good night."

Pratt's good-humoured, smiling face puzzled the housekeeper. She allowed herself to be backed out, and the door closed behind her.

Two Scenes

Matters had not been very pleasant in the neighbourhood of Mrs Lloyd that night Polly had escaped by being a prisoner; but the butler had been reduced, between fear of his wife and a burst of passion from his master, into a state of semi-idiocy; while the rest of the servants, after one or two encounters, had had a meeting, and declared—being, for the most part, newly engaged in consequence of the young heir's return—that if that woman was to do as she liked in the house, they'd serve their month and then go.

But it was on retiring for the night that the butler came in for the full torrent of his wife's anger.

"It sha'n't go on!" she exclaimed, fiercely, as she banged a chair down in the centre of the room, and seated herself. "Here do I stop till every light's out. That boy whom we worshipped almost, who's been our every thought, to come home at last like a prodigal son—backwards, and begin to waste his patrimony in this way."

"'Sh! 'sh!" said the butler.

"'Sh yourself!" exclaimed Mrs Lloyd, angrily.

"But, my dear, he's master here," the butler ventured to say.

"Is he indeed!" exclaimed Mrs Lloyd. "I'll see about that."

"Oh, for goodness' sake—for Heaven's sake—pray don't do anything rash, Martha," said the butler, imploringly. "Think—think of the consequences."

"Consequences—you miserable coward, you; I haven't patience with you."

"But we are old now, Martha; and what could we do if anything happened to us here? Pray, pray think. After thirty years in this place; and we should never get another. Pray, pray don't speak."

"Hold your tongue! Do you think, after bringing him up and rearing him as we did when he was delicate, and nursing him through measles and scarlatina, and making a man of him as we have, taking care of the pence, and saving and scratching together, that I'm going to be trampled under foot by him?"

"But, Martha—"

"Hold your tongue, I say. Bringing home here his evil companions, for whom nothing's good enough; and they must have the best wines, and turn my dining-room into a tap-room with their nasty smoke. I won't have it, I tell you—I won't have it."

"But, Martha, dear, you are so rash; come to bed now, and sleep on it all."

"Not till every light is out in this house will I stir. Sitting smoking, and diceing, and gambling there at this time of night."

"Were they, my dear?" said the butler, mildly.

"Yes, with gold by their sides, playing for sovereigns; and that black-looking captain had actually got a five-pound note on the table. We shall all come to ruin."

"Yes, that we shall, if you forget your place," said the butler, pitifully, as he gave his pillow a punch.

"Forget my place, indeed!" retorted his wife; "have I been plotting and planning all these years for nothing? Have I brought matters to this pitch to be treated in this way, to be turned upon by an ungrateful boy, with his rough, sea-going ways? This isn't the quarter-deck of a ship—do you hear what I say?—this isn't the quarter-deck of a ship."

"No, my dear, of course it isn't," said the butler, mildly—"it's our bedroom," he added to himself.

"But I'll bring him to himself in the morning, see if I don't," she said, folding her arms, and speaking fiercely. "I'll soon let him know who I am—an overbearing, obstinate, mad—are you asleep, Lloyd?"

"No, my dear, I'm listening."

"Now, look here; I have my plans about Polly."

"Yes, dear."

"And, mind this, if that fellow Humphrey attempts to approach her again—"

"Poor Humphrey!" sighed the butler.

"Ah!" exclaimed his wife, "what was I about to marry such a milksop? Did you know that he was making up to her?"

"I thought he cared for the girl, my dear."

"You fool! you idiot, Lloyd! and not to tell me. Have you no brains at all?"

"I'm afraid not much, my dear," said the butler, pitifully: "what little I had has been pretty well muddled with trouble, and upset, and dread, and one thing and another."

"Lloyd!" exclaimed the housekeeper, "if ever I hear you speak again like that—"

She did not finish her sentence, but her eyes flashed as she looked full in his, holding the candle over him the while.

"Now, look here," she said, more temperately. "I shall have a talk with my gentleman in the morning."

"What, poor Humphrey?"

"Poor Humphrey, no. But mind this—he's not to come near Polly."

"But you don't think—"

"Never mind what I think, you mind what I say, and leave me to bring things round. If she don't know what's good for her, I do; and I shall have my way."

The butler sighed.

"Now, look here, I shall have some words of a sort with my fine gentleman in the morning."

"No, no, Martha, don't—pray don't; let things be now; we can't alter them."

"Can't we?" said Mrs Lloyd, viciously—"I'll see about that."

"But, Martha, dear, I'm fifteen years older than you, and if anything happened it would break my heart—there!" he exclaimed, vehemently. "I'd sooner go down to Trevass Rocks, and jump off into the sea, and end it all, than that anything should happen to us now—after all these years."

Mrs Lloyd did not speak for a few minutes. Then, hearing a voice downstairs, she opened the door gently, and listened, to make out that it was only laughter from the smoking-room, and she closed the door once more.

"If ever there was a coward, Lloyd, you are one," she said, with a bitter sneer.

"Yes," said the butler. "I suppose I am, for I can't bear the idea of anything happening now. Then people say we're unnatural to poor Humphrey."

"Poor Humphrey again!" exclaimed Mrs Lloyd, angrily; "let people talk about what they understand. I should like for any one to say anything to me."

"But Martha," said Lloyd, after a pause. "Well?"

"You'll not be rash in the morning—don't peril our position here out of an angry feeling."

"You go to sleep," was the uncompromising response.

And sighing wearily, the butler did go to sleep, his wife sitting listening hour after hour till nearly two, when there was the sound of a door opening, a burst of voices, steps in the hall, "Good nights!" loudly uttered, Pratt going upstairs to his room, whistling number one of the Lancers-quadrilles with all his might. Then came the closing of bedroom doors and silence.

Mrs Lloyd sat for ten minutes more, then, taking her candle, she walked softly downstairs; went round dining- and drawing-rooms and study, examining locks, bolts, and shutters, and then went to the butler's pantry, gave a drag at the handle of the iron plate-closet, to satisfy herself that all was right there, and lastly made for the smoking-room.

"Like a public-house," she muttered, as she crossed the hall, turned the handle with a snatch, and threw open the door, to find herself face to face with Trevor, who was sitting at a table writing a letter.

"Mrs Lloyd!"

"Not gone to bed!"

The couple looked angrily at each other for a few moments, and then Trevor said, sternly—

"Why are you downstairs at this time of the night, Mrs Lloyd?"

"The morning you mean, sir," said the housekeeper. "What am I down for?" she continued, angrily; "to see that the house is safe—that there's no fire left about—that doors are fastened, so that the house I've watched over all these years isn't destroyed by carelessness, and all going to rack and ruin."

Trevor jumped up with an angry exclamation on his lips; but he checked it, and then spoke, quite calmly—

"Mrs Lloyd, I should be perfectly justified in speaking to you perhaps in a way in which you have never been spoken to before."

"Pray do, then, Master—sir," jerked out Mrs Lloyd, looking white with anger.

"In half a dozen things during the past evening you have wilfully disobeyed my orders. Why was this?"

"To protect your interests and property," exclaimed the housekeeper.

"Giving me credit for not knowing my own mind, and making me look absurd in the eyes of my friends."

"I didn't mean to do anything of the kind, sir," said Mrs Lloyd, stoutly.

"I'll grant that; and that you did it through ignorance," said Trevor.

"I don't want to see the place I've taken care of for years go to ruin," said Mrs Lloyd.

"I'll grant that too," said Trevor, "and that you and your husband have been most faithful servants, and are ready at any time to give an account of your stewardship. I feel your zeal in my interests, but you must learn to see, Mrs Lloyd, that you can carry it too far. I daresay, too, that for all these years you and your husband have felt like mistress and master of the house, and that it seems hard to give up to the new rule, and to render the obedience that I shall exact; but, Mrs Lloyd, you are a woman of sound common sense, and you must see that your conduct to me has been anything but what it should be."

"I've never had a thought but for your benefit!" exclaimed Mrs Lloyd.

"I believe it, Mrs Lloyd—I know it; but tell me frankly that you feel you have erred, and no more shall be said."

Mrs Lloyd gave a gulp, and stood watching the fine, well-built man before her.

"It grieves me, I assure you, to have to speak as I do, Mrs Lloyd," continued Trevor; "but you must see that things are altered now."

"And that you forget all the past, Master Dick," cried Mrs Lloyd, with a wild sob, "and that those who have done everything for you may now be turned out of the house in their old age and go and beg their bread, while you make merry with your friends."

"Come—come—come, Mrs Lloyd," said Trevor, advancing to her, and laying his hand caressingly on her shoulder, "you don't believe that; you have too much respect for your old master's son to think he would grow up such an ingrate—so utterly void of common feeling. He has not forgotten who took the place of his mother—who nursed him—who tended him through many an illness, and was always more a friend than a servant. He has come back a man—I hope a generous one—accustomed to command, and be obeyed. He wishes you to keep your position of confidential trust, and the thought of making any change has never entered his mind. All he wishes is that you should make an effort to see the necessity for taking the place necessitated by the relative positions in which we now find ourselves; and he tells you, Mrs Lloyd, that you may rest assured while Penreife stands there is always a home for you and for your husband."

As he touched her a shiver ran through the woman's frame; the inimical aspect faded out, and she looked admiringly in his face, her own working the while, as his grave words were uttered, till, sobbing violently, she threw her arms round his neck, kissed him passionately again and again, and then sank upon the floor to cover her face with her hands.

"There—there, nurse," he said, taking her hand and raising her. "Let this show you I've not forgotten old times. This is to be the seal of a compact for the future,"—he kissed her gravely on the forehead. "Now, nurse, you will believe in your master for the future, and you see your way?"

"Yes, sir," she said, looking appealingly in his face.

"We thoroughly understand each other?"

"Yes, sir; and I'll try never to thwart you again."

"You'll let me be master in my own house?" he said, his handsome face lighting up with a smile.

"Yes, indeed, I will, sir," sobbed the woman; "and—and—you're not angry with me—for—for—"

"For what—about the wine?"

"No, sir, for the liberty I took just now."

"Oh no," he said; "it was a minute's relapse to old times. And now," he continued, taking her hand, to lead her to the door, "it is very late, and I must finish my letter. Good night, nurse."

"Good night, sir—and—God bless you!" she exclaimed, passionately.

And the door closed between them—another woman seeming to be the one who went upstairs.

"Sing Heigh—Sing Ho!"

Trevor's letter was sent off by one of the grooms by eight o'clock; for, accustomed to late watches and short nights at sea, the master of Penreife was down betimes, eagerly inspecting his stables and horses, and ending by making inquiries for Humphrey Lloyd, to find that he was away somewhere or another to look after the game.

Donning a wideawake, and looking about as unlike a naval officer as could be, he summoned the butler, to name half-past nine as the breakfast hour, and then, with little Polly watching him from one of the windows, he strode off across the lawn.

Polly sighed as she looked after him, and then she started, for a couple of hands were laid upon her shoulder, and turning hastily, it was to confront Mrs Lloyd, whose harsh countenance wore quite a smile as she gazed fixedly in the girl's blushing face, and then kissed her on the forehead.

"He's a fine, handsome-looking man, isn't he, child?" said the housekeeper. "Don't you think so?"

"Yes, aunt," said the girl, naïvely; "I was thinking so as I saw him go across the lawn."

Which was the simple truth, though, all the same, Miss Polly had been comparing him, somewhat to his disadvantage, with Humphrey.

"Good girl," said Mrs Lloyd. "You must get yourself a silk dress, child—a nice light one."

"Thank you, aunt," said the girl, flushing with pleasure.

"Yes, he's a fine young fellow, and as good and noble as he is high."

"I'm sure he must be, aunt," said the girl. "He spoke so nicely to me."

"When?—where?" said Mrs Lloyd, eagerly.

"Yesterday, aunt, when I took in that silver cup."

"Ah?" said Mrs Lloyd. "Yes, she'll be a lucky girl who wins him."

"Yes, that she will, aunt," said the girl, enthusiastically. "He's very rich, isn't he?"

"Very, my dear; and his wife will be the finest lady in the county, with dresses, and carriages, and parties, and a town-house, I daresay."

"I hope he'll marry some one who loves him very much," said the girl, simply.

"Of course he will, child. Why, any girl could love him. She ought to jump at the chance of having such a man. And now I must go, child. I was rather cross to you last night. I was worried with the preparations, and it did not look well for me to come and see that fellow with his hands through the window; but that won't happen again. A little flirting's all very well for once in a girl's life, but there must be no more of it, and I know I shan't have to speak any more."

She hurried out of the room before the girl could reply, leaving her with her little forehead wrinkled by the puzzling, troubled thoughts which buzzed through her brain.

"Aunt must mean something," she said to herself. "I wonder what she really does mean. She can't really—oh, nonsense, what a little goose I am!"

Polly's pretty little face puckered with a smile, and she took up her work, waiting to be called for breakfast, and sat wondering the while what Humphrey was doing.

Humphrey was away down by the disputed piece of land, and Trevor soon forgot all about him; for, crossing a field and leaping a stile, he stood in one of the winding lanes of the neighbourhood; then crossing it, and leaping another stile, he began to make his way along the side of a steep valley, when he stopped short; for, from amongst the trees in front, rang out, clear and musical—

"There came a lady along the strand,
Her fair hair bound with a golden band,
Sing heigh!"

And a second voice—

"Sing ho!"

Then the two, sweetly blended together, repeated the refrain, "Oh, Tiny!" cried the voice, "here's one pretty enough to make even Aunt Matty look pleasant. Oh, my gracious!" she exclaimed, dropping her little trowel, for Trevor had come into sight.

"Don't be alarmed, pray!" he said, laughing. "But really I did not know we had such sweet song-birds in the woods."

"It was very rude to listen, Mr Trevor; and it isn't nice to pay compliments to strangers," said Fin, nodding her saucy head.

"Then," said Trevor, taking the hand slightly withheld, "I shall be rude again only in one thing—listening; for we must be strangers no more, seeing that we are such near neighbours. Miss Rea," he said, taking Tiny's hand in turn, and looking earnestly in her timid eyes, "you were not hurt yesterday?"

"Oh no, not in the least," was the reply.

"We are indebted to your friends, too, for taking compassion upon us in our misfortune."

"Don't name that," he said, hastily. "I am glad the carriage came up in time. By the way, Miss Rea, I am glad we have met, I want to clear up a little unpleasantly that occurred yesterday."

"Oh, of course," said Fin. "Why, we ought to have cut you this morning."

"No, no," said Trevor, laughing, "that would be too cruel I am really very, very sorry about it all; and I have sent a letter over to Sir Hampton this morning, apologising for my hasty words."

"Oh, have you?" said Fin, clapping her hands, and making a bound off the moss; "how nice! I mean," she added, demurely, "how correct."

Fin whispered her sister, who was growing flushed and troubled by the eager and impressive way in which Trevor spoke to her.

"It would be such a pity," he said, walking on by her side, "if any little trifle like that in dispute should be allowed to disturb the peace, and break what would, I am sure, be a charming intimacy!"

"Why, the great, handsome wretch is making love to her," said Fin to herself. "Oh, what a shame! I hate him already."

"I know—I feel sure papa will only be too glad—too ready to make amends," said Tiny, who was growing more confused; for every time she spoke and ventured to glance at her companion, it was to meet his eyes gazing into hers with a depth of tenderness that pleased while it troubled her, and made her little heart behave in the most absurdly fluttering fashion. He looked so frank and handsome—so different in his brown tweeds and carelessly put-on hat to the carefully dressed dandies, their companions of the day before.

"I have told Sir Hampton that I mean to call this afternoon to ask him to shake hands with me. Do you think I may?" he said, with another look.

"I don't know—I think so—oh yes! pray call," said Tiny, confused, and blushing more than ever.

"Thank you, I will," he said, earnestly, "and you will be at home?"

"I forbid thee—no, thou must not come," said Fin, in a mock-serious tone, "And why not?" said Trevor, turning upon her.

"Because Aunt Matty hates the sight of young men, and papa will be ready to eat you."

"Why, bless your bright, merry little face," cried Trevor, enthusiastically, and catching Fin's hands in his. "Do you know what I feel as if I could do?"

"No, of course not," cried Fin, trying to frown, and looking bewitching.

"Why, catch you up and kiss you a dozen times for a merry little woodland fay," cried Trevor.

"Oh, gracious!" cried Fin, snatching away her hands, and retreating behind her sister.

"Don't be alarmed, little maiden," said Trevor, laughing; "I won't do so."

"I should think not," cried Fin.

"Sailors' manners," said Trevor, laughing, as he walked on by their side.

"Do you know how old I am, sir?" said Fin, austerely.

"I should say nearly sixteen," said Trevor, glancing at her sister.

"Seventeen and a half, sir," said Fin, with dignity on her forehead, and a laugh at each corner of her little mouth.

"Then it will be a sin if Nature ever lets you get a day older," said Trevor, laughing.

"Thank you, sir," said Fin, with a mock curtsey.

"Is she always as merry as this?" said Trevor to Tiny, who glanced at him again, to once more lower her eyes in confusion, he looked at her so earnestly.

"Yes; but you must not heed what she says," was the reply.

"I'm very wicked in my remarks, Mr Trevor," said Fin; "and now, sir, if you please, we are going this way to dig up ferns—so good morning."

"That is my direction," said Trevor, quietly; "and as I am only your neighbour, surely you need not treat me as a stranger."

"Tiny, it's all your fault," said Fin, maliciously; "so if Aunt Matty scolds, you may take the blame. I would make him carry the basket, though."

"Yes, pray let me," said Trevor, holding out his hand.

"Thank you, no," said Tiny, recovering herself, and speaking with a very sweet assumption of maidenly dignity. "If Mr Trevor will excuse us, I think we will return now to breakfast. I feel sure that papa will gladly receive you this afternoon."

"And you will be at home?" said Trevor, earnestly.

"I cannot say," said Tiny, quietly; "but I hope the little unpleasantly will be removed."

"You do hope that?" said downright Trevor.

"Yes—of course," said Tiny, ingenuously opening her soft eyes, and meeting his this time without a blush. "It would be so unpleasant—so unneighbourly for there to be dissension between us," and she held out her hand. "Good morning, Mr Trevor."

If he might only have kissed it! But it would have been enough to stamp him as a boor, and he contented himself with pressing it tenderly as he bent over it.

"Good morning, Mr Trevor," said Fin, holding out her hand in turn, and she gazed at him out of her laughing, mischievous eyes, till a dull red glow spread over his bronzed cheeks, and he squeezed her fingers so that she winced with pain.

"Good morning," he said. "Eh—what is it?"

"Oh, dear!" cried Fin, shutting her eyes, "here's that horrid, solemn-looking little man coming, just in the way we want to go."

"Then, let me introduce you," said Trevor, laughing, as Pratt came sauntering along, whistling and cutting off fern leaves with his stick, till he saw the group in front, when he became preternaturally solemn.

"Pratt, let me introduce you to my neighbours. Miss Rea—Miss Finetta Rea—my old friend, Frank Pratt."

"Pratt! What a disgusting name!" said Fin to herself, as, with a tender display of respect that his friend did not fail to notice, Trevor performed the little ceremony out there amid the gleaming sunbeams; and then they parted.

"Oh, Tiny, isn't he delicious?" cried Fin, as soon as they were out of hearing. "Isn't he grand?"

"Hush, Fin! How can you?" said her sister.

"How can I? So," said Fin, throwing her arms round her sister, and kissing her. "He's head over heels in love with you. What fun! And I hate him for it like poison, because I want him myself."

"Fin, dear, don't, pray. Suppose any one heard you."

"Don't care if they did. Ugh! I'm as jealous as an Eastern sultana I shall stab you some night with a bodkin. But, I say, isn't the solemn man fun?"

"I don't see it," said Tiny, glad of a diversion.

"I think he's a regular little cad."

"Slang again, Fin!"

"Yes, it's because I'm cross and want my breakfast," and she hurried her sister along.

"Ahem!" said Pratt, as soon as they were alone in the lane.

"Franky," cried Trevor, clutching his friend by the arm, "did you ever see a sweeter girl in your life?"

"What, than that little Miss who laughed at me?" said Frank.

"No, no; the other. I declare she's a perfect angel. I never saw so much sweetness in my life before. I—"

"Phew—phew—phew—phew—phew—phew—phew—phew!" whistled Pratt.

"Don't be a fool, Franky."

"But 'tis my nature to," said Pratt.

"Listen, man; I really do believe that there is something true about fellows falling in love at first sight, and that sort of thing; I do indeed."

"So do I," said Pratt.

"What do you mean?"

"Oh, come now, that's rich. To go and get hooked like that, before you've been at home a month! Well, that comes of going to sea, and being out of the way of civilised beings from year's end to year's end. I say, there's a romance beginning here—tyrannical heavy father, and the rest of it."

"Nonsense!" cried Trevor. "Come along, old boy; I'm as hungry as a hunter. By Jove, though, I came out on purpose to find Humphrey."

"And only met a goddess in the dell," said Pratt.

And the two young men returned to breakfast.

A Ceremonious Call

"How could I be such an ass as to ask them down?" said Trevor, aloud, as he stood at the dining-room window directly after lunch.

"And then such an ass as to say so out loud?" said a voice behind him; Frank Pratt having returned to the room, and his footsteps being inaudible on the thick Turkey carpet.

"Ah, Frank?" said Trevor, turning sharply, "you there!"

"Yes, sir," said Pratt, solemnly, "I am here—for the present. Will you have the goodness to order a carriage, or a cart, or something, to convey my portmanteau to Saint Kitt's, and I'll be off by the night train."

"Be off—night train—what the deuce do you mean?"

"Mean? Why, that you were just accusing yourself of being a fool for firing me down; and—"

"Don't, Franky—don't be a donkey I'm worried and bothered, old man. Help me: don't get in my way."

"I that moment proposed getting out of it," said Pratt, quietly.

"Tut, tut, tut!—you know I didn't mean you. Look here, Frank, I want to go out this afternoon—to make a call."

Pratt made a grimace, and an attempt to feel his friend's pulse.

"No, no; don't play the fool now," said Trevor. "You know I've only just got those two down, and it would be so rude to leave them."

"And you don't want to take them—with you?"

"No, certainly not," exclaimed Trevor, hastily.

"But they have been introduced," said Pratt.

"To whom—where?" said Trevor.

"Oh, my dear, transparent, young sea deity," said Pratt, laying his hand on Trevor's shoulder. "It is so easy to see through you. Of course you don't want to go straight off to Sir Hampton Court's this afternoon."

"Well, and if I do, what then?"

"Nothing, whatever," said Pratt. "She really is nice; I own it."

"Don't humbug, Frank. Of course I want to call there. I want to patch up that unpleasantly. I want to be on good terms with my neighbours."

"Hadn't you better have only a week's holiday down here, and then be off again to sea?"

"Will you help me, Franky, or won't you?"

"I will. Now, then, what is it? Get up something to amuse Van and Flick till you come back?"

"Yes, that's it. Do that for me, there's a dear old fellow."

"What should you think the hour or so worth to you?"

"Worth? I don't understand you."

"Would you stand a five-pound note for the freedom?"

"Half a dozen, you mercenary little limb of the law."

"Hold hard, there! or, in your nautical parlance, avast there! I don't want the money—only to lose. If I play billiards with Van he's sure to beat me, and he knows it; therefore, he won't play me without he thinks he can win some money. Give me a fiver to lose to him, and I'll warrant he won't leave the billiard-room till he has got every shilling."

"Here—take ten pounds," said Trevor, hastily; "and go on, there's a good fellow."

"No; five will do for him," said Frank. "And now I shall have to play my best, to make it last."

"Frank, old boy, you're a trump. I don't know what I should have done without you."

"I always was a young man who could make himself generally useful," said Pratt. "Good luck to you, old boy!"

He sighed, though, and looked rather gloomy as he went out to seek the friends whom he had left in the smoking-room, where Vanleigh was in anything but a good humour, and had been pouring a host of complaints into Sir Felix's ear. It was foolish of them to come down to such an out-of-the-way place; they should be eaten up with ennui. Why didn't Trevor order horses round? The wines weren't good; and he hadn't smoked such bad weeds for years.

"Must make the best of a bad bargain," said Sir Felix. "Must stay— week."

"Oh! we'll stay a month now we are here," said Vanleigh; "let's punish him somehow. What do you say to having a smoke outside?"

"I'm 'greeable," said Sir Felix; and they passed out through the window.

Five minutes after Pratt entered the room, with—

"Now, Vanleigh, I'll play a—Hallo! where the deuce are they?"

He walked hastily into the billiard-room, expecting to find a game begun; but, of course, they were not there.

"Gone to write letters," he muttered; and he went into the library.

Then he entered the drawing-room, the dining-room, the conservatory. Ran up and knocked at their bedroom doors, and then ran down again.

"Having a weed in the garden," said Pratt, "of course. How provoking!"

He took a hat and ran out to the summer-house, garden chairs being set out beneath the various favourite trees, and at last caught sight of a couple of figures in the distance, evidently making for the sea.

"That must be them," he said; and he started off in full chase.

Meanwhile Trevor had hurried off; and as he left the house, Mrs Lloyd came into the hall, and then watched him from a side window.

"Yes!" she said; "he's gone that way again—I thought he would. He's sure to meet her."

Mrs Lloyd was quite right; for a quarter of a mile out of the grounds, and down the principal lane, he saw a white dress, and his heart gave a bound, but only to calm down in its throbbing as he saw that it was little Polly, who advanced to meet him with a very warm blush on her face.

"Hallo! little maid," he said, heartily—"out for a walk?"

"Yes, sir," said Polly, all in a flutter. "I've been—"

"I see, picking wild flowers," said Trevor. "Well, come, give me one for my coat."

The girl hesitated, and then took a cornflower from her little bouquet.

"Thanks," he said, smiling. "But I shan't pay you for it with a kiss. I ought to, though, oughtn't I?"

"Oh, no—please no!" said the girl, with a frightened look, and she glanced round.

"What?" said Trevor, "is there some one coming? There, run away; and tell your aunt to take care of you."

The girl hurried away, and Trevor walked on, to come suddenly upon Humphrey, leaning upon his thistle staff, at a turn of the road.

"Ah, Humphrey," he said, "going your rounds? I want to have a talk to you to-morrow."

There was a hard, stern look on the young man's face as he involuntarily saluted his master; but Trevor did not notice it, and turning down the lane which led to Tolcarne, he began to tap his teeth with the stick he carried, and run over in his own mind what he should say, till he reached the new gates, walked up to the house, and was shown into the presence of the knight's sister.

Miss Matilda Rea did not like Cornwall, principally for theological reasons. She preferred her brother's town-house in Russell Square, because she was within reach of the minister she "sat under"—a gentleman who, she said, "was the only one in London to awaken her stagnant belief."

The fact was that Aunt Matty was a lady who required a zest with her worship—she liked pickles with her prayers, and her friend the minister furnished them—verbal pickles, of course, and very hot.

But there were other reasons why she did not like Cornwall; there were no flagstones; the people did not take to her visitations; her prospects of getting a suitable companion grew less; and lastly, Cornwall did not agree with her dog.

Aunt Matty was dividing her time between nursing Pepine, who was very shivery about the hind legs, and reading small pieces out of a "serious" book—tiny bits which she took like lozenges, and then closed her eyes, and mentally sucked them, so as to get the goodness by degrees. In fact, she was so economical with her "goody" books, that one would last her for years.

"Mr Trevor!" said the servant, loudly, and then—"I'll tell Sir Hampton, sir, that you are here."

Aunt Matty raised her eyes, and Pepine barked virulently at the stranger, as her mistress half rose and then pointed rather severely to a chair.

"He can't be nice," said Aunt Matty to herself, "or Pepine would not bark." Then aloud—"Sir Hampton will, I have no doubt, soon be here."

"Have I the pleasure of addressing Lady Rea?" said Trevor, with a smile.

Pepine barked again.

"What an insult!" thought Aunt Matty. "Did she look like the mother of two great girls?"

In truth, she really did not.

"I am Sir Hampton's sister," she said, stiffly—"Miss Matilda Rea."

A Friendly Call

There was a pause of the kind that may be called cold for a few moments in Sir Hampton's drawing-room. Then Trevor spoke—

"I beg pardon, I'm sure," he said, frankly; "I hope my name is not unknown to you."

"I think I have heard my brother mention it," said Aunt Matty, stiffly. "Hush, Pepine I don't bark!" when, as a matter of course, the dog barked more furiously than before.

"I've just come back from sea," said Trevor, to break the chill.

"Indeed," said Aunt Matty, freezing a little harder; and added to herself, "A most objectionable person." Then aloud, "Pepine must not bark so, hush! hush!"

"Oh, for goodness' sake, Matty, do send that cross little wretch away," cried Lady Rea, bursting into the room. "Mr Richard Trevor, is it?" she said, her plump countenance breaking into a pleasant smile as she gazed up at her visitor. "I'm very glad to see you," she continued, holding out both hands, "and I hope we shall be very good neighbours."

"I hope we shall, indeed," said Trevor, shaking the little lady's hands very heartily, and thinking what a homely, pleasant face it was.

"And aren't you glad to get back? Did you enjoy yourself at sea? I hope you didn't get wrecked!" said Lady Rea, in a breath.

"No; I reached home safe and sound," said Trevor.

"We do have such storms on this coast sometimes. I've told Edward to look for his master. Hampy's always about his grounds."

"My sister means she has sent for Sir Hampton," said Miss Matilda, frigidly. In fact, the cold was intense, and showed in her nose.

"Yes, I've sent for Sir Hampton," said Lady Rea, feeling that she had made a slip. "The girls will be here, too, directly. You have met them?"

Miss Matilda darted a look of horror at her sister; but it missed her, and the little lady prattled on.

"They told me about meeting you twice; and, oh!—here, darlings!—Mr Trevor's come to give us a neighbourly call."

They came forward—Tiny to offer her hand in a quiet, unaffected manner, though a little blush would make its way into her cheek as her eyes met Trevor's, and she felt the gentle pressure of his hand; Fin to screw up her face into a very prim expression, shake hands, and then retire, after the fashion taught by the mistress of deportment at her last school.

"I wish that old griffin would go," thought Trevor, as the conversation went on about the sea, the country and its pursuits—a conversation which Aunt Matty thought to be flighty, and wanting in ballast—which she supplied.

But Aunt Matty did not mean to go, and dealt out more than one snub keen enough to have given offence to the young sailor, but for the genial looks of Lady Rea and the efforts of Fin, who, to her sister's trouble, grew spiteful as soon as her aunt snubbed her ladyship, and became reckless in her speech.

Aunt Matty thought it was quite time for "the seafaring person," as she mentally termed him, to go. She had never known a visit of ceremony last so long. On the contrary side, Trevor forgot all about its being a visit of ceremony: he was near his deity—for a warm attachment for the sweet, gentle girl was growing fast—and he liked the merry laughing eyes of Fin.

"By the way, Mr Trevor," said Lady Rea. "I hear you've got beautiful horses."

"Oh, I don't know," said Trevor. "I tried to get good ones."

"I'm told they are lovely. The girls are just beginning riding—papa has had horses sent down for them."

"I hope they are quiet and well broken," said Trevor, with an anxious glance at Tiny.

"I don't think, Fanny, that Mr Trevor can care to know about our simple domestic matters—our horses, for instance," said Miss Matilda, now solid ice.

"Oh, sailors always love horses, aunty," said Fin, colouring a little; and then mischievously, as she sent an arrow at Trevor, "because they can't ride them."

Aunt Matty's lips parted, but no words came; and to calm her ruffled feelings she took a little dog—in strokes.

"Your daughter is right," said Trevor, "I do love horses; and," he said, laughing at Fin, "I do try to ride them."

"I hope you'll look at the girls' horses, then, Mr Trevor," said Lady Rea. "As you understand them, you'd be able to tell whether they are safe. I don't half like the idea of the girls mounting such wild beasts as horses often are. As for me, I wouldn't ride on one for the world."

The idea of plump little Lady Rea in a riding-habit, mounted on a horse, like a long-draped pincushion, was too much. Tiny coloured. Aunt Matty looked horrified. Trevor grew hot and bit his lip, caught Fin's eye, and then that young lady, who had held her handkerchief to her mouth, burst out laughing.

"Dear me!" exclaimed Lady Rea, good-humouredly. "What have I said now?—something very stupid, I'm sure. But you must not mind me, Mr Trevor, for I do make such foolish mistakes."

Miss Matilda took hold of the two sides of the light shawl thrown over her angular shoulders, and gave it a sawing motion to work it higher up towards her neck, a shuddering sensation, like that caused by a cold current of air, having evidently attacked her spine.

"I think it was a foolish mistake, Fanny," she said, in a voice acid enough to corrode any person's temper, "to doubt Sir Hampton's Judgment with respect to the horses he would choose for his daughters' use."

Fin began to bristle on the instant; her bright eyes flashed, and the laughing dimples fled as if in dismay, as she threw down her challenge to her aunt.

"Why, aunt," said the girl, quickly, "one of the grooms said pa didn't hardly know a horse's head from its tail."

"Oh, Fin, my dear!" cried mamma.

"Which of the grooms made use of that insolent remark?" cried Aunt Matty. "If I have any influence with your papa, that man will be discharged on the instant."

"I think it was Thomas, aunt, who makes so much fuss over Pepine," said Fin, maliciously.

"I'm quite sure that Thomas is too respectable and well-conducted a servant to say such a thing," said Aunt Matty. "It was my doing that your papa engaged him; for he came with a letter of introduction from the Reverend Caius Carney, who spoke very highly indeed of his honesty and pious ways."

"Oh, aunty," cried Fin, "and he swears like a trooper!"

Aunt Matilda went into a semi-cataleptic state, so rigid did she grow; and her hand, with which she was taking a little more dog by friction, closed so sharply on the scruff of the little terrier's neck, that it yelped aloud.

"You mustn't say so, my dear, if he does," said Lady Rea, rather sadly.

And to turn the conversation, Trevor asked her if she liked flowers.

"Oh yes, Mr Trevor," she exclaimed, beaming once more. "And you've got some lovely gladioluses—li—oli," she added, correcting herself, and glancing from one to the other like a tutored child, "in your grounds, of a colour we can't get. May I beg a few?"

"The gardener shall send in as many as you wish for, Lady Rea— anything in my place is at your service."

Poor Tiny! His eager, earnest words began to wake up such a curious little tremor in her breast. It was all so new—so strange. Now she told herself she was foolish, childish, and that she was giving way to silly, romantic fancies; only Fin was evidently thinking something too, and gave her all sorts of malicious looks. As for Aunt Matty, she sat now with her eyes closed, sucking a mental lozenge about patience; and Fin's championship was in abeyance for the rest of the visit—the conversation being principally between Lady Rea and their visitor.

"It's very kind of you to say so, I'm sure," said Lady Rea. "We saw them, you know, when we went over your place, once or twice, for Mrs Lloyd was good enough to say we might. And a very beautiful place it is."

"It's a dear old home, Lady Rea, indeed," said Trevor, enthusiastically.

"Though you must have found it very *sad*," said Lady Rea.

"No," said Trevor, frankly; "it would be mockery in me to say so. My parents died when I was so very young, that I never could feel their loss: I hardly knew what it was to have any one to love."

"Let him look at her now, if he dare," thought Fin, with her eyes sparkling.

But Trevor did not dare; he only gazed in Lady Rea's pleasant face, and she made Aunt Matty shiver—firstly, by laying her hand in a soothing way upon the young man's arm; secondly, by saying she would put herself under an obligation to this dreadful seafaring person, by accepting his offer of flowers; and thirdly, by the following terribly imprudent speech—

"I'm sure I don't know where dear papa can be gone; but as he's not here, Mr Trevor, you must let me say that whenever you feel dull and lonely, you must come up here and have a chat, and some music, or something of that sort. We shall always be delighted to see you."

"Er-rum! Er-rum!" came from the garden.

"Oh! here's papa!" cried Lady Rea. "I'm glad he's come!"

"Er-rum!" came again, and then steps and voices were heard in the conservatory—voices which made Trevor rise and look annoyed.

The next moment Sir Hampton ushered two gentlemen into the drawing-room through the conservatory.

"Lady Rea—Tiny dear," he said, loudly—"er-rum, let me make you known to my friends—Sir Felix Landells and Captain Vanleigh."

Aunt Matty is Cross

Sir Hampton started as his eyes fell upon Trevor, and his pink complexion began to grow red.

"Oh, Fin!" whispered Tiny, heedless of the admiring gaze of Vanleigh, who now advanced; while after saluting Lady Rea, Landells turned to Fin.

"This is Mr Trevor, called to see us, dear," said Lady Rea.

"Er-rum!" went Sir Hampton, and he bristled visibly; but Trevor approached with extended hand.

"Sir Hampton," he said, "I came to apologise for my very hasty behaviour to you. I'm afraid I gave you a very bad opinion of your neighbour."

"Er-rum! I—er? I—er-rum," said and coughed Sir Hampton, hesitating; but there was the hand of amity stretched out, and he was obliged to take it—moving with great dignity, and looking at Trevor as if he had just pardoned a malefactor for committing some heinous crime.

"Didn't 'spect to see; here," said Sir Felix, making play with his glass at everybody in turn.

"The surprise is mutual," said Trevor.

"Odd coincidence," said Vanleigh, who had crossed now to Miss Matilda, like a good diplomatist. "We were walking, after you ran away from us, and met Sir Hampton."

"Er-rum—Mr Trevor," said Sir Hampton, pompously, "I am in your debt; your friends here were kind enough to give my daughters and myself the use of your carriage after a very—er-rum—narrow escape from a terrible—er-rum—catastrophe. I am very much obliged."

"Don't name it, Sir Hampton, pray," said Trevor. "Out here in this place, we are all obliged to rely upon one another for a little help. I shall have to beg favours of you, some day, I hope."

"Er-rum—you are very good," said Sir Hampton, stiffly.

"Yes, Hampton, dear," said Lady Rea, "Mr Trevor is really very kind: he has promised us a lot of those beautiful gladioli that you admired so when you went over Penreife grounds."

Sir Hampton bowed to Trevor, and looked daggers at his wife, who glanced then at Fin, as much as to say—"What have I done now!"

"A particularly fine specimen, I should say," Vanleigh was heard to remark. "Do you think so?" said Miss Matilda.

"I should say perfectly pure," said Vanleigh, stooping to caress Pepine, who snarled and tried to bite.

"Fie, Pepine, then!" said Miss Matilda. "Don't be afraid of him, Captain Vanleigh."

"I am not," said Vanleigh, showing his white teeth, and taking the terrier in his hands. "Look here, Landells, what should you say of this dog?"

Sir Felix fixed his glass, and crossed to his friend.

"'Markably fine terrier," said Sir Felix, "most decidedly."

And he touched Pepine, and was bitten spitefully on the glove.

"You remember the dog you sent to the Palace Show?"

"'Member perfectly," said Sir Felix; "splen' collection."

"But did you see a finer bred specimen than that—say frankly?"

"Nothing like it; 'fectly sure of it."

"There, Miss Rea," said Vanleigh, "and Landells is one of the finest amateur judges of dogs in the country."

"Is he really?" said Miss Matilda, smiling.

"Oh yes," said Vanleigh. "What should you think that dog was worth, Landells?"

"Any money," said Sir Felix; "five at least."

"But I gave ten pounds for it," said Miss Matilda, indignantly.

"Exactly," said Vanleigh. "Then you obtained it at a great bargain."

"But he said five pounds," said Miss Matilda.

"Exactly, my dear madam," said Vanleigh. "That is the judge's fashion— five pounds a paw; twenty pounds."

"Oh, I see!" said Miss Matilda, and Trevor turned aside, for he had encountered Fin's laughing eyes, and her pinched-up mouth had said dumbly—

"My! What a fib!"

After a little more conversation, the trio took their leave, and there was peace between the dwellers at Penreife and Tolcarne for many days to come.

"Er-rum," said Sir Hampton, as soon as they were alone. "I am not very agreeably impressed with this Mr Trevor."

"Aren't you, dear?" said Lady Rea; "and I thought him such a nice, gentlemanly, frank fellow, and so did the girls."

"Sadly wanting in manners," said Aunt Matty. "Quite as you said, Hampton—rough and uncultivated."

Sir Hampton nodded his head approvingly.

"But he don't call out 'avast!' and 'Ship ahoy!' and 'Haul in slack,' as you said he would, aunty," said Fin.

"Finetta, I never made use of any such language," said Miss Matilda.

"Then it must have been I," said Fin. "I know somebody said so."

"Most gentlemanly men the friends you introduced, Hampton—especially Captain Vanleigh."

"And the dog-fancier with the glass," put in Fin, in an undertone; but her aunt heard her.

"Hampton," she said, viciously, "I am unwilling to make complaints, but I am sorry to say that the treatment I receive from Finetta is anything but becoming. Several times this afternoon her remarks to me have been such as when I was a little girl I should never have thought of using, and I should have been severely reprimanded if I had said a tithe."

"Why, I thought tithes were parsons' payments, aunty," said Fin, merrily; and Aunt Matty stopped short, Lady Rea turned away to smile, and Sir Hampton actually chuckled.

Miss Matilda gathered up her skirts, and taking Pepine under her arm, was marching out of the room.

"Please, aunt, I'm very sorry," said Fin. "I'm afraid I'm a very naughty little girl, and shall have to be punished—Papa, can I have any dinner?"

"Er-rum. Matilda," said Sir Hampton, "I am going on the lawn. Will you come?"

Aunt Matty was mollified, and took his arm.

"You shouldn't, Fin, indeed," said Tiny.

"My darling, I must beg of you not," said Lady Rea, piteously.

"Then she shan't snub my darling, dear mamma," said Fin, kissing her. "I'm never saucy to Aunt Matty only when she says rude things to you; treating me like a child, too! Oh, mamma, if you ever find me growing into a sour old maid, pray poison me with something hidden in a spoonful of currant jam."

Proposals

"If you wish it, Hampton, of course have it; but I think the money that it will cost might very well be given to some missionary fund," said Miss Matilda.

"Er-rum! When I want your advice, Matty, I shall ask it," said Sir Hampton. "I must keep up my dignity in the county."

"You could do it in no better way, Hampton, than by subscribing to the South Sea Islander Society—'Sir Hampton Rea, twenty guineas,' in the county paper, would add more to your dignity than giving a dinner party."

This was at breakfast, and Fin cast malicious glances at her sister, who was blushing, and bending over her plate.

"Fanny!—er-rum!" continued Sir Hampton, not seeming to notice his sister, "we'll say Friday. You will send invitations to— er-rum—let me see!"

"Stop a minute, Hampy dear," cried her ladyship, making a scuffle to get at something. "There—oh! now, how tiresome—that cream jug always gets in the way. Thank you, Fin, my dear; take it up with a spoon—it isn't hurt."

"Oh, ma dear," cried Fin, "the cream will taste of hot washerwoman and mangles. You can't use it now."

"Oh, I'll drink it, my dear—oh!" she added, in a low voice, "Aunt Matty will think it such waste."

"Are you ready, Fanny?" said Sir Hampton, rolling his head in his stiff cravat.

"One moment, Hampy," said her ladyship, getting her pencil and tablets. "My memory is so bad now, I must put them down."

"Then—er-rum—first we'll say—"

"Oh, one moment, Hampy; this tiresome pencil's got no point again."

"Take mine, ma dear," said Fin.

"Thank you, my love. Now, pa."

"Er-rum," said Sir Hampton—"first, then, we'll have er—er—Sir Felix Landells."

Aunt Matty bowed her head approvingly.

"E, double L, S," said Lady Rea, writing. "Don't shake me, Fin, there's a dear."

For Lady Rea had come undone at the back of her dress, and Fin was busy with a pin at her collar.

"Er-rum!" continued Sir Hampton. "Next we'll have Captain Vanleigh."

And he looked hard at Tiny, who bent lower over her plate.

"Van, I—tut-tut-tut, how do you spell leigh, e first or i first?" said Lady Rea.

"Shall I write them down for you, Fanny?" said Aunt Matty.

"No, thank you, Matty," said Lady Rea, who was getting into a knot. "There, I shall know what that means."

"Er-rum!" said Sir Hampton; "Mr Mervyn."

"La! Hampy," cried Lady Rea, looking up, "you haven't said Mr Trevor."

"Mister—er-rum—Mervyn!" exclaimed Sir Hampton, sharply.

"Oh, there, my dear, don't fly at me like that," cried Lady Rea. "M, e, r, v, i—"

"Y Fanny, y," said Aunt Matty, with a shudder.

"Oh yes, y, of course," said Lady Rea, good-humouredly; "y, n, Mervyn. Next?"

The girls bent their heads—Tiny over her breakfast, Fin smoothing the rather tousled hair of her mother.

"Er-rum, I suppose I must ask this—er-rum—Trevor."

"Surely, Hampton," exclaimed Aunt Matty, "you will not think of inviting that objectionable person."

Fin glanced at her sister, whose face was crimson, and Lady Rea looked pained. "Matty, my dear, I think you are wrong. I..."

"Have you got that name down, Lady Rea?" said Sir Hampton.

"No, dear; but I soon will have," said her ladyship, making her pencil scramble over the tablet.

"Er-rum!" ejaculated Sir Hampton, rising, puffing himself out, and walking slowly up and down the room; "a man in my position is obliged to make sacrifices, and ask people to whom he objects. In the event of my contesting the county such a man as this—er-rum—this—er-rum—Trevor would be useful I thank you, Matty; you mean, er—mean—rum, well. Put his name down, Fanny."

"I have, my love," said Lady Rea, beaming at her children.

"Hampton, I protest against this outrage," cried Aunt Matty, "after the marked way in which he has—"

"Tiny, come and cut some flowers," said Fin; and her sister gladly beat a retreat, Fin whispering as they went—"Will he ask the little man?"

"Now, Matty," said Sir Hampton, "have the goodness to proceed; and in future, when you enter upon such subjects, have the kindness to—er-rum—remember that I am not deaf."

"I say, Hampton, after the marked way in which that 'seafaring person' has behaved to Valentina, it is most indiscreet to ask him here."

"Oh, Matty," cried Lady Rea, "I'm sure that young man is as nice as can be."

"If that was what you intended to say, Matilda—er-rum—it would have been most indecent before those children," said Sir Hampton, pompously.

"In—"

Aunt Matty could not say it, the word was too outrageous.

"I feel bound—er-rum—bound," said Sir Hampton, with emphasis, "to ask the young man, as a proprietor, even as we might ask a tenant, Fanny."

"Yes, my love."

"Put down that lawyer as well, Mr—er, er—Mr—" he got the name out with great disgust at last, "Pratt," and carefully wiped his mouth afterwards.

"You'll be sorry for this, Hampton," said Miss Matilda, shaking with virtuous indignation, so that some frozen dewdrops in her head-dress quivered again, and Pepine, who had been surreptitiously nursed under a canopy of table-cloth, received, in her excitement, such a heavy nip from his mistress's knees, that he uttered an awful howl.

"Er-rum—sorry?"

"Yes, sorry. That objectionable person is always hanging about the house like—like—like a vagrant; and those girls never go for a walk without being accosted by him or his companion. If you have any eyes, you ought to see."

"Oh, Matty, pray don't," said Lady Rea, appealingly.

"Er-rum! Silence, Fanny," said Sir Hampton. "And as for your remarks, Matilda, they are uncalled for. My children would not, I am sure, encourage the—er-rum—advances of that person; and Lady Rea would be one of the first to crush any—er-rum—thing of the kind."

"Indeed!" said Aunt Matty, spitefully. "That—er-rum—will do," said Sir Hampton. "Fanny, those will be our guests. See that the dinner is worthy of our position."

He went out like a stout, elderly emperor of florid habit, and, as soon after as was possible, Lady Rea beat a retreat, leaving Aunt Matty taking dog, after her habit, in strokes with one hand, holding a pocket handkerchief cake in the other; "and looking," Edward the footman, said in the kitchen, after removing the breakfast things, "like a bilious image getting ready for a fit."

Sir Hampton's study was horticulture that morning; and, after swallowing a page on the manipulation of the roots of espaliers and pyramid trees, he was about to go out and attack Sanders, the gardener, when Edward announced Sir Felix Landells and Captain Vanleigh on business, and they were shown in.

"Really—hope not deranging—untimely call," said Sir Felix.

"We will not detain you long, Sir Hampton," said Vanleigh, with a great show of deference.

"Er-rum, gentlemen," said Sir Hampton, whose face shone with pride, "in these rural—er-rum—districts, when one is—er-rum—far from society and town, sociability and hospitality should, er—"

"Go hand in hand—exactly," said Vanleigh, smiling.

"Er-rum, I am very glad to see you, gentlemen," said Sir Hampton. "Oddly—er-rum—oddly enough, we were discussing a little dinner for Friday. Could you—er-rum—both, both—er—honour us with your company?"

And he looked from one to the other.

"Well," said Vanleigh, hesitating, and glancing at Sir Felix, "it depends somewhat on—Would you like to speak out, Landells?"

"'Sure you, no. Do it so much better. Pray go on."

And the young man turned crimson.

"Not pre-engaged, I hope?" said Sir Hampton.

"Well, Sir Hampton," said Vanleigh, modestly, after a pause, during which he sat with his eyes on the carpet, "this is all so new to me, and you have confused me so with your kind invitation, that my business—our business—comes doubly hard to us to state."

"Er-rum—pray go on," said Sir Hampton, smiling condescendingly, for all this was sweet to his soul; two scions of aristocratic houses with sense enough to respect his position in life. Captain Vanleigh might have borrowed a hundred pounds on the instant had he liked; but he was playing for higher stakes.

"Then, if you won't speak, Landells, I must," said Vanleigh, who seemed overcome with confusion. "No doubt there is a proper etiquette to be observed in such cases, but I confess I am too agitated to recall it, and I merely appeal to you, Sir Hampton, as a gentleman and a parent."

Sir Hampton bowed, and uttered a cough that seemed wrapped up in cotton wool, it was so soft.

"The fact is, Sir Hampton, we have been here now three weeks—Landells and I—and we have been so charmed, so taken with your sweet daughters, that, in this hurried, confused way—I tell you, in short, we thought it right, as gentlemen, to come first and tell you, to ask you for your permission to visit more frequently, to be more in their society—to, in short, make formal proposals for their hands."

There was another soft cough, and Vanleigh continued—

"I hope I am forgiven, Landells, for my awkward way?"

"Yes. Pray go on; capital," said Landells, who was perspiring profusely.

"It is only fair to say how we are placed in the world, Sir Hampton. My friend there, Sir Felix, has his eight thousand per annum; and it will increase. For myself, I am but a poor officer of the Guards."

"Er-rum! a gentleman is never poor," said Sir Hampton, with dignity.

"I think I can say no more, Sir Hampton," said Vanleigh, bowing to the compliment. "You see now my hesitation about the dinner; for, of course, if you refuse to regard our application favourably, to-morrow we should—eh, Landells?"

"Back—town—certainly," said Sir Felix, wiping his face.

"Er-rum!" said Sir Hampton, rising, and placing a hand in his breast. "Gentlemen, you take me by surprise, and you ask a great deal in—er-rum—I say you ask a great deal—I, er-rum, I—honoured by your—er-rum—proposals—and—and—er-rum, if I express myself badly, it is a father's emotion. In short, I—er-rum—gentlemen—I, er-rum, give both my full consent to visit here as often as you wish, and Lady Rea and my daughters shall be acquainted with your proposals. I can, er-rum, say no more now. Let us join the ladies."

Sir Felix, with tears in his eyes, took and wrung the old man's hand, and, as the friends followed him out, Vanleigh bestowed upon the young baronet a most solemn, but very vulgar, wink.

An Interview with Barney Sturt

"Couldn't you make it a four-wheeler, Sam," said Mrs Jenkles, one evening, "and take me up and bring us all back together?"

"Now, lookye here, old lady," said Sam, "I don't want to be hard, nor I don't want to be soft, but what I says is this here—Where's it going to end?"

"What *do* you mean, Sam?" exclaimed Mrs Jenkles.

"What I says, my dear—Where's it going to end? You've got over me about the money, and you've got over me about the lodgings. You're allus going to Mrs Lane to tea, as I knows they don't find; and now you wants me to give up my 'ansom, borrer a four-wheeler, and lose 'bout a pound as I should make in fares; and what I says is—Where's it going to end?"

"Sam, Sam, Sam," said Mrs Jenkles, "when did you ever go out with your cab for about a couple of hours and make a pound?"

Sam stood rubbing his nose, and there was a droll twinkle in his eye as he replied—

"Well, I might make a pound, you know."

"Now don't talk stuff, Sam, but go to the yard and change your cab, take me up there, and bring us all back comfortable."

"You're argoing it, you are, missus," said Sam. "That's the way—order your kerridge. 'Sam,' says you, 'the kerridge at six.' 'Yes, mum,' says I. 'Oppery or dinner party?' 'Only to make a hevening call, Sam,' says you. 'Werry good, mum,' says I."

"If you want me to go up there by myself, Sam, and fetch them, I'll go, and we can get back somehow by the 'bus; but I thought you'd like to come up and see that those ladies and your wife weren't insulted."

"I should jest like to catch anybody at it, that's all," said Sam, sharply.

"I didn't mean to say anything, Sam," continued Mrs Jenkles; "for I thought if we'd got such a man as you with us, no one would dare to interfere."

"Now, look here," said Sam, "I never did come across such an old snail as you are, missus; I like the allus being at home part of it, but it's the hiding as I don't like. Now, look here, I never does nothing without coming and telling you all about it; and as for you, why, you've allus got something in the way for me to find out."

"What's the use of me bothering you with trifles, Sam, when you've got plenty of troubles on your mind? I would tell you if it was anything you need know."

"Well, come now, what's it all mean bout Miss Lane?" said Sam.

"Only, dear, that since those people have found that Mrs Lane meant to leave, they've turned very strange, and the poor child's quite frightened and timid like."

"Now, why couldn't you say so at first," said Sam, "instead of dodging and hiding, and making a blind man's buffer of me? That's it, is it? Mr Barney of the betting ring—'Ten to one bar one'—means to be nasty, does he? Well, all I've got to say is, just let him try it on, that's all!"

"Now, there it is," said Mrs Jenkles; "that's just what I want to avoid. Tell you about it, and you want to do the very thing as will upset that poor girl; and oh! Sam, do be careful, she—"

Mrs Jenkles added something in a whisper.

"I'll be careful enough," said Sam; "and look here—how long shall you be?"

"I'm ready now, Sam," said his wife.

"Yes, but I've got to go down to the yard, and get the keb changed, take me 'bout three quarters of an hour, it will, and then I'm back."

Sam went off, muttering to himself; the only words audible being—

"Jest let him, that's all!"

And within the prescribed time he was driving Mrs Jenkles up to Mrs Lane's wretched lodgings.

Mrs Jenkles passed in, after a word or two with her husband, and saw at a glance Barney of the black chin smoking in his shop, and Mrs Barney looking over his shoulder. She took no notice of them, and went upstairs, to find Mrs Lane looking very pale and much excited, holding Netta's hand.

"And how's my pretty to-night?" said Mrs Jenkles, after a quick glance had passed between her and the mother.

"Quite—quite well," said the girl, placing both her hands in those of Mrs Jenkles, and holding her face to be kissed; but her unnaturally bright eyes and flushed face contradicted her words, and she kept glancing timidly towards the door.

"That's right, my dear," said Mrs Jenkles. "Ah! and I see you've got the trunk packed, and all ready. I've got some flowers for you at home, and everything waiting; so don't you go looking like that."

"She has been a little frightened today," said Mrs Lane; "the people downstairs—"

"Oh, don't you mind them," said Mrs Jenkles. "They don't like losing good lodgers, now it comes to the point, with all their grumbling. Have you paid your bit of rent?"

"Yes," said Mrs Lane; and she glanced anxiously at her child, whose alarm seemed to increase.

"I see," said Mrs Jenkles, in her most business-like way. "Now, look here, the thing is to get it over quickly. Have you got everything there?" and she pointed to a trunk and carpet-bag.

"Yes, everything," said Mrs Lane.

"Then I'll call up Sam to take them down to the cab."

"No, no—stop!" exclaimed Netta. "Oh! mamma, had we not better stop? That man—what he said this morning!"

"There, there, my pretty," said Mrs Jenkles, "don't you be alarmed. You leave it to me."

Then going to the window, she signalled to Sam, who was busy tying knots in his shabby whipthong.

As Mrs Jenkles turned from the window, the door was thrown open, and Mrs Sturt, looking very aggressive, entered the room, closely followed by her lord, smoking his black pipe of strong, rank tobacco.

Netta shrank timidly back into her seat, catching at her mothers hand, while the result of the tobacco-smoke was to set her coughing painfully.

"Now if you please," said Mrs Sturt, "I want to know what this means?"

And she pointed to the trunk and the other manifest signs of departure.

"I told you a week ago, Mrs Sturt, that we intended to leave," said Mrs Lane, speaking with a forced calmness, as she pressed her child's hand encouragingly.

"And so you think a week's notice is enough after the way as we've been troubled to get our bit of rent?" said Mrs Sturt, raising her voice. "Are we to be left with our place empty, after harbouring a pack of lodgers with no more gratitude than—than—than nothing?" continued the woman, at a loss for a simile.

"I have nothing to do with that," said Mrs Lane, with dignity. "Mrs Sturt, I have rigidly kept to the arrangement I made with you, and you have no right to expect more."

"Oh, haven't I?" said the woman. "Do you hear that, Barney? I'll just let 'em see!"

Barney growled, and showed his teeth.

"Lookye here," he said, hoarsely; "you aint agoing to leave here, so now then. And you, missus," tinning to Mrs Jenkles, "you're gallus clever, you are; but you may let your lodgings to some one else."

Netta's clutch of her mother's hand grew convulsive, and her face wore so horrified an expression that Mrs Jenkles did not reply to the challenge directed at her, but stepped to the poor girl's side.

"Don't you be frightened, my dear," she whispered; and then to herself—"Why don't Sam come?"

"Mr Sturt," said Mrs Lane, firmly in voice, though she trembled as she spoke to the fellow, "you have no right to try and force us to stay if we wish to leave."

"Oh! aint I," said Barney. "I'll let you see about that. Here, give us that," he said, turning to snatch a paper from his wife's hand. "Let alone what he telled me too, about yer—"

"He! Who?" exclaimed Mrs Lane, excitedly,

Netta started from her chair.

"Never you mind," said Barney, showing his great teeth in a grin. "You think I don't know all about yer, now, don't yer? But you're precious mistaken!"

"But tell me, man, has any one—"

"There, there, it's all right, Mrs Lane—you've got to stop here, that's what you've got to do. What have you got to say to that, for another thing?"

As Barney spoke, he thrust the paper down before Mrs Lane, and went on smoking furiously.

"What's this? I don't owe you anything," said Mrs Lane, whose courage seemed failing.

"Don't owe us anything, indeed!" said Mrs Sturt, in her vinegary voice; "why, there's seven pun' ten, and seven for grosheries!"

"Oh! this is cruel as it's scandalous and false!" cried Mrs Lane, in reply to Mrs Jenkles's look. "I do not owe a shilling."

"Which you do—there!" cried Mrs Sturt; "and not a thing goes off these premises till it's paid."

"And they don't go off, nor them nayther, when it is paid," said Barney, grinning offensively. "So now, Mrs What's-yer-name, you'd better be off!"

Mrs Jenkles had been very quiet, but her face had been growing red and fiery during all this, and she gave a sigh of relief as she patted Netta on the shoulder; for at that moment Sam came slowly into the room, closed the door, and bowed and smiled to Mrs Lane and her daughter.

"Sam," said Mrs Jenkles; and then she stopped almost aghast at her husband's proceedings, for with a sharp flourish of the hand, he knocked Barney's pipe from his mouth, the stem breaking close to his teeth, and he looking perfectly astonished at the cabman's daring.

"What are yer smoking like that for, here? Can't yer see it makes the young lady cough?"

"I'll—" exclaimed Barney, rushing at Sam menacingly; and Netta uttered a shriek.

"Don't you mind him, Miss," said Sam, laughing, "it's only his fun. It's a little playful way he's got with him, that's all. Which is the boxes?"

"That trunk, and the carpet-bag, Sam," said Mrs Jenkles; and Sam advanced to them.

"Hadn't we better give up?" said Mrs Lane, pitifully; and she glanced at Netta who trembled violently.

"I should think not, indeed," said Mrs Jenkles. "Don't you be afraid— they daren't stop you."

"But we just dare," said Mrs Sturt, furiously. "Not a thing goes off till my bill's paid."

"And they don't go off when it is! now then," said Barney.

"Don't let him touch those things," said Mrs Sturt.

"Sam, you take that trunk down directly," said Mrs Jenkles. "Now, my dear; come along."

"All right," said Sam, and he advanced to the trunk; but Barney pushed himself forward, and sat down upon the box; while, as Mrs Jenkles placed her arm round Netta, and led her towards the door, Mrs Sturt jerked herself to it, and placed her back against the panels.

"You're a nice 'un, you are, Barney Sturt, Esquire, of the suburban races," said Sam, good-temperedly; "but it aint no good, so get up, and let's go quietly."

Barney growled out an oath, and showed his teeth, as Mrs Lane came up to Sam, and laid her hand on his shoulder.

"Thank you much," she said, with a shudder; "but I give up: we cannot go."

"Believe you can't," said Barney, grinning. "D'yer hear that, cabby?"

"Yes, I hear," said Sam, gruffly; "and if it weren't that I don't want to make a row afore the ladies, I'd have you off that trunk afore you knew where you was. And as to leaving the box alone, my missus said I was to take it down to the keb. Is it to go, old lady?"

"Yes, certainly," said Mrs Jenkles, with flashing eyes.

"Now, Barney, d'yer hear?" said Sam.

"Who do you call Barney? You don't know me," said he.

"Oh no," said Sam; "I don't know you. I didn't give yer a lift in my 'ansom, and drive yer away down at 'Ampton, when the mob had torn yer clothes into rags for welching, and they was going to pitch yer in the Thames, eh?"

Barney scowled, and shuffled about on his seat.

"Now, then," said Sam; "are you going to get up?"

"No," said Barney.

"Mrs Jenkles, pray end this scene!" exclaimed Mrs Lane, pitifully—"for her sake," she added in a whisper.

"I'll end it, mum," said Sam.

And he gave a sharp whistle, with the result that the door was opened so violently that Mrs Sturt was jerked forward against Sam, the cause being a policeman, who now stood in the entry, with the further effect that Barney leaped off the trunk, and stood looking aghast.

Mrs Jenkles gave a sigh of relief, and a gratified look at her husband.

"Here's the case, policeman," said Sam. "Ladies here wants to leave these lodgings: they've given notice and paid their rent; but the missus here brings out a bill for things as the lady says she's never had, and wants to stop their boxes. It's county court, aint it? They can't stop the clothes?"

"Nobody wants to stop no boxes," said Barney, uneasily. "Only it was precious shabby on 'em going like this."

"Then you don't want to stop the boxes, eh?" said Sam.

Mrs Sturt gave her husband a sharp dig with her elbow.

"Be quiet, can't you!" he snarled; and then to Sam, "'course I don't."

"Then ketch hold o' t'other end," said Sam, placing the bag on the trunk.

And like a lamb Barney helped to bear his late lodger's impedimenta downstairs, and then to place them on the cab, as Mrs Jenkles led Netta half fainting from the room.

Five minutes after, Sam had banged-to the rattling door, shutting in the little party, climbed to his box, and settled himself in his place, with a good-humoured nod to the policeman, who stood beating his gloves together, while Barney stood at the side of his wife.

"Here's the price of a pint for you, Barney," said Sam, throwing him a couple of pence—money which Barney instantly secured; and then, vowing vengeance against the donor, he slunk off in the opposite direction; but only to double round by a back street, and track the cab like a dog, till he saw it set down its inmates at the humble little home of Mrs Jenkles.

Frank Pratt's Cross-Examination, and Après

Captain Vanleigh had declared solemnly that Penreife was "the deucedest dullest place" he ever saw in his life; and Sir Felix said it was "'nough to kill 'fler;" but, all the same, there was no talk to Trevor of moving; they lounged about the house chatting to each other, and consumed their host's cigars to a wonderful extent; they ate his dinners and drank his wine; and Vanleigh generally contrived to go to bed a few guineas richer every night from the whist table.

Pratt protested against the play, but Trevor laughed at him.

"My dear boy," he said, "why not let such matters take their course? Van is my guest; surely I should be a bad host if I did not let him win a little spare cash. Have you anything else to grumble about?"

"Heaps," said Pratt, trying to put his little legs on a chair in front of the garden seat where he and his friend were having a morning cigar; but they were too short, and he gave up the attempt.

"Go on, then," said Trevor, lazily, "have your grumble out."

"Hadn't I better go back to town?" said Pratt, sharply.

"Why, are you not comfortable?"

"Yes—no—yes—no. I'm precious uncomfortable. I see too much," said Pratt.

"Well, let's hear what you see that makes you so uncomfortable," said Trevor, carelessly.

"Dick, old boy," said Pratt, "you won't be offended with me for what I say?"

"Not I," was the answer.

"What are you thinking about?" said Pratt, watching the other's face.

"I was only thinking about you, and wondering why, if you don't like what you see, you can't close your eyes."

"That's what you are doing, Dick!" said Pratt, eagerly.

"My dear Frank, have you discovered powder barrels beneath the house—is there a new plot?"

"Don't be so foolish, Dick. Why don't you let those two fellows go?"

"Because they are my guests, and stay as long as they like."

"And are doing their very best to undermine your happiness."

"Nonsense, man."

"Dick, old fellow, answer me honestly. Don't you care a great deal for that little girl up at Tolcarne?"

There was a few moments' pause, during which the colour came into Trevor's cheek.

"Honestly, I do," he said at last. "Well, and what of that?"

"Well, Dick, are you blind? Van's making all the play that he can, and father and aunt favour him. He's there nearly every day. He's there now."

Trevor gave a start, and turned round to face his friend, his lips twitching and fingers working; but he burst out laughing the next moment.

"Anything else, Franky?"

"Laugh away," said Pratt, who looked nettled—"only give me credit for my warning when you find I am right."

"That I will," said Trevor. "Now then, go on! What's the next plot against my peace of mind?"

"Suppose I ask you a question or two!"

"All right—go on!"

"Have you noticed anything wrong with Humphrey?"

"Been precious sulky lately."

"Sulky! The fellow's looked daggers at you, and has barely answered you civilly."

"Well, he has been queer, certainly."

"Why is it?" said Pratt.

"Bilious—out of order—how should I know?"

"The poor fellow's in love!"

"Poor Strephon," said Trevor, idly.

"And he sees a powerful rival in the path," continued Pratt.

"The deuce he does!" said Trevor, laughing. "Is that Van, too? But hang it, Frank!" he cried, starting up, "seriously, I won't stand any nonsense of that kind. If Van's been making love to that little lass, I'll put a stop to it. Why, now I think of it, I did see him looking at her!"

"No!" said Pratt, quietly. "It isn't Van—he's too busy at Tolcarne!"

"Silence, croaker!" cried, Trevor, laughing in a constrained fashion. "But, come—who is the powerful rival?"

"Dick, old fellow, I'm one of those, and no humbug, who have a habit of trying to ferret out other people's motives."

"Don't preach, Franky. Is it Flick? because if it is, the girl's laughing at him."

"No," said Pratt; "it isn't Flick."

"Then who the deuce is it?"

"You!"

Trevor burst into a hearty laugh.

"Why, Frank!" he exclaimed, "if ever there was a mare's-nesting old humbug, it's you. Why, whatever put that in your head?"

Pratt sat looking at him in silence for a few moments.

"Dick," he said, "if ever there was a deliciously unsuspicious, trusting fellow, you are he."

"Never mind about that," said Trevor. "I want to get this silly notion out of your head."

"And I want to get it into yours."

"Well, we'll both try," said Trevor. "You begin: I'll settle you after."

"To begin, then," said Pratt. "You've several times met that girl in the lane yonder."

"Yes; now you mention it—I have."

"About the time when you've been going up to Tolcarne?"

"Yes; and it was evident that she was there to meet Humphrey. Why, I laughed and joked the pretty little lass about it."

"Yes; and did you ever meet Humphrey afterwards?"

"Bravo! my little cross-examining barrister. Yes I did—two or three times. I'm not sworn, mind," added Trevor, laughing.

"True men don't need swearing," said Pratt.

"Thanks for the compliment. Well?"

"How did Humphrey look?"

"Well—yes—now you mention it—to be sure! He looked black as thunder. Oh, but, Franky, I'll soon clear that up. I wouldn't hurt the poor lad's feelings for the world."

"Wait a bit," said Pratt. "What, more mystery? Well, go on."

"Did it ever strike you as strange that you should encounter a pretty, well-spoken little girl like that in your walks?"

"No; I told you I thought she was out to see Humphrey."

"Or that you should meet her in the passages at home here, to bring you letters, or messages from Mrs Lloyd?"

"Well, now you mention it, yes: it has struck me as odd once or twice."

"Never struck you that the girl came of her own accord?"

"Never, and I'm sure she never did. She rather avoided me than not; so come, Master Counsellor, you're out there."

"Did it never strike you that she was sent?"

Trevor did not answer, but sat gazing in his friend's face for a few moments, as if he were trying to catch his drift, and then in a flash he seemed to read all the other meant; for his brow grew cloudy, and he sat down hastily, then got up, and took a few strides up and down before reseating himself.

"Well," said Pratt, "can you see it?"

"I see what you mean, Franky; but I can't quite think it. The old woman would never have the impudence to plan such a thing."

"Dick, old fellow, it's as plain as the day. She's made up her mind that her little niece shall be mistress of Penreife, and she is playing her cards accordingly."

"Then I'm afraid, if that is her game, she'll lose the trick."

"Dick, old fellow," said Pratt, "you're not annoyed?"

"But I am—deucedly annoyed—not with you, Franky; but don't say any more now, I mean to think it over."

"Being a friend to an unsuspicious man is about the most unpleasant post on the face of the earth," said Pratt, moralising, as he saw his friend stride away. "Everybody hates you for enlightening him, and even he cannot forgive you for waking him from his pleasant dreams. Now where has he gone?—oh, to bully that plotting old woman. Well, I've done right, I think; and now I'll have my stroll."

Frank Pratt started off to do what he called "a bit of melancholy Jaques," in the pleasant woodland lanes; and was not long in finding an agreeable perch, where he seated himself, lit his big pipe, and began communing with himself till the pipe was smoked out; and then he sat on and thought without it, till a coming light footstep took his attention.

"Now I make a solemn affidavit," he said, "that I did not come here to play the spy upon anybody's actions. If they choose to come and act under my very nose, why, I must see the play. Who's this?"

"This" proved to be little Polly, who walked quickly by him, glancing suspiciously round as she continued her walk.

"Scene the first!" said Pratt; "enter village maiden with flowers. To her village lover," he continued as a heavy step was heard. "No, by Jove! It's Dick."

He was right, for Trevor came along at a swinging pace, and apparently in a few moments he would overtake the girl.

"If I didn't believe Dick Trevor to be as open as the day, how suspicious that would look!" thought Pratt.

Trevor passed on without seeing him, and then there was a pause. The sun's rays darted through the overhanging boughs; birds flitted and sang their little love songs overhead; and in a half-dreamy way Pratt sat thinking upon his perch till voices and coming footsteps once more aroused him.

"It's them!" he said to himself. "I'll go."

He made as if to descend, but it struck him that he should be seen if he moved, and he sat still watching—to see at the end of a few moments Tiny

Rea coming along the footpath, evidently looking agitated as she walked on in advance.

"She's never seen Dick and her together!" Pratt said, mentally; and he felt as if he could have run and spoken to the girl; but that which next met his eyes made him utter a low, deep sigh, and he looked as if made of the mossy stone upon which he sat, as Fin Rea followed her sister, hanging on Mr Mervyns arm, and gazing eagerly in his face, while he evidently told her something which was of interest.

They passed slowly by, as if in no hurry to overtake Tiny; and Pratt watched them till quite out of sight, when he got down in a heavy, stunned fashion, to go slowly farther and farther into the wood, where he threw himself down amongst the ferns, and buried his face in his hands, as he groaned —

"More than old enough to be her father!"

Misunderstanding

Meanwhile Trevor had gone along the lane, evidently meaning to make a call at Tolcarne. He was walking with his head bent down, thinking very deeply over what Pratt had said, when he stopped short with a start; for there, just in front, and gazing at him in a startled way, was little Polly.

He nodded to her and passed on; but ere he had gone a dozen yards, he turned sharp round and retraced his steps, calling to the girl to stop.

"I'll get to the bottom of it at once," he said. "Here, Polly."

The little girl turned, and stood trembling before him, her face like fire, but her eyes full of tears.

"Did you call me, sir?" she faltered.

"Yes, my little maid, I want a few words with you."

"Oh, sir, please—pray don't speak to me!" faltered the girl, bursting into tears.

"Why, you silly child, what are you afraid of?" cried Trevor, catching her by the wrist. "Look here, tell me this, and don't be afraid."

"No—no, sir," faltered the girl.

"Tell me now, honestly—there, there, stop that crying, for goodness' sake! Any one would think I was an ogre. I hate to see a woman crying."

"Please, sir, I am trying," sobbed the girl.

"Now, then, I want to know this—you have often met me here—do you come to meet Humphrey?"

"No, sir."

"Then why the deuce—there—there, I don't mean that—tell me why you do come?"

"Aunt sends me to walk here, sir; but please don't say I told you, or she will be so angry."

"Then you don't want to come and walk here?"

"Oh no, sir! I would much rather not," exclaimed the girl, eagerly.

"Your aunt sends you, then?" said Trevor, looking at her searchingly, while she gazed up in his eyes like a dove before a hawk.

"Ye-yes, sir!"

"Do you know why?"

The girl's face grew fiery red now, even to the roots of her hair, and as she looked appealingly at him, he flung her hand angrily from him.

"There, go back," he exclaimed. "I'm not cross with you, but—there, go home."

The girl sprang away, evidently frightened to death, and weeping bitterly, to pass these people—she could not tell whom—as she held down her head; but Trevor saw, and he knew that they saw him, and must have witnessed part of the interview; for the party consisted of Tiny Rea, her sister, and Mr Mervyn.

"Was ever anything so provoking?" muttered Trevor, as they bowed and passed, taking a turning that led in another direction. "Oh! this is unbearable."

For a moment he stood irresolute, hesitating as to whether he should hurry after them; but he was, to use his own words, too much taken aback, and ended by following a narrow pathway into the woods, down which he had not gone half a dozen yards before he became aware that there had been another spectator to his interview with Polly, and that no less a person than Humphrey.

"What the devil are you doing there, sir?" roared Trevor, who was half beside himself with a rage which grew hotter as the bluff young Cornishman stood leaning on his gun, and said, sturdily—

"Watching you, sir."

"Watching me?"

"Yes, sir. I did not mean to, but I was obliged when I saw what I did."

"Then you saw me talking to that girl?"

"Yes, sir, I did; and you had no right to do so."

"How dare you speak to me like that, sir?" roared Trevor; and thoroughly roused now, he caught the young keeper by the throat, and for a few moments the ferns were trampled under foot as they wrestled together, till the veins stood up in knots in Humphrey's white forehead, as his hat fell off, and, grinding his teeth together, he put out his strength, and, with all the skill of a Cornish wrestler, threw Trevor heavily on his back.

"You would have it," said the keeper, hoarsely. "You made me forget my place; so don't blame me for it. Have I hurt you, sir?"

The rage had departed as quickly as it came, and the young man went down on one knee by Trevor, who was half-stunned, but recovered himself quickly, and got up.

"No. I'm not much hurt," he said, hoarsely.

"You made me do it, sir," said Humphrey, pitifully. "You shouldn't have laid hands on me, sir—it made me mad."

"Made you mad!" said Trevor, angrily. "This is a pretty way to serve your master."

"You're no master of mine, sir, from now," cried Humphrey. "I can't stand to serve you no more. I'd have stuck to you, sir, through thick and thin, if you'd been a gentleman to me, but—"

"Do you dare to say I've not been a gentleman to you, you scoundrel?" cried Trevor, menacingly, as he clenched his fists.

"Now, don't 'ee, sir," cried Humphrey, appealingly. "I don't want to hurt you, and if you drive me to it I shall do you a mischief."

"You thick-headed, jealous dolt!" cried Trevor, restraining himself with difficulty. "How can you be such an ass?"

"I don't blame you, sir," cried Humphrey, "not so much as that silly old woman who has set it all going."

"Then it is all true?" cried Trevor, angrily. "Humphrey," he said, "you're as great a fool as that mother of yours; and—there, I'll speak out, though you don't deserve it: as to little Polly, you great dolt, I never said a tender word to her in my life."

"Why, I saw you with her hand in yours, not ten minutes ago," cried Humphrey, indignantly.

"I've been calling you fool and dolt, Humphrey," said Trevor, cooling down, "when I've been both to let my passion get the better of me, as it has. There's a wretched mistake over this altogether; and more mischief done," he continued, bitterly, "than you can imagine. You think, then, that Mrs Lloyd has that idea in her head?"

"Think, sir!" cried the keeper, hotly, "I know it. Hasn't she forbidden me to speak to the poor girl? Hasn't she half-broken her heart?"

"Humphrey," said Trevor, "you had good reason for feeling angry, but not with me."

Humphrey looked at him searchingly.

"You doubt me?" said Trevor.

"Will you say it again, sir?" cried the young man, pitifully—"will you swear it?"

"I give you my word of honour as a gentleman, Humphrey, that I have never given the girl a thought; and that this afternoon, when I spoke to her, it was to ask her if she came there to meet you; and she owned her aunt had sent her."

"Master Dick—Master Dick!" cried the young man in a choking voice, "will you forgive me, sir? If I had known that, sir, I'd sooner have cut my right hand off than have done what I did."

"It was all a mistake, Humphrey. There—that will do."

"But I said, sir, you were no master of mine—Master Dick—Mr Trevor, sir. We were boys together here—at the old place—don't send me away!"

"There, go now; that will do. Yes, it's all right, Humphrey. I'm not angry. Send you away? No, certainly not; only go now, and don't make a scene," said Trevor, incoherently, his eyes the while turned in another direction; for he had heard footsteps, and at the turn of the lane he could see through the trees that Mr Mervyn was coming, with his two companions.

Trevor hurried off through the wood, so as to gain the path a hundred yards in advance, and then he sauntered along so as to meet them.

"If I can get a few words with her I can explain," he said; and then they were close at hand.

"Ah, Mr Trevor!" cried Mervyn, gaily, for he seemed elated, and he held out his hand.

Before Trevor could take it, Fin had looked straight before her and marched on, her little lips pinched together, and her arm tight in that of her sister; while Tiny met Trevor's gaze in one short, sad look—piteous, reproachful, and heartbroken—before she hurried away.

Invitations

Trevor returned home in no very enviable frame of mind. The look Tiny Rea had given him troubled him more than he could express, and he felt ready to rail at Fortune for the tricks she had played him. Old Lloyd came, smiling and deferential, into the room with some letters, which his master snatched up and threw on the table.

"In which room are Captain Vanleigh and Sir Felix?"

"I think they're gone up to Tolcarne, sir," said the butler.

Worse and worse: they were evidently liked there, too, and that was the reason why they prolonged their stay without a word of leaving.

"Is there anything I can get for you, sir?" said the butler.

"No," said Trevor, sharply.

And he walked out of the room, to encounter Mrs Lloyd, who was ready to smile and give him a curtsey; but he passed her with such an expression of anger that the blood flushed into her face, and she stood looking after him as, with his letters crumpled in his hand, he walked out into the grounds, to think over what he should next do.

"I'll send them both away," he thought. "That old woman's insolence is intolerable. It's plain enough. Pratt's right. Where is the little humbug? Out of the way just when I want him. I'll give that old woman such a setting down one of these days—but I have not time now."

He sat very still for a time, thinking of what he should do—Tiny's soft eyes haunting him the while, with their sad reproachful look.

He had seen very little of her, but, sailor-like, his heart had gone with a bound to her who had won it; and he was even now accusing himself of being dilatory in his love.

"Yes," he said, "I do love her, and very dearly. I'll see her, tell her frankly all, take her into my counsel, and she will believe me. I'm sure she will, and forgive me too. Humph! Forgive me for doing nothing. But I must talk to the old gentleman—propose in due form, ask his permission to visit his daughter, and the rest of it. Heigho! what a lot of formality there is in this life! I think I may cope with her, though. She looked so gently reproachful I could wait; but no, I mustn't do that. I'll call this afternoon and suffer the griffin. But those two fellows, why should they go up this morning? Evident that they did not see the ladies, for they were out. No wonder Van takes to making calls, seeing how I've neglected him and Flick. I wish Pratt were here. Where did he go?"

"Thy slave obeys," said Pratt, who had approached unobserved upon the soft turf! "Should you have liked Van to hear what you said just now?"

"No. Was I talking aloud?" said Trevor.

"You were, and very fast," was the reply.

"But what's the matter, Franky? What's the letter?"

And he pointed to an open missive in his friend's hand.

"It's about that I've come to you," said Pratt. "Read."

Trevor took the note, glanced over it, and found it was an invitation to Mr Frank Pratt to dine at Tolcarne on the following Friday. This brought Trevor's thoughts back to the letters Lloyd had given him, and he hastily took them from his pocket, to find a similar invitation to the one Pratt had had placed in his hand.

"That's lucky," he said, brightening.

"Lucky—why?" said Pratt.

"Because I want to go. But why are you looking so doleful?"

"Natural aspect, Dick. I only came to tell you I should not go."

"Not go! Why?"

"Because I am going back to town."

"Are you upset, Franky? Is anything wrong? I've been rude, I suppose, and said something that put you out this morning."

"No—oh no!"

"But I'm sure that must have been it. But really, old fellow, I was much obliged. Franky, you were quite right—it is as you say; so if I said anything when I was hipped, forgive me."

"Dick, old fellow," cried Pratt, grasping the extended hand, "don't talk of forgiveness to me. I have been here too long; this idle life don't suit me, and I've got to work."

"Work, then, and help me through my troubles. I can't spare you."

"Dick, old fellow, I feel that I must go. Don't ask me why."

"No, I won't ask you why," said Trevor, eyeing him curiously; "but, to oblige me, stay over this Friday, and go with me to the dinner."

Pratt hesitated a moment.

"Well, I will," he said; and the conversation ended.

During the intervening days Trevor was too much excited to say anything to Mrs Lloyd. He called at Tolcarne twice, but the ladies were out. He tried every walk in the neighbourhood, but without avail; and at last, blaming himself bitterly for his neglect of his guests, and thinking that the opportunity he sought must come on the Friday, he determined to try and make up for the past by attending to Vanleigh and Landells.

"I'll talk to Lady Rea about it—that's; how I'll manage," he said. "She's a good, motherly soul, and will set me right, I'm sure. I know—tell her I want advice and counsel; ask her to help me counteract Mrs Lloyd's designs."

Trevor laughed over what he considered the depth of his plans, and after dinner that night was in excellent spirits, losing thirty guineas to Vanleigh in a cheery way that made Pratt shudder for his recklessness, and bite his lips with annoyance at the cool manner in which the money was swept up.

"By the way," said Trevor, as they sat smoking, "what do you say to a sail to-morrow?—the yacht's in trim now, and the weather delightful."

"Thanks—no," said Vanleigh. "I don't think we can go, eh, Landells?"

"Jove!—no; drive, you know, with the old gentleman."

Trevor looked inquiringly from one to the other.

"Fact is," said Vanleigh, coolly, "Sir Hampton Rea has asked us to join him in a little picnic excursion to the north coast—drive over, you know, to-morrow. Yes, Thursday," he said, looking at his little note-book—one which usually did duty for betting purposes—"Yes, Thursday, and Friday we all dine there, of course."

"Yes, of course," said Trevor, in a quiet, constrained way, which made Sir Felix, who had already felt rather hot and confused, colour like a girl.

"Mustn't mind our running away from you so much, Trevor," continued Vanleigh, with a smile, which the former felt carried a sneer, and an allusion to his own playing of the absentee. "Fact is, the old gentleman seems to be rather taken with Flick here."

"'Sure you, no," said Sir Felix, excitedly; "it's the other way, Trevor. Makes no end of Van, showing him over grounds, asking 'vice, you know, and that sort of thing."

"I am glad you find the place so much more agreeable than you expected," said Trevor, gravely.

"Never s' jolly in m' life, Trevor," said Sir Felix, excitedly, and speaking nervously and fast. "Fine old fellow, S' Hampton. Fitting up b'liard-room. 'L have game after come back."

"Take another cigar," said Trevor, and his voice was very deep, as he seemed now to be exerting himself all that he could to make up for his past neglect to those whom he had invited down as his friends. "Vanleigh, you are taking nothing."

"I'm doing admirably, dear boy," said the captain, in the most affectionate of tones; and then to himself—"What does that little cad mean by watching me as he does?"

He smiled pleasantly, though, all the while, and when, to pass the time away, and conceal his trouble, Trevor once more proposed cards, the captain condescended to take "that little cad" as his partner, and between them they won fifty pounds of Trevor and Sir Felix—the latter throwing the cards petulantly down, and vowing he would play no more.

"Good night, dear boy," said Vanleigh, rising and yawning a few minutes after smilingly taking his winnings. "It's past one, and we shall be having our respected friend, Mrs Lloyd, to send us to bed."

A sharp retort was on Trevor's lip, but he checked it, and with a courtesy that was grave in spite of his efforts, wished him good night, saying—

"There is no fear of that; Mrs Lloyd and I understand each other pretty well now."

"Ya-as, exactly," said Vanleigh; and he went out whistling softly.

"Good night, Trevor," said Sir Felix, in turn. "'Fraid we're doocid bad comp'ny. Too bad, I'm sure, going 'way as we do."

"Good night, Flick," said Trevor, smiling; and then, as the door closed, he turned to find Pratt leaning against the chimneypiece, counting over his winnings. "Well, my lad!" continued Trevor, trying to be gay.

"Twenty-five pounds, Dick," said Pratt, laying the money on the table. "I shan't take that."

"Nonsense, man," said Trevor; "keep it till Van wins it back. But what's the matter? Have you found another of your mare's-nests?"

"I was thinking, Dick," said Pratt, gravely, "that you must be very sorry you asked any of us here."

Trevor's lips parted to speak; but without a word he wrung his friend's hand, took his candle, and hastily left the room.

Before Dinner

It was a busy day at Tolcarne, that of the dinner party. The picnic had not been a success. In fact, at one time, when very much bored by the attentions of Vanleigh, Tiny had gazed out to sea at a pretty little yacht gliding by, and longed to be on board—innocent, poor girl! of the fact that Dick Trevor was lying on the deck with a powerful lorgnette, seeing the party distinctly, and plainly making out the captain leaning on the rock by her side.

Fin, too, was no wiser—though, for quite a quarter of an hour Frank Pratt was gazing, with knitted brow, through a second lorgnette at the little rocky cove where Sir Felix Landells was pestering her with attentions, and evidently labouring under the impression that unless she partook of lobster salad every five minutes she must feel faint.

Aunt Matty was the only really happy person in the party. She had, to the dismay of all, announced her intention of going, feeling sure that the change would benefit Pepine; and the way in which Vanleigh and Landells tried in emulation to gratify her whims was most flattering to her.

Not that she was deceived by the attentions, and imagined them extorted by her charms; she knew well enough the visitors' aims, and was gratified at their discernment.

"They know how much depends upon my opinion," she said to herself; and she smiled graciously upon them both as one carried Pepine down the rocks, the other her shawl, and gave his arm; ending by playfully sending them afterwards to the girls.

"Old girl's warm, I know," said Vanleigh to himself.

"We must keep in with the old nymph, Van," said Sir Felix to him at the end of the day; just about the same time that Tiny was crying silently in her bedroom; and Fin striding up and down like a small tragedy queen.

"He's a born idiot, Tiny!" she exclaimed; "and what pa can mean by making such a fuss over him, and telling me it's a proud thing to become a lady of title, I don't know. Ahem!—Lady Landells—fine, isn't it? I don't see that dear ma's any happier for being Lady Rea."

"Papa seems infatuated with them," said Tiny, bitterly.

"Yes; and when he found that black captain paying you such attention, I saw him smile and rub his hands."

"Oh, don't Fin!" exclaimed Tiny, shuddering.

"I believe he's a regular Bluebeard. Look at the little blue-black dots all over his chin. I shouldn't be at all surprised if he's got half a dozen wives in a sort of Madame Tussaud's Blue Chamber of Horrors, preserved in waxwork."

"Pray don't be so foolish, Fin."

"Foolish? I don't call it foolish to talk about our future husbands."

"Fin!" cried her sister.

"Well, you see if that isn't what pa means! I saw Aunt Matty smirking about it and petting the captain; and ma was almost in tears about their goings on."

"Oh, Fin! don't talk so," said Tiny, sadly; "I shall never marry."

"Till you say Yes at the altar, and the bevy of beauteous bridesmaids dissolve in tears," laughed Fin. "I say, though, Tiny, I'm not going to be bought and sold like a heroine of romance. I wouldn't have that Sir Felix—no, not if he was ten thousand baronets; and if you listen to Bluebeard, Tiny, you are no sister of mine."

"Do you think papa seriously thinks anything of the kind?"

"I'm sure of it, dear, and—and—and—oh! Tiny, Tiny—I do feel so very, very miserable!"

To the surprise of her sister, she threw herself in her arms, and they indulged in the sweet feminine luxury of a good cry, ending by Fin declaring that she shouldn't go back to her own room; and more than once, even in sleep, the pillows upon which the two pretty little flushed faces lay, side by side, were wet with tears that stole from beneath their eyelids in their troubled dreams.

And now the day of the dinner had arrived, and Lady Rea had had such a furiously red face that Sir Hampton told her she ought to be ashamed of herself, and made the poor little woman, who had been fretting herself to death to do honour to his guests, shed tears of vexation.

Next there was a furious ringing of Sir Hampton's bell, about six o'clock, and a demand whether the house was to smell of cabbage like that.

As the odour did not pass away, Sir Hampton sought his lady, who had gone to dress, and again made her shed tears by exclaiming against his mansion being made to smell like a cookshop.

"It's that dreadful prize kitchener, Hampton, dear," said poor Lady Rea. "The smell comes into the house instead of going up the chimney."

"It's nothing of the sort—its your stupid servants!" exclaimed the knight, and he bounced off to his room to prepare for the banquet.

"I've a good mind to make myself ugly as sin, Tiny," said Fin, pettishly. But she did not, for she looked very piquante in her palest of pale blue diaphanous dresses, while her sister looked very sweet and charming in white.

"Why, Tiny, you look quite poorly," cried Fin, in alarm. "Pray, don't look like that, or that wretch Trevor will see that you've been fretting. If he prefers little servant-girls to my dear sister, let him have them."

"Fin, dear, you hurt me," said Tiny, simply; and there was such a tender, reproachful look in her sweet eyes that Fin gave a gulp, and, regardless of her get-up, threw herself on her sister's breast.

"I'm such a thoughtless wretch, Tiny; I won't say so any more."

"Please, Miss, your par says are you a coming down?" said the maid sent to summon them; and they went down, to find Sir Hampton in so violently stiff a cravat, that the wonder was how it was possible that it could be tied in a bow, and the spectator at last came to the conclusion that it had been starched after it was on.

Aunt Matty had, in her Irish poplin, a dress that was fearfully and wonderfully made, and dated back to about a quarter of a century before. It was of the colour of the herb whose perfume it exhaled—lavender; and every time you approached her you began to think of damask—not roses, but table-cloths and household linen, put away in great drawers, in a country house.

This is not a wardrobe style of story, but we must stay to mention the costume of Frances, Lady Rea, who came into the room with her cheeks redder than ever, although she had tried cold water, hot water, lavender water, and every cooling liquid she could think of. She was in peony red—a stiff silk of Sir Hampton's own choice, and she sought his eye, trembling lest he should be displeased; but as he emitted a crackle, produced by his cravat, as he bent his head in satisfactory assent, a bright smile shot across the pleasant face, dimpling it all over, and she exclaimed—

"Lor', my dears, how well you look. There, they may come now as soon as they like."

"Mind your dress, Fanny," said Aunt Matty, austerely, as she sat minding her own. "Sh!"

She held up her fan to command silence, as Sir Hampton cleared his throat, chuckled violently, and spoke—

"Er-rum, I think our guests will not find our circle much less attractive than—er-rum!—Ah, here they are!"

After Dinner

Sir Hampton was right—the visitors had arrived; and almost directly after the ordinary greetings, during which Tiny never raised her eyes, and Fin was so short that Sir Hampton darted an angry glance at her, the dinner was announced. Trevor took in Lady Rea; Vanleigh, Tiny; Landells, Fin; and Pratt, Aunt Matty—Sir Hampton bringing up the rear.

The dinner was good, and passed off with no greater mishaps than a slight distribution of the saccharine juices in a dish in the second course down the back of Aunt Matilda's poplin—Edward being the offender; but the sweetly gracious smile with which the lady bore her affliction was charming, and Fin looked her astonishment at her sister.

But the dinner was not a pleasant one, even if good; there was too much, "Thompson, that hock to Sir Felix Landells;" "Thompson, the dry champagne to Captain Vanleigh"—it was hard work to Sir Hampton not to add "of the Guards;" "Thompson, let Mr Trevor taste that Clos-Vougeot;" and it was a relief when the ladies rose.

"If he will talk about his cellar, Felix, punish it," whispered Vanleigh, as they drew closer; but Sir Felix Landells's thoughts were in the drawing-room, and though Sir Hampton persisted in talking about his cellar—how many dozens of this he had laid down, how many dozens of that; how he had been favoured by getting a few dozens of Sir Magnum O'pus's port at the sale, and so on ad infinitum—Sir Felix refrained from looking upon the wine when it was red; and as soon as etiquette allowed they joined the ladies in the drawing-room, where Trevor had the mortification of seeing Vanleigh resume his position by Tiny, while Landells loomed over Fin like an aristocratic poplar by a rose-bush.

Trevor consoled himself, though, by sitting down by pleasant Lady Rea, while Sir Hampton crackled at Pratt, talked politics to him, and his ideas of Parliament, and Aunt Matty fanned herself, as she treated Pepine to the sensation of lavender poplin as a couch.

"What a nice little man your friend is, Mr Trevor," began Lady Rea; "I declare he's the nicest, sensiblest man I ever met."

"I'm glad you like him, Lady Rea," said Trevor, earnestly; "but I want to talk to you."

"There isn't anything the matter, is there?" said Lady Rea, anxiously.

Trevor looked at her for an instant, and saw that in her face which quickened his resolve, already spumed into action by the markedly favoured attentions of Vanleigh to the elder daughter of the house.

"Lady Rea," he said, "I'm in trouble."

"I'm so sorry," she said, with simple, genuine condolence. "Can I help you?"

"Indeed you can," said Trevor; and he proceeded to tell her what he had discovered respecting Mrs Lloyd's designs.

"Well, I never knew such impudence!" cried Lady Rea, indignantly.

"You will sing now to oblige me," said Vanleigh; but for the time, Tiny declined, and Fin was carried off to the piano by Sir Felix.

"Do you know 'Won't you tell me why, Robin?'" said Sir Felix, beaming down at the little maiden.

"Yes," said Fin, sharply.

"Then do sing it."

"I shall sing 'Maggie's Secret' instead," said Fin, sending the colour flushing into her sister's face, as she rattled it out, with tremendous aplomb given to the words—

So I tell them they needn't come wooing to me.

Meanwhile, Trevor went on pouring his troubles into Lady Rea's attentive ears, as Sir Hampton prosed, Aunt Matty dozed with a smile on her countenance, Pepine snoozed in her lap in a satin tent made of his mistress's fan, and Poor Tiny longed for the hour when she could be alone.

"Lady Rea," said Trevor, at last, "I will not attempt to conceal my feelings—I think you can guess them, when I tell you that my trouble is that your daughter passed me in the wood talking to—questioning the little girl I have mentioned, and I read that in her face which seemed to say that she despised me."

"Then that's what's made Tiny so low-spirited for the last few days," said Lady Rea.

"God bless you for that!" said Trevor, in a low, hoarse voice, "you've made me very happy. Lady Rea, will you take my part? If I have no opportunity of explaining, will you do it for me? I am very blunt, I know—

recollect I am a sailor; so forgive me if I tell you that since I first met Miss Rea, I have scarcely ceased to think about her."

"I'm not cross with you for it," said Lady Rea, "and I will tell Tiny; but you mustn't ask me to interfere—I couldn't think of doing so. There," she whispered, "go and talk to her yourself."

And she gave the young fellow so pleasant a look, as their eyes met, that he knew that if the matter depended upon her, Tiny Rea would be his wife.

But there was no opportunity as yet, for Tiny had been unwillingly led to the piano, vacated by Fin, Sir Felix being buttonholed by Sir Hampton, and Pratt taking his place, and talking to the sharp-tongued little maid in a way that made her exclaim—

"How solemn you are!"

"Hush!" said Pratt. "Listen! What a sweet voice!"

"Yes, Tiny can sing nicely," replied Fin.

And they listened, as did Trevor, while, in a sweet, low voice, Tiny sang a pathetic old ballad with such pathos that a strangely sweet sense of melancholy crept over Trevor, and he stood gazing at her till the last note had ceased to thrill his nerves, when Vanleigh led her to her seat, and crossed to pay his court to Aunt Matty, awakened by the song.

"Now," whispered Lady Rea, "go and tell her how it was."

In strict obedience to the indiscreet advice, Trevor crossed to where Tiny was seated, offered his arm, and together they strolled into the handsome conservatory.

"Miss Rea," said Trevor, plunging at once in medias res, as Tiny made one or two constrained replies to his remarks, "I have been explaining to Lady Rea what trouble I am in."

"Trouble, Mr Trevor?" said Tiny, coldly.

"Yes: how I had ventured to hope that I had won the friendship of two ladies, and with the vanity, or weakness, of a sailor, I trusted that that friendship would ripen into something warmer."

"Mr Trevor," said Tiny, her voice trembling, "I must request—"

"Tiny, dear Tiny," cried Trevor, passionately, "I may have but a few moments to speak to you. Don't misjudge me, I have explained all to Lady Rea, and she will tell you. If I am mad and vain in hoping, forgive me—I cannot help it, for I love you dearly; and this that I see—these attentions—these visits—madden me."

"Mr Trevor, pray—pray don't say more!" exclaimed Tiny, glancing in the direction of the drawing-room.

"I must—I cannot help it," he whispered, passionately. "Tell me my love is without hope, and I will go back to sea and trouble you no more; but give me one little word, tell me if only that we are friends again, and that you will not misjudge me, or think of me as you did the other day in the wood. Tell me—confess this: you thought me wrong?"

"I had no right to judge you, Mr Trevor," said Tiny, in a trembling voice; "but—but my sister—and I—"

"Tiny," whispered Trevor, catching her land in his, "my darling, I could not have a thought that you might not read. Give me one word—one look. Heaven bless you for this."

Young men are so thoughtless, so full of the blind habits of the sand-hiding ostrich at such times, and so wrapped up was Richard Trevor, sailor and natural unspoiled man, in the soft, gentle look directed at him from Tiny's timid, humid eyes, that, regardless of the fact that they were close to the drawing-room, the chances are that he might have gone farther than kissing the little blue-veined hand he held in his, had not, from behind a clump of camellias, a harsh voice suddenly exclaimed—

"Now, then, am I right?"

Sir Hampton Rea and Aunt Matty appeared upon the scene.

Dear Aunt Matty had had her way, and was satisfied. Quiet as she was, she had her suspicions of Trevor's earnest talk to Lady Rea; and when Vanleigh drew her attention to the fact that the two imprudent young people had strolled off into the conservatory, by saying, "I suppose Miss Rea finds the room too close?" she gave him a significant look.

"Sit down and hold Pepine for me, Captain Vanleigh," she said, in a low voice, "and I'll soon put a stop to that."

Vanleigh said something very naughty, sotto voce, and then, as he felt bound to flatter Aunt Matty, he seated himself, and nursed the wretched little dog, while Aunt Matty made her way to Sir Hampton, who was deep in a political speech, to which Sir Felix kept saying "Ya-as" and "Ver' true," eyeing Fin the while through his glass.

Fin's sharp eyes detected something wrong, and she tried a flank movement.

"Go and tell my sister I want her directly, Mr Pratt," she said—"in the conservatory."

It was too late; Aunt Matty's forced march had done it.

"Eh! what? Er-rum!" ejaculated Sir Hampton.

Then he followed his sister out into the conservatory, where she made the before-mentioned remark, and Sir Hampton, turning port wine colour, caught his daughter by the wrist.

"Go to bed this instant!" he exclaimed, reverting in his rage to the punishment inflicted years before. "As to you, sir—"

"Excuse me, Sir Hampton," said Trevor, boldly.

"Let me speak," said Aunt Matty, with great dignity. "Hampton, this is neither the time nor the place to have words about the works of the wicked. I warned you, but you would not take heed. Valentina, you are not to go to bed, but to return to the drawing-room as if nothing had happened. Hampton, you must not disturb your other guests—the strangers sojourning in peace within your gates."

At a time like this Aunt Matty was too much for Sir Hampton. She had girded herself as she would have termed it; and when Aunt Matty girded herself her words were like a strong solution of tracts, and she became a sort of moral watering-pot, with which she sprinkled the wicked and quenched their anger. Sir Hampton never so much as said "Er-rum!" at such times, and now seeing the wisdom of her words, he picked two or three flowers, and walked back into the drawing-room with Tiny, the poor girl trying hard to conceal her agitation.

Trevor was about to follow, but Aunt Matty stopped him.

"Sit down there, young man," she said, severely.

"If you wish to speak to me, certainly," said Trevor, politely; "but what I have to say must be to Sir Hampton, with all respect to you."

"Sit down there for five minutes, young man, and then you can return."

Trevor fumed—the position was so ridiculous; but he accepted it, glancing the while at his watch, and then fighting hard to preserve his gravity before the stiff figure in whose presence he sat. For, in spite of the annoyance, a feeling of joyous hilarity had come upon the offender against decorum: he knew that Tiny loved him, and doubtless a few words of explanation would be listened to when Sir Hampton was cool, and then all would come right.

"I think the five minutes are up, Miss Rea," said Trevor, rising. "Perhaps you will take my arm, and we can stroll back as if nothing had happened. I will see Sir Hampton in the morning."

Aunt Matty bowed, and then, wearing the aspect of some jointless phenomenon, she stalked by his side back into the drawing-room, where, in spite of the efforts of Lady Rea and Vanleigh, nothing could disperse the gloom that had fallen; and the party broke up with the departure of the gentlemen, who walked home on account of the beauty of the night—Vanleigh talking incessantly, and Trevor quiet, but striving hard to conceal his triumph.

"I'll ease him as much as possible," Trevor had said to himself, àpropos of Vanleigh.

"Poor brute! he little thinks how he's shelved," said Vanleigh to Landells.

"Little girl's pos'tively b'witching," said Landells.

"Who, Miss Rea?"

"Jove! No—sister. Sharp and bright as lit' needle."

"Just suit you, there, Flick."

"Ya-as."

"It came to a climax, then, Dick, eh?" said Pratt.

"Franky, old boy, I'm the happiest dog under the sun."

These fragments of conversation took place at odd times that night; and the next morning, soon after breakfast, Trevor made an excuse to his friends, and started for Tolcarne.

"Gone to get his congé, Flick," said Vanleigh.

"Poor Trevor! Sorry. Not bad 'fler," said Sir Felix.

"Bah! every man for himself. But we shall have to clear out after this. We'll go and stay at Saint Francis, and when the old boy finds we are there, he'll ask us up to Tolcarne."

"But seems so shabby to poor Trevor," said Sir Felix.

"Pooh, nonsense! Every man has his crosses in this way. Let's get out somewhere, though, so as not to be at hand when the poor beggar comes back; he'll be in a towering fury. I hope he won't make an ass of himself, and force a quarrel on me."

Speaking to Papa

Meanwhile Trevor was on his way to Tolcarne, where he was shown into the library. He felt flushed and excited, but he had come with the confidence of a conqueror; and, besides, he could feel that he was no ineligible parti for the young lady.

"Poor Franky, I know he's bitten by that little fairy," he said, as he waited impatiently—the "directly" of Edward, who had announced that Sir Hampton was in the garden and would come, having extended to ten minutes.

"Hang the formality of these things!" said Trevor. "I could talk to that dear little woman, Lady Rea, by the hour without feeling uncomfortable; but as to pater—well, there; it's only once in a man's life. Here he is."

The door leading into a farther passage opened this moment, and Trevor rose; but instead of encountering fierce Sir Hampton, in skipped petite Fin, to run up to him flushed and excited, but with her eyes sparkling with pleasure.

She placed both her little hands in his, and her words came in hurried jerks, as she exclaimed—

"Tiny told me all about it—last night—Oh, I'm so glad!"

"That's right, little fairy," laughed Trevor, smiling down on the pleasant little *face*.

"But there's been such a rumpus, and I came to tell you before pa came."

"Indeed," said Trevor, retaining the little hands, though there was no effort made to remove them.

"Yes, pa's been raging and bullying poor Tiny so. Those friends of yours came and proposed for us, and papa said they might come, and he is horribly cross about it. But you won't give way?"

"Do I look as if I would?" said Trevor.

"No; and I am glad, because I think you do like Tiny."

"Like?"

"Well, love her, then. Ma likes you, too."

"And little Fin?"

"There's little Fin's answer," said the girl, with tears in her eyes, and she held up her face and kissed him with quiet gravity. "Oh, let me go," she cried, and she struggled from his arms and fled, leaving him to turn round and face Sir Hampton and Aunt Matty, who had entered by the other door.

"What does this mean, sir?" exclaimed Sir Hampton, furiously. "Er-rum! I am astounded!"

"Merely, Sir Hampton, that your daughter was willing to accord to me the licence that she would to a brother."

Aunt Matty was heard to mutter something about vulgar assurance, and Trevor flushed as Sir Hampton motioned him to a chair, took one, and crossed his legs; but he was determined not to be angry, and he went on—

"Our meetings, so far, Sir Hampton, have been unfortunate, and I have come over this morning to try and set myself at one with you. I presume I am to speak before Miss Rea?"

"My sister is in my confidence, and is my adviser," said Sir Hampton, in the tone he had prepared for the magisterial bench.

"Then, Sir Hampton, speaking as a frank, blunt sailor, I humbly ask your pardon for any lapses of politeness wherein I have been guilty, and also beg of you to forgive me for my conduct last night."

"A perfect outrage—barbarous," said Aunt Matty.

"Er-rum!—Matilda, let the young man speak," said Sir Hampton, magisterially.

"It was, I am aware, very foolish of me, but I was carried away by my feelings. Sir Hampton Rea, I love your daughter, Valentina."

"Absurd!" exclaimed Miss Matilda, who remained standing.

"I ventured to tell her so last night, in explaining away a little misapprehension that had existed between us."

"I never heard such assurance!" said Miss Matilda.

"Matty—er-rum! Matilda, I mean, have the goodness not to interrupt the pris—I mean—er-rum—the statement that is being made."

"If I could feel warrant for such a proceeding," continued Trevor, calmly, "I intended to speak to you this morning, and ask your consent, even as I spoke to Lady Rea last night, before I addressed your daughter."

"Just like Fanny—encouraging it!" muttered Aunt Matty.

"Go on, sir, I am listening," said Sir Hampton, telling himself this was quite a preparation for the bench.

"I came, then, Sir Hampton, to formally propose for your daughter's hand. Though comparatively a stranger to you, I am well known here—of one of the most ancient county families—and I have eight thousand a year. That, Sir Hampton, is putting the matter in a plain, business-like form. If I am wanting in the proper etiquette, my excuse is my seafaring life."

"Exactly," said Aunt Matty, satirically.

The words "prisoner at the bar" were on Sir Hampton's lips, but he did not utter them; he only rolled his words nice and round, and infused as much dignity as was possible into his tones. "The young man" had insulted him, but he could afford to treat him with dignified composure.

"Mr Trevor," he began, "I have listened to your remarks with patience"— magisterial here, very—"I have, er-rum I heard your application. For your friends' sake, I was willing to condone"—capital magisterial word, and he liked it so much that he said it again—"er-rum! to condone that which was past. Er-rum! but under the circumstances, near neighbours as we are, I think it better that all communication"—the clearest magisterial tone here, and repeated—"er-rum! communication between us should cease."

"Decidedly!" put in Aunt Matty, arranging her mittens.

"Er-rum—hear me out, sir"—a magisterial wave of the hand here, and a quiet settling down into the chair, as of one about to pass sentence—"Er-rum—as to your formal matrimonial proposals, they are quite out of the question. Captain Vanleigh has honoured me by proposing for my daughter Valentina's hand, and he is accepted."

"By the young lady?" exclaimed Trevor.

"Er-rum! there is no occasion for us to enter upon that point, Mr Trevor, for—tut! tut! what do you want here, Lady Rea?—this is business."

"Fanny!" exclaimed Miss Matilda, as her sister-in-law entered the room, walked up to Trevor, shook hands very warmly, and then accepted the chair he vacated on her behalf.

"Thank you, Mr Trevor. Matty, I think any of my husband's affairs that are business for you, are business for me," said Lady Rea, firmly; "and as I know why Mr Trevor has visited us this morning, I came down."

Aunt Matty looked yellow with anger, and for a few moments Sir Hampton's magisterial dignity was so upset that he could only ejaculate "Er-rum" three times at a few seconds' interval. It was awful, this manifestation of firmness on his wife's part, and he could only glare fiercely.

"What have you been saying to Mr Trevor?" said Lady Rea, earnestly.

"Sir Hampton informs me that the young lady is irrevocably engaged to Captain Vanleigh," said Trevor, quietly. "May I appeal to Miss Rea?"

"My daughters will leave us to discriminate as to—er-rum—what is good for them," said Sir Hampton, stiffly. "Mr Trevor, we must bring this very unpleasant interview to an end. Sir—er-rum!—you have heard my—er-rum—ultimatum!"

Aunt Matty bowed, and smiled a wintry smile, that was as cold as her steely eyes.

Trevor directed a piteous look at Lady Rea, and without a moment's hesitation she exclaimed—

"It's all stuff and nonsense, Hampy! I won't stand by and see either of my darlings made miserable!"

"Frances!" exclaimed Aunt Matty.

"Er-rum!" exclaimed Sir Hampton, and he sent at his wife a withering look.

"You can say what you like," cried the little lady, ruffling up like a very bantam hen in defence of her chicks; and now, for the first time, Trevor saw a trace of Fin. "I say I won't stand by and see my darlings made miserable. Tiny told me not ten minutes ago, crying up in her own room as if her heart would break, that she would sooner die than listen to Captain Vandells."

"Vanleigh," said Aunt Matilda, contemptuously.

"Vandells, or Vanleigh, or Vandunk, I don't care a button what his ugly Dutch name is!" cried Lady Rea, angrily; "and I say it shan't go on!"

"Hampton!" began Aunt Matty, "do you intend—"

"Didn't I tell you not to interfere, Matilda?" exclaimed Sir Hampton, pettishly.

Aunt Matty darted an indignant glance at him, gathered up her skirts, and sailed out of the room, Sir Hampton wiping his perspiring brow.

"I thank you for your kindness, Lady Rea," said Trevor. "I will go now; perhaps another time Sir Hampton will accord me an interview."

"No; don't you go, my dear boy," said Lady Rea, earnestly, and she took his hand. "I give way in nearly everything, but I'm not going to give way in this."

"Fanny, this is foolishness," said Sir Hampton, who looked as if in a state of collapse.

"It's such foolishness as this that makes people happy," said Lady Rea; "and if Mr Trevor loves my darling, as I know she loves him, no one shall stand in their way."

"But, Fanny," said Sir Hampton, "I..."

"Look here, Hampy, you used to be very fond of me. Now, how would you have liked my father to make me marry some one else?"

"May I come in?" said a little voice; and Fin peeped in, entered, and closed the door. "I saw Aunt Matty go, so I came. Oh, pa, dear, Tiny is in such trouble—how could you?"

She seated herself on his knee, nestled up to him, and the knight began to stroke her hair.

"There now," said Fin, "I knew pa would be a dear kind old dad, as soon as he knew about Tiny. There now, I may fetch her down."

"No, no, Finetta, certainly not, I..."

Fin was gone.

"There, Hampy," said Lady Rea, going up to him, "you do love your children."

"I don't like it—I—I protest against it!" exclaimed Sir Hampton, struggling against the bonds his woman folk had wreathed around him.

"Sir Hampton," said Trevor, holding out his hand, "say you relent."

"And—er-rum!—how the deuce—devil am I to face those gentlemen?" exclaimed Sir Hampton.

"I'll see them," said Lady Rea, firmly. "Here's Tiny."

In effect that young lady entered, red-eyed, wet-cheeked, and blushing, to throw herself on her father's breast, and cling there sobbing violently, while Fin took the precaution to lock the door.

"I don't like it, Tiny, I—er-rum!—I..."

"Oh, dear papa, I could not marry him," sobbed Tiny—and her emotion was so excessive that Sir Hampton grew frightened, and soothed and petted her till her sobs grew less violent, when Trevor approached and took her hand, and unresistingly drew her to him, till she hid her face in his breast.

Then there was a fine scene. Poor Lady Rea ran up to them, kissed Tiny, and tried to kiss Trevor, but could not reach, till he bent lower. After which she broke into a violent fit of sobbing, and plumped herself down in the nearest chair, Fin tending her for a moment, and then fetching Sir Hampton to her side, to ask forgiveness.

Next there was a general display of pocket-handkerchiefs. Fin gave a hysterical hurrah, and kissed everybody in turn, ending by exclaiming, as she sobbed aloud—

"And now we're all happy!"

In fact there were smiles upon every face but Sir Hampton's, and he, feebly saying he did not like it, was left alone as the party adjourned to the drawing-room.

"Lady Rea, I have you to thank for this," said Trevor, affectionately. "How am I ever to show it?"

"By being very, very, very kind to my darling there," said Lady Rea, pitifully; "for you're a bad, cruel man to come and win away her love."

Then, of course, there was a great deal more kissing, ending in a burst of merriment; for Fin dashed, wet-eyed, to the piano, and rattled off, "Haste to the Wedding," running into Mendelssohn's "Wedding March," till Tiny went and closed the instrument.

At that moment Edward, the footman, knocked at the door, and entered, saying to Lady Rea—

"If you please, m'lady, Miss Matilda's took bad, and wants the doctor. Who shall I send?"

"Gracious, Edward! what is it?" said Lady Rea.

"Please, m'lady, they think it's spasms," said the footman.

Lady Rea ran out, and the doctor was sent for from St Kitt's; but, by the time he arrived, Aunt Matty's spasms were better.

And so Richard Trevor, master of Penreife, became engaged to Valentina Rea, of Tolcarne.

Very Dreamy

Trevor heard it afterwards from Fin, how that mamma saw Captain Vanleigh when he called with Sir Felix; Sir Hampton leaving a note, and—so Fin declared—hiding in the gardener's toolhouse till the visit was over; and that she had, at the earnest wish of Sir Felix, seen him in the drawing-room.

"Where he made the most downright booby of himself you ever saw," said Fin.

And the result was that one morning, after the most elaborate fencing had been going on between Trevor and his guests, one vieing with the other in politeness, Pratt met his old schoolfellow on his return from Tolcarne with—

"Thank goodness, Dick, there's peace in the grove."

"What do you mean, Franky?" said Trevor, who was rather uneasy at having heard from Lady Rea that Sir Felix and Vanleigh had been up to the house while he was away with the girls, and had a long interview with Sir Hampton and Aunt Matty.

"Mean, Dick? Why, that the telegram has come at last—message from St Kitt's—Vanleigh and Flick wanted directly in town—so sorry couldn't stop to say good-bye, and that sort of thing."

"Then they are gone?"

"Yes. I ordered round the waggonette; and Mrs Lloyd seems in ecstasies at the clear-out, and is getting ready to bestow a benediction on me—for I must be off next."

"Nonsense, Franky; you are happy enough here."

"No, old fellow—this Sybarite's life is spoiling me, and I must go."

"Why not follow my example, Franky?" said Trevor, laughing.

Pratt shrugged his shoulders, and the matter dropped for the time being.

The next evening the Reas dined at Penreife in great state and dignity—all but Aunt Matty, who steadily refused pardon, and turned her back upon

Trevor; while Sir Hampton preserved a dignified composure upon the matter, as if submitting of necessity; for—

"Mark my words, Hampton," his sister had said, "this ridiculous marriage will never take place. I should as soon expect Finetta to be espoused by that wretched little companion of the seafaring man."

Sir Hampton grunted, and went to the dinner, which he thoroughly enjoyed, and softened a good deal over his wine; after which, the evening being delicious, he allowed himself to be inveigled into the grounds, where Trevor asked his advice respecting some new forcing-houses which he proposed having, listening to him with deference; and at last, when they strolled in through the open drawing-room window, Sir Hampton said aloud—

"Er-rum—yes, Trevor, I'll come over with Sanders—say Wednesday—and he shall mark out the lines on the same plan as mine. I think I can put you in the way of many improvements."

Directly after, he was settled in an easy-chair, with his handkerchief spread upon his knees, thinking—with his eyes closed; and while he thought, everybody spoke in a whisper, for it was a custom with Sir Hampton Rea to think for half an hour after dinner—with his eyes closed: he never took a nap.

Lady Rea, looking rosy, round, and warm, was presiding at the tea-table; and Tiny, blushing and happy, was rearranging some flowers, Frank Pratt helping her in a loving, deferential manner, very different from his general easy-going way; while Fin had caught Trevor by the arm, led him into the far window, and forced him back into a chair, before which she stood, holding up a menacing finger.

"I'm ashamed of you, Dick—I am indeed," she said, sharply.

"Ashamed!" he exclaimed. "Why?"

"Such cunning, such artfulness! I didn't give you credit for it."

"What do you mean?"

"Coaxing pa round like that, when you no more want hothouses than I do. There, go away, sir; I'm disgusted. Look! ma's beckoning to you."

In effect, Lady Rea was cautiously making signals from the tea-tray; and on Trevor going to her, Pratt slowly crossed to the window, and began to talk to Fin.

"Do you know, Miss Rea, I find I've been here six weeks," he said awkwardly.

"You don't say so, Mr Pratt," said Fin, quietly.

Pratt stared, and went on.

"The time has gone like magic."

"Has it really?" said Fin, demurely.

"Yes," said Pratt a little bitterly; "and as I have decided upon returning to town in a day or two, I thought I'd take this opportunity of saying good-bye."

"I think its the very best thing you can do, Mr Pratt," said Fin, sharply.

"What, say good-bye?"

"No, go back to town. You will be industrious there. See what's come to your poor friend by mooning about in the country."

She nodded her saucy head in the direction of Trevor, who was bending over Tiny—she looking shyly conscious and happy—while Lady Rea beamed upon them both; and Sir Hampton thought so deeply with his eyes closed, that he emitted something much like a stertorous snore.

"Yes, dear old Dick's very happy," said Pratt, gravely. "Rich, loved, and with the fixture all sunshine. She's a sweet girl."

"Yes, a rose—with a thorn of a sister, ready to pester her husband," said Fin. "Yes, Mr Pratt, you had better go. It is not good for young men to be idle."

"So I have been thinking," said Pratt—"especially poor fellows like myself."

"How is our little friend?" said Fin, maliciously.

"What little friend?"

"The little, round-cheeked niece of Mrs Lloyd—Polly, isn't her name?"

"Really, I don't know, Miss Rea," said Pratt, smiling.

"Fie, Mr Pratt!" said Fin. "Why, you are always being seen with her in the lane. Is it true you are to be engaged?"

Pratt looked at her sharply.

"Does it give you so much pleasure to tease?" he said, quietly.

"Tease? I thought it was a settled thing."

"I don't think you did," said Pratt, quietly.

"Well," said Fin, laughing, "Mr Mervyn told me the other day that—oh, look at that now!"

The last words were said by Fin to herself; for as she mentioned Mr Mervyn's name Pratt turned slowly away, and going to a table began to turn over the leaves of a book.

In the meantime Lady Rea had had a few words with Trevor.

"I declare I felt quite frightened of her, my dear."

"It's her way only," said Trevor, smiling. "She nursed me like a mother, Lady Rea; and she and her husband have for years done almost as they liked here, only checked by the agent and my poor father's executors, who seem to have come down once a year to look at the place so long as they lived; but they have both gone now."

"She looked dreadfully cross, though, at Tiny—just as if, my dear, she was horribly jealous of her. And now, Richard, my dear, you won't be offended if I ask a favour of you?"

"Certainly not," said Trevor, in the same low whisper in which the conversation was carried on.

"Then make her send that niece of hers away. After what you told me, I'm sure it would be for the best; because while she is here the poor woman will always be thinking of her disappointed plans."

"Well, but," said Trevor, smiling, "I was thinking of hurrying on her marriage with my keeper, Humphrey; the poor fellow is desperately fond of her, and, as far as I can make out, the feeling is mutual."

"Oh, if that's it," said Lady Rea, "pray don't do anything to make the young people unhappy."

"Yes, Trevor," said Sir Hampton, "fifty feet by twenty will be the size."

The conversation was carried on henceforth in voices pitched now in the normal key.

The distance was so short that it was decided to walk back through the moonlit lane, and as Trevor and Pratt accompanied the party, it was a matter of course that Fin should walk papa off first, Lady Rea following with Pratt, and Tiny lingering behind in the silvered arcades—dreamy, loving, too happy to speak, and feeling that if life would but always be the same, how could they ever tire?

Here, in the rugged lane, all was black darkness, and the gnarled tree trunks seemed to spring from sable velvet. A few yards farther, a sheaf of silver arrows seemed shot down through the foliage upon the laced ferns that rose like a tiny forest of palms; down by their side there was the rippling tinkle of water, gurgling amongst stones; and again a few steps, and a pool shone like molten silver. Above all, the air was soft, humid, and balmy; and love seemed breathed in the gentle wind that barely stirred the leaves. They had no need to talk, for it was very sweet; and they could foresee no black clouds to come sweeping across their horizon.

Tolcarne gates at last, new and crest-crowned — good-bye — and then out cigars, and a matter-of-fact walk back, the young men both too dreamy to speak. And after a brief "Good night, Dick, old fellow" — "Good night, Franky, old boy," each sought his room — Trevor thinking the while of Lady Rea's words, and how that he had hardly seen Polly lately, while he had been too happy in his love to so much as think of Mrs Lloyd and her baffled plans. For her part, she seemed to have avoided him ever since she had heard of the engagement that he had made.

"Ah, well," he said, smiling, as he gazed from the open window at the moonlit shimmering sea, "all these things come right in the end. What need have I to trouble, with life so pleasurably spread out before me? Heigho! I don't deserve such good luck; but I think I can bear it like a good man and true. I wonder, though, whether Frank really cares for little Fin!"

Ten minutes after, Trevor was dreaming happily of his love, without a sign of cloud or storm in his sunlit fancies; but they were gathering fast the while.

A Little Confession

But Mrs Lloyd, though quiet for a time, and letting matters rest till the termination of Vanleigh and Sir Felix Landells's visit, was anything but dormant.

The fact was, that Vanleigh had been in the way upon more than one occasion. When Polly had been sent for a walk in the hope of enchanting the "young master," Vanleigh had met her, and been so attentive that the girl had come back at last, sobbing and almost defiant, telling her aunt that sooner than be so treated she would run away back to the mountains in Wales.

This put a stop to it for the time, and Aunt Lloyd waited, hearing rumours that the two London visitors were engaged to the young ladies of Tolcarne, and rubbing her hands thereon, for these were threatened rivals out of the way.

Her encounters with Trevor had been few and far between; but all seemed satisfactory, and, to use her own words, she "bided her time."

When the news came to her ears, endorsed by the sudden departure of the visitors, and further confirmed by the many visits to Tolcarne, and lastly by the coming of the Reas to Penreife, that Trevor was engaged to Valentina Rea, the woman was furious.

"It shan't go on, Lloyd—I won't have it. I'll put a stop to it. He shall marry Polly, or—"

"Martha, Martha!" cried her husband, wringing his hands—"you will ruin us."

"Ruin! I'll ruin him—an upstart! I'll have him on his knees to me. After the way in which I brought him up, to turn upon me like this. He shall marry Polly!"

"How can you be so mad?" groaned Lloyd. "Oh, Martha, think of our old age."

"Think!" said Mrs Lloyd, contemptuously, "I do think. Mad? Isn't a girl with the blood of the Lloyds in her veins better than the daughter of an upstart London merchant? There—hold your tongue; and don't you interfere. I'm not going to be stopped in my plans, so I tell you. Lloyd, are you asleep?"

"No," said her husband, with a heavy sigh, "I wish I was, so as to forget my troubles."

"You dolt!" exclaimed Mrs Lloyd. "Have you seen Humphrey hanging about lately?"

There was no answer.

"I say, have you seen Humphrey hanging about or talking to Polly lately? I don't want to think the girl artful; but she has been very quiet, and I hardly like it. Lloyd, do you hear what I say?"

There was a long-drawn breath for reply, and Mrs Lloyd went on making her plans—giving her husband the credit of being asleep.

But the latter was very wide awake, and he had seen something that night of which he did not wish to tell. For while Mrs Lloyd had been busy with the company that evening, there had come a soft tap on the housekeeper's room window, whose effect was to make little Polly turn violently red in the face, begin to tremble, then, after listening at the door, steal out, little thinking that the butler had seen her go.

Of course it was very artful and very wrong, but it is an acknowledged fact that there is a certain magnetism in love; and, to go back to the simile before used, when the loadstone came what could the industrious little needle do?

The next morning, after breakfast, Mrs Lloyd called Polly to her.

"Found out at last," thought poor Polly.

She went shivering up to her very stern-countenanced aunt, with the recollection of twenty sweet but stolen meetings on her conscience.

"Go and put on your white muslin dress and blue ribbons, Polly," said her aunt.

"Are we going out, aunt?" faltered the girl.

"You are, my dear," said Mrs Lloyd; "so put on your hat—the new one, mind."

"Please, aunt, I'd rather not go," faltered the girl.

"Go and dress yourself this minute," exclaimed the housekeeper, firmly: "and look here, if you dare to cry, and make those eyes red, I'll punish you."

Polly shivered, went to her room, and came back, looking as pretty a little rustic rosebud as could be seen for miles around.

"Ah," said Mrs Lloyd, hanging about her with a grim smile on her face, to give a pull at a plait here, a brush at a fold there, and ending by smoothing the girl's soft hair—"if he can resist that, he's no man."

"Please, aunt, what do you mean?" pleaded the girl. "Don't send me out again."

"There are no captains about now, goose, are there?" said the housekeeper, angrily.

"No, aunt, dear," faltered the girl; "but don't send me out. What do you mean?"

"What do I mean?" exclaimed Mrs Lloyd; "as if you didn't know what I mean. To raise the house of Lloyd, child—to make you mistress of Penreife—"

"Oh, aunt!"

"Instead of letting you throw yourself away upon a common servant."

"Aunt—aunt, dear!" cried the girl, piteously.

But the woman stopped her.

"Not another word. Now, look here—do I speak plain?"

"Yes, aunt."

"Hush!—no crying. You are to be Mrs Richard Trevor, with a handsome husband, and plenty of money. If you don't know what's good for you, I do. Now go out for a walk; and when he meets you, if you don't smile on him, and lead him on, I'll—I'll—There, I believe I shall poison you!"

The girl turned, shivering, from the fierce-looking face, as if believing the threat, and hurried out of the house.

"If Humphrey don't take me away I shall go and drown myself," she cried, with a sob. "Oh, it's dreadful! He will hate me for this, and if Mr Richard sees me, what will he think!"

Poor Polly's life had been a very hard one. So accustomed was she to blindly obey, that it never occurred to her that she might take any other route than the one so often indicated by her aunt; and she went as usual—ready to cry, but not daring, and thinking bitterly of her position.

"If I had only been a man," she thought, "I'd run away to sea, and—here he is."

"Ah, little maiden," exclaimed Trevor—for Mrs Lloyd had timed the matter well—"why, how bright and pretty you look!"

"Please, sir, I'm very sorry," faltered the girl.

"Sorry! Why? Have you come out here," he continued, suspiciously, "to meet Humphrey?"

"Please, sir—no, sir," said the girl, looking appealingly in his frank face.

"Having a walk then, eh?"

"Please, sir, aunt sent me," said the girl.

"Polly, my little maid, I believe you are a good girl," said Trevor, his face growing dark—"there, don't cry, I'm not angry with you. Speak out, and trust me. You are not afraid of me?"

"Oh no, sir. Humphrey says you're so good and kind," said the girl.

"Thanks to Humphrey for his good opinion," said Trevor. "But, now, tell me plainly, what does all this mean?"

"Please, sir, I dursen't," sobbed the girl.

"Nonsense, child! Tell me directly."

"Aunt would kill me," sobbed Polly.

"Stuff, child! Now, be a good, sensible little girl, and fancy I'm Humphrey."

"Oh, sir—please, sir, I couldn't do that."

"Come, come, speak out. Now, do you come of your own accord for these walks?"

"No, sir. I—I—Aunt makes me."

"I thought so—I supposed so," said Trevor. "And why do you come?"

"Oh, sir, don't ask me, please—don't ask me," sobbed Polly, now crying out-right.

"Now, look here, my little girl; if you'll speak plainly perhaps I can help you. Once more, why do you come here? There, there, don't cry."

"Oh, please, sir, it's—it's aunt's doing."

"Well, well, child, speak," said Trevor, and he took the girl's hand. "It makes me cross when you will keep on crying."

"Pray, sir, don't—pray, don't," she sobbed, trying to withdraw her hand. "Oh! what shall I do?"

"Speak put," said Trevor.

"Aunt—aunt thinks, sir—wants, sir—you to marry me, sir; and oh!" she cried, throwing herself on her knees, and holding up her little hands as in prayer, "I do hate you so—I do, indeed!"

"Thank you, little one," exclaimed Trevor, laughing merrily. "There, Polly, get up before you stain that pretty dress with the moss. Wipe your little eyes, and leave off hating me as soon as you can, and you shall marry Humphrey."

"Oh, sir!" faltered Polly, rising.

"There, little one, go and walk about till your eyes are not red; and if you should see Humphrey down by the long copse, where they are repairing the ditches, tell him I shall want to see him about three—no, stop, say this evening. I am going for a drive."

Polly hesitated a moment, and then caught and kissed his hand, shrinking back the next moment, ashamed at her boldness.

"There, I thought you would not hate me," said Trevor. "I'll go back at once and see your aunt. You shan't be unhappy any more, little maiden."

"Oh, pray, sir!" cried Polly again.

"I'm master here, my child; and I won't have anybody about me made unhappy if I can stay it. Now, trot along."

The girl gave him one timid glance, and then went on, while he turned in the direction of Penreife.

Before he had gone far, though, he turned back, with a smile on his lip.

"I'll wager a sovereign," he thought, "that Humphrey was not down at the long copse, but pretty close at hand, watching for the safety of his sweetheart."

He walked sharply back to a curve in the woodland path, and found that he was right; for some distance ahead he caught sight of Polly's pretty muslin dress, and across it there was plainly visible a bar of what resembled olive velveteen.

"Eight," said Trevor, smiling. "Well, why shouldn't they be happy too? Now, then, to have it out with Mrs Lloyd."

A Revelation

"If you please," said a hard, cold voice.

And Richard Trevor started to find himself face to face with the object of his remark, one which he had uttered aloud.

Trevor stood for a moment looking round; but they were quite alone, and standing now in the lane where Mr Mervyn captured Fin Rea in the rugged tree far up the rocky bank.

"You had better return to the house, Mrs Lloyd," said Trevor, coldly. "I want to speak to you."

"You can speak now, if you please," said the woman, in a low, suppressed voice. "I don't suppose you would like the servants to know."

Trevor was getting angry, and he took a step towards the woman, and held up a finger.

"You have been watching me, Mrs Lloyd."

"Yes," she said, coolly—"I came on purpose."

"You sent that poor girl here, then, Mrs Lloyd, and you have been playing the spy?"

"You can call it any hard names you like, Mr Richard," said the woman, defiantly.

She rolled her white apron round her arms, tightened her lips until they formed a thin livid line, and looked at him without flinching.

Trevor bit his lip to keep down his rising passion, and then went on—

"Mrs Lloyd," he said, "I thought we had made a truce. Mind, you are the one who breaks it, not I."

The woman laughed mockingly.

"We may as well understand one another," said Trevor; "so speak out. You have been forcing that poor girl, day after day, to throw herself in my way—have you not?"

"Yes."

She nodded her head many times, as she said the word with quite a sharp hiss.

"You wanted me to take a fancy to her?"

"Yes."

"To marry her?"

"Yes."

"And make her the mistress of Penreife?"

"Yes; and I mean to do it."

Trevor stared at her, in wonder at the effrontery displayed.

"And, in your foolish vanity, you thought such a thing possible?"

"Yes."

"Regardless of the poor girl's feelings?"

"Yes—yes—yes!" said Mrs Lloyd, slowly. "I know what is for her good—and yours."

"Mrs Lloyd," said Trevor, coldly, "I would gladly keep to my promise with you, that you should never leave Penreife. If harm to your prospects comes of this, don't blame me. You had better go back to the house."

He turned, as if to walk away; but she caught him sharply by the wrist.

"Stop!" she cried, angrily. "Tell me this. Have you been trying to make an engagement with that wax doll up at Tolcarne?"

"You insolent old—There go back, Mrs Lloyd," he cried, checking himself. "You must be mad."

"Mad? Yes, enough to make me, you wild, ungrateful boy," she cried, her fingers tightening round his wrist, so that it would have taken a violent effort to free himself. "Stop, and listen to me."

Trevor looked at her, his anger cooling; for he thought the housekeeper was suffering from mental excitement brought on by the disappointment consequent upon the failure of her plans.

"What do you want to say?" he said, quietly.

"A great deal. Ah, you see, you must listen. Now tell me—that Miss Rea, have you been talking to her father and mother?"

"Yes," said Trevor, thinking it better to humour her till he could get her back to the house.

"Then go and break it all off—at once. Do you hear—at once."

"And why, pray?" said Trevor, smiling—the position, now that his anger had passed, seeming ridiculous.

"Because you are to marry little Mary, as I wish," said Mrs Lloyd, in a quick whisper.

"The parties, neither of them being agreed. Come, Mrs Lloyd, let's get back to the house."

"Richard," cried the woman, shaking his arm—"listen. Do you hear me? How dare you laugh at me like this?"

"Come, Mrs Lloyd—come, nurse, what are you thinking about?" said Trevor, good-humouredly. But he was beginning to fret under the opposition.

"Of your fixture—of your good, boy. Now, listen to me, Richard. I have long planned this out. I have brought Mary here, educated her, and prepared her for it."

"And now she has fallen in love with Humphrey, and they are going to marry," said Trevor, laughing.

But the smile passed away as he saw the malignant look in the woman's face.

"Humphrey!" she exclaimed, and as she uttered the name she spat upon the ground—"Humphrey shall go. Humphrey shall not stay here. I hate him! His being here is a curse to me."

"Her own son. The woman is crazy," thought Trevor; and he looked anxiously in her eyes.

"Mrs Lloyd," he began; but she caught him by the other wrist, and her strength in her excitement was prodigious.

"Richard," she exclaimed, "will you mind me—will you do as I wish, and marry Polly?"

"Come to the house, and let's talk about it there, nurse," he said, kindly.

"No—no! here—here! I say you *shall* have her, or, mark me, you shall rue it. There, I know what you think; but I'm as sane as you are—more sane, for you would throw yourself away, and I won't let you."

"Come, Mrs Lloyd, there must be an end to this. Come to the house."

"Stay where you are, boy," she cried, with her eyes flashing. "Will you obey me?"

"No—no—no," said Trevor, impatiently, and he tried to extricate himself. "Nurse, you are mad."

"Don't call me nurse," she cried, viciously. "Do as I bid you, or I'll make you rue it till your deathbed. But, no, I can't do that. Richard, you shall mind me—you shall obey me in this. I have a right to be minded."

"Mrs Lloyd, you have gone to the extent of your right, and beyond it; from henceforth you and your husband must find another home. You shall have a comfortable income, but this cannot go on. There, I cannot leave you in this way—come up to the house."

He tried to lead her, but she broke away.

"You will have it then?" she hissed, in a hoarse whisper. "Richard, is this the way you treat your mother?"

"My—"

Trevor started back to the extent of their arms, looking at the woman aghast. The fancy that she was distraught had passed away during the last few minutes, and there was such an air of decision and truth in her words and looks that he staggered beneath the shock. The past, her determined action, her opposition to his will—so different to the behaviour of a dependent, and explained at the time on the score of old service—and many little words and looks, notably her passionate embrace on the night of the encounter in the study, all came back to him like a flash, and he could find no words for quite a minute.

"It's a lie!" he said at last. "Woman, how dare you? My father was too honourable a gentleman ever to descend to a low intrigue with one of his servants."

"Yes," said the woman, "and Martha Jane Lloyd was too good a wife to have listened to him if he had."

"Then," cried Trevor, in a fury, "how dare you say what you did?"

"Because, my boy, it is the truth. You are my flesh and blood."

"You are mad!" exclaimed Trevor. "Loose my wrist, woman, or I shall hurt you."

He looked sharply round, but there was no help at hand; for his first impulse was to tie her wrists, and have her carried to the house. But she prisoned one of his the tighter, by placing her other bony hand a little higher.

"*I'm* not mad, Richard," she said, quietly; "and when you hear me, you will see that you must mind me; for, at a word from me, all your riches would be swept away, and you might change places with your keeper."

"Humphrey!" ejaculated Richard, his brain in a whirl of doubt. "Tell me—what do you mean?"

"Only this," said the woman, hoarsely. "That Mrs Trevor and I had sons almost together. Humphrey and you were the two boys. Do you understand?"

"No," said Richard, fiercely. "Go on."

"I got my sister, Dinah Price, from Caerwmlych to come and be nurse for both, for I was in the house—the maid Jane, as they called me then. Do you want to hear more?"

"Go on," said Richard, in a hoarse whisper.

"One day I sat thinking. There was death in the house, Richard, and I was wondering about the fixture—how hard it would be if my fine boy should grow up to poverty through the changes that might take place, and me perhaps sent away by a new mistress. I was jealous, too, of the Trevors' boy, petted and pampered and waited upon, while my darling had to take his chance. I tell you it made me nearly mad sometimes, for I was ill and weak; and I think the devil came and tempted me, knowing how I was."

"Go on," said Richard; for she stopped, and the great drops of sweat were standing on his brow.

"One day, boy, I felt that I could bear it no longer. Dinah had gone down to the kitchen to join the servants watching the funeral; and I sat thinking, when the Trevors' baby cried, and no one went. I had you on my knee, Richard, nursing you, and I went up, innocently enough, to quiet the motherless little bairn, and as I saw it lying alone there in its cradle, my heart yearned over the poor little thing, and I took it in my arms, when it nestled to my breast so pitifully, that I nursed it as I did you, and sat there with you both in my arms."

Her voice was very husky now; but her words came firmly, and bore the impress of truth.

"It was then, Richard, that the temptation came; for all at once, as I looked down upon you both, the thought came, and I shivered. Then all opened out before me—a bright life, wealth, position, a great future for the helpless babe I held; and I said why should it not be for my boy. I shrank from it for a moment, not more. Then it seemed so easy, so sure, that I did not hesitate. In two minutes you had on the little master's night-gown, and he wore yours; and I laid *you*, Dick—my boy—my flesh and blood, in the cradle, and stole downstairs with theirs."

There was a faint rustle amongst the leaves overhead; but no one heeded, and the woman went on.

"As soon as I got down, shivering with fear, a sort of hysterical fit came over me, and I got worse; I grew so feverish that I had to lie down, and I was ill for weeks; but that passed off, and the struggle began. Ah, Richard, boy, your poor mother bore it all for you—that you might be rich and happy, while she suffered the tortures of hell; her heart yearning to take you to her heart, hearing you cry as she lay awake at nights with a stranger nursed at her breast. But that passed off when you both grew bigger; and you know how I treated you after, as I saw you grow up. People said I was hard to Humphrey. Perhaps I was, but I was never hard to you; and many a night I've cried myself to sleep with joy, when I have found you loving and affectionate, soothing me for the jealous tortures I suffered because I could not call you mine. But I said 'no, there is no going back; you have made him, let it be.'"

"And Lloyd?" said Richard, hoarsely—"did he know of this?"

"Yes, I told him, and he would have confessed; but he did not dare. My boy, when you spoke to me that night in your room—when for the first time for years I kissed you, I felt that I must tell you all."

"It's monstrous!" cried Richard, and his face looked ten years older. "But, no; I won't believe it—it can't be true."

"Not true!" exclaimed Mrs Lloyd, with her sallow cheeks flushing. "Ask your father. Is it so hard," she added, bitterly, "to find that you have a father and mother alive instead of in the grave?"

"It is impossible!" cried Richard.

"Hush, hold your tongue!" she said, angrily. "You know the secret now—keep it. What is it to a soul? I never had the heart to send Humphrey away, but treated him well. Send him away now—give him money to go away. He'll soon forget Polly. You must marry her; and Richard—say a kind word to me," she whispered, softening, "kiss me once—once only, my boy—your mother—before she goes back to be your servant, and to hold her peace for ever."

She crept closer to him, as he stood staring straight away, her thin hands rested on his shoulders, and she gazed up into his eyes, with her face working and growing strangely young, even as his tinned old.

"Dick, my darling, handsome son, kiss me—once only. And you'll marry her, won't you, and make her happy? One kiss, my own boy."

She uttered a hoarse cry, for he looked down at her with a look of loathing, and thrust her away.

"Mother? No!" he cried. "I can't call you that. Woman, you thought to bless me, and what you have done comes upon me like a curse. Don't touch me. Don't come near me. Take away your hands. I cannot bear it."

She clung to him; but he tore her hands away, and pushed her from him.

"Dick," she cried, throwing herself on her knees to him, and embracing his knees. "Your mother. One loving word."

"I can't," he gasped—"I can't. It is too much. An impostor—a pretender; and now to be an outcast! My God! what have I done that I should suffer this? Oh, Tiny! My love—my love!"

Those last words seemed torn from his breast in a low, hoarse whisper, as, breaking from the prostrate woman, he rushed away, right into the woods—the undergrowth bending and snapping as he passed on; till, with a groan of despair, he threw himself upon the earth, and lay there, in the deep shade, with his face buried in his hands.

With the Owner

How long Richard lay there he did not know. To him, it seemed like a year of torment, during which, in a wildly fevered state, he went over, again and again, the narrative he had heard; tried to find a flaw in it, but in vain. It was too true—too circumstantial; and at last, in a dazed, heavy way, he raised his haggard face, with his hair roughened, and wrinkled brow, to see Humphrey sitting upon a fallen tree by his side.

"Ah, Humphrey," he said, in a calm, sad voice. "How long have you been there?"

"Ever since, sir," said the young man. "I followed you."

"Then you heard?"

"Every word, sir. I couldn't help it, though. I didn't want to listen."

Richard bowed his head, and remained with his chin upon his breast.

"I had left Polly, sir—God bless her! she'd made me very happy with what she said—and I was taking a short cut back to try and catch you, sir, when I came upon you sudden like."

"Yes," said Richard, looking him full in the face. "But it was no fault of mine. I thought I was too happy for it to last. But I'll be a man over it. Humphrey," he exclaimed, rousing himself, "they educated me to be a gentleman, and I won't belie them there. Once for all, I am very sorry, and I'll make you every restitution in my power."

"Well, sir, I did wonder why she was always so hard to me: but I don't understand you, sir," said Humphrey, quietly.

"Don't sir me, man," exclaimed Richard, passionately.

"Don't be cross with me about it, Master Dick," said Humphrey, smiling; "'taint my fault."

"No, no, my good fellow, I know. Oh, it was monstrous!"

He turned away his head.

"Do you think it's all true, Master Richard," said Humphrey, quietly; "it seems so wild-like."

"True enough. Oh yes, it's true. But there, we won't talk."

"But I think we'd better, sir."

"Haven't I told you that I'll make you restitution, man—give up all?"

"Master Richard," said Humphrey, with a happy smile on his face, "you've give up to me my little love, and made me feel as if there was nothing else in the world I'd care to have. Look ye here, sir, it's stunned me like; it's hard, you know, to understand. I'm only a poor fellow like, come what may; and if I had the place—oh, you know, it just sounds like so much nonsense!—what could me and Polly do with it, when we could be happier at the lodge? It makes me laugh—it do indeed, sir. You, you see, have been made a scholar, and have your big friends—been made a gentleman, in fact—and nothing would ever make one of me. Let's go on, then, as we are, sir. I'm willing. Only sometimes Polly, maybe, 'll want a new dress, or a ribbon, or something of that kind; and then, if I ask you, you'll give me half a sovereign, or may be a sovereign, eh?"

"Half a sovereign—a sovereign! Why, man, can you not realise that you have from now eight thousand a year?"

"No, sir, that I can't," said Humphrey, smiling pleasantly. "I never was good at figures. Dogs, you know, or horses, or anything in the farming line, I'm pretty tidy at; but figures bothers me. Let things stop as they are, sir; I won't say a word, even to Polly."

"Humphrey," said Richard, holding out his hand, "you always were a good, true, simple-hearted fellow."

"I hope so, sir," said Humphrey, giving his horny palm a rub down his cord breeches before taking the extended hand, "and that's what makes it right that we should go on as we are. Nature knew it, sir, and that's how it was the change came about—you being the clever one, and best suited for the estate. I'm glad of one thing, though."

"What's that?" said Richard, wringing the extended hand.

"Why, I know now, sir, why Mrs Lloyd was always so down on me—she always was down on me, awful—regular hated me, like. Ah, the times I've cried over it as a boy! Nobody ever seemed to love me like till now, sir—till now."

Humphrey beamed as he slapped his broad chest; and his simple words seemed to corroborate those of Mrs Lloyd, till the last ray of hope was crushed from Richard's breast.

"No, Humphrey," he said, gravely, though every word cost him a pang, "I cannot stay here as an impostor. The place is yours, I give up all."

"That you just won't, sir," said Humphrey. "Why, I should be a brute beast if I let you. Come, come, let it go for a day or two, and think it over. It won't trouble me. I don't want it. I'm only glad of one thing—I've got somebody on the hip, and she won't say no now."

"I want no thinking, Humphrey; and we can still be friends. Come up to the house."

"And what would Miss Tiny say?"

If Humphrey had stabbed him with the iron-pointed staff he carried, he could not have given him greater pain; and his eyes wore a strange piteous aspect as they gazed upon the young keeper's face,

"You've got her to think about too, sir," said Humphrey, "same as I have. Oh no, Master Richard, it wouldn't never, never do."

"Come up to the house, Humphrey—come up to the house."

And then, without another word, but closely followed by his late servant, Richard strode hastily through the wood, whose briars and twigs in the unaccustomed path seemed now to take the part of fate, and lashed and tore him in his reckless passage, till his face was smeared with the blood which he had wiped hastily away.

"Has Mrs Lloyd come back from her walk?" said Richard to the staring footman.

"Yes, sir, two hours ago," said the man.

"Go into the study, Humphrey Trevor," said Richard, quietly; and then to himself, "Poor woman! and it was done for me."

In Transition

It was a hard fight, and the temptation was strong upon him to hide the truth. Humphrey would be content—he did not want to take his place; and he sat opposite to him now in the study, upon the very edge of the chair. Oh, it was ridiculous that he should have to give the place up to such a man—one whom he had to order before he could get him to sit down in his presence. And even when he felt that his mind was made up, and he was stoically determined to do that which was right, the rightful heir would keep upsetting his plans.

"You see, it would be so foolish, Master Dick."

"I can't help that, Humphrey. You must have your rights. I will not be a party to the imposture."

"Hadn't you better see a lawyer about it all?"

To be sure. There was Pratt—a barrister—he might give good advice.

Richard rang the bell and a servant came. "Ask Mr Pratt to be kind enough to step here."

"If you please, sir, Mr Pratt's gone, sir. I put his letter on your table. Yes, there it is, sir."

Richard started.

"The rats desert the sinking ship," he muttered; and then blushed for his doubt of his friend.

"When did he go?"

"Hour ago, sir. Telegraph come from Saint Kitt's, sir; and he wrote that letter, sir, for you, while they got the dogcart ready to take him to the station."

"That will do."

He tore open the letter, which enclosed the telegram from a friend in chambers—

"Come directly. A good brief for you. Don't lose the chance."

The hastily-scrawled letter was as follows:—

"Dear Dick,—Don't blame me for going. I must take work when it comes; and honestly, for reasons I can't explain, I am glad to go.—Yours, F.P."

"Must be genuine," thought Richard. "Well, it has happened at a good time. I'm glad he has gone."

Then a thought struck him.

He and Humphrey might divide the estate. But, no, he drove it away; he would be honest.

"Shall I go over to Saint Kitt's and fetch Mr Lawyer Dancer, sir?" said Humphrey.

"Say no more about it, for Heaven's sake!" exclaimed Richard. "I want no advice—I want nothing—only this, Humphrey, that you will forgive those old people—my—my parents. Let them have money to the end of their days, even if it is not deserved."

"Oh, but Master Richard."

"And promise me that you will not allow any prosecution and punishment to be held over their heads."

"Is it likely, Master Richard?" said Humphrey, laughing.

"Now let me have a few hours to myself, to collect my thoughts, and write a few letters."

Humphrey leaped from his chair.

"'Bout draining the little meadow, sir?" he said. "Shall I set the men on? The tiles is come."

Richard's face contracted with pain, and then a bitter smile crossed it.

"My dear Humphrey," he said, taking his hand, "can you not realise your position? You are master here."

"No, sir," cried Humphrey, flinging down his hat, and then picking it up—"I'll be blessed if I can. This has put my head all in a buzz, like bees swarming, and I can't understand it a bit."

He left the room, and Richard gave a sigh of relief, seating himself at his table, and taking up a pen to write; but only to rest his head upon his hand, and stare before him, dazed—crushed.

"Please, sir, Mrs Lloyd says can you make it convenient to see her?" said the footman; and then he started back, astounded at his master's anger.

"No," roared Richard, "I will see no one. Let me be left alone."

Then he hastily wrote a letter to Pratt, and fastened it down before dropping it in the letter-bag, and threw it into the hall.

He had hardly finished before, knocking first softly, Lloyd opened the door, to stand trembling before him.

Richard pointed to the door.

"Go," he said, hoarsely. "I can't talk to you now. Another time—in a week—in a month—wait until then."

"But—"

"Go—for Heaven's sake, go!" cried Richard, frantically.

He was left alone.

Next came a note in pencil from Mrs Lloyd.

> "My dearest Boy—Forgive me; it was for your sake I did all this. Pray be careful, for I fear Humphrey has some suspicion. Do see me, and give me your advice.
> "M.J.L."

"Poor woman!" he muttered, tearing the note bit by bit into tiny fragments. "Her plan is destroyed, save that this niece—my fair cousin, Polly—will sit in the seat she intended, without poor Humphrey is spoiled by prosperity. Poor fellow! It will be a hard trial for him.

"Be careful?" he said, laughing in a strange, harsh fashion. "Does she think I am going to remain her accomplice in this horrible fraud?"

He sat down, then, to think; but his brain was in a whirl, and he gave up in despair.

At last he woke up to the fact that it was growing late, and he remembered that he was to have accompanied the Reas on an expedition that afternoon, and now it was past six. They must have been and returned.

What would poor Tiny think?

A cold, chilling feeling of despair came over him now. What would she think? Yes, how would she take it? All must be over between them now—at least, for some years to come.

A servant announced dinner, and he bade him send it back. Locking the door after him, he sat down in an easy-chair, conscious that several times there had been knocks at the door, but paying no heed whatever.

Night fell, and he had not moved; and then, in a strange, fitful, dreamy fashion, the night passed away.

He must have dozed at times, he knew; for his thoughts had wandered off into dreams, and the dreams had trailed off in turn into thoughts; and now it was morning, for the grey light was streaming through the antique casement, and a feint glow overhead told of the rising sun.

He threw open the windows, and the cool morning breeze, fresh from the Atlantic, seemed to calm and refresh him. His thoughts grew more collected; and at last he left the window, and went out into the hall, to seek his bedroom.

A bitter smile crossed his lip as he noticed the luxurious air of wealth about him, and then a sigh drew his attention to the fact that the cause of all his agony had been watching at his door the night through, and was now on her knees stretching out her hands as if in supplication for pardon.

"Oh, my boy—my boy, what are you going to do," she groaned.

"Do?" he said, bitterly, as she crept to his feet. "Act like the gentleman you wanted me to be."

"What do you mean, Richard—my son? There, I give up about Polly. I'll never say another word. You shall do as you like."

"I need not ask you if what you told me yesterday was true," he said, calmly. "Well, we must make amends."

"How? What do you mean?" she said, starting up.

"Mean? Why, by giving up everything to the rightful owner, and leaving him possession at once."

"Richard," she cried, passionately, catching him by the arm, "you would not be so mad "

"I shall be so honest," he said.

"What, give up—give up everything to Humphrey?"

"Everything," he said, coldly, "and at once."

"You're mad—mad!" gasped Mrs Lloyd. "And after all I have done for you—to make you a gentleman."

"These are its effects," he said, bitterly. "You made me a gentleman—I wish to act as one."

"But, Richard—think—your father—your old mother—we shall be turned out in disgrace—to starve," she cried, piteously.

"Mother, I cannot help the disgrace," he said, coldly. "I would save you if I could, but the disgrace would be greater to keep up this horrible imposture."

"Hush!" she whispered, "the servants will soon be down—they may hear us. Oh, you cannot mean, Richard, what you say."

"I told Humphrey yesterday," continued Richard, "that I begged he would care for you; but that is only for the present. As soon as I can find means to earn my bread, I will keep you both myself; so that you shall be spared the disgrace of taking alms from the man you wronged."

"Fool—idiot—mad boy!" hissed Mrs Lloyd, seizing his arm angrily, and shaking it. "You shall not act like this. I've been nearly thirty years building this up, and do you think I will have it crushed down like that? Say a word if you dare!"

"If I dare!" exclaimed Richard. "Do you know that Humphrey does more than suspect, that he knows all—heard all from your own lips in the lane yesterday?"

Mrs Lloyd's jaw dropped.

"The true-hearted, honest fellow refused to take advantage of his position."

"Of course, yes," cried Mrs Lloyd. "We'll pay him out, and let him go. Yes, he shall have Polly," she added, with a look of pleasure on her troubled face.

"Enough of this," said Richard, firmly. "Loose my arm. Some day I may be able to talk to you again. Now, go to your room, and make arrangements either for leaving, or make your peace with your new lord. He loves little Polly, and that will act as a shield for you."

"I say you shall not give in," cried Mrs Lloyd, in a hoarse, angry voice.

But he dragged his arm free, and dashed up the stairs.

Mistaken Zeal

In the course of the morning Richard grew calmer. He had a long interview with Humphrey, giving him plenty of advice as to his future proceedings; and then sending for Mr Mervyn, whom Humphrey happened to mention as a gentleman in whom he had great confidence.

But the messenger was not needed, for Mr Mervyn was coming up the drive, and he was sent on another errand, with a couple of notes to Penreife—one to Sir Hampton, the other to Tiny.

"I was on my way here, Mr Trevor," he began.

"My name is Richard Lloyd, Mr Mervyn," said Richard, quietly.

"Yes—yes," said Mr Mervyn, "I have heard. It is all over the place."

"So soon?" said Richard, bitterly.

"Yes; and directly I heard," said Mervyn, "I came up. But, my dear sir, it's like a romance; it can't be true."

"It's true enough," said Richard, coldly.

"But under the circumstances, Mr Trev—Lloyd," said Mervyn, "Mr Humphrey here won't press—"

"That's what I want Master Richard here to understand," said Humphrey. "As I says to him yesterday, sir, what's the good of it to me?"

"Exactly," said Mervyn, "right is right; but as Mr Trev—Lloyd is innocent in the matter, and has made engagements and the rest of it, why not come to some arrangement satisfactory to both?"

"Mr Mervyn, you are sent for here as the friend of Mr Humphrey Trevor."

"Exactly, Mr Tre—Lloyd. I beg your pardon, but my tongue is not so quick of apprehension as my brain."

"I want you to advise and help him in his novel position."

"I will," said Mervyn, frankly; "but I should like to advise and help you too. You see, Mr Tre—there—Mr Richard, you have possession."

"I give it up," said Richard.

"But you might hold it, and give friend Humphrey here a great deal of trouble."

"Mr Mervyn, I claim to be still a gentleman, whatever my birth," said Richard, haughtily. "Will you act as Humphrey's friend?"

"I will."

"Then understand this, sir. I have had a hard fight, and I have come through the temptation, I hope, like a man. I now resign everything to Mr Humphrey Trevor here. I ask his pardon for usurping his rights, and I beg his forbearance towards my poor father and mother. I will not make this cruel injury to him worse by any opposition."

Humphrey shuffled in his seat, and tried to speak, but he only wiped his damp face, and looked helplessly at the man he was bound to oust.

"You see, Mr Mervyn," continued Richard, "Mr Trevor's will be a peculiar position."

"Yes," said Mervyn; "but had you not better get some legal advice?"

"What for?" said Richard. "Can anything be plainer? As I said, Mr Trevor's will be a peculiar position. He will be the mark of the designing, and he will need a staunch friend at his side. Will you be that friend?"

"I will," said Mervyn, wringing his hand. "Yours too, my dear fellow, if you'll let me. But," he added, in a whisper, "Miss Rea?"

A spasm of pain shot across Richard's face, and he was about to speak when Humphrey turned to him.

"Master Richard," he said, in a husky voice, "we was boys together, and played together almost like brothers. This here comes to me stunning, like. You say it's mine. Well, it aint my fault. I don't want it. Keep it all, if you like; if not, let's share and share alike."

The last words fell on empty air, for Richard had waved his hand to both, and hurried out of the room.

That evening, with beating heart, he walked towards Tolcarne gates. He had been busy amongst his papers, tearing up and making ready for that which he had to do on the morrow; and now, more agitated than he would own, he sought the lane where so many happy hours had been spent to see if Tiny Rea would grant him the interview he had written to ask for, that he might say good-bye.

It was a soft, balmy night, and the stars seemed to look sadly down through the trees as he leaned against a mass of lichen-covered granite, pink here and there with the pretty stonecrop of the place, waiting, for she was behind time.

"Will she come," he said, "now that I am a beggar without a shilling, save that which I could earn? Oh, shame! shame! shame! How could I doubt her?"

No, he would not doubt her; she could not have cared about his money. She was too sweet and loving and gentle. And what should he say—wait? No, he dared not. He could only—only—leave her free, that she might—

"Oh, my darling!" he groaned; and he laid his broad forehead upon the hard, rugged stone, weeping now like a child.

The clouds came across the sky, blotting out one by one the glistening stars; a chilly mist swept along the valley from the sea, and all around was dark and cold as the future of his blasted life. For the minutes glided into hours, and she came not—came not to say one gentle, loving word—one God-speed to send him on his way; and at last, heart-broken, he staggered to the great floral gate, held the chilly rails, kissed the iron, and gazed with passionate longing up at the now darkened house, and then walked slowly away, stunned by the violence of his grief.

The wind was rising fast, and coming in heavy soughs from off the sea. As he reached the lodge gates at Penreife he paused, staring before him in a helpless way, till a heavy squall smote him, and with it a sharp shower of rain, whose drops seemed to cool his forehead and rouse him to action.

Starting off, with great strides, he took the short cut, and made for the sea, where the fields ended suddenly, their short, thyme-scented grass seeming to have been cut where there was a fall of full four hundred feet, down past a rugged, piled-up wall of granite, to the white-veined rock, polished by the restless sea below. To any one unaccustomed to the coast a walk there on a dark night meant death, either by mutilation on the cruel rocks, always seeming to be studded with great gouts of crimson blood, where the sea anemones clung in hundreds, or else by drowning in the deep, clear water, when the tide was up, and the waves played amidst the long, chocolate strands of fucus and bladder-wrack, waving to and fro.

It was going to be a wild night, but it seemed in keeping with the chaos of his mind. Far out on the sea, softly rising to and fro in the thick darkness, were the lights of the fishing-boats, as a score or so lay drifting with their herring-nets; and in his heart there was not a rough fisher there whose lot he did not envy.

"And she could not come!" he groaned, as he stood there, with bare head. "Oh, my love—my love! To go without one gentle word, far, far away, and but yesterday so happy!"

The wind increased in force, and, with the gathering strength of the tide, the waves came rushing in, to beat in thunder against the rocks far beneath his feet; and then, with a rush, the fine salt spray was whirled up, and swept in his face, as he gazed straight out to sea.

At another time he might have shuddered, standing thus upon the edge of that great cliff, with—just dimly seen in its more intense blackness—the rugged headland that stretched like a buttress into the sea upon his left. But now the horrors of the place seemed welcome, and he felt, as a smile came on his dripping features, that it would be pleasant to leap from where he stood right off at once into oblivion.

It seemed so easy, such a quiet way of getting rest from the turmoil and trouble of the future, that the feeling seemed to grow upon him.

"No," he said at last; "that would be a coward's end. I've done one brave thing to-day; and now, old friend, you shall have me again to toss upon your waves, but it shall be as your master, not as a slave."

As he spoke he raised his hands and stretched them out, when he heard a hoarse cry behind him, and as he sharply turned and stepped back, something seemed to come out of the darkness, seize him by the throat, and the next moment he was over the cliff, suspended above eternity.

Then there was an awful silence, only broken by the roar, thud, and hiss of the waves below, as they rushed in, broke upon the rocks, and then fled back in foamy spray.

Richard's fingers were dug into the short, velvet turf, and he hung there, with his legs rigid, afraid to move, and wondering whether those were friendly or inimical hands that clutched his throat. It seemed an age of horror before the silence was broken, and then came a panting voice, which he knew as Humphrey's, to sob, as it were, in his ear—

"Master Dick, don't be scar'd. I've got you tight, but I can't move. Get your nerve, and then shift your hands one at a time to me."

Without a moment's hesitation, Richard did so, with the damp gathering on his brow the while.

"That's brave, sir. Now get your toes in the cracks of the granite somewhere—gently, don't hurry—I won't let go, though I can't move."

Richard obeyed, drew himself up an inch, then another, and another, felt that he was saved—then made a slip, and all seemed over, but Humphrey held to him with all his strength, and once more Richard tried, tearing hands and knees with the exertion, till he got his chest above the cliff edge, then was halfway up, and crawled safely on, to fall over panting on his side.

"Quick, Master Richard, your hand!" shouted Humphrey.

And the saved had to turn saver, for the keeper had been drawn closer and closer to the edge by Richard's efforts, and but for a sudden snatch, and the exercise of all his strength, the new owner of Penreife would have glided off the slippery grass into the darkness beneath.

"Safe," muttered Humphrey, rising. "Give me your hand, Master Richard. I thought, when I followed you, you meant to leap off."

"No, Humphrey," said Richard, sadly, "I will not throw my worthless life away. It is such glimpses of death as that we have just seen that teach the value of life. Goodnight; don't speak to me again."

Humphrey obeyed, and followed him in silence to the house.

The next morning, as soon as the letters had been brought in, Richard took his—a single one—and, without a word to a soul, carried a small portmanteau to the stable-yard, waited while the horse was put to, and then had himself driven off.

As he passed the lodge a note was put into his hand by a boy. An hour later he was in the train, and the destination of that train was the big metropolis, where most men come who mean to begin afresh.

Correspondence

It never struck Richard that some of his behaviour was verging on the Quixotic. His only thought now was that he was degraded from his high estate, and that the woman whom he had loved with all his heart—did love still—had turned from him in his poverty and distress.

At such times men are not disposed to fairly analyse the motives of others; and Richard was anything but an unbiased judge, as he knit his brow, told himself that he had the fight to begin now, and determined to take help from no one who had known him in his prosperity.

With this feeling strong upon him he dismissed the man who had driven him over; and, to the utter astonishment of the Saint Kitt's station-master, took a third-class ticket for London, and entered a compartment wherein were a soldier with a bottle, a sailor just landed, an old lady with several bundles, bound on a visit to her boy in London—a gentleman, she informed everybody, who kept a public—and the customary rural third-class passengers.

And then the long, dreary journey began, Richard making up his mind to suit himself to the company amongst whom he was thrown, and failing dismally; for both soldier and sailor, whose idea of enjoyment seemed to be that they must get hopelessly intoxicated as soon as possible, took it as an offence that he would not "take a pull" of rum out of the bottle belonging to the son of Neptune, and of gin from that of the son of Mars.

To make up for this, Richard tried to be civil to a couple of rustic lasses, who received all his little bits of matter-of-fact politeness and conversation with giggles and glances at a young Devonian in the corner of the carriage, till his brickdust-coloured visage became the colour of one of his own ruddy ploughed fields, and he announced that "for zigzpence he'd poonch that chap's yed."

Hereupon the old lady with the bundles loudly proclaimed a wish that her "zun" was there; and ended by hoping that, if "this young man" (meaning Richard) intended to make himself unpleasant, he would go into another carriage.

It was hard—just at a time, too, when Richard's temper seemed to be angular and sore—when the slightest verbal touch made him wince. But he set his teeth, bore a good deal of vulgar banter with patience, and was able to compliment himself grimly for his forbearance during the long ride along that single line of Cornish railway that is one incessant series of scaffold-like viaducts, over some of the most charming little valleys in our isle.

After passing Plymouth, the old lady became so sociable that she dropped asleep against our traveller. The rustics had given place to a tall traveller; and the soldier and sailor grew hilariously friendly after replenishing their bottles at Plymouth. And so, fighting hard to put the past in its proper place—behind—the train bore Richard onward to his goal.

Just before nearing Paddington Station, Trevor took out his pocket-book, and the rugged, hard look upon his face was softened. He glanced round the compartment, to see that half his fellow-passengers were asleep, the soldier drunk, the stout old lady with the bundles busy hunting for her railway ticket, and the sailor disconsolately trying to drain a little more rum out of his bottle.

By this time Trevor had grown weary of the long journey—so tedious on the hard third-class seats—in spite of his determination; and a sigh would once or twice escape, as recollections of his old first-class luxury intruded.

"I'll hold to it, though," he muttered.

And, determined to go on in his course, he opened his pocket-book, and drew from it a letter which he had received from Tolcarne. It was not long, but it sent the blood dancing through his veins, and nerved him for the fight to come. It run as follows:—

> "Dearest Dick—What shall I say to you in this your great
> trouble? Can I say more than that I would give anything
> to be by your side, to try and advise—at all events, to try
> and help and comfort? Papa was very angry when your
> letter came, and read it to Aunt Matty; but let that pass, as I
> tell you only, Dick, that you have a friend in dear mamma,
> who stood up for you as nobly as did darling little Fin,
> who had been in unaccountably low spirits before. I tried
> so hard, Dick, to come to you—to answer your letter and
> scold you; but they would not let me stir. I dare not tell you
> what they said; you must guess when I tell you that I was
> a dreadfully disobedient child, and Aunt Matty declared
> that no good could ever come to a girl who set herself up
> in opposition to her father and aunt. Poor dear mamma
> was left out of it altogether. I say all this, Dick, for fear

you should think I fell away from you in your trouble, and would not come to you as you wished; but my heart was with you all the time. And now, Dick, darling, to be more matter-of-fact, what is all this to us? You could not help it; and whether you are Richard Trevor or Richard Lloyd by name, how does it alter you in the eyes of her to whom you said so much? Dick, you don't know me, or you would never have sent me that cruel letter, so full of your dreadful determination. Oh, Dick, do you think—can you think—I wish to be free? You taught me to love you, and you cannot undo your work. For shame, to write in that desponding tone because of this accident. It was very wicked and dreadful of Mrs Lloyd, but you could not help it; and now you have so nobly determined to make restitution to poor Humphrey, let it all go. My Dick only stands out more nobly than ever. You have your profession, sir—go back to that, and they will only be too proud to have you; but don't go long voyages, or where there are storms. I lay awake all night listening to the wind, and thinking how thankful I ought to be that you were ashore, Dick, and all the time I felt prouder than ever of my own boy. Oh, Dick, never talk to me of freedom! Nothing can make me change. Even if I saw with my own poor little crying eyes that you cared for me no more, I could not leave off loving; and, dear Dick—dearest Dick—don't think me bold and unmaidenly if I say now what I should not have dared to say if you had not been in trouble—Dick, recollect this—that there is some one waiting your own time, when, rich or poor, you shall ask her to come to you, when and where you will, and she will be your own little wife—Tiny.

"P.S.—Pin has looked over my shoulder, and read all this as I wrote it; and she says it is quite right, besides sending her dear love to brother Dick."

Trevor's forehead went down on his hands as he finished, his face was very pale, and a strange look was in his eyes as he re-perused the note.

"God bless her!" he muttered. "I will do something, and I believe she will wait for me; but I can't drag her down to share my poverty. But there, I won't curse it, when I see how it brings out the pure metal from the fire. I can't go back to the sea, though. Pooh! what chance have I—a poor penniless servant's son—how should I get a ship. Why, my rank has been obtained by imposture."

The rugged, hard look came back, but the sight of an enclosure once more smoothed his forehead.

"Here's dear little Fin," he said to himself. "Well, after all, it's very sweet to find out how true some hearts can be."

Saying this to himself, he opened and read a little jerky scrawl from Fin:—

"My own dear Brother Dick,—I sent you a message by Tiny, but I thought I'd write too, so as to show you that little people can be as staunch as big. Never mind about the nasty money, or the troublesome estate—you can't have everything; and I tell you, sir, that you've won what is worth a thousand Penreifes—my darling little Tiny's heart—you great, ugly monster! Dear Dick, I'm so sorry for you, but I can't cry a bit—only pat you on the back and say, 'Never mind.' I'll take care of Tiny for you, in spite of Aunt Matty—a wicked old woman!—for if she didn't look up from a goody-goody book, and say that she'd always expected it, and she was very glad. Ma sends her love to you, and says she shall come across to Penreife to see you, the first time papa goes over to Saint Kitt's. She would come now, only she wants to keep peace and quietness in the house. They're against you now, but it will soon blow over. If it don't, we'll win over Aunt Matty to our side by presenting her with dogs. By the way, Pepine has a cold: he sneezed twice yesterday, and his tail is all limp. Goodbye, Dick.—Your affectionate sister,
"Tiи Rеа.

Richard's eyes brightened as he read this, and then carefully bestowed it in his pocket-book.

He then took out and read again the letter that had come by post:—

"My dear old Dick,—Had yours and its thunderclap. Gave me a bad headache. Hang it all! if it's true, what a predicament for a fellow to find out that he's somebody else—'Not myself at all,' as the song says! But you have possession, Dick; and, speaking as a lawyer, I should say, let them prove it on the other side. Don't you go running about and telling people you've no right to the property; for, after all, it may only be an hallucination of that old woman's brain. What a dreadful creature! Why, if she isn't your mother—and really, I think she can't be—I should feel disposed to prosecute her; and I should like to hold the brief. Don't be in too great a hurry to give up, but, on the contrary, hold on tight; for that's a fine estate, and very jolly, so long as you could keep off the locusts. On looking back, though, there are a good many strange things crop up—the wonderful display of interest in dear Master Dick, and all the rest of it. Looks bad—very bad—and like the truth Dick. But, as I said before, legally you've got possession, and if I can help you to keep it—no, hang it, Dick! if the place isn't yours, old boy, give it up. There, you see how suitable I am for a barrister. I could never fight a bad cause. But, as I said before, give it up, every inch of it. I wouldn't have my old man Dick with the faintest suspicion of a dirty trick in his nature. Cheer up, old fellow, there's another side to everything. That Sybaritish life was spoiling you. Why, my dear boy, you've no idea how jolly it is to be poor. Hang the wealth! a fico for it! Come up and stay with me in chambers, while we talk the matter over, and conspire as to whether we shall set the Thames on fire at high or low water, above bridge or below. Meanwhile, we'll banquet, my boy, feast on chops—hot chops—and drink cold beady beer out of pewters. Ah, you pampered old Roman Emperor, living on your tin, what do you know of real life? Setting aside metaphysics, Dick, old boy, come up to me, and lay your stricken head upon this manly bosom; thrust your fist into this little purse, and go shares as long as there is anything belonging to, yours truly,

"Frank Pratt.

"P.S.—I should have liked to see Tolcarne again. Pleasant, dreamy time that. Of course you will see no more of the little girls?"

"Poor old Frank," said Richard, refolding the letter. "I believe he cared for little Fin."

There was no time for dreaming, with the bustle of Paddington Station to encounter; and making his way into the hotel, he passed a restless, dreamless night.

New Lodgings

Richard was pretty decided in his ways. Hotel living would not suit him now; and soon after breakfast he took his little valise, earned a look of contempt from the hotel porter by saying that he did not require a cab, and set off to walk from Paddington to Frank's chambers in the Temple; where he arrived tired and hot, to climb the dreary-looking stone stairs, and read on the door the legend written upon a wafered-up paper, "Back in five minutes."

With all the patience of a man accustomed to watch, Richard up-ended his portmanteau, and sat and waited hour after hour. Then he went out, and obtained some lunch, returning to find the paper untouched.

Sitting down this time with a newspaper to while away the time, he tried to read, but not a word fixed itself upon his mind; and he sat once more thinking, till at last, weary and low-spirited, he walked out into the Strand, the portmanteau feeling very heavy, but his determination strong as ever.

"Keb, sir—keb, sir," said a voice at his elbow; for he was passing the stand in Saint Clement's Churchyard.

"No, my man—no."

"Better take—why, I'm blest!"

The remark was so emphatic that Richard looked the speaker in the face.

"Don't you remember me, sir—axdent, sir—op'site your club, sir—me as knocked the lady down, sir?"

"Oh yes," said Richard, "I remember you now. Not hurt, was she?"

"On'y shook, sir. But jump in, sir. Let me drive yer, sir. Here, I'll take the portmanter."

"No, no," said Richard, "I don't want to ride, I—there, confound it, man, what are you about?"

"No, 'fence, sir—I on'y wanted to drive a gent as was so kind as you was. Odd, aint it, sir? That there lady lives along o' me, at my house, now—lodges, you know—'partments to let, furnished."

"Apartments!" cried Richard, eagerly; "do you know of any apartments?"

"Plenty out Jermyn Street way, sir."

"No, no; I mean cheap lodgings."

"What, for a gent like you, sir?" said Sam Jenkles.

"No, no—I'm no gentleman," said Richard, bitterly; "only a poor man. I want cheap rooms."

"Really, sir?" said Sam, rubbing his nose viciously.

"Yes, really, my man. Can you tell me of any?"

"You jump in, sir, and I'll run you up home in no time."

"But I—"

"My missus knows everybody 'bout us as has rooms to let—quiet lodgings, you know, sir; six bob a week style—cheap."

"No, no; give me your address, and I'll walk."

"No you don't, sir, along o' that portmanter. Now, I do wonder at a gent like you being so obstinit."

Richard still hesitated; but it was an opportunity not to be lost, and, before he had time to thoroughly make up his mind, Sam had hoisted the portmanteau on the roof, afterwards holding open the flap of the cab.

"It's all right, sir; jump in, sir. Ratty wants a run, and you can't carry that there portmanter."

"A bad beginning," muttered Richard.

Then he stepped into the cab, and the apron was banged to, Sam hopped on to his perch, and away they rattled along the Strand into Fleet Street, and up Chancery Lane.

"He's a-going it to-day, sir, aint he?" said a voice; and Richard turned sharply round, to see Sam Jenkles's happy-looking face grinning through the trap. "He's as fresh as a daisy."

The little trapdoor was rattled down again, for other vehicles were coming, and Sam's hands were needed at the reins, the more especially that Ratty began to display the strangeness of his disposition by laying down his ears, whisking his tail, and trying hard to turn the cab round and round, clay-mill fashion. But this was got over, the rest of the journey performed in peace, and Sam drew up shortly at the door of his little home, the two front windows of which had been turned into gardens, as far as the sills were concerned, with miniature green palings, gate and all, the whole sheltering a fine flourishing display of geraniums and fuchsias, reflected in window-panes as clean as hands could make them.

"Why, this would do capitally," said Richard, taken by the aspect of the place.

"Dessay it would, sir," said Sam, grinning; "but our rooms is let. But come in, sir, and see the missus—she'll pick you out somewhere nice and clean. But, hallo! what's up?"

Richard had seen that which brought the exclamation from Sam's lips, and stepped forward to help.

For, about a dozen yards down the quiet little street, Mrs Lane was supporting Netta, the pair returning evidently from a walk, and the latter being overcome.

"Thank you—a little faint—went too far," said Mrs Lane, as Richard ran up to where she was sustaining her daughter. "Netta, darling, only a few yards farther. Try, dear."

"She has fainted," said Richard. "Here, let me carry her."

Before Mrs Lane could speak, Richard had taken the light figure in his arms, and, guided by the frightened mother, bore it to Sam's door.

"That's right, sir, in there," said Sam, eagerly—"fust door on the left's the parly. Poor gal!"

This last was in an undertone, as the young man easily bore his burden in—finding, though, that a pair of large dark eyes had unclosed, and were gazing timidly in his, while a deep blush overspread cheek and forehead.

"There," said Richard, laying her lightly down upon the couch, and helping to arrange the pillows with all a woman's tenderness. "You look weak and ill, my dear, and—and—I beg pardon," he said, hesitating, as he met Mrs Lane's gaze, "I think we have met before."

Mrs Lane turned white, and shrank away.

"Of course," said Richard, smiling. "My friend here, who drove me up, told me you lodged with him."

Mrs Lane did not speak, only bowed her head over Netta.

"If I can do anything, pray ask me," said Richard, backing to the door, and nearly overturning bustling Mrs Jenkles, who came hurrying in with—

"Oh, my dear, you've been overdoing it—I beg your pardon, sir."

"My fault, I think," said Richard.

And with another glance at the great dark eyes following him, he backed into the passage—this time upon Sam, who had carried in the portmanteau.

"If you wouldn't mind, sir," said Sam—"our back room here's on'y a kitchen; but we lets our parlour, as you see. There," he said, leading the way, "that's my cheer, sir; and the wife 'll come and talk to you dreckly, I dessay. I must go back on to the rank."

"One moment," said Richard.

"There, sir, I don't want paying for a bit of a job like this," said Sam. "Oh, well, if you will pay, I shall put that down to the lodgers' nex' ride."

"They are your lodgers, then?"

"Yes, sir; and it all come out of that old Ratty when I knocked Mrs Lane over."

"But the young lady?"

"Thanky, sir, for calling her so; that's just what she is."

"Is she an invalid?"

"Feard so, sir," said Sam, in a hoarse whisper. "I don't like her looks at all. But I can't stop, sir; the missus 'll be here, and I hope she'll know of a place as suits."

The next moment, Sam Jenkles was gone, and Richard sat looking round at the bright candlesticks and saucepan-lids, hardly able to realise the fact that but a day or two before he was the master of Penreife, for what had taken place seemed to be back years ago.

His musings were interrupted by the entry of Mrs Jenkles, who stood curtseying and smoothing her apron.

"Is she better?" said Richard, anxiously.

"Yes, sir, she's quite well again now," said Mrs Jenkles. "She's weak, sir—rather delicate health; and Sam—that is my husband—said you wanted apartments, sir."

"And that you would be able to find me some," said Richard, smiling.

"I don't think we've anything good enough about here, sir, for a gentleman like you."

"For a poor man like me, you mean. Now look here, Mrs—Mrs—"

"Jenkles, sir."

"Mrs Jenkles. I can afford to pay six or seven shillings a-week, that is all."

"Then there's Mrs Fiddison, sir, nearly opposite. Very clean and respectable. Bedroom and sitting-room, where a young gentleman left only about a week ago. He played a long brass thing, sir, at one of the theatres, and used to practise it at home; and that's why he left."

"That will do, I daresay," exclaimed Richard, who, in the first blush of his determination, was stern as an ascetic, and would have said Yes to the lodgings if Mrs Jenkles had proposed a couple of neatly furnished cellars.

The result was that the cabman's wife went over with him to Mrs Fiddison's, and introduced him to that lady, who was dressed in sombre black, held a widow's cap in her hand, and was evidently determined to keep up the supply, for there were at least six arranged about the little parlour into which she led the way.

Not Musical

Mrs Fiddison was a tall, thin lady, who was supposed to be a widow from her display of caps; but the fact was that she had no right to the matronly prefix, she being a blighted flower—a faded rosebud, on whom the sun of love had never shone; and the consequence was that her head drooped upon its stalk, hung over weakly on one shoulder, while a dewdrop-like tear stood in one eye; and, like carbonic acid gas concealed in soda-water, she always had an indefinite number of sighs waiting to escape from her lips.

She smiled sadly at Richard, and waved him to a chair, to have taken which would have caused the immolation of a widow's cap—which, however, Mrs Fiddison rescued, and perched awry upon her head, to be out of the way.

"This gentleman wants apartments, Mrs F.," said Mrs Jenkles.

"Mine are to let," said Mrs Fiddison, sadly; "but does the gentleman play anything brass?"

Richard stared, and then remembered about the last lodger.

"Oh, dear, no," he said, smiling.

"Because I don't think I could bear it again, let alone the neighbours' lodgers," said Mrs Fiddison. "I might put up with strings, or wood, but I could not manage brass."

"I do not play any instrument," said Richard, looking at the lady in a troubled way, as her head drooped over the cap she was making, and she gazed at it like a weeping widow on a funeral card.

"So many orchestral gentlemen live about here," said Mrs Fiddison. "You can hear the double bass quite plain at Cheadley's, next door but one; but Waggly's have given the kettledrum notice."

"Indeed," said Richard, glancing at Mrs Jenkles, who stood smoothing her apron.

"Yes," said Mrs Fiddison, holding out the white crape starched grief before him, so that he might see the effect of her handiwork. "The last new pattern, sir."

Richard stared at Mrs Jenkles, and that lady came to his assistance.

"Mrs F. makes weeds for a wholesale house, sir."

"They ought to be called flowers of grief, Mrs Jenkles," said the lady. "A nice quiet, genteel business, sir; and if you don't object to the smell of the crape, you'd not know there was anything going on in the house."

"Oh, I'm sure I shouldn't mind," said Richard.

"Prr-oooomp!" went something which sounded like young thunder coming up in the cellar.

"That's the double bass at Cheadley's, sir," said Mrs Fiddison; "and, as I was a-saying, you'll find the rooms very quiet, for Waggly's have given the kettledrum notice. Mrs Waggly said she was sure it was that made her have the bile so bad; and I shouldn't wonder if it was."

"And the terms," said Richard.

"You are sure you don't play anything brass, sir?" said Mrs Fiddison, looking at him with her head all on one side, as if to say, "Now, don't deceive a weak woman!"

"Indeed, I am not musical at all," said Richard, smiling.

"Because it isn't pleasant, sir, for a landlady who wishes to make things comfortable," continued Mrs Fiddison, smiling at the cap—which she had now put on her left fist—as if it were a face.

"It can't be, of course." said Richard, getting impatient.

"Mr Took, my last lodger, sir, played the rumboon; and sometimes of a morning, when he was doing his octaves, it used to quite make my brain buzz."

"I think the rooms would suit me," said Richard, glancing round.

"Thank you, sir," said Mrs Fiddison, wiping one eye with a scrap of crape. "You can see the marks all over the wall now."

"Marks—wall?" said Richard.

"Ah, you don't understand the rumboon, sir," said Mrs Fiddison, pointing with a pair of scissors to various little dents and scratches on the wall, as she still held up the widow's cap. "Those places are what he used to make when he shot the thing out to get his low notes—doing his octaves, sir."

"Indeed," said Richard, recalling the action of the trombone player in the marine band on board his last ship.

"Perhaps you'd like to see the bedroom, sir?"

"Would you mind seeing that for me, Mrs Jenkles?" said Richard.

"It's plain, sir, but everything at Mrs Fiddison's here is as clean as hands can make it," said Mrs Jenkles, glancing from one to the other.

"Then it will do," said Richard. "And the terms?"

"Seven shillings my last lodger paid me, sir," said Mrs Fiddison, drooping more and more, and evidently now much impressed by one of Richard's boots. "I did hope to get seven and six for them now, as there's a new table-cover."

Richard glanced at the new cotton check on the table.

"Then I'll pay you seven and sixpence," he said.

"The last being full of holes he made when smoking," said Mrs Fiddison.

"Then that's settled," said Richard. "Mrs—Mrs—"

"Jenkles, sir," said the cabman's wife, smiling.

"Mrs Jenkles, I'm much obliged to you for your trouble," he said.

"And so am I," said Mrs Fiddison, removing a tear once more with a scrap of crape. "My dear," she continued, fixing a band to the cap, and holding it out—"isn't that sweet!"

Mrs Jenkles nodded.

"I think the gentleman wants the rooms at once," she said, glancing at Richard.

"Yes, that I do," he replied. "I'll fetch my portmanteau over directly."

"Oh, dear!" ejaculated Mrs Fiddison—"so soon."

And with some show of haste, she took a widow's cap off a painted plaster Milton on the chimneypiece, another from Shakespeare, and revealed, by the removal of a third, the celebrated Highland laddie, in blue and red porcelain, taking leave of a green Highland lass, with a china sheep sticking to one of her unstockinged legs.

Half an hour after, Richard was sitting by the open window, looking across the street at where a thin, white hand was busy watering the fuchsias and geraniums in the window, and from time to time he caught a glimpse of Netta's sweet, sad face.

Then he drew back, for two men came along the street. The first, black-browed and evil-eyed, he recollected as the fellow with whom he had had the encounter on the race day, and this man paused for a moment as he reached Sam Jenkles's door, turned sharply round, pointed at it, and then went on; the second, nodding shortly as he came up, raised his hand, and knocked, standing glancing sharply up and down the street, while Richard mentally exclaimed—"What does he want here?" Then the door opened, there was a short parley with Mrs Jenkles, and the man entered, leaving Richard puzzled and wondering, as he said, half aloud—

"What could these men be doing here?"

Between Friends

A fortnight passed away.

It was a difficult matter to do—to make up his mind as to the future; but after a struggle, Richard arrived at something like the course he would pursue. He must live, and he felt that he had a right to his pay as an officer; so that would suffice for his modest wants.

Then, as to the old people. He wrote a quiet, calm letter to the old butler, saying that some time in the future he would come down and see them, or else ask them to join him. That he would do his duty by them, and see that they did not come to want; but at present the wound was too raw, and he felt that it would be better for all parties that they should not meet.

Another letter he despatched to Mr Mervyn, asking him once more to be a friend and guide to Humphrey; and, above all, to use his influence to prevent injury befalling Stephen and Martha Lloyd.

His next letter was a harder one to write, for it was to Valentina Rea. It was a struggle, but he did it; for the man was now fully roused in spirit, and he told himself that if ever he was called upon to act as a man of honour it was now. He told her, then, that he never loved her more dearly than now; that he should always remember her words in the letter he treasured up, but that he felt it would be like blighting her young life to hold her to her promise. If, in the future, he could claim her, he would; but he knew that father—soon, perhaps, mother—would be against it, for he could at present see no hope in his future career.

But all the same, he signed himself hers till death; sent his dear love to "little Fin;" and then, having posted his letters, he felt better, and went to seek out Frank Pratt.

"He won't turn out a fine weather friend, of that I'm sure," he said, as he went up, the staircase in the Temple, to be seized by both hands as soon as he entered, and have to submit to a couple of minutes' shaking.

"Why, Dick, old man, this does one good!" exclaimed Pratt. "Now, then, a steak and stout, or a chop and Bass, two pipes, and a grand debauch at night, eh?"

"What debauch?" said Richard, smiling.

"Front row of the pit, my boy. Absolute freedom; comfort of the stalls without having to dress. Nobody waiting to seize your 'overcoat, sir.' Good view of the stage; and, when the curtain's down, time and opportunity to pity the curled darlings of society, who stand, in melancholy row, with their backs to the orchestra, fiddling their crush hats, and staring up at the audience through eyeglasses that blind."

"And meet Flick and Vanleigh."

"Who cares?" said Pratt, forcing his friend into a well-worn easy chair, and taking away hat and stick. "Isn't that a lovely chair, Dick? I've worked that chair into that shape—moulded it, sir, into the form of my figure, and worn off all its awkward corners. Pipe?—there you are. 'Bacco?—there you are. Whisky?—there you are. And there's a light. Have a dressing-gown and slippers?"

"No, no—thanks," said Dick, laughing.

But his face twitched as, after filling and trying to light a pipe, he laid it hastily down, wrung Pratt's hand, and then started up and walked to the window, to stand gazing out at the dirty walls before him.

Before he had been there a moment, a friendly hand was laid upon his shoulder and Pratt got hold of his hand, standing behind him without a word, till he turned again and walked back to his seat.

"Don't mind me, Franky, I'm very sore yet."

"I know, I know," said Pratt, feelingly. "It's hard—cursed hard! I'd say damned hard, only as a straightforward man I object to swearing. But where's your bag, portmanteau, luggage?"

"Oh, that's all right," said Richard, lighting his pipe, and smoking.

"What do you mean by all right? Where shall I send for them?"

"Send for them?"

"Send for them—yes. You've come to stay?"

"Yes, for an hour or two."

"Dick," cried Pratt, bringing his fist down upon the table with a bang, "if you are such a sneak as to go and stay anywhere else, I'll cut you."

"My dear Frank, don't be foolish, I've taken lodgings."

"Then give them up."

"Nonsense, man! But listen to me. You don't blame me for giving up?"

"I don't know, Dick—I don't know," said Pratt. "I've lain in bed ruminating again and again; and one time I say it's noble and manly, and the next time I call you a fool."

Richard laughed.

"You see, old fellow, I'm a lawyer. I've been educating myself with cases, and the consequence is that I think cases. Here, then, I say, is a man in possession of a great estate; somebody tells him what may be a cock-and-bull tale—like a melodrama at the Vic, or a story in penny numbers—about a mysterious changeling and the rest of it, and he throws up at once."

"Yes," said Richard.

"Speaking still as a man fed upon cases I say, then, give me proofs—papers, documents, something I can tie up with red tape, make abstracts of, or set a solicitor to prepare a brief from. I'm afraid you've done wrong, Dick, I am indeed."

"No, you are not, Franky," said Richard, quietly. "Now speak as a man who has not been getting up cases—speak as the lad who was always ready to share his tips at school. No, no, Franky; the more I think of it, the more I feel convinced that I have behaved—as I cannot be a gentleman—like a man of honour."

"Gentleman—cannot be a gentleman!" said Pratt, puffing out his cheeks, and threatening his friend with one finger, as if he were in the witness-box. "What do you mean, sir? Now, be careful. Do you call Vanleigh a gentleman?"

"Oh yes," said Richard, smiling.

"Then I don't," said Pratt, sharply. "I saw the fellow yesterday, and he cut me dead."

"Indeed?"

"Yes, and no wonder. He was talking to a black-looking ruffian who bothers me."

"Bothers you?"

"Yes, I know I've seen him before, and I can't make out where."

"Was it at the steeplechase?" said Richard, quietly.

"You've hit it, Dick," cried Pratt. "That's the man. Why weren't you called to the bar? But I say, why did you name him? You know something—you've seen them together."

"I have."

"Um!" said Pratt, looking hard at his friend. "Then what does it mean?"

"Can't say," said Richard, quietly—"only that it don't concern us."

"I don't know that," said Pratt; "it may, and strongly. But tell me this, how long have you been in town?"

"A fortnight."

"A fortnight, and not been here!"

"I have been three times," said Richard, "and you were always out."

"How provoking! But you might have written. The fact is, Dick, I'm busy. All that work that was held back from me for so long is coming now. I was a bit lucky with my first case."

Which was a fact, for he had carried it through in triumph, and solicitors were sending in briefs.

"I have been busy, too—making up my mind what to do."

"Then look here, Dick, old fellow. I'm getting a banking account—do you hear? a banking account—and if you don't come to me whenever you want funds, we are friends no more."

"Franky," said Richard, huskily, "I knew you were a friend, or I should not have come to your chambers for the fourth time. But what did you mean about Vanleigh's affairs concerning us?"

"Well, only that they may. You know they are in town, of course?"

"Why, yes; I met Van the other day. Flick is sure to be near him."

"Yes, as long as Flicky has any money to spare—afterwards Van will be out. But I mean them."

"Whom?" said Richard, starting. "Our Tolcarne friends—Russell Square, you know," said Pratt, reddening slightly.

"No," said Richard, hoarsely, "I did not know it."

"Yes, they have been up a week."

"How did you know it?"

"Well," said Pratt, reddening a little more, "I—that is—well, there, I walked past the house, and saw them at the window."

"You've watched it, then, Franky?" said Richard, quietly.

"Well, yes, if you like to call it so; and I've seen Van and Flick go there twice. How did they know that you had—well, come to grief?"

Richard shook his head.

"I'll tell you. Depend upon it, that amiable spinster aunt, who loved you like poison, sent them word, and also of their return to town."

"Possibly," said Richard, in the same low, husky voice.

"Dick, old fellow, I don't think you've done quite right in giving up all," said Pratt. "You had some one else to think of besides yourself."

"For Heaven's sake, don't talk to me now," said Richard, hoarsely. "The task is getting harder than I thought; but if that fellow dares—Oh, it's absurd!"

He stood for a few moments with his fists clenched, and the thoughts of Vanleigh's dark, handsome face, and his visit to the little Pentonville street, seemed to run in a confused way through his brain, till he forced them aside, and, with assumed composure, filled his glass, and tossed it off at a draught.

He was proceeding to repeat it, when Pratt laid a hand upon his arm.

"Don't do that, old fellow," he said, quietly. "If there's work to be done, it's the cool head that does it; drink's only the spur, and the spurred beast soonest flags. Let you and me talk it over. Two heads are better than one, and that one only Van's. Dick, old fellow, what are you going to do?"

Lady Rea's State of Mind

Frank Pratt was quite right, the Rea family were in town; and thanks to Aunt Matilda, who had sent to Captain Vanleigh a notification of all that had taken place, that gentleman and his companion had resumed their visits; and had, in the course of a few days, become quite at home.

Lady Rea had felt disposed to rebel at first, but Vanleigh completely disarmed the little lady by his frank behaviour.

"You see, Lady Rea," he said to her one day, in private, "I cannot help feeling that you look upon me rather as an intruder."

"Really, Captain Van—"

"Pray hear me out, dear Lady Rea," he said, in protestation. "You prefer poor Trevor as your son-in-law—I must call him Trevor still."

"He was as good and gentlemanly a—"

"He was, Lady Rea—he was indeed," said Vanleigh, warmly, "and no one lamented his fall more than I did."

"It was very, very sad," said Lady Rea.

"And you must own, dear Lady Rea that as soon as I heard of the attachment between Trevor—I must still call him Trevor, you see—and your daughter, I immediately withdrew all pretensions."

"Yes, you did do that," said Lady Rea.

"Exactly," said Vanleigh. "Well, then, now the coast is once more clear, and the engagement at an end—"

"But it isn't," said Lady Rea.

"Excuse me, my dear Lady Rea—I have Sir Hampton's assurance that it is so. He tells me that Trevor—poor old Trevor—resigned his pretensions in the most gentlemanly way."

"Yes, he did," said Lady Rea; "and it was very foolish of him, too."

"Doubtless," said Vanleigh, with a smile; "but still, under the circumstances, how could he have done otherwise? Ah, Lady Rea, it was a very sad blow to his friends."

"It's very kind of you to say so, Captain Vanleigh," said Lady Rea.

"Don't say that," replied Vanleigh. "But now, Lady Rea, let me try and set myself in a better position with you. Of course you must know that I love Miss Rea?"

"Well, yes—I suppose so," said the little lady.

"Then let us be friends," said Vanleigh. "I am coming merely as a visitor—a friend of the family; and what I have to ask of you is this, that I may be treated with consideration."

"Oh, of course, Captain Vanleigh."

"If in the future Miss Rea can bring herself to look upon my pretensions with favour, I shall be the happiest man alive. If she cannot—well, I will be patient, and blame no one."

"He was very nice, my dear," said Lady Rea to her daughter. "No one could have been more so; but I told him I didn't think there was any hope."

"Of course there isn't, ma, dear," said Fin; "and it's very indecent of him to come as he does, and so soon after Richard's misfortune; but I know how it all was—Aunt Matty did it."

"Aunt Matty did it, my dear?"

"Yes, ma. Wrote to Captain Vanleigh at his club, and told him all about how pa said poor Richard was not to be mentioned in the house, and how we were all brought up to town for change."

"I don't think Aunt Matty would do anything so foolish, my dear," said mamma.

"Then how came they to call as soon as we had been up two days?" said Fin. "Aunt Matty would do anything she thought was for our welfare, even if it was to poison us."

"Oh, Fin, my dear!"

"Well, I can't help it, ma, dear; she is so tiresome. Aunt Matty is so good; I'm glad I'm not, for it does make you so miserable and uncharitable. Oh, ma, darling, what a dreadfully wicked little woman you must be!"

"Oh, my dear!"

"I'm sure Aunt Matty thinks you are. I often see her looking painfully righteous at you when you are reading the newspaper or a story, while she is studying 'Falling Leaves from the Tree of Life,' or 'The Daily Dredge.'"

"My dear Fin, don't talk so," said Lady Rea. "Aunt Matty means all for the best."

"Yes, ma, dear," said Fin, with a sigh, "that's it. If she only meant things for the second best, I wouldn't care, for then one might perhaps be comfortable."

"But, my dear, don't talk so," said Lady Rea; "and I think you are misjudging Aunt Matty about her sending to Captain Vanleigh."

"Oh no, ma, dear," cried Fin. "It's quite right. That dreadful noodle, Sir Felix, let it all out to me just now in the dining-room, while the Captain was upstairs with you."

"Has he been speaking to you, then?" said Lady Rea, eagerly.

"Yes, ma," said Fin, coolly; but there was a pretty rosy flush in her little cheek.

"What did he say, dear?"

"He-haw, he-haw, he-haw-w-w-w!" said Fin, seriously.

"Fin!"

"Well, it sounded like it, ma," said Fin, "for I never did meet such a donkey."

"But, my dear Fin—"

"Well, I know, ma," exclaimed Fin, "it's rude of me; but I'm naturally rude. I've got what Aunt Matty would call the mark of the beast on me, and it makes me wicked."

"Tut, tut, tut! Fin, my dear," said Lady Rea, drawing her child to her, till Fin lay with her head resting against her, but with her face averted. "Now, come, tell me all about it. I don't like you to have secrets from me."

"Well, ma, he met me, and begged for five minutes' interview."

"Well, my dear?"

"Well, ma, I told him it was of no use, for I knew what he was going to say."

"Oh, Fin, my dear child, I'm afraid they neglected your etiquette very much at school."

"No, they didn't, ma," said Fin, with her eyes twinkling—"they were always sowing me with it; but I was stony ground, as Aunt Matty would say, and it never took root. Oh, ma, if you had only seen what a donkey he looked!—and he smelt all over the room, just like one of Rimmel's young men. Then," continued Fin, speaking fast and excitedly, "he went on talking stuff—said he'd lay his title and fortune at my feet; that he'd give the world to win my heart, and I told him I hadn't got one; said he should wait patiently, and kept on talk, talk, talk—all stuff that he had evidently been learning up for the occasion; and I'd have given anything to have been able to pull his ears and rumple his hair, only he might have thought it rude."

"Oh yes, my dear," said mamma, innocently.

"And at last I said I didn't think I should ever accept any one, for I hated men; and then he sighed, and looked at me side-wise, and wanted to take my hand; and I ran out of the room, and that's all."

"But, Fin, my dear—"

"Oh, I know, ma, it was horribly rude; but I hate him. Pf! I can smell him now."

Lady Rea sighed.

"And now, I suppose," said Fin, "we are to be pestered—poor Tiny and your humble servant; they'll follow us to church, get sittings where they can watch us, and carry on a regular siege. I wish them joy of it!"

Lady Rea only sighed, and stroked the glossy head, till Fin suddenly jumped up, and ran out of the room; but only to come back at the end of a minute, and stand nodding her head.

"Well, my dear, what is it?" said Lady Rea.

"You'll have to put your foot down, mamma," said Fin, sharply.

Lady Rea glanced at her little member, which, in its delicate kid boot, looked too gentle to crush a fly; and she sighed.

"A nice state of affairs!" said Fin.

"There's Tiny, up in her bedroom crying herself into a decline, and Aunt Matty in the study with papa conspiring against our happiness, because it's for our good. Now, mark my words, mamma—there'll be a regular plot laid to marry Tiny to that odious Bluebeard of a Captain, and if you don't stop it I shall."

Lady Rea sat, with wrinkled brow, looking puzzled at the little decisive figure before her; and then, as Fin went out with a whisk of all her light skirts, she sat for a few moments thinking, and then went up to her elder daughter's room.

Frank a Visitor

Richard felt very sanguine of success during the first weeks of his stay in London. He was young, ardent, active, and a good sailor. Some employment would be easily obtained, he thought, in the merchant service; and he only stipulated mentally for one thing—no matter how low was his beginning, he must have something to look forward to in the future—he must be able to rise. But as the days glided into weeks, and the weeks into months, he was obliged to own that it was not so easy to find an opening as he had expected, and night after night he returned to his solitary lodgings weary and disheartened.

Mrs Fiddison sighed, and said he was very nice—so quiet; her place did not seem the same. And certainly the young fellow was very quiet, spending a great deal of his time in writing and thinking; and more than once he caught himself watching the opposite window, and wondering what connexion there could be between Vanleigh and his neighbours.

This watching led to his meeting the soft dark eyes of Netta, as she busied herself at times over her flowers, watering them carefully, removing dead leaves and blossoms, and evidently tending them with the love of one who longs for the sweet breath of the country.

Then came a smile and a bow, and Netta shrank away from the window, and Richard did not see her for a week.

Then she was there again, showing herself timidly, and as their eyes met the how was given, and returned this time before the poor girl shrank away; and as days passed on this little intercourse grew regular, till it was a matter of course for Richard to look out at a certain hour for his pretty neighbour, and she would be there.

This went on till she would grow bold enough to sit there close to the flowers, her sad face just seen behind the little group of leaves and blossoms; and, glad of the companionship, Richard got in the habit of drawing his table to the open window, and read or wrote there, to look up occasionally and exchange a smile.

"I don't see why I shouldn't know more of them," he said to himself, one morning; and the next time a donkey-drawn barrow laden with Covent

Garden sweets passed, Richard bought a couple of pots of lush-blossomed geraniums, delivered them to Mrs Jenkles, and sent them to Miss Lane, with his hope that she was in better health.

Mrs Jenkles took the pots gladly, but shook her head at the donor.

"Is she so ill?" said Richard, anxiously.

"I'm afraid so, sir," said Mrs Jenkles. "Her cough is so bad."

As she spoke, plainly enough heard from the upper room came the painful endorsement of the woman's words.

Richard went across the way thoughtfully; and as he looked from his place a few minutes after, it was to see his plants placed in the best position in the window; and he caught a grateful look directed at him by his little neighbour, "Poor girl!" said Richard.

A very strange feeling of depression came over him as his thoughts went from her to one he loved; and he sighed as he sat making comparisons between them.

An hour after, Mrs Fiddison came in, with her head on one side, a widow's cap in one hand, a crape bow in the other, and a note in her mouth, which gave her a good deal the look of a mourning spaniel, set to fetch and carry.

Mrs Fiddison did not speak, only dropped the note on the table, gave Richard a very meaning look, and left the roam.

"What does the woman mean?" he said, as he took up the note. "And what's this?"

"This" was a simple little note from Netta Lane, written in a ladylike hand, and well worded, thanking him for the flowers, and telling him that "mamma" was very grateful to him for the attention.

A week after, and Richard had called upon them; and again before a week had elapsed, he was visiting regularly, and sitting reading to mother and daughter as they plied their needles.

Then came walks, and an occasional ride into the country, and soon afterwards Frank Pratt called upon his old friend, to find him leading Netta quietly into the Jenkles's house, and Pratt stood whistling for a moment before knocking at Mrs Fiddison's door, and asking leave to wait till his friend came across.

Mrs Fiddison had a widow's cap cocked very rakishly over one ear, and she further disarranged it to rub the ear as she examined the visitor, before feeling satisfied that he had no designs on any of the property in the place, and admitting him to Richard's sanctum.

At the end of half an hour Richard came over.

"Ah, Franky!" he exclaimed, "this is a pleasure."

"Is it?" said Pratt.

"Is it?—of course it is; but what are you staring at?"

"You. Seems a nice girl over the way."

"Poor darling!—yes," said Richard, earnestly.

"Got as far as that, has it?" said Pratt, quietly.

"I don't understand you," said Richard, staring hard.

"Suppose not," said Pratt, bitterly. "Way of the world; though I didn't expect to see it in you."

"'Rede me this riddle,' as Carlyle says," exclaimed Richard. "What do you mean, man?"

"Only that it's as well to be off with the old love before you begin with the new."

"Why, Franky, what a donkey you are!" said Richard, laughing. "You don't think that I—that they—that—that—well, that I am paying attentions to that young lady—Miss Lane?"

"Well, it looks like it," said Pratt, grimly.

"Why, my dear boy, nothing has ever been farther from my thoughts," said Richard. "It's absurd."

"Does the young lady think so too?"

Richard started.

"Well, really—I never looked at it in that light. But, oh, it's ridiculous. Only a few neighbourly attentions; and, besides, the poor girl's in a most precarious state of health."

"Hum!" said Pratt. "Well, don't make the girl think you mean anything. Who are they?"

"I asked no questions, of course—how could I? They are quite ladies, though, in a most impecunious state."

"Hum!" said Frank, thoughtfully, and he rose from his chair to make himself comfortable after his way; that is to say, he placed his feet in the seat, and sat on the back—treatment at which Mrs Fiddison's modest furniture groaned. "Old lady object to this?"

Frank tapped the case of his big pipe, as he drew it from his pocket in company with a vile-scented tobacco pouch.

"Oh no, I'm licenced," said Richard, dreamily; for his thoughts were upon his friend's words, and he felt as if he had unwittingly been doing a great wrong.

"I'm going to take this up, Dick," said Pratt, after smoking a few minutes in silence.

"Take what up?" said Richard, starting.

"This affair of yours, and these people."

"I don't understand you."

"Perhaps not," said Pratt, shortly. "But look here, Dick, you're not going to break faith with some one."

"Break faith, Frank!" exclaimed Richard, angrily. "There is no engagement now. The poor girl is free till I have made such a fortune"— he smiled bitterly—"as will enable me once more to propose. There, there, don't say another word, Franky, old man, it cuts—deeper than you think. I wouldn't say this much to another man living. But as for that poor child over the way, I have never had a thought towards her beyond pity."

"Which is near akin to love," muttered Frank. Then aloud—"All right, Dick. I could not help noticing it; but be careful. Little girls' hearts are made of tender stuff—some of them," he said, speaking ruefully—"when they are touched by fine, tall, good-looking fellows."

"Pish!" ejaculated Richard. "Change the subject."

"Going to," said Pratt, filling his pipe afresh, and smoking once more furiously. "Better open that window, these pokey rooms so soon get full. That's right. Now, then, for a change. Look here, old fellow, you know I'm going ahead now, actually refusing briefs. Do you hear, you unbelieving-looking dog?—refusing briefs, and only taking the best cases."

"Bravo!" said Richard, trying to smile cheerily.

"I'm getting warm, Dick—making money. Q.C. some day, my boy—perhaps. But seriously, Dick, old fellow, I am going ahead at a rate that surprises no one more than yours truly. When I'd have given my ears for a good case, and would have studied it night and day, the beggars wouldn't have given me one to save my life, even if I'd have done it for nothing. Now, when I'm so pressed that it's hard work to get them up, they come and beg me to take briefs. This very morning, one came from a big firm of solicitors at ten o'clock, marked fifty guineas, and I refused it. At one o'clock, hang me if they didn't come back with it, marked a hundred, and a fellow with it, hat in hand, ready, if I'd refused again, to offer me more."

"Frank," cried Richard, jumping up, and shaking his friend warmly by the hand, "no one is more delighted than I am."

"Mind what you're up to," said Pratt, who had nearly been tilted off his perch by his friend's energy. "But I say, it don't seem like it."

"Why?"

"Because you won't share in it. Now, look here, Dick, old fellow, you must want money, and it's too bad that you won't take it."

"I don't want it, Frank—I don't, indeed," cried Richard, hastily. "Living as I do, I have enough and to spare. I tell you, I like the change."

"Gammon," said Pratt, shortly. "It's very well to talk about liking to be poor, and no one knows what poverty is better than I; but I like money as well as most men. I used to eat chaff, Dick; but I like corn, and wine, and oil, and honey better. Now, look here, Dick, once for all—if you want money, and don't come to me for it, you are no true friend."

"Franky," said Richard, turning away his face, "if ever I want money, I'll come to you and ask for it. As matters are, I have always a few shillings to spare."

As he spoke, he got up hastily, lit a pipe, and began to smoke; while Mrs Fiddison in the next room, heaved a sigh, took off her shoes, and went on tiptoe through the little house, opening every door and window, after carefully covering up all her widows' caps.

"There is one thing about noise," she said to herself, "it don't make the millinery smell."

"I knocked off a few days ago," said Frank, from out of a cloud.

"You are working too hard," said Richard, anxiously.

"'Bliged to," said Pratt. "Took a change—ran down to Cornwall."

Richard started slightly, and smoked hard.

"Thought I'd have a look at the old place, Dick—see how matters were going on."

Silence on the part of Richard, and Pratt breathed more freely; for he had expected to be stopped.

"First man I ran against was that Mervyn, along with the chap who was upset in the cab accident in Pall Mall, and gave you his card—a Mr John Barnard, solicitor, in Furnival's Inn—cousin or something of Mervyn's— knew me by sight, and somehow we got to be very sociable. Don't much like Mervyn, though. Good sort of fellow all the same—charitable, and so on."

Richard smoked his pipe in silence longing to hear more of his old home, though every word respecting it came like a stab.

"Heard all about Penreife," continued Pratt, talking in a careless, matter-of-fact way. "Our friend Humphrey is being courted, it seems, by everybody. Half the county been to call upon him, and congratulate him on his rise. I expected to find the fellow off his head when I saw him; but he was just the same—begged me to condescend to come and stay with him, which of course I didn't, and as good as told me he was horribly bored, and anything but happy."

There was a pause here, filled up by smoking.

"The old people are still there, and they say the new owner's very kind to them; but our little friend Polly's away at a good school, where she is to stay till the wedding. Humphrey wants to see you."

Richard winced.

"Asked me to try and bring about a meeting, and sent all sorts of kind messages."

Richard remained silent.

"Says he feels like as if he had deprived you of your birthright; and as for the people about, they say, Dick,"—Pratt paused for a few moments to light his pipe afresh—"they say, Dick, that you acted like a fool."

Richard faced round quietly, and looked straight at his friend.

"Do you think, Frank, that I acted like a fool?"

Pratt smoked for a moment or two, then he turned one of his fingers into a tobacco stopper, and lastly removed his pipe.

"Well, speaking as counsel, whose opinion is that you ought to have waited, and left the matter to the law to sift, I say yes."

"But speaking as my old friend, Frank Pratt," said Richard, "and as an honest man?"

"Well, we won't discuss that," said Frank, hopping off his perch. "Good-bye, old chap."

He shook hands hastily, and left the house, glancing up once at Sam Jenkles's upper window, and then, without appearing to notice him, taking a side glance at Barney of the black muzzle, who was making a meal off a scrap of hay, with his shoulders lending polish to a public-house board at the corner.

"There's some little game being played up here," said Frank to himself. "I'll have a talk to Barnard."

A Proposal

Frank Pratt had no sooner gone than Richard began to stride hastily up and down the little room, to the great endangering of Mrs Fiddison's furniture. As he neared the window he glanced across, to see Netta sitting there at work, and a faint smile and blush greeted him.

"Poor girl," he muttered. "But, no, it's nonsense. She can't think it. Absurd! She's so young—so ill. There, it's childish, and I should be a vain fool if I thought so."

He stood thinking for a few moments, and as he paused there was the rattle of wheels in the street, and Sam Jenkles drove his hansom to the door and stopped, gave the horse in charge of a boy, and went in.

The next minute Richard had crossed too, for a plan had been formed on the instant.

Mrs Jenkles met him at the door, and at his wish led him to where Sam was seated at a table, hurriedly discussing a hot meal.

"Drops in, sir, if ever I drives a fare in this direction, and the missus generally has a snack for me. Eh, sir? Oh no, sir. All right, I'll wait," he said, in answer to a question or two.

And then Richard ascended the stairs, knocked and entered, to find that mother and daughter had just risen from their needlework, Mrs Lane to look grave, Netta with a bright look in her eyes, and too vivid a red in either cheek.

"Ah, you busy people," he said, cheerily, "what an example you do set me! How's our little friend to-day?"

The bright look of joy in Netta's face faded slightly as she heard their visitor speak of her as he would of some child, but there was a happy, contented aspect once more as she placed her hand in his, and felt his frank pressure.

"Mrs Lane," said Richard, speaking gaily, "I'm like the little boy in the story—I'm idle, and want some one to come and play with me, but I hope for better luck than he."

Mother and daughter looked at him wonderingly.

"I've come to tell you," he said, "that the sun shines brightly overhead; there's a deep blue sky, and silvery clouds floating across it; and six or seven miles out northward there are sweet-scented wild flowers, waving green trees, all delicious shade; the music of song-birds, the hum of insects, and views that will gladden your hearts after seeing nothing but smoke and chimneypots. I am Nature's ambassador, and I am here to say 'Come.'"

As he spoke the work fell from Netta's hands, her eyes dilated, and a look of intense glad longing shone from her soft, oval face, while she hung upon her mother's lips, till, hearing her words, the tears gathered in her eyes, and she bent her head to conceal them.

Mrs Lane's words were very few; they were grateful, but they told of work to be done by a certain time, and she said it was impossible.

"But it would do you both good. Miss Netta there wants a change badly," said Richard; "and you haven't heard half my plan. Jenkles has his cab at the door, and I propose a drive right out into the country, and when we get back you will ask me to tea. It will be a squeeze, but you will forgive that."

Poor Mrs Lane's face looked drawn in its pitiful aspect. She felt that such a trip would be like so much new life to her child, but she could not go, and she shook her head.

"It may not be etiquette, perhaps," said Richard, quietly, "but I shall ask you to waive that, and let me take Netta here. You know it will do her good, and she will have Mr Jenkles, as well as your humble servant, to take care of her."

Mrs Lane looked him searchingly in the face, which was as open as the day, and then, glancing at Netta, she saw her parted lips and look of intense longing. The refusal that had been imminent passed away, and laying her hand upon the young man's arm, she said, softly—

"I will trust you."

There was something almost painful in the look of joy in Netta's face as, with trembling eagerness, she threw her arms round her mother, and then, with the excitement of a child, hurried away to put on hat and mantle.

"I shall be back directly," she exclaimed.

Richard's heart gave one heavy painful throb as he turned for an instant at the door.

Mrs Lane laid her hand upon his arm as soon as they were alone, and once more looked searchingly into his face.

"I ought not to do this," she said, pitifully. "You're almost a stranger; but it is giving her what she has so little of—pleasure; more, it is like giving her life. You know—you see how ill she is?"

"Poor child, yes," said Richard.

"Child!"

"Yes," said Richard, gravely. "I have always looked upon her as a child—or, at least, as a young, innocent girl. Mrs Lane, I tell you frankly, for I think I can read your feelings—every look, every attention of mine towards that poor girl has been the result of pity. If you could read me, I think you would never suspect me of trifling."

"I am ready to trust you," she said. "You will not be late. The night air would be dangerous for her—hush!"

"I'm ready!" exclaimed Netta, joyfully.

As she appeared framed in the doorway of the inner room, her dark hair cast back, eyes sparkling, and the flush as of health upon her cheeks, and lips parted to show her pure white teeth, Richard's heart gave another painful throb, and he thought of Frank Pratt's words, for it was no child that stood before him, but a very beautiful woman.

"You'll be back before dark, my darling?" said Mrs Lane, tenderly.

"Oh yes," cried Netta, excitedly. "Mr Lloyd will take such care of me; but—"

The joy faded out of her countenance, and she clung to her mother, looking from her to the work.

"What is it, my dear?" said Mrs Lane, stroking her soft dark hair.

"It's cruel to go and leave you here at work," sobbed the girl.

"What! when you are going to get strength, and coming back more ready to help me?" said Mrs Lane, cheerfully. "There, go along! Take care of her, Mr Lloyd."

Richard had been to the head of the stairs, and spoken to Sam, who was already on his box; and as the young man offered his arm, Netta took it, with the warm, soft blush returning, and she stole a look of timid love at the tall, handsome man who was to be her protector.

The next minute she was in the cab, Richard had taken his place at her side, and Sam essayed to start as the good-bye nods were given.

"Lor!" said Mrs Jenkles, her woman's instinct coming to the fore, "what a lovely pair they do make!"

At the same moment, on the opposite side of the way, a lady with a widow's cap cocked back on her head, gazed from behind a curtain, wiped her eyes on a piece of crape, and said, with a sigh—

"And him the handsomest and quietest lodger I ever had!"

Meanwhile, in answer to every appeal from Sam Jenkles, Ratty was laying his ears back, wagging his tail, and biting at nothing.

"Don't you be skeared, Miss," said Sam, through the little roof-trap, "it's on'y his fun. Get on with yer, Ratty—I'm blowed if I aint ashamed on yer. Jest ketch hold of his head, and lead him arf a dozen yards, will yer, mate?" he continued, addressing a man, after they had struggled to the end of the street. "Thanky."

For the leading had the desired effect, and Ratty went off at a trot to Pentonville Hill.

"Blest if I don't believe that was Barney," said Sam to himself, looking back, and he was quite right, for that gentleman it was; and as soon as the cab was out of sight he had taken a puppy out of one pocket of his velveteen coat, looked at it, put it back, and then slouched off to where he could take an omnibus, on whose roof he rode to Piccadilly, where he descended, made his way into Jermyn Street, and then stopping at a private house, rang softly, took the puppy out of his pocket, a dirty card from another, and waited till the door was answered.

"Tell the captain as I've brought the dawg," he said to the servant, who left him standing outside; but returned soon after, to usher him into the presence of Captain Vanleigh, who smiled and rubbed his hands softly, as he wished Tiny Rea could have been witness of that which had been brought to him as news.

In the Woods

The captain would have been more elate if he had been able to follow the fortunes of Sam Jenkles's cab; for having received his instructions, Sam bowled along by Euston Square in the direction of the Hampstead Road, till he had to go at a foot's pace on account of some alteration to the roadway, the result being that for a few moments the cab was abreast of a barouche containing four ladies, one of whom started, and said, in a quick whisper—

"Oh, look, Tiny, that's the church with the figures I told you about."

But Fin Rea was too late, her sister was leaning over the side of the carriage, gazing intently at Sam Jenkles's cab, and the dark-haired girl, with the wondrous colour and look of animation, looking so lovingly in her companion's face; and as the carriage swept on, unseen by the occupants of the cab, poor Tiny sank back, not fainting, but with a pitiful sigh and a look of stony despair that made Fin clasp her hands, as she set her little white teeth together, and muttered—

"The wretch!"

Lady Rea saw nothing of this; but Aunt Matty, who was beside her, did, and a look of quiet triumph came into her withered features. But nothing was said, and as for the cab, it rolled on and on quickly, till it came to the tree-shadowed hill beneath Lady Coutts' park, and then, after a long walk up to the top of Highgate Hill, on and on again, till London was far behind, the soft green meads and the sheltered lanes reached; and while Sam pulled up at a roadside public-house, amongst half a dozen fragrant, high-laden hay carts, Richard led off his charge, with sinking heart, over a stile, and away midst waving cornfields, bright with poppy and bugloss; and by hedges wreathed with great white convolvuli, and the twining, tendrilled bryonies, or wild clematis.

Richard was grave, and his heart sank as he saw the joyous air of the young girl by his side, felt the light touch of her little hand, and when he met her eyes read in them so much gentle, trusting love, that he felt as if he had been a scoundrel to her, and that he was about to blight her life.

He was not a vain man, and he had used no arts to gain the sympathy that it was easy to read in the sweet face beside him but he could not help telling himself that it was but too plain; and he groaned in his heart as he thought of that which he had determined to say.

"Hark, listen!" cried the girl, as a lark rose from the corn close by. "Isn't it beautiful? How different to those poor caged things in our street. Look, too, at the green there—four, five, twenty different tints upon those trees. Oh, you are losing half the beauties of those banks! Look at them, scarlet with poppies! There, too, the crimson valerian. How beautiful the foxgloves are! Why, there's a white one. Who'd ever think that London could be so near!"

She stopped, panting, and held her hand to her side.

"You are tired?" he said, anxiously.

"Oh no," she said, darting a grateful look in return for his sympathy—"it is nothing. I feel as if I should like to set off and run, but I think sometimes I am not so strong as I used to be. Mamma says I have outgrown my strength; but it is my cough."

She said these last words plaintively, and there was a sad, pinched look in her face as she gazed up at him; but it lit up again directly as she met his eager, earnest eyes fixed upon her, and her trembling little hand stole farther through his arm.

"That's right," he said, patting it—"lean on me. I'm big and strong."

"May I?" she said, softly.

"To be sure," he answered.

"It's very kind of you," she whispered, "and I like it. I go out so little, and yet I long to; and if I don't stay here long, I shall have seen so little of the world."

"Netta, my child," he exclaimed, "what are you saying?"

The girl's other hand was laid upon his arm, as they stood beneath a shady tree, and she looked up at him in a dreamy way.

"I think sometimes," she said, slowly, "that I shall not be here long. It's my cough, I suppose. It's so pleasant to feel, though, that people—some one cares for me; only it makes me feel that I shall not want to go."

"Come, come, this is nonsense," he said, cheerily. "Why, you're not an invalid."

"I should be, I think, if we were rich," she said, sadly. "But let's go on along by that high sand bank, where the flowers are growing; and here is a wood all deep shades of green."

"But you will be tired?"

"No, no; you said I might rest on you. I should not be weak if I could live out here, and dear mamma were not compelled to work. Poor mamma!"

They walked on in silence, and she leaned more heavily upon his arm. Twice their eyes met, and as Netta's fell before those of her companion it was not until they had told the sweet, pure love of her young heart. They were no fiery, rapturous glances—no looks of passionate ecstasy; but the soft, beaming maiden love of an innocent, trusting girl, whose young heart was opening, like a flower, to offer its fragrant sweets to the man who had first spoken gentle words to her—words that had seemed to her, who had not had girlhood's joys, like the words of love. And that young heart had opened under the influence, like the scented rosebud in the sun; but there was a fatal canker there, and as the flower bloomed, the withering was at hand.

"Let us stop here," cried Netta, drinking in the beauty of the scene; "it is like being young again, when we were so happy—when mamma watched for papa's coming, and there seemed no trouble in life. Oh, it has been a cruel time!"

She shuddered, and clung to the arm which supported her.

"This is very wrong of me," she said, looking up, and smiling the next moment. "I ought not to talk of the past like that."

"Shall we sit down here?" he said, pointing to a fallen tree trunk.

Then, with the low hum of the insects round them, they entered the edge of the wood.

He sat looking at her in silence for a few moments, and twice her eyes were raised to his with so appealing and tender a look that he felt unmanned. He had brought her there to tell her something, and her love disarmed him; so that he snatched at a chance to put off that which he wished to say.

"You were telling me of the happy past," he said. "Your were well off once?"

"Yes, and so happy," said the girl, her eyes filling with tears. "I ought not, perhaps, to tell you, though."

"You may trust me, Netta," he said, taking her hand.

"I always felt that I could," she cried, eagerly, as her face flushed more deeply, and her hand trembled in his; for he had again called her Netta, and her heart throbbed with joy, even though he was so grave. "Shall I tell you?"

"Yes—tell me; but are you weary?"

"Oh, no, no," she said, excitedly. "But I must not mention names. Mamma wishes ours kept secret, for she is very proud. Papa is an officer, and as I remember him first, he was so handsome, even as mamma was beautiful. We used to live in a pretty cottage, just outside town, and papa was so kind. But how it came about I never knew, he gradually grew cold, and hard, and stern, so that I was afraid of him when he came to see us, and he used to be angry to mamma, and then stay away for weeks together, then months, till at last we rarely saw him. The pretty cottage was sold, with everything in it—even my presents; and mamma and I lived in lodgings. And then trouble used to come about money; for poor mamma would be half distracted when none was sent her, and this dreadful neglected state went on, till mamma said she could bear it no more. Then she used to go out and give lessons; but that was terribly precarious work, and soon after she used to work with her needle."

"And your father?" said Richard.

"Never came," said Netta—"at least, very rarely. But I ought not to tell you more."

"Can you not trust me?" he said, with a smile.

"Oh, yes, yes, yes," cried the girl, impetuously, and she nestled closer to him. "I can trust you. It was like this:—Papa was a Roman Catholic, and mamma had always brought me up in her own Protestant religion; and by degrees I found out he had made a point of that, and had told mamma that their marriage was void, as it had only been performed according to one church. He used to write and tell her that he was free, and that if she would give up every claim on him, and promise to write to that effect, he would settle a regular income upon her."

"And your mamma?"

"I heard her say once to herself that it would be disgracing me, and that she would sooner we starved. That is why we have worked so hard, and had to live in such dreadful places," said the girl, shuddering.

"My poor child!" he said, tenderly. "Yours has been a hard life, and you so delicate."

"I shall grow strong now," she said, half shyly; "but why do you call me child?"

She looked up in his face with a smile, half playful, half tender—a look that made him shiver.

"You are not cross with me?" she said, gazing at him piteously.

"Cross? No," he said, gently.

And he once more took her hand, trying hard to begin that which he had brought her there to tell, but as far off as ever. At the end of a minute, though, she gave him the opportunity, by saying naïvely—

"You have never told me anything about yourself. Mamma wondered what you were—so different to everybody we meet."

"Let me tell you, Netta," he said, earnestly. "And promise me this—that we are still to be great friends."

She looked at him wonderingly.

"Yes, of course," she said. "Why should we not be? You have always been so kind."

He paused for a moment or two; and then, there in the calm of that shadowy wood, with the sunbeams coming like golden arrows through the leafy boughs, and the distant twitter of some bird for interruption, he told her of his own life and troubles, watching her bright, animated face as she listened eagerly, sometimes laying her hand confidingly upon his arm, till his tale approached the chapters of his love; and now, impassioned in his earnestness, he half forgot the listener at his side, till, in the midst of his declaration of love and trust and fidelity to Valentina Rea, he became aware of a faint sigh, and he had just time to catch the poor girl as she was slipping from the tree trunk to the ground.

"Poor child!" he said, raising her in his arms, gazing in the pale face, and kissing her forehead. "It was a cruel kindness, for Heaven knows I never thought of this."

He sat holding her for a few moments, as animation came slowly back, till at last her eyes opened, looking wonderingly in his; and then, as recollection returned, she put up her two hands as if in prayer, and said, piteously—

"Take me home—please, take me home."

"Netta, my child," cried Richard, sinking at her feet, "recollect your promise—that we were to be friends. I have hurt you—I have wounded you. I call God to witness that I never meant it!"

A sad smile quivered for a moment on her poor white lips, as he kissed her hands again and again; and then, as the full reality of all she had heard came upon her, she uttered a low, heart-breaking wail, and sank upon the ground amidst the ferns and grass, covered her face with her hands, and sobbed aloud.

"My God, what have I done?" exclaimed Richard, hoarsely. "Netta, my child, I tried to be kind to you, and it has all turned to gall and bitterness. For Heaven's sake, tell me you forgive me—that you do not think me base and cruel. Netta, pray—pray speak to me."

She dropped her hands in her lap, and raised her blank white face to his.

"You believe me?" he cried, hoarsely.

"Yes, yes," she said, piteously. "It was my fault. I thought—I thought—"

"Hush, my poor darling!" he whispered, "I know what you would say. I should have known better."

"No," she said, sweetly, and her trembling voice was so piteous that the tears rose to the strong man's eyes. "It was I who should have known better, Richard—I, who have only a few short months to stay on earth."

"Netta!" he cried, and his voice was wild and strange.

"Yes, it is true," she said, simply—"it is quite true; but you came like sunshine to my poor dark life, and I could not help it—I thought you loved me."

"And I do, my child, dearly, as I would a sister!" he exclaimed, passionately, as he raised her up, and kissed her forehead. "Netta, I would have given my right hand sooner than have caused you pain."

"Don't blame yourself," she said, softly, extricating herself from his arms; "I should have known better. Take me home—take me home!"

She caught at his arm after trying to walk alone, and looked pitifully in his face.

"You see," she whispered, "it was a dream—a dream; but so bright, and now—"

She reeled, and would have fallen but for the strong arm flung round her; and Richard held her for a few moments till she recovered.

"Richard," she whispered, sadly, "forgive me if I was unmaidenly and bold; but it seemed so short a time that I should be here, that I could not act as others do. But take me home—take me home."

She seemed half fainting, and raised he handkerchief to her lips, to take it down stained with blood. Then, shuddering slightly, she turned her face to his, smile faintly, and laid one little thin hand upon his breast, before hanging almost inanimate upon his arm.

Richard uttered a groan as he raised her in his arms, and bore her rapidly into the lane, where, at the distance of a hundred yards, stood the cab, with Batty grazing comfortably, and Sam Jenkles dozing on his box.

"Taken ill—quick!" gasped Richard, as he lifted his burden into the vehicle. "Quick—London—the first doctor's."

The Use of Money

That evening Frank Pratt was busily preparing himself for a City dinner, when Richard rushed panting into the room, haggard, his face covered with perspiration, and a look of despair in his eyes that frightened his friend.

"Why, Dick, old man," he cried, catching his hands, "what is it?"

"Money, Frank—give me money—ten—twenty—fifty pounds; doctors—doctors. I've killed her—killed her!" he groaned.

Pratt asked no questions, but unlocking a desk, he took out and placed five crisp bank notes in his friend's hand.

"I knew you would," panted Richard. "God bless you, Frank! Best doctor—consumption?"

"Morley, Cavendish Square," said Pratt, with sharp brevity.

Then waving his hand, Richard dashed from the room; while Pratt quietly sat down, half-dressed, to think it out, which meant to light his pipe.

Meanwhile his friend had rushed down, taken Sam Jenkles's cab, which was waiting, and, as he was being driven through the streets, went over the incidents of his return—how they had called on a suburban surgeon, who had administered a styptic, and ordered them to go back very gently—how Mrs Lane had met him with a look of reproachful agony in her eyes, as he lifted out the half insensible girl, and bore her upstairs; and then, as he turned to go, after laying poor Netta on the bed, she had held out her hands to him, taking his in hers, and kissing them—so unmanning him that he had sunk upon his knees by her side, and hid his face.

He could hardly recall the rest—only that he had had to go to four doctors before he could find one ready to come to the shabby street; and when at last he had been brought to the poor girl's bedside, he had recommended the hospital.

It was this that had sent the young man to Frank Pratt's for money, the value of which he now thoroughly realised for the first time in his life.

The old white-haired physician came with him at once—Ratty, the horse, never once causing trouble; and Netta gave the messenger a grateful smile, as she saw the mission upon which he had been. Then, with his mind in a whirl, Richard waited to see the physician, taking him over into his own rooms, that his questions might be unheard.

"But she will recover?" said Richard, eagerly.

The old physician shook his head.

"It is but a matter of time," he said, gravely. "I can do nothing. Quiet, change, nutritious food, are the best doctors for a case like hers. A southern climate might benefit her a little; but it would be cruelty to send her away from home, and might do more harm than good. The poor girl is in a deep decline."

Richard was alone. What an end to the pleasant day he had projected!—one which should do his poor little neighbour good, and wherein at the same time he could quietly tell her of his position, and so stop at once any nascent idea she might have that he was seeking to win her love. How could he know, he asked himself, that matters had gone so far—that the poor child really cared for him—for him, who had not a disloyal thought to Valentina Rea; who, like the poor sufferer, lay that night wakeful, and with a weary, gnawing pain at her heart—in the one case mingled of hopeless misery, in the other tinged with bitterness, and a feeling new to her—anger against the author of her pain.

Thus the days glided by, with Netta lying dangerously ill, too weak to be moved. Richard was over a dozen times a day, asking after her health, and he had insisted upon Mrs Lane taking money for the necessities of the case. Then came a day when a fly stopped at the door; and Richard from his window, expecting to see a fresh doctor, saw a quiet-looking man step out, enter, stay a quarter of an hour, and then return; and when, an hour later, he went over himself, it was to find Mrs Lane deeply agitated, and with traces of tears upon her face; but she made no confidant of him.

At last, while he was sitting writing one day, there came a letter for him, with Frank Pratt for bearer. It had come to his chambers by post, he said, enclosed in another, asking him to forward it.

Frank went away as soon as he had delivered it, seeming troubled; and on Richard opening the note, he found these words:—

> "I think it right to tell you what you have done, though no one knows that I have written. I did trust you, Richard Trevor; for I thought you a true, good man, who would be as faithful to my dear sister as she would have been to you. If any one had told me you would give her up directly for somebody else, I could have struck him. But

I'll tell you what you've done, for you ought to know it for your punishment: you've broken the heart of the dearest, sweetest sister that ever lived, and I hate you with all mine.

"Fin Rea.

"P.S.—Tiny's very ill, almost seriously, and all through you."

He had hardly read the note a second time, when Mrs Fiddison came in dolefully, to say that Mrs Jenkles wanted to speak to him; and upon that lady being admitted, it was to say, with a curtsey—

"If you please, sir, Mrs Lane says Miss Netta has been begging for you to be sent for, if you'd come."

Richard rose to follow the messenger, who said, softly—

"You must be very quiet, sir, for she's greatly changed."

In the Square Called Russell

There's plenty of room in Russell Square for a walk, without the promenaders being seen by those without, either in the houses or on the pavement.

Russell Square had grown very attractive to Frank Pratt of late, and he used to smoke cigars there at all sorts of hours. He had been seen by the milk there at 6:15, railway time; Z 17 had glanced suspiciously at him at one a.m.; while the crossing-sweeper said she "knowed that there little stumpy gent by heart."

It was one afternoon about three, though, that Pratt was sauntering along one side of the square, when he saw Vanleigh and Sir Felix go slowly up to Sir Hampton's house; and a pang shot through the little fellow, as envy, hatred, malice, and all uncharitableness took possession of his heart.

"Lucky beggars!" he groaned.

He felt better, though, the next minute, for the servant who answered the door had evidently said "Not at home!" card-cases had been withdrawn, and then the visitors had languidly descended the steps and continued their way.

"Lucky beggars!" said Pratt again. "Heigho! what a donkey I am to wander about here. Poor Dick, though, it's to do him a good turn."

He crossed the road to the railings of the garden, and as he walked there he cast a very languishing look up at the great, grim house, almost fancying he heard "Er-rum!" proceed from an open window; and if he had not said his presence there was on account of his friend, any looker-on would have vowed it was in his own interests.

He walked slowly on, thinking about Cornwall, and another visit he had projected there; of Fin Rea; about Richard and his disappointments; about his pretty neighbour; and lastly of a case he had in hand, when a little toy dog rushed amongst the shrubs inside the railings, and began snapping and barking at him with all the virulence of an old acquaintance.

"Get out, you little wretch!" thought Pratt, and then he fancied he recognised the dog.

"Why, it's Pepine!" he mentally exclaimed.

And if any doubt remained it was solved by a voice crying—

"Naughty Pepine, come here directly!"

Then through the trees he caught a glimpse of a lavender dress gracefully draping an iron seat.

It was not the dog that made Frank Pratt flee with rapid strides, till a thought made him check his steps.

"Suppose some one else was walking there!"

In the hope that it might be possible, Pratt went slowly on, taking advantage of every break in the trees to peer anxiously through the railings, seeing, however, nothing but nursemaids in charge of naughty children, whom it was necessary to correct by screwing their arms at the sockets—a beneficial practice, no doubt, but whose good was not apparent at the time. There was a perambulator being propelled by a nursemaid reading the *Family Herald*, while the two children it contained were fast asleep—one hanging forward, sustained by a strap, and looking like a fat Punch in a state of congestion; the other leaning over the side, and having a red place ground in its ear by the perambulator wheel. Farther on there were more children, playing alone at throwing dirt, their protectress being engaged in a flirtation with a butcher in blue with a round, bullet head, whose well-oiled hair shone in the afternoon sun.

Pratt walked on, getting hopeless as he progressed, for soon he would come within range of Pepine, and perhaps be discovered when—What was that?

A sharp, short little cough that could be no other than Fin's; and there, through the trees, were she and her sister, Tiny resting on Fin's arm, and walking very slowly.

There was an opening in the shrubs farther on; and hurrying to this, though it was dangerously near Pepine and Aunt Matty, Pratt waited the coming of the sisters.

Alas, for human hopes!—they had turned back, and he had to hurry after them for some distance before he could find an opening sufficiently clear to display his figure, when he hazarded a cough; and on Fin looking sharply round, he followed it up with a "How d'ye do, Miss Rea?"

"It's Mr Pratt!" he heard Fin whisper. And then came back a quiet response.

"Do you always walk like this—within prison bars?" said Pratt, walking on parallel with them.

"It can't be prison when one holds the keys, Mr Pratt," said Fin, sharply.

"You'll let me shake hands?" he said, after a pause. "I never see you now."

"How can you?" said Fin, sharply, "when you never call."

"What was the use of my calling, when your servant could only speak me one speech?" said Pratt.

"And pray, what was that?" said Fin, with her nose in the air. "Not at home."

Fin gave her foot a little stamp on the gravel, and whispered to her sister. By this time they had reached the gate, just as a nursemaid unlocked it to pass through with her charge.

"Thanks," said Pratt, quietly. And, walking in, he was the next moment with Fin and her sister; the former looking defiant, and half drawing back her hand, the latter so pale and ill that, forgetting Fin, Pratt took both her hands affectionately, as, with a husky voice, he exclaimed—

"My dear Miss Rea, I didn't know you had been so ill."

Tiny answered with a gentle smile; and Fin, who had been setting up all the thorns about her, ready to tear and lacerate this intruder, now looked quite humid of eye, and shook hands warmly.

"I—I didn't know you'd be so glad to see me," said Pratt, flushing with pleasure.

"I didn't say I was," said Fin, archly.

"You looked so," it was on Pratt's lips to say; but he checked it, and they strolled on—away from Aunt Matty, after Fin had mischievously proposed that Pratt should go and see her—till Tiny complained of fatigue and sat down.

Here was an opportunity not to be lost; and, after a little solicitation, Fin consented to leave her sister and walk on, conditionally that they kept in sight.

Pratt, on the strength of his prosperity, had determined to sound his little companion; but before they had gone a dozen yards, he found that his own affairs were to be of no account.

"What's become of that wretch of a friend of yours?" said Fin, sharply.

"Do you mean Sir Felix Landells?" said Pratt, borrowing a shaft from her own quiver.

"No, I don't," said Fin, flushing scarlet, "nor any such silly donkey, I mean—"

Pratt would have gone down on his knees in the gravel, only there was a nursemaid close by, and a big, fat child was sucking its thumb, and staring at them; but he burst out, in a husky voice—

"Oh, Miss Rea—Finetta—pray, pray say that again."

"Indeed, I shall do no such thing," said Fin, sharply, and becoming more red—"why should I?"

"Because it makes me so happy," said Pratt. "I thought it was to be he."

"Then you ought to be ashamed of yourself," said Fin. "A nice feeling of respect you must have for me, to couple me with that scented dandy."

"Finetta, don't be hard upon me," gasped Pratt—"I can't talk now. If I had you in a witness-box I could go ahead, but I feel now as if I were going to lose my case."

"What stuff are you talking?" said Fin, whose breast was panting.

"I was trying to tell you that I loved you with my whole heart," said Pratt, earnestly; "even as I learned to love you down in Cornwall, when I was such a poor, miserable beggar that I wouldn't have told you for the world."

"And now you're in Jumbles *versus* Hankey, and the great cotton case."

"Why, how did you know?" cried Pratt.

"I always read the law reports in the *Times*" said Fin, demurely.

Pratt choked; he felt blind; then the railings seemed to be dancing with the trees, and the little children to be transformed into cherubs, attended by angels, with triumphant perambulating cars. He felt as if he wanted to do something frantic; and it was a minute before he came to himself, and could see that the tears were running down Fin's cheeks.

"Thank you," he said at last. "Finetta—Fin—may I call you Fin? dearest Fin, say I may."

"No, no, no," jerked out Fin, hysterically—"you mustn't do anything of the kind. Pa wouldn't approve, and Aunt Matty hates you, and—and—and I'm nearly sure I do."

"Go on hating me like this, then," cried Pratt, rapturously. "Oh, darling, you've made me so happy!"

"I haven't," protested Fin, "and I can't, and I won't. How can I, when poor darling Tiny has been so treated by that odious wretch?"

"What—Vanleigh?"

"No, you know what I mean; but he's an odious wretch, too. It's abominable. Mr Trevor ought to be hung."

"Why?" said Pratt.

"Why?" echoed Fin. "Hasn't he jilted my poor darling, and behaved cruelly to her, after winning her heart, just as all men do?"

"No," said Pratt, stoutly.

"What!" cried Fin, "didn't I see him out with her himself, and hasn't somebody been at our house dropping hints about it—unwillingly, of course—and made pa delighted, and Aunt Matty malicious? while poor mamma has done nothing but cry, because she liked and believed in your nice friend. As to poor Tiny, she was dangerously ill for a time."

"I don't care," said Pratt, vehemently; and he arranged an imaginary wig, and waved some non-existent papers in the air. "Matters may be against my client—I mean Dick; but I'll stake my life on his honour. I say Richard Trevor—Lloyd, as he calls himself now—is a true man of honour. Look how he gave up the estate! See how he yielded his pretensions to Miss Rea's hand! And do you dare to tell me that this is a man who would stoop to a flirtation, or worse, when he owns to being cut up by the loss he has sustained? I say it's impossible, and that the person who would dare to charge my cli—friend, Richard Trevor, alias Lloyd, with such duplicity is—"

"What?" said Fin, sharply. That one little word went through Frank Pratt. He cooled on the instant, the flush of excitement passed away, and, in a crestfallen manner, he groaned—

"That's just like me. What a fool I am! Now you'll be cross with me."

"No, I shan't," said Fin, demurely. "I like it. It's nice of you to stand up for your friend. I like a man to be a trump."

Fin's face was like scarlet as soon as she made this admission; and to qualify it, she hurriedly exclaimed—

"You may like him if you please; but till I see him cleared I shall hate him bitterly; and—and—and—I don't know how he ought to be punished. He'll be punished enough, though, by losing my sweet sister. Why didn't you like her, instead of some one else?" she said, archly.

"Don't ask me," said Pratt. "I'm so happy, I shall do something foolish."

"You haven't anything to be happy about," said Fin; "for I'm going to devote myself to Tiny, and if they force her into this hateful marriage, I mean to be a nun."

"What marriage?" said Pratt.

"Why, with that Bluebeard of a captain."

"And are they pushing that on?"

"Yes," said Fin, "and it's abominable. It will kill her."

"No, it won't!" said Pratt, coolly.

"Then you're a wretch!" said Fin, with flashing eyes. "I say it will."

"And I say it won't," said Pratt; "because it must never come off."

Fin stared at him.

"I'll see to that," said Pratt, confidently. "I have a friend busy about Master Captain Vanleigh. But, oh!" he exclaimed, as the recollection of one Barnard, solicitor, brought up a gentleman of the name of Mervyn—"but, oh! I say, tell me this, Fin—Mr Mervyn—you know—there wasn't ever—anything—eh?"

"Oh, you goose!" cried Fin, stamping her foot. "Mr Mervyn—dear Mr Mervyn, of all people in the world!—who used to treat us like as if we were his little girls. Oh, Mr Pratt, I did think you had some sense in your head."

"Oh no," said Pratt, solemnly; "never—not a morsel."

Then they looked at one another, and laughed; but only for Fin to turn preternaturally serious.

"I must go back to Tiny now," she said.

"But when shall I see you again?" urged Pratt.

"Perhaps never," said Fin—"unless you can come about once a week, on a Friday afternoon, here in the square, and tell me some news that will do poor Tiny good."

"I may come and say good-bye to her, then?" said Pratt, getting hold for a moment of the little half-withdrawn hand.

"Yes, if you like. No—here's Aunt Matty."

In fact her herald approached in the shape of Pepine, who no sooner caught sight of the retreating form of Pratt, than he made a dash at him, chasing him ignominiously to the gate, where he stood barking long after his quarry had gone. But Pepine was no gainer in the end, for during the next week Fin never neglected an opportunity of administering to him a furtive thump.

Netta's Appeal

Richard felt very bitter as he followed Mrs Jenkles across the road. Mingled with pity for the poor girl he was about to visit, there was a sense of resentment; for she seemed to have been the cause of pain and sorrow to one he dearly loved. And yet, how innocent and gentle she was—how unlike any one he had met before! Pity may or may not be akin to love, but certainly it was very strong in Richard's breast at the present moment.

"If you'll step in the kitchen just a moment, sir, I'll see if you can go up," said Mrs Jenkles, smoothing her apron.

She ushered the visitor into the clean, bright place, where Sam was seated by the fireside, looking very hard at his pipe.

"How do, sir, how do?" he said. "Take a cheer, sir."

"Thanks, no, Sam, I'll stand," said Richard, quietly. "But where's your pipe?"

"There it hangs, sir," said Sam, folding his arms and looking at it.

"No tobacco?"

"Plenty, sir," said Sam; "but I've put the pipe out at home, sir: cos why? It sets that poor gal a-coughing, and that spoils it. It's a wonder, aint it, as doctors can't do more?"

Further converse was cut short by the entrance of Mrs Jenkles, who beckoned their visitor to come, and he followed her upstairs to the neat little front room, where a pang shot through Richard as he saw the change. Netta was half lying on a couch, propped up by pillows, and beside her, on a table, were the two plants he had sent across, evidently carefully tended,—not a withered leaf to be seen amongst their luxuriant foliage, while she who had made them her care lay there, white, shrunken, and so changed.

There was a bright smile of pleasure flickering about her lips, and a ray of gladness flashing from her eyes, as she held out her hands to him—hands that he caught in his and kissed, as he sank on his knees by her side.

"My poor girl!" he exclaimed, huskily, "is it so bad as this?"

"I'm so glad you are come," she whispered; and then she lay gazing at him, as if her very soul were passing from her eyes to his. "I've longed and prayed so for this. I thought once that it wasn't to be—that I was never to see you again; but I'm better now."

"Better—yes; and you'll soon grow strong and well again."

"Do you think so?" she said, looking at him wistfully, while an incredulous smile was upon her lips. "But don't let's talk of that. Sit down by me, where I can see you—I've so much to say."

He drew a chair to her side, and, as he did so, he saw that they were alone, for Mrs Lane had gone out softly directly he had entered. Then sitting down, the note which he had received fell from his pocket, and lay half beneath the couch.

"You are not angry with me for sending for you?" said the girl, piteously. "Why do you frown?"

"Did I frown?" he said, gently. "It was only a passing thought. There, now, let's have a quiet, long chat."

"Yes," she said, eagerly. "I want to thank you for being so kind to us—for the fruit and flowers, and all you have done for mamma. As for me," she continued, laying her hand in his, "I shall be so ungrateful."

"No, no, I cannot believe that."

"Yes," she said, smiling, "you have done so much to make me well, and in return I shall die."

"My dear child, you must not talk like this," exclaimed Richard, with an involuntary shiver. "You must get well and strong again."

She shook her head sadly, and then lay gazing up into his eyes.

"Netta," he said, gently, "you have thought a great deal about me since you have been ill."

"Yes—oh yes," she said.

"Looking back, then, do you blame me—do you think I was cruel, and led you on to think I loved you?"

"No," she said, and her hand closed almost convulsively on his. "I don't think so now. I have thought it all over, and it was my folly and weakness. I seem to have grown old since then, and to have become so much wiser. That's all past now; but I want you to tell me, first, that you did not think me forward then, and strange."

"My child," said Richard, "I have felt that the blame has been on my side, and it has caused me many a pang."

"But it is all past now," said Netta, eagerly. "I know—I can see plainly enough. You knew better how ill I was than I did, and pitied and were very sorry for me; and it seemed so sweet to me that—that I could not help watching for you—feeling glad when you came. But that's all past now, and you said we could be friends."

"Indeed, yes," he said, gazing into the great, brilliant eyes; but in a sad, dreamy way, for he could read but too plainly the coming end.

"And you forgive me—quite forgive me?" she murmured.

"My poor child, I have nothing to forgive," he said, leaning over and kissing her forehead.

"Thank you," she murmured, closing her eyes; and she lay silent for a few moments. Then, brightening, she said, "Now tell me again about her."

He remained silent, and she repeated her request—almost impatiently.

"Tell me her name."

He looked at her wonderingly for a few moments, before he answered, softly—

"Valentina."

"Valentina," said Netta, smiling. "Yes, a pretty name—Valentina. I shall love it as I love her."

"You love her?"

"Yes, though I have never seen her. Did you not tell me that she loved you? You think me strange," she continued, smiling in his face, "but I am not. Why, if you could have loved me, I could not have stayed, and you would have been unhappy. It is for the best, and I shall know that you are content."

"Netta," said Richard, hoarsely, "you must not talk like this."

"Why not?" she said, wonderingly. "All the trouble seems past to me. Now I know you feel for me—I believe you like me. Everybody seems kind to me now, and that foolish little dream has quite passed away. Come, tell me about her. I should like to know her. Would she come to see me—if she knew that I was dying?"

"Yes, I feel sure she would, if she knew all," said Richard, sadly. "She is everything that is gentle and good, and would have loved you dearly, Netta. You may meet yet."

"I should like to see her," said the girl, enthusiastically, "that I might tell her how noble and good you are. There, you see how I make an idol of my brother Richard."

He started, and looked hard at her.

"Yes," she said, "brother Richard—you were behaving like a dear brother to me, only I could not understand. I never had a brother, but you will be one to me still. You will not stay away, Richard, even if I love you, for it is a chastened love now—one that I need not feel ashamed to own. You'll not stay away, but come and sit with me, and read to me, as you did before?"

He shook his head sadly.

"Yes—yes, you will come," she cried, putting her hands together. "I shall have something to live for then—a little longer—and we can sit and talk of her—of Valentina. If you stay away—I—I—shall—die."

It was no fiction of the lips, and Richard knew it, as her voice grew weaker, and she seemed to droop. The mark was upon her face, telling that she was one of those soon to fall. Her pitiful appeal went to his heart; and raising her in his arms, he pillowed her head upon his shoulder, and kissed her quivering, pallid lips, as in a voice broken with emotion he muttered in the familiar old scriptural words—

"God do so to me, and more also, my poor stricken lamb, if I do not try and smooth your poor, thorny path."

Once, and once only, did her poor, thin lips respond to his caress. Then, her transparent, white hand was passed lightly over his forehead; her eyes closed, and with a faint sigh of content, she lay quite still, her fluttering breath telling, at the end of a few minutes, that she had, thoroughly exhausted, fallen asleep.

Waiting for News

The weeks went on, and glided into months. Frank Pratt had been as punctual as the clock in his visits to Russell Square, but his love matters made no progress. Unless he had something to communicate affecting Tiny, Fin would hardly stay a minute. Then, too, at times, there were checks caused by the presence of Aunt Matty, when Pratt would return to his chambers disconsolate, and yet happy at having had a glimpse of the darling of his heart.

Once, when he had entered strongly into his affairs, and spoke of trying to renew his acquaintance in a straightforward way with the family—

"Because I should not be ashamed to meet Sir Hampton now," he said.

Fin responded coolly—

"I'm afraid I hate you very much, Mr Pratt."

"Hate me! Why?" he exclaimed.

"Because you're so unfeeling."

"Unfeeling?"

"You think so much of yourself, and your silly love nonsense, when poor Tiny is persecuted and tortured by that hateful Vanleigh, who only wants her money. I believe he'd ill-treat her before they'd been married a month. He looks like a wife-beater."

"But they never persecute you," said Pratt.

"Don't they? Why, only this morning pa told me that he should expect me to receive Sir Felix Landells; while ma cried, and Aunt Matty nodded her head approvingly."

"And—and what did you say?" cried Pratt.

"I gave Pepine a vicious kick, and walked out of the room. And now, sir, if you please, how about all your fine promises? What have you done all these months? Have you got that wicked wretch Trevor back his property? Come, speak!"

"No," said Pratt, "I went down on Tuesday to see how things were, and Master Humphrey seems settling down comfortably enough. Quite the country squire."

"Serve Richard Trevor right," said Fin. "And now, about that girl? Does he go to see her still?"

Pratt was silent.

"How dare you stand there like that, Frank, and not answer me?" cried Fin.

"Call me Frank again, darling, and I'll say anything you wish."

"I won't," said Fin. "You shall tell me without."

"I don't like telling tales about poor Dick," said Pratt.

"If you care for me, sir, it's your duty to tell me the honest truth about everything. Am I less than Richard Trevor?"

Bodily, of course, she was; but as she meant in his regards, he said she was all the world to him.

"Now, then," said Fin, "does he go to see that girl now?"

"Yes," said Pratt; "but I'm sure it's all in innocence. The poor girl is in a dying state. I went to see her with him once, and a sweeter creature you never saw."

"Then she has captivated you, too?" cried Fin, viciously.

"Oh, come—I say!" exclaimed Pratt. "Fin, that goes right to my heart."

"And now about Vanleigh. You've boasted over and over again that you could produce something which would put a stop to his pretensions—where is it?"

"You are so hard on a poor fellow," said Pratt. "I am trying my best, and I feel quite sure that he has no right to pretend to the hand of your sister; but then, you know, before one makes such a charge, there must be good personal and documentary evidence."

"Well," exclaimed Pin, "and where is it?"

"I haven't got it yet," said Pratt; "but I have tried very, very hard. I shall succeed, though, yet, I know."

"And while you are succeeding, poor Tiny is to be sacrificed?"

"Oh no; not so bad as that. I don't despair of seeing Dick back at Penreife, and your dear sister its mistress."

"Then I do," cried Pin, bitterly; "for she's drifting into a state of melancholy, and will let them persuade her to do what they wish. She thinks Richard has given her up, and deceived her; and soon she won't care whether she lives or dies."

"But, Fin—" said Pratt.

"Miss Rea, if you please, Mr Pratt," said the girl, formally.

"Don't be hard on me," he pleaded. "I'm trying my best, and if I can only get some one to speak, I shall have the whole thing at my finger's ends."

"Then the sooner you do the better," said Fin, sharply. "Good-bye."

"One moment, dear," whispered Pratt.

"Well, what is it?" said Fin.

"Give me one kind look, you beautiful little darling," whispered Pratt.

Fin made a grimace, and then, as if in spite of herself, her bright eyes beamed on him for a moment ere she withdrew them.

"And now tell me this," whispered Pratt; "if they say any more to you about Landells, or if he speaks to you, you'll—you'll—you'll—"

"There, good-bye!" cried Fin. "How can you be such a goose? I haven't patience with you—good-bye."

There was a look accompanying that good-bye that sent a thrill through Frank Pratt, and he went back to his musty briefs as light as if treading on air.

On reaching his chambers, though, it was to find Barnard, the solicitor, waiting for him.

"Well, what news?" was Pratt's greeting.

"Nothing more," was the reply. "I've sent, and I've been myself. That this Vanleigh has compromised himself in some way, so that his marriage is impossible, I feel convinced; but a solution of the matter can only come from one pair of lips."

"Well?"

"And they remain obstinately silent."

A Visit

And the months glided on. Winter came, and in its turn gave place to the promise of spring; that came, though, with its harsh eastern blasts that threatened to extinguish the frail lamp of life still burning opposite Richard's rooms.

He had responded to Pin's letter soon after its receipt, but he had heard no more. His attempts at obtaining an engagement had proved failures still; and so he had accepted his fate, and spent his time reading hard, his sole pleasures being a visit across the road, or a dinner with Frank Pratt.

Of the acts of the Rea family he knew little, save that they had wintered in Cornwall, from which a letter came occasionally from Humphrey or Mr Mervyn, both sent to the care of Frank Pratt, Esq.; and in his, Humphrey had twice over expressed a wish to divide the property with his old companion.

"I don't see why you shouldn't do so," Pratt had said. "It's Quixotic not to accept his offer."

"Aut Caesar, aut nullus," was Richard's reply. "No, Franky, I'm too proud. I could never go to Cornwall again but as master. Those days are gone."

"But, Dick, old man!"

"My dear Franky," said Richard, dropping something of the misanthropical bitterness that had come over him of late, "I am quite content as I am—content to wait; some of these days a chance will turn up. I'll abide my time."

"He's gone back to her," said Pratt, shaking his head. "Poor old Dick!— some people would misjudge him cruelly. Well, time will show."

Pratt was quite right, Richard had gone back to Netta; for it promised to be a fine afternoon, and on such days it had grown to be his custom to devote the few shillings he could spare from his scanty income to the payment of Sam Jenkles.

It was so this day. Sam was at the door by two, with the old horse brushed up, and every worn buckle shining. Then Richard would go upstairs, to find Netta with a bright spot in each cheek, and an eager welcome in her eye. She had gained ground during the autumn, but in the winter it had all been lost; and now the time had come when Richard raised her in his arms, and had to carry her—grown so light—down to the cab, wherein he tenderly placed her, and took her for one of the drives of which she was never weary.

It seemed a strange taste, but her desire was always for the same spot— the little wood where the fallen tree was lying. Here, on sunny days, she would sit for an hour, while he read to her; and then the quiet, slow journey was taken back, when the little ceremony had to be gone through in reverse, there was a grateful pressure of the hand, and Richard took his leave.

Twenty or thirty times was this little excursion made, and always with a foreboding on Richard's part that it was to be the last. But still she lingered, brightening with the balmy April weather that came by fits, and then fading again under the chilling blasts.

By some means Netta had informed herself of the return of the Rea family to town for the season, and she prepared to execute a little plan that had been long deferred. She had possessed herself of the note sent by Fin— the note which Richard had let fall. Probably Mrs Jenkles was the bearer of her messages, and had obtained the information she required. Suffice it that Tiny Rea, now somewhat recovered, but still pale and dejected, received one morning a note, which she read, and then placed in her mother's hands.

It was as follows:—

> "I have heard so often of your beauty, goodness, and your
> many acts of kindness, that I have been tempted to ask
> you to come once and see me before I pass away. I would
> say *pray* come, but I think your gentle heart will listen to
> my simple appeal. Come to me, and say good-bye.
> "Netta Lane."

Here followed the address.

"It's some poor creature in great distress, my dear, who has heard of us. We'll go this afternoon, and take her something."

"Would you go, mamma?" faltered Tiny, whose heart told her whom the letter was from.

"Certainly, my dear. I shouldn't rest to-night if I'd left such an appeal as that unanswered, let alone enjoy our At Home; though there isn't much enjoyment to be got out of those affairs, with everybody drinking tea on the stairs, and ten times as many people as we've room for."

"Then you would go, mamma?"

"Certainly, darling. It's an awkward time for her to send, but we'll go; and oh, my darling, pray, pray try and look bright. You make me wretched."

"I do—I will try, mamma!" exclaimed Tiny, suppressing a sob. "But tell me, is Captain Vanleigh going to be here to-night?"

"I—I was obliged to send him an invitation, my darling," said Lady Rea, pitifully. "Your papa stood at my side while I wrote it. If—if—he—Mr Trevor had stood firm to you, they should have cut me in pieces before I'd have done it; but as it is, what can I do?"

Tiny made no reply; and directly after luncheon the carriage came round, and, being left at the corner of the narrow street, Lady Rea and her daughter made their way on foot to the house of Mrs Jenkles.

Mrs Lane met them, and said it was her daughter's wish to see Miss Rea alone, if she would condescend to go up and see her; and a minute after, with a mist floating before her eyes, and a singing in her ears, Tiny stood near Netta's couch, as the poor girl lay, with clasped fingers, gazing up at the graceful, fashionably-dressed girl.

Tiny maintained a haughty silence for a few minutes. This was the girl for whom she had been forsaken. She felt sure of it. How could it be otherwise? But the letter said that she was dying. Fin had told her of Pratt's assurances; and, as the mist cleared away, so melted the hauteur, for she could not look upon the soft, sweet face before her with anger; and if he loved her, should not she do the same? The two girls gazed in each other's eyes for a few moments, and then, with a smile, Netta held out one hand.

"Thank you for coming," she said. "I have wanted to see you for months, and I was afraid I should not live long enough. Do you know why?"

"No—I cannot tell," said Tiny, in a choking voice; for she, too, could see for herself the truth of what had been said.

"I wanted to see the beautiful girl that he loves—her of whom he has so often talked—and to tell you that you have misjudged him, if you think as your sister thinks in the letter she sent."

"Letter?" exclaimed Tiny.

"Yes, this," said the girl, producing one from her bosom. "Oh, Miss Rea, how can you slight his noble love? If you only knew! You both misjudge him. Look at me, dear. I am here now; perhaps to-morrow, or the next day, I shall be gone. But I do not think I could have died without seeing you face to face, and telling you that he has been true, and noble, and faithful to you. You might not have believed me if I had been different; but now, ready to go away, you know mine are true words, when I tell you Richard Lloyd has been to me as a brother."

"Oh, I believe, I believe!" sobbed Tiny, sinking on her knees beside the couch. "But it is too late—too late!"

"No, no," whispered Netta, "it is not too late. Make him happy. Send to him to come to you. He is too proud and poor to come himself. But I know his story: how he lost all through being so honourable and good. Tiny—you see I know your name; why, he has described you to me so often that I should have known *you*—send for him, and bless him. You could not love such a one as he too well."

"Too late!" sobbed Tiny. "It is too late."

She started up, and turned as if to go; but only to push her hair back from her forehead, lean over Netta's couch and kiss her, as a pair of thin, weak arms closed round her neck. Then, tearing herself away, she hurried from the house with Lady Rea, who vainly questioned her as to the cause of her agitation.

"I asked the woman, who is very ladylike, my dear, but she said her daughter would explain; so I waited till you came down; and now," said the little ruffled dame, "you do nothing but cry."

"Don't ask me now, mamma, dear," sobbed Tiny, covering her face with her hands. "Another time I'll tell you all."

"Very well, my darling," said Lady Rea, resignedly. "But, pray, try now and look brighter. Papa will be terribly put out if he finds you so; for he said you told him yesterday you would do as he wished about Captain Vanleigh, and Aunt Matty has been quite affectionate to me ever since."

"Mamma, dear, do you think it will make you happier?"

"I don't know, my dear," said Lady Rea. "I blame myself sometimes for not being more determined; but I'm obliged to own that Captain Vanleigh has been very patient, and he must care for you."

Tiny shuddered again, and her sobs became so violent that Lady Rea drew up the carriage window, for a few minutes being quite alarmed. At length, though, the poor girl grew calm, and seemed to make an effort over herself as they neared home, just as Fin crossed the road from the square garden, looking as innocent as if she had not had half an hour's talk with Frank Pratt.

At Home

"And what do you mean to do, Tiny?" said Fin, as she stood by her sister's side, dressed for the evening. "Papa told me about it, and nearly boxed my ears because I said it was a shame; and he ended by saying if I did not follow your example, and listen to Sir Felix, he would keep me on bread and water; and then I laughed out loud, and he left the room in a fury. How could you be so weak?"

"I don't know," faltered Tiny, "only that I was very miserable. Constant dropping will wear a stone."

"Then the stone must be very soft. Withdraw your promise," cried Fin. "Do as I do. I'll be as obedient a child as I can, but I will not be married against my will."

"Please, Miss, somebody's downstairs already," said their maid, entering the room. "And Edward says Sir Hampton's in a towering passion because there was no one but him in the drawing-room."

"Isn't mamma there?" cried Fin.

"No, Miss, her ladyship was dressed, and going down; but her primrose satin came undone—give way at the hooks and eyes—and she had to go back to change it."

"Tell Edward to say we'll be down in a moment," said Fin.

Hurrying the girl out of the room, she turned to Tiny, who stood looking pale and stunned.

"It wasn't true, Fin!" she said, pitifully, as her face began to work. "He wasn't deceitful. I saw her to-day."

"Saw whom?" exclaimed Fin, in wonder.

"That poor girl. She sent for me—she is dying; and oh, Fin, darling, I feel as if my heart would break!"

She sank sobbing on her sister's shoulder, sadly disarranging poor Fin's dress; but that was forgotten as, with eager haste, the little maiden tried hard to soothe and comfort her.

"If ma won't fight for you, Tiny, I will," she cried, impetuously. "I declare its too bad. I don't half know what you are talking about; but Frank—I mean Mr Pratt, always sticks up for his friend. Ugh! I wish I'd been near when that wicked Mrs Lloyd changed the babies, I'd have knocked her head off."

At this moment there was a knock at the bedroom door.

"Coming—coming—coming—coming!" said Fin, in a crescendo,

Then running to the door, she opened it once more to the maid.

"Please, Miss—"

"Bother—bother—bother!" cried Fin. "Don't you see Miss Rea's poorly? Go and say we'll be down soon."

"But, please, Miss, Sir Hampton sent Edward for me, and jumped on me horrid. He said it was my fault you weren't dressed, and your dear ma looks quite frightened with the people coming."

"Go and say we'll come down as soon as my sister's better—there!"

She half pushed the girl from the room, and then turned to Tiny.

"Now, look here, Tiny—you're very fond of that wicked Richard Trevor, bad as he's behaved to you."

Tiny gave her a pitiful look.

"Then I say, once for all, it would be a piece of horrible wickedness for you to let papa frighten you into this engagement. Now, tell me directly how it was. You ought to have told me before. If you had been a good, wise sister, you would."

"Oh, Tin, I could not tell you!" said Tiny, plaintively. "You had just come in from the square, and looked so happy about—"

"I didn't—I wasn't—I hate him; and I won't listen to him any more till you are happy," burst out Fin.

Tiny smiled.

"Papa sent for me into his study, and took my hand, and sat down by me. He was so gentle and kind. He said he wanted to see us both settled in a position which should give us the entrée into good society; for he said that, after all, he knew well enough people did not care for him, as he'd been a tradesman."

Fin gave her head a jerk.

"He told me he had given way about—about—"

"Yes, yes—go on—I know," said Tin.

"And that if he had not lost his position he should never have opposed the match; but as that was all over, he begged me to consent to receive Captain Vanleigh's attentions. And, oh, Fin, he knew about the attentions to that poor girl, and told me of it."

"Then some spiteful spy must have told him that," cried Fin. "Oh, Aunt Matty."

"He talked to me for an hour, Fin, so kindly all the time—said it would be for the best, and that it would make him happy and me too, he was sure; and at last I gave way. For oh, Fin, darling, I had no hope yesterday—nothing, I felt, to live for; and I thought that if I could make him satisfied, and dear ma happy, that was all I need care to do."

"Then you were a wicked, weak little coward," said Fin, "I'd have died sooner than given way. There, here they are again for us; and now I suppose we are to meet those people to-night."

"Yes; papa said he should write to Captain Vanleigh."

"And Sir Felix, of course. Madame, your humble servant—Finetta, Lady Landells. There, we're coming down now. Miss Rea is better," she said, in answer to a knock at the door.

Tiny turned to the glass, and smoothed her hair, while Fin went and stood behind her, holding her waist.

"What are you going to do?" she said, sharply.

Tiny shook her head.

"Masterly inactivity—that's the thing," cried Fin. "Do nothing; let things drift, same as I do. It can't go on, I'm sure it can't. There, let's go down, for poor dear mamma's sake, and I'll be buffer all the evening. Whenever Bluebeard comes near you, I'll get between, and we'll have a long talk to-morrow."

The two girls went down, to find many of the visitors arrived; and the news of Tiny's indisposition having spread, she was surrounded directly with kind inquirers. But she hardly heard a word that was said to her, for her timid eyes were wandering round the room, to see if the object of her dread had arrived; and then, noticing his absence, she sank back in a fauteuil with a sigh of relief.

Fin mounted guard by her side, and snubbed the down off the wings of several butterflies who came fluttering about them, her little lips tightening into a thin smile as Sir Felix and Vanleigh were announced.

Directly they had freed themselves from their host and hostess, they made their way to the corner of the great drawing-room, now ablaze with gas and candles, where the sisters were together; and, in spite of Fin's diplomacy, she found Vanleigh too much for her, as he quietly put aside her vicious little thrusts, and ended by interposing himself between her and Tiny—Fin being carried off by Sir Felix, whose face wore quite a puzzled expression, so verbally nettled was his little prize.

Aunt Matty met them, carrying with her a halo of lavender wherever she went, and exhaling the sad fragrance in every direction as she moved. Pepine was poorly in bed, so that his mistress was able to devote the whole of her attention to those with whom she came in contact.

"Ah, Sir Felix!" she exclaimed, "and so you've captured my saucy little bird of a niece. You'll have to clip her wings some day," she continued, playfully.

As she spoke she tapped Fin on each shoulder—from whence the imaginary wings doubtless sprang—with her fan, while aunt and niece gazed in each other's eyes.

"Yes, exactly," said Sir Felix, smiling feebly.

But somehow he did not feel comfortable, and in spite of his after-efforts to lead Fin into conversation, he failed.

The end of it was that the little maid telegraphed to another admirer, and had herself carried back to where she had left her sister; but Tiny was gone.

In fact, as soon as they were left alone, Vanleigh had quietly offered his arm.

"This room is too hot for you, Valentina," he said. "Let me take you out of the crowd."

"Masterly inactivity," Fin had said, and the words seemed to ring in Tiny's ears, as, unable to refuse, she suffered herself to be led through the crowded rooms, past Lady Rea, who nodded and smiled—past Aunt Matty, who came up, tapped the Captain on the middle shirt stud with her fan, and pinched her niece's cheek, as she smiled at her like a wintry apple—past Sir Hampton, who came behind her, and whispered, a faint "Er-rum."

"Thank you, Tiny: good girl!"—out on to the great broad staircase, now a complete conservatory of exotics where the air was perfectly cool by comparison; and there Vanleigh found her a seat smiling occasionally at the new-comers who kept thronging upstairs to where Lady Rea was receiving—Sir Hampton now keeping an eye upon the couple, a flight of stain below him, and nodding encouragement whenever his eyes met those of his child.

"I received Sir Hampton's note yesterday," said Vanleigh at last, speaking slowly, and in a suppressed voice, as the guests passed on. "Don't start—I am not going to make a scene. I only wish to tell you how happy you have made me, and that you shall find me patient and watchful of your every wish."

"Masterly inactivity," thought Tiny.

"I am going to wait—to let you see that heretofore you have misjudged me. And now let me assure you that I am not going to presume upon the consent I have received."

He waited, and she felt obliged to speak.

"Captain Vanleigh," faltered Tiny, "it was at my father's wish that I gave way, and consented to receive your visits. It is only fair to tell you that you are seeking to gain one who does not—who can never care for you."

"My dear Valentina," he said, smiling, "I am quite content. I know your sweet, gentle nature better than you know it yourself. And now for once, and once only, I am going to revert to an unpleasant theme, begging you first to forgive me for touching a wound that I know still throbs."

"Captain Vanleigh!"

"It is odd, is it not," he said, speaking with a mingling of profound tenderness and respect—"this talking of such things in a crowd? I only wished to say this once, that you do not know me. I am going to prove my love by patience. Valentina, dearest, you have been wasting the sweetness of your heart on an unworthy object."

She tried to rise; but his hand rested on her arm, and detained her.

"I pain you; but I must tell you, sweet one, that he whom you cared for, no sooner left your side than he sought consolation with another, forsaking a love that is meet for the best on earth—a love of which I feel myself unworthy. Stay, not a syllable. Those were cruel words, but the words of truth. Now we understand one another, let us draw a veil over the past, never to refer to it again. You will know me better soon."

As he spoke, there was a little bustle in the hall, where visitors were constantly arriving; and as Vanleigh stood gazing down in the pale, frightened face before him, watching the struggle that was going on, a plainly dressed woman brushed by the servant, who tried to stay her, and reached the stairs.

"Forgive me, Valentina," whispered Vanleigh, bending over her. "I touched the wound but to try and heal it. My future life shall be all devotion; and in the happiness to come you will—"

Tiny half rose; and he was about offering his arm to conduct her back to the drawing-room, when a voice below arrested him.

"Don't stop me! I must see him. I know he is here."

"But you can't, you know. Here, Edward!"

It was one of the servants who called, but he was too late; the strange visitor had already reached the landing as Sir Hampton hurried down, aghast at such a daring interruption.

At that moment the woman uttered a cry of joy, and darted towards where Vanleigh stood with his companion.

"Oh, Arthur!" she cried, "they would not bring a message. I was obliged to force my way in."

"Who is this madwoman?" cried Vanleigh, turning of a waxy pallor, while Tiny clung to the balustrade for support.

"Yes; mad—almost!" cried the woman, with a piteous cry. "But come—come at once! She is praying to see you once more. Arthur, Arthur," she panted, sinking at his knees, and clasping them, "for God's sake, come—our darling is on the point of death!"

"Who is this woman? Er-rum—Edward—James!" cried Sir Hampton, "where are the police?"

"Don't touch me!" cried the unwelcome visitor, starting to her feet; and her words came panting from her breast. "Quiet, Arthur, or it's too late! Sir," she cried, turning to Sir Hampton, whose hand was on her arm, "I am Captain Vanleigh's wife!"

Too Late

Frank Pratt, the successful barrister, saw a portion of the scene from the pavement outside, where he formed one of the little crowd by the awning. He had been restlessly walking up and down, watching the lights and shadows on the blinds. He had gazed in at the open door at what seemed to him a paradise, as he heard the music and hum of conversation, scented the fragrance from flower and perfumes that floated out, and then called himself a miserable little beggar.

"Never mind," he said at last, lighting his pipe, and looking longingly at one of the tall obelisks by the door of a neighbouring mansion, and thinking what a capital perch it would make for him to sit and look on from — "never mind, bless her, she'll snub them like fun."

He felt better then, and saw Sir Felix and Vanleigh go up the carpeted steps without a pang. Ten times over he made up his mind to go and have a quiet little tavern supper, and then to his chambers and read; but he could not tear himself away; and so it was that he saw the arrival of the uninvited guest, and in the confusion that ensued witnessed something of what followed, standing aside to let Vanleigh come hurrying out, holding his neglected wife by the hand, furious, and yet too horror-stricken and remorseful to speak to her.

"A cab!" he shouted; and a minute after they entered, and the shabby screw was whipped into a gallop, and going in the direction of Pentonville.

Earlier in the evening Netta had seemed brighter, and had eaten heartily of some fruit Richard had fetched for her from Covent Garden. She was very weak, but she had begged to be dressed, and was lying upon the little couch; while Mrs Jenkles, after helping, had gone down into the kitchen, where Sam was sitting at his tea, to look at him very fixedly, and then her face began to twitch and work.

"She aint worse, is she?" said Sam, in an awe-stricken whisper.

"Oh, Sam, Sam," sobbed the poor woman, bursting into tears; "and her so young, too. It's very, very sad."

"I shan't go out to-night, then," said Sam, a little more hoarsely than usual. "Ratty may have a holiday. It's a hill wind as blows nobody any good. If I do go to have a smoke, old woman, I shall be standing across the road in Mother Fiddison's doorway."

"Oh, Sam, it's very, very sad," sobbed Mrs Jenkles again; "and her so young. If it had been her mother or me!"

"Stow that, old gal," said Sam, with a choke. "If there's e'er a woman as can't be spared outer this here wicked world of pore cabmen and hard fares, it's you. What'd become o' me?"

"Oh, Sam," sobbed Mrs Jenkles from inside her apron.

"I should go to the bad in a week, old gal. I should never pass a corner public without dropping in; and at the end of six months there'd be a procession o' cabs follering a subscription funeral, raised by threepenny bits and tanners; and every cabby on the ranks'd have a little crape bow on his whip in memory o' Sam Jenkles, as drunk hisself to death."

"Don't, pray, Sam," sobbed his wife.

"It's true enough, missus; and I b'lieve the chaps 'd be sorry; while as for old Ratty, I b'lieve he'd cry."

"Sam!" sobbed his wife.

"I wonder," said Sam, dolefully, "whether they'd let the old 'oss follow like they do the soldiers, with my whip and boots hanging one side, and my old 'at on the other. Sh! here's Mrs Lane."

"Mrs Jenkles," cried their lodger, hurriedly, "go and ask Mr Lloyd to come over. She wants to see him."

"Is she worse, ma'am?"

The mother's lip quivered for reply; but after stifling a sob, she gasped—

"And ask Mr Reston, the doctor, to step in."

"I'll run for him, mum, while the missus fetches Mr Lloyd," said Sam, hurrying away.

A few minutes after, Richard ascended to Netta's room, to be received with a smile of pleasure, and he took the seat to which the poor girl pointed.

"Are you better to-night, my dear?" he said, kissing her gravely.

"Yes, much," she said, retaining his hand and keeping it pinioned between hers. "I want you to sit and talk to me to-night—mamma will like to hear—about our rides, and the woods and flowers. Ah, how little I've seen of the country and the flowers!"

She started as she caught a sigh from Mrs Lane.

"You could not help it, dear," she said, hastily. "Don't think me ungrateful. Come and kiss me, and tell me you don't."

Mrs Lane bent over her, and kissed her poor thin lips; and though the fount was nearly dry, a couple of burning tears fell upon the face of her child.

"If I could only be at rest about you," said Netta, drawing her mother closer to her, "I could be so happy. There, we've asked Mr Lloyd to come, and here is a welcome."

She half playfully pointed to a chair, and once more took Richard's hand between both hers, listening to him as he tried to talk cheerfully, not so much of the past as of trips to come, till, meeting her eyes, and seeing in them the sad, reproachful gaze of one who said "Why this deceit?" his voice grew husky, and he was silent.

"What's that?" said Netta, suddenly, as she heard steps below. "Oh, mamma, you have sent for him again—why did you?"

There was tender love in the reproachful smile—one which faded as the doctor entered, and Richard gave up his place to him.

He made but a brief stay, and was followed out of the room by Mrs Lane.

"Sit down again, Richard," said the girl, fondly. "Take those," she said, pointing to a pair of scissors on the table. "Now cut off that long piece of hair."

As she spoke she separated a long, dark brown tress and smilingly bent towards him as he divided it from her head.

"There," she said, smiling, as she knotted it together like so much silk; "give that to Tiny—some day—and tell her it was sent by one who had prayed night and day for her happiness and yours."

"Oh, my poor child!" groaned Richard, as he placed her gift in his pocket-book.

"And, Richard, when you are happy together, talk about me sometimes; you'll bring her to see where they have laid me—where I lie asleep?"

"For God's sake, do not talk like this, my darling!" he exclaimed; "I cannot bear it!"

"I must," she said, excitedly. "I must, the time is so short. Tell her, Richard," she whispered, earnestly, "that I loved you very dearly; for I did not know then about her. But tell her it was so innocent and dear a love, that

I think God's angels would not blame me for it. I would not talk so now, Richard, but I am dying."

He started up to run for help, but she feebly restrained him.

"No, no, don't go; it is not yet," she whispered. "Stay with me even when it's growing dark. Promise me you will stay and hold my hand till the last. I shall not feel so afraid then, and I don't think it can be wrong. I used to think once about you, so strong and brave; how in the future you would take care of me, and that I should never be afraid again. Then I used to sit and whisper your name, and stop from my work to kiss the flowers you sent me, every leaf and every blossom, and whisper to it, 'You are my darling's gift.' Was this wrong of me? I could not help it. No one knew, and I have been so different to others. My life has been all work and sorrow—her sorrow—and those were my happy moments."

"My poor darling!" was all he could utter; and the words came like a groan.

"Don't trouble about it," she whispered; "I'm not sorry to die. You have made me so happy. I feel as if I may take those tender words from you now, Richard. You called me darling twice to-night. Kiss me once again."

Tiny's name was on his lips as he bent over her, and raised the little frail form in his arms; and hers were wreathed around his neck as he pressed his lips to hers twice—lips which responded to the caress.

As he laid her tenderly back upon her pillow, she retained one of his broad, nervous hands, pressed her lips to it once, and then placed it feebly beneath her cheek, lying with her eyes half-closed, and her voice coming in a faint whisper as she said—

"I don't think she would be angry if she knew all. Ah, mother darling, I did not know you had come back. Come here."

For Mrs Lane was sitting in the corner of the room by the door, with her face buried in her hands.

She came and sat at the foot of the couch, unable to restrain her sobs.

"I could not help loving him, dear," she said, smiling; "he is so good and true. It was not the same love I have for you. Richard, you'll be rich again some day. You'll be kind to her?"

"Rich or poor, on my soul I will!" he exclaimed.

"She has worked so hard for me," said Netta, feebly. Then starting with a wildly anxious look upon her face, she uttered a strange, passionate cry as of one in intense mental agony.

"My child—my poor child!" cried Mrs Lane, throwing herself on her knees by the couch.

"Why—why did I not think of it before?" cried Netta, wildly. "I ought to have thought—Oh, it will be too late."

"What is it—what can I do?" cried Mrs Lane.

"Papa—papa—papa!" wailed the girl; "I must see papa."

Mrs Lane sank in a heap with her head bowed down upon her knees.

"I—I must see papa," wailed Netta again—"I did not think before—I have something to say—it only came just now. Oh, mother, you will fetch him before it is too late."

Mrs Lane started up and gazed wildly at her guest.

"Can I go? Can I do anything?" he exclaimed.

"No, no, stay with me," wailed Netta; "he would not come for you. Mamma, you will go. Dear mother, bring him here."

Without another word, Mrs Lane ran into the next room and hurried on her things, returning to kiss the anxious, flushed face gazing so wistfully at her.

"You will not leave her?" she said, hoarsely.

"No, he will not go," moaned Netta; "but be quick—be quick."

Richard's heart beat fast, for, as he was left alone, Netta's eyes closed and a terrible pallor succeeded the flush. He was about to rise and summon Mrs Jenkles, but Netta divined his intention, and uttered a feeble protest.

"You said you would not leave me. I am only tired. It is of no use."

She lay there with her cheek pillowed on his hand, and her eyes closed, but her lips moved gently; and as in that feebly-lighted room the solemn silence seemed to grow more painful, Richard felt a strange thrill of awe pass through him: for he knew that the words she softly whispered to herself were words of prayer.

After a time, Mrs Jenkles softly opened the door and peered in.

"Can I do anything for you, my dear?" she said, gently.

"Yes," said Netta, in a faint whisper; "come here. Kiss me and say good-bye," she continued, after a pause. "Now go and tell Sam I have prayed for a blessing on you both for your kindness to the poor creature you found in such distress."

Mrs Jenkles's sorrow, in spite of herself, found vent in a wail; and she hurried out of the room to weep alone by her own fireside.

Then an hour passed without a change, only that twice over the great soft, dilated eyes opened widely to gaze wonderingly about till they rested on Richard, when a faint smile came on the poor wan face, the thin cheek nestled down into the strong man's hand, and a faint sigh of content fluttered from the lips of the dying girl.

It must have been nearly eleven when Netta opened her eyes widely.

"They are very long," she said, in a harsh, cracked voice—"Very long; he must come soon. Why did I not think of it before?"

"She must soon return," said Richard. "Shall I send?"

"No, no! It would be no use," she whispered; and her great loving eyes rested fondly on his for a moment. "Do not let go of my hand, and I shall not feel afraid."

She sank back once more, but only to start at the end of a few moments.

"He's coming—yes, he's coming now."

Richard strained his ears to listen, but there was not a sound; but as a smile of content came once more upon the anxious features, there was the roll of distant cab wheels, and he knew that the senses of the dying girl were preternaturally quickened.

The next minute the wheels stopped at the door, and there were steps on the stairs.

"He has come!" cried the girl, joyfully. "Lift me up in your arms, Richard, that I may see him."

As he responded to her wish, and held her up with her head resting upon his shoulder, the door opened, and, to his intense astonishment, the handsome man of fashion, looking sallow, haggard, and ten years older, with the great drops of sweat upon his face, and his hair clinging wetly to his brow, half staggered into the room.

"Papa, dear papa!" wailed the girl, stretching out one hand; and with a groan, as he read in her wasted features the coming end, he stumbled forward, to sink crushed and humbled to his knees before the face of death.

"My poor child!" he groaned.

"I knew—you would come," moaned the girl, faintly. "Mother—quick—papa—kind to her—once more—suffered so—so much—"

With her last strength, her trembling little fingers placed those of Vanleigh upon the hand of his neglected, forsaken wife; and then, as a shudder ran through her frame, her nerveless arm dropped, and her head turned away to sink pillowed on Richard's arm. There was a smile upon her lip, as her eyes were bent fixedly upon his, and then as he gazed he saw that their loving light faded, to give place to a far-off, awful stare, and a deep groan burst from the young man's breast.

Vanleigh started up at that, exclaiming wildly—

"Quick—a doctor—the nearest physician—do you hear!"

"It is too late," said Richard, sadly. "Your child is dead."

Three Months After

"Why did you come, Humphrey? Why did you hunt me out?" cried Richard, in answer to a speech made by the broad-shouldered West-country-man, who had been ushered in by Mrs Fiddison.

"Because I wanted to see you, Master Dick. I've written, and you won't answer; so I got Mr Pratt there to tell me where you were, and here I am."

Richard stood frowning for a few moments; but there was something so bright and frank in the face before him that a sunshiny look came in his own, and he shook hands heartily.

"Come, sir, that does one good," cried Humphrey. "I *am* glad I've come."

"Well, I am glad to see you, Humphrey; but yet—"

"I know, sir—I know," said Humphrey. "I could tell you exactly what you feel—a bit of envy-like; but there, bless your heart, if it wasn't for Polly and the thoughts of her, I should be a miserable man."

"Well, you've got plenty to make you miserable," said Richard.

"Ah, you may smile, sir—I know what you mean; but I have, all the same. I tell you, I was a deal happier man without the estate than I am with it. Old Lloyd and Mrs Lloyd—begging your pardon for speaking so of them—look sneering-like at me; so do the quality; hang them, they're civil enough, but I can see them sneer. They look down on me, of course. I'm not one of their sort. I'm ignorant, and can't talk to them. I get on well enough with the young fellows, shooting, and so on; but I always feel as if I ought to load their guns, and I can't help saying 'sir' to every one of them."

"But I thought Mr Mervyn—"

"Mr Mervyn's as good and kind a gentleman as ever lived, and he's wanted to learn me all sort of things; but I can't take to them—I can't, indeed, sir. Then there's Polly: she's at a fine school, and, poor lass, she's miserable, and writes to me how glad she'll be to get away. It's all wrong, sir. What's the good of a horse to a man as can't ride, or a yacht to a man as can't sail it? I've got Penreife, and I go in and out of it feeling quite ashamed-like, just as if I was a fish out of water. I tell you, Master Dick, upon my sivvy, what with feeling uncomfortable about ousting you, and being sneered at on the sly, and bothered with the company and invitations, and hints to dress different, and learn this, and learn that, I haven't had a happy day since you left. I don't like it, and I don't want it. Damn the estate!—there!"

"Why, my dear fellow, you'll soon get used to it if you make up your mind. Why, you're in your old keeper's clothes."

"Of course I am. Why shouldn't I be? There's no one up here I know, so I thought I'd be comfortable-like, and I thought—I thought I should be better in them to come and see you. And now, sir, how's it with you?"

"Oh, pretty well, Humphrey. I've got the command of a schooner, and I'm going on a voyage to India."

"No, no—don't go, Master Dick—don't. Come down into Cornwall again."

Richard shook his head.

"Nonsense, sir; why, lookye here. Here am I, Humphrey Lloyd—"

"Trevor," said Richard.

"Hang the name!" said Humphrey, "it's always bothering me. I more often sign Lloyd than Trevor, which is about the awkwardest name there ever was to write. Ah, Master Dick, it was a bad day's work for me when there was that change."

"Nonsense, man."

"Ah, but it was; and I tell you what: if it wasn't for my darling little lassie, I should take to drinking to drown my cares—But, look here, Master Richard—they wanted me to take that name, too—Richard—but I wouldn't stand that. Well, look here, sir, why don't you come down, and put your foot in the old place again? What's being born got to do with it? We couldn't help being born; we didn't want to be, I dessay; and we couldn't help what they did with us in our cradles."

"Of course not, Humphrey."

"Well, look here, sir; you grew into a gentleman, I grew into a common man. Well, then, what's stupider than trying to make me what I didn't grow into, and you into a common man? It's rubbish: we're neither of us no good as we are."

Richard laughed—rather bitterly, though.

"Polly and I have had it all over, sir. I went down to her school-place, poor little lass. She's very unhappy, and we came to the conclusion that with the cottage nicely papered and painted, and a hundred a year, we should be as happy as the day's long. So come, Master Richard—there's the place nohow for want of you. Come down, and take possession."

"Humphrey, if ever there was a fellow born with the soul of a gentleman, it's you. But no; there is such a thing in a man as pride, and I have too much to accept your offer; and, besides, I have made an engagement."

"Not to be married, sir?"

"No, no; my ship, man, my ship."

"Oh!" said Humphrey; "because I was thinking, sir. There's Miss Rea, you know."

"What about her?" said Richard, sharply.

"Oh, only that she's down at Tolcarne now, sir. They say she's been better lately. There was some talk about her being engaged to an officer—that captain, sir, as come down and stayed with us—you, I mean—but they say that's all broken off, because he was married already. His wife fetched him, and he's gone off in a regiment to India."

Richard remained silent.

"Well, come—look here, Master Dick, you say you won't take the place back?"

"Certainly not."

"Then let's go halves."

"Humphrey, it is yours by right; keep it," said Richard, decisively.

"Well, come then, sir, we were boys together, you won't refuse to do your old companion a good turn?"

"Anything consistent that you ask me to do, Humphrey, I'll do with pleasure."

"Then come down and be my best man at my wedding."

Richard hesitated, for there was a battle going on within his breast. He longed—longed intensely to go down and see Cornwall again. Tiny Rea was there—he might see her. Yes, and make himself more wretched than ever, for he could not speak to her. It would be madness to go—and yet once—to see the old place before he left England—just for a few hours. And why should he not see Tiny, just to tell her of his unaltered faith? He felt that he would give the world to go, and yet pride kept him back, "All right—I'll walk in, Mrs Fiddison," said a voice, and Frank Pratt entered.

"Well, Dick, old man, how are you? Ah, Humphrey, I told you I should turn up some time."

"I'm trying to get Master Dick here, sir, to come down and be my best man at the wedding."

"Well, he'll do that for you, surely," said Pratt, quietly. "Go down, Dick. I've promised Humphrey to go. I said I would directly he asked."

Pratt looked very solemn over it; but there was tremendous exultation in his heart as he thought of seeing Pin, for the family had left Russell Square directly after the unpleasant éclaircissement.

"He'll come, Humphrey. There, I'll promise for him, and so you may make your mind happy."

"But just say you will, Master Dick," said Humphrey, rising.

"Well, I will, Humphrey," said Richard, holding out his hand, though he repented the next moment, as his successor took his leave.

"Seen Mrs Vanleigh lately?" said Pratt, as soon as they were alone.

"Poor woman! no, not for two days. I must call."

"Van's behaving very well now that it's too late. There's a regular allowance for her at his army agents. I didn't believe a man could have changed so as he did. It was that fever did it, coming upon the shock. Poor wretch! I never saw a man so stricken down as he was at the poor girl's funeral."

He caught Richard's eye.

"There, what a blundering ass I am, Dick, old man. It's my trade to rout out all sorts of old sores. But, mum, I won't say any more. How's our friend the cabby?"

"Oh, quite well!"

"And Madame?"

"Excellently well. They say that perhaps Mrs Vanleigh is coming to stay with them again; but I don't think it would be wise for the poor woman to do so."

"Quite right," said Pratt. "Well, I must be off and work. I've got an Indian case on—Jeefee Rustam versus Tomkins, and two or three more things to get out of the way before I go down to Cornwall. By the way, I met our languid friend, Flick, at the dub yesterday."

"Well?"

"He cut me, sir. Looked bayonets, lance-points, and sabres at me. Heigho! Well, we can't all win. Ta-ta."

"Good-bye."

"Cornwall, mind."

Richard nodded, and he was left alone, to make up his mind a dozen times that he could not go down to the old place without a great sacrifice of dignity, and as often something seemed to whisper him that he must go; and to that faint whisper he lent an attentive ear, for the desire grew so strong at last that he found himself unable to resist.

A Fellow-Traveller

"Don't mind telling you now," said Frank Pratt, sitting back in the railway carriage, with his hands under his head, and great puffs of smoke issuing from between his lips as he stared at Richard, who was gazing quietly at the pleasant Devon prospect past which they flew.

"Don't mind telling me what?" said Richard, dreamily.

"That I never expected to get you down here. Dick, old man, I've felt like a steam-tug fussing about a big ship these last few days. However, I've got you out of dock at last."

"Yes," said Richard, dreamily, "you've got me out of dock at last."

They relapsed into silence for a time, Pratt sitting watching his friend, and noting more than ever the change that had come over him during the last few months. There were lines in his forehead that did not exist before, and a look of staid, settled melancholy, very different from the calm, insouciant air that used to pervade his countenance.

"Poor old Dick," muttered Pratt, laying aside his pipe; "I mustn't let him look down like this." Then aloud, "Dick, old boy, I'm going to preach to you."

Richard turned to him with a sad smile.

"Go on, then," he said.

"I will," said Pratt. "Never mind the text or the sequence of what I say. I only wanted to talk to you, old fellow, about life."

"I was just then thinking about death," said Richard, quietly.

"About death?"

"I was visiting in spirit the little corner at Highgate where that poor girl lies, and thinking of a wish she expressed."

"What was that?"

Richard shook his head, and they were silent as the train rushed on.

"Life is a strange mystery, Dick," said Pratt at last, laying his hand on his friend's knee; "and I know it is giving you great pain to come down here and see others happy. It is to give them pleasure you are coming down?"

Richard nodded.

"Last time we were down here together, Dick, I was one of the most miserable little beggars under the sun. I don't mind owning it now."

His friend grew more attentive.

"You were happy then, old fellow, and very hard you tried to make others so too, but I was miserable."

"Why?"

"Because I was poor—a perfect beggar, without a prospect of rising, and I had found out that in this queer little body of mine there was a very soft heart. Dick, old boy, the wheel of fortune has given a strange turn since then. I've gone up and you have gone down, and 'pon my soul, old fellow, I'm very, very sorry."

"Nonsense, Franky," said Richard, speaking cheerfully. "If ever a man was glad, I am, at your prosperity. But you don't look so very cheerful, after all."

"How can I?" said Frank, dolefully, "with you on my mind for one thing, and the lion's mouth gaping for my unlucky head."

"Lion's mouth?"

"Yes, Dick; I'm going to Tolcarne to pop my head in; and, to make matters worse, there's a horrible, sphinxy griffin sits and guards the lion's den."

"You mean that you are going to propose for little Fin?"

"I am, Dick, I am," said Pratt, excitedly. "I wouldn't have said a word if I had kept poor, but with my rising income—"

"And some one's permission?"

"Bless her, yes; she says she hates me, and always shall, till her sister's happy, but I may ask papa, so as to get rid of poor Flick and his persecutions. I believe the poor chap cares for her; but I can't afford to let him have her, and make her miserable—eh, Dick?"

"Frank, old fellow, I wish you joy, and I'm glad of it, for she's a dear little girl."

"Oh, that don't express it within a hundred," said Pratt. "Dear little girl! That's the smallest of small beer, while she's the finest vintage of champagne. But, I say, Dick, old fellow, you've got to help me over this."

"I? How?"

"She says she shall hate me till her sister's happy; and, Dick, old fellow, there's only one way of making Valentina Rea happy, and that you know. There—there—I've done. Don't look at me like that. Fortune's wheel keeps turning on: I shall be down in the mud again soon, and you cock-a-hoop on the top. Do you stick to your purpose of not going on to-night?"

"Yes, I shall go on in the morning from Plymouth, be present at the wedding, and then come away."

"But you'll go and see the old people? Dick, recollect Mrs Lloyd did all out of love and pride in her boy."

"Yes, I have made up my mind to go and see them," said Richard, quietly. "I'll try and be a dutiful son."

"And if I can manage it, you shall be a dutiful friend and brother-in-law too, my boy," muttered Pratt, as he sank back in his seat, relit his pipe, and smoked in peace.

Plymouth platform was in a state of bustle on the arrival of the train. The friends had alighted from their coupé, inquired about the early morning train for Penzance, pointed out their light luggage toon obsequious porter, whose words buzzed with z's, and were about to make their way to the great hotel, when Pratt's attention was taken by a little grey, voluble old woman, very neatly and primly dressed in blue print, with a scarlet shawl, and a wonderful sugar-loaf beaver hat upon her head. She was in trouble about her railway ticket, two bundles tied up in blue handkerchiefs, and a large, green umbrella.

"I can't find it, young man; I teclare to cootness, look you, I can't find it."

"Very sorry, ma'am," said the ticket collector, who had followed her from the regular platform; "then you'll have to pay from Bristol."

"Put look you," cried the old lady, "I tid pay once and cot the ticket, look you, and I put it somewhere to pe safe."

"Have you searched all your pockets?" said Richard.

"Yes, young man," said the old lady; "I've only cot one, look you— there!" and she dragged up her dress to display a great olive green pocket as big as a saddle-bag, out of which, after placing a bundle in Pratt's hands and the umbrella in Richard's to hold, she turned out a heterogeneous assortment of nutmegs, thimbles, reels of cotton, pieces of wax-candle, ginger, a bodkin case, pincushions, housewives, and, as the auctioneers say, other articles too numerous to mention.

"It don't seem to be there," said Richard, kindly.

"No, young man, it isn't. I hunted it all over, look you, and I must have peen robbed."

"Well, ma'am, I'm very sorry," said the collector, "but you must pay again."

"I teclare to cootness, young man, I can't, and I won't. I shall have no money to come pack."

"Can't help that," said the collector, civilly enough. "I must do my duty, ma'am."

"How much is it?" said Richard.

"From Bristol, third-class, sir, eight and tenpence."

"Look you, young man, I shall pe ruined," cried the old woman, tearfully.

"I'll pay it," said Richard, thrusting his hand into his pocket.

"You're a tear, coot poy, pless you," cried the old lady; and to the amusement of all on the platform, she went on tiptoe, reached up to Richard, and gave him a sounding kiss. "Pless you for it. Coot teeds are never thrown away."

"I hope you are a witch, Mother Hubbard," said Pratt, laughing. "Here's your bundle. Don't forget to do him a good turn."

Richard took out the money, and the collector was about to write a receipt, when it suddenly occurred to the young man to open the umbrella, which he did with some difficulty, and the missing ticket fell out.

"There," cried the old lady, joyfully, "I knew I put it somewhere to pe safe. Thank you, young man, and pless you all the same; for, look you, it was as coot a teed as if you had tone it."

"Don't say any more, mother," said Richard, laughing. "Good-bye."

A Quiet Wedding

There was just time to snatch a hasty breakfast the next morning before starting for the station, and after a short journey they mounted into the dog-cart which Humphrey had sent to meet them. By comparing times, Pratt, who had taken all the management upon himself, found that he could execute a little plan he had been hatching; and when they neared Penreife, after a chat with the groom about the preparations, he proposed to Richard that they should alight, send the vehicle on, and take the short cut by the lanes.

"If you like," said Richard, quietly; and the sadness that had seemed to hang over him more and more as they neared their journey's end now half unmanned him.

"I thought you'd like better to walk up to the old place alone," said Frank, "instead of having a third person with us."

"Thank you, Frank, thank you," said Richard, in a voice that was husky with emotion. "It was a mistake to come."

"No, no, a kindness to Humphrey and me."

"I—I—thought I could stand it better, and not behave like such a weak fool," said Richard. "There, it's over now. Let's get through our task, so that I may go back."

"You must wait for me, you know, Dick," said Frank, cheerily. "There, cheer up, old man, it isn't for ever and a day. Try and be hopeful, and put on a bright face before the wedding folks. It's all going to be as quiet as possible—a couple of carriages to the church and back. Your old people will be there. Say a kind word to them—there, you know how to do it."

"I'll try and act like a man, Frank, hard as it will be. But you've set me a bitter task."

"Then you shall have some sweet to take with it," said Pratt to himself. Then aloud, "Ah, how nice this old lane looks. I never saw the ferns brighter or richer. How the sun shines through the trees. What a lovely morning, Dick! I say," he gabbled on in a hasty way, "look at that tiny waterfall. What a change, Dick, from Fountain Court, Temple."

"Why did you come this way?" groaned Richard, as he strove hard to fight down the emotion caused by the recollections that pervaded his memory.

That lane was hallowed to him: but a quarter of a mile farther was the old woman's cottage where he had encountered the sisters; there was the place where he had walked one evening with Tiny; there—oh, there was a happy memory clinging to every tree and mossy block of granite; and but for the strong effort he made, he could have wandered out of the path, thrown himself down amongst the ferns, and cried like a child.

Meanwhile, Pratt chatted excitedly.

"Bless the dear old place. Why, Dick, that's where I saw my little Fin looking so disdainfully at me, coming round the sharp turn there; and, look here, that's my old perch, where I've had many a jolly pipe."

He caught his friend suddenly by the arm, in a strangely-excited fashion, and turned him round, as he pointed to the grey, lichen-covered monolith of granite.

"Dick, old man, I could smoke a pipe there now, and sit and whistle like a bird. I say, Dick, how comical a fellow would look up there in his wig and gown, and—thank goodness!"

He said those last two words to himself with a sigh of relief, as, turning round, there, timed to a moment by his vile machinations and those of Fin, the sisters came, basket and fern trowel in hand, from amongst the trees, just as if time had been standing still, and no troubles had intervened.

To two of the party the surprise was complete. Richard stopped short, rigid and firm; while Tiny, as soon as her eyes rested upon him, turned pale, her basket fell to the ground, and uttering a faint cry of pain, she pressed her hand to her side and tottered back.

Conventional feelings, rigid determination, everything went down before nature then. With one bound Richard was at Tiny's side, and the next moment, with a cry of joy, the poor girl's arms were round his neck, and she was sobbing on his breast.

The probabilities are that had the insane behaviour of Frank Pratt been seen, he would have lost caste at the bar; for, dashing down his hat and an expensive meerschaum, which was shivered to atoms on the granite path, he executed a wild breakdown, brought his foot to the earth with a flop, and then rushed at Fin; but only to be disappointed, for she was clinging to and sobbing over Dick—that is, as far up as she could reach, crying—

"Oh, you dear, good darling, Dick—pray, pray don't go on breaking her poor heart any more."

"I say," said Pratt, reproachfully, as Richard bent down and kissed the little maid, "what have I done? Ain't I nobody?"

"Oh, go away now," cried Fin, "There, you may have one, if nobody's looking. Now, that will do;" and, after suffering a kiss, she returned it with a push.

"Time's up, Dick, come. You shall see her again," said Pratt, looking ruefully at his meerschaum scraps, as he dusted his hat. Then followed a little whispering with Pin, and he caught his friend's arm, as his fellow-conspirator led her sister away.

"This is madness," groaned Richard, as he yielded to his friend's touch, and they walked rapidly away. "Oh, Franky, you contrived this."

"To be sure I did," said Pratt, grinning; "and you shall have another dose to cure you both, if you are good. But, quick; now, then, look a man. Here we are."

Richard walked steadily up to the house, where he was pleased to find that all the servants' faces were new. Humphrey met him at the door, and Mr and Mrs Lloyd were in the hall ready to approach timidly, as the young man gravely kissed the late housekeeper, and shook hands with Lloyd.

Polly was in the drawing-room, for it was to be a very homely, unconventional marriage; and she blushed warmly on encountering the former owner of the place.

"I wish you every happiness, my dear," said Richard, to set her at ease; and he bent down and kissed her. "Humphrey has told me of your good little heart."

"And you will listen to him, Mr Lloy—Trevor?" said the girl, mixing the two names together.

"Time to go," said Humphrey; and he handed Polly, Mrs Lloyd, and her husband into the first carriage, which was kept back while he, Richard, and Pratt entered the other, and were driven off to the church.

In spite of the endeavours to keep the affair quiet, the little churchyard was crowded, and it was a harder trial for Richard even than he had expected, to hear the whisperings, and receive the friendly nods and bows from so many of those who knew him well.

But he bore it all in a calm, manly fashion; shook hands warmly with Mr Mervyn, who had come with a white favour in his button-hole; stood best man to Humphrey; and after little Polly, but a week before at school, had been given away by her uncle, and, the wedding over, the carriage had driven back with the bride and bridegroom, he took his place again quite calmly, shook hands with those who clustered round, and was driven away.

Everything went off well; and at the simple wedding breakfast, when called upon, Richard, in a very manly speech, wished health and happiness to the bride and bridegroom. Humphrey responded, broke down, tried again, broke down again, and then, leaving his place, crossed to where Richard sat, grasped his hand, and in a voice choking with emotion, exclaimed—

"Master Dick, I'm speaking for my wife as well as myself when I tell you that, if you wish us to be a happy couple, you must come back to your own."

Richard rose, and returned the strong grasp; but before he could utter a word Pratt brought his hand down bang upon the table, exclaiming—

"Mother Hubbard, by Jove!"

Every face was directed at the door, where, standing, in her black hat and scarlet shawl, with her hands resting upon the horn handle of her umbrella, was the little grey old woman of Plymouth Station.

"It's dear Aunt Price," cried Polly, jumping up; and, regardless of her finery, she ran to the severe-looking old lady, hugged her affectionately, and then began to unpin her shawl, and take off her hat. "Oh, aunty, I'm *so* glad you've come."

"And are you married, look you?" said the old lady.

"Married, yes," cried Humphrey, heartily; "we couldn't wait, you know, or it would have been too late. Give's your umbrella, and come and sit down. Why didn't you come last night?"

"It was too far, my poy," said the old lady; "and I was tired. It's a long way, look you, from Caerwmlych, and I'm a very old woman now. Well, Lloyd—well, Chane, you're both looking older than when I was here last, close upon thirty years ago, and nursed you through two illnesses."

"We are quite well," said Mrs Lloyd; "but didn't expect you here."

"P'r'abs not, p'r'abs not," said the old lady; "put Polly here wrote to me to come, and I thought it was time, for she's peen telling me strange news, look you."

Lloyd shuffled in his chair, Mrs Lloyd was silent, and Richard's brow knit as he glanced across the table at Pratt, while Humphrey busied himself in supplying the old lady's plate.

"I cot Polly's letter, look you, and I teclare to cootness, if I'd been tead and perried, I think I should have cot up and t come, look you. And so you're married to Humphrey! Ah, well, he was a tisacreeable paby; but he's grown, look you, into a fine lad, and I wish you poth choy."

The old lady took a glass of wine and ate a little, and then grew more garrulous than ever, while no one else seemed disposed to speak.

"And I'm glad to see you again," said the old lady, looking at Richard. "I tidn't expect it when I left you at the railway place; and yet I seemed to know you again, look you. I felt I knew the face, and I teclare to cootness I couldn't tell where I'd seen it, but I rememper now."

"Come, aunt, darling," said Polly, "make a good breakfast."

"Tinner you mean, child," said the old lady.

"Well, dinner, dear," said Polly, "because I want a long talk with you before we go."

"You're coing away, then?"

"Yes, aunt, for a month; but you'll stay till we come back?"

"Well, I ton't know, look you," said the old lady, sturdily. "Chane Lloyd and I never tid get on well together; but if Mr Richard Trevor there isn't too prout to ask a poor old woman off the mountains—who nursed his poor mother, and tantled him in her arms when he was a paby—I teclare to cootness I will stay."

A dead silence fell upon the group at the table. Humphrey seemed uncomfortable, Polly clung to his arm, Mrs Lloyd looked white and downcast, and her husband glanced at the door, and motioned a servant who was entering to retire.

Richard broke the silence, after giving a reassuring smile to Humphrey and his wife, by saying, gravely—

"I would ask you to stay with pleasure, Mrs Price, if I were master here, but you are mistaken. There sits Mr Humphrey Trevor; I am your own kith and kin, Richard Lloyd."

"Chut!—chut!—chut!" exclaimed the old lady, starting up and speaking angrily, as she pointed at him with one finger. "Who ever saw a Lloyd or a

Price with a nose like that? Ton't tell me! You're Mr Richard Trevor, your father's son, and as much like him, look you, as two peas."

The Lloyds rose, Mrs Lloyd looking like ashes as she clung to her husband's arm; while Pratt left his place, and stood behind the chair of his friend.

"I'd forgotten all about it, look you," said the old lady, prattling away, "till Polly wrote to me from her school; and then it all came back about Chane Lloyd and her paby, and her having the fever when her mistress died. Why, look you, tidn't I go up to the nursery after peing town to see the funeral, and find Chane Lloyd hat peen up there, and put her paby in the young master's cratle? and, look you, titn't I go town to chite her, and find her all off her heat, and she was ill for weeks? I thought she'd tone it without knowing, or, peing wild-like, had liked to see her little one in the young master's clothes. I put that all right again, and nursed poth pabies till she cot well. Lloyd—Trevor—tidn't I see them poth as soon as they came into the worlt, and to you think I ton't know them? Why, look at them!"

She turned to Pratt, who was nearest to her; but she cried out in alarm, for the little fellow had caught her in his arms and kissed her on both cheeks, as he cried—

"It isn't Mother Hubbard, Dick, but the good fairy out of the story-book. God bless you! old lady, for this. Here, Humphrey, see to your mother."

But Humphrey was pumping away at both Richard Trevor's arms, as he cried, excitedly—

"Hooray! Master Dick. I never felt so happy in my life. Polly, lass, we shall get the cottage after all."

He saw the next moment, though, that Mrs Lloyd had fainted dead away; and his were the arms that carried her to her bedroom, while Polly crept to the old Welshwoman's side.

"I came, look you, Master Richard, to put all this right," said the old lady. "Putt it was all nonsense, I teclare to cootness. Anypody might have seen."

"I—I thank you—I'm contused—dazed, rather," said Trevor, looking from one to the other. "Polly, my poor girl, I'll try to make up to you for this disappointment."

"I'm not disappointed, please, Mr Richard, sir," said Mrs Humphrey, bobbing a curtsey, and then trying a boarding-school salute and failing, and blushing terribly.

"I'm very happy indeed, and I'm sure Humphrey is—he said so, and he always tells the truth. And if you please, sir, aunt and I will go now into the housekeeper's room."

"That you won't, if I have any influence with some one here," said Pratt. "No, my pretty little wife; you and your brick of a husband shall go off in triumph; and oh, by Jove! here's the present I brought down for you."

Frank Pratt's present was a handsome ring, and he was placing it above the plain one already on her finger, when Humphrey came back.

"She's all right again," he said, huskily. "I was obliged to come away, for she wanted to go on her knees—and I couldn't stand it. Polly—Aunt Price—she wants you both. Master Dick, sir, isn't this a day?"

Conclusion

Everybody said, as a matter of course, afterwards, that the whole affair was perfectly absurd, and that anybody could see with half an eye that Humphrey was not a Trevor. All the same, though, he had been accepted for many months as the owner of the estate.

The young couple went off on their wedding trip, for Mrs Lloyd's illness was of only a transitory nature; and soon after the carriage had taken them to the station, the old housekeeper sent a message to Trevor, asking leave to see him.

What took place at that interview Richard Trevor never said; but the result was that a couple of hours after she and her husband had left the place, having refused Trevor's offer to let them stay, though living on his bounty to the end.

In writing, it needs but a stroke of the pen to carry the reader now to a year ago or the reverse; so let us say that a year has elapsed, and there is once more a dinner-party at Penreife, where there are visitors staying. It is to meet them that Sir Hampton and Lady Rea are coming from Tolcarne. One of the visitors is with her sister beneath one of the shady trees on the lawn; and the other, a little solemn-looking man, her husband, has been making a tour of the place with Richard Trevor.

They stopped at the pretty keeper's lodge, with its little farm, to drink new milk, tempered from a flask, offered in glasses by pretty Mrs Humphrey Lloyd, who looked wonderfully important with the new baby. Then they visited the stables, where an old friend was enjoying a pipe after seeing to the comforts of the horses; for Sam Jenkles, when poor Ratty was obstinate for the last time, and insisted upon dying of old age in the road instead of at peace in the stables, gladly accepted the offer made to him to take the superintendence of the little stud at Penreife; while his wife lived in one of the prettiest cottages on the estate, and was always busy at the house during company times.

Sam's news when he came down was that Mrs Fiddison had changed her name, having been proposed to by a widower who fancied she was one of the bereaved; also that one Barney had got into some little difficulty with the police, and had gone abroad for change of air.

On returning to the house for dressing, the ladies were already prepared, and the gentlemen had only time to hurry on their things before there was a loud "Er-rum" in the hall, and Sir Hampton Rea was ready to button-hole his sons-in-law, telling the Cornish one that the new greenhouse was a great success, and that Sanders should come over the next day to see the wistaria.

As for Lady Rea, she was being heartily kissed, every kiss budding into a smile on her pleasant face, till Tiny made the discovery that the plump, affectionate little dame was coming undone, when she had her whisked away and pinned, volubly telling her daughter the while that Pepine was so ill, Aunt Matty had not the heart to come.

At eleven precisely the last "Er-rum" is heard in the hall, and peace— truly a blessed peace—falls on the pleasant Cornish home.

Three months after we have the return visit, Richard Trevor and Valentina, his wife, being up at Frank Pratt's old-fashioned house at Highgate, where the only trouble happy little Fin can complain of is that Frank is so bunted by the solicitors that he has no peace. Fin has quite made up her mind that he will be Lord Chancellor; but Frank thinks it more than doubtful, and is very fond of teasing his wife, his great coup being to tell her that she asked him to marry her at last.

There is a quiet, grave look in the faces of Richard and his wife, for they have paid two visits that day—one to the living, one to the dead.

Mrs Vanleigh is living in a pleasant little cottage in a Highgate lane, and from her they learn that Sir Felix Landells marries the daughter of an earl in a few weeks; also that Captain, now Major, Vanleigh is still in India, where he is likely to stay; but that he writes regularly to his neglected wife, and has devoted himself heart and soul to his profession.

The visit to the dead was made in Highgate Cemetery, where there is a neat little railing round a grave—green in summer, purple in spring with violets; and as husband and wife stand hand in hand there, the tears of the latter fall fast, while his eyes are blurred and misty as he pictures the past, and seems to see the slight, fragile form slowly wasting day by day, till once more, for the thousandth time, he conjures up the dimly-lit room, and the solemn scene wherein he was an actor. He knows that the long, dark tress of hair lies upon his wife's bosom; and he knows, too, that in her gentle heart there is no tinge of jealous feeling, or want of faith; for as he raises his head with a muttered "God rest her!" he meets the loving look of a sweet, trusting pair of eyes. Lastly, they gaze together at the simple headstone, but his are even now too blurred to read the simple inscription—"Netta."